IN
ASHES
LIE

THE ONYX COURT BOOK II

MARIE
BRENNAN

In Ashes Lie
Print edition ISBN: 9781785650758
E-book edition ISBN: 9781785650765

Published by Titan Books
A division of Titan Publishing Group Ltd
144 Southwark Street, London SE1 0UP

First edition: June 2016
2 4 6 8 10 9 7 5 3 1

A CIP catalogue record for this title is available from the British Library.

Printed and bound in Great Britain by CPI Group Ltd.

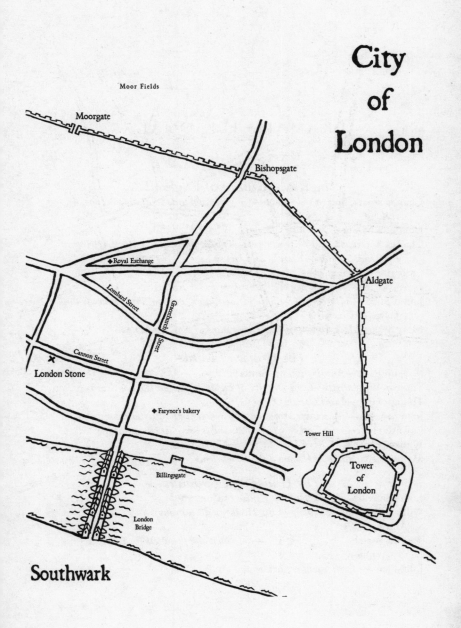

DRAMATIS PERSONAE

The Royal Family of England

Charles Stuart, first of that name—*King of England, Scotland, France, and Ireland*

Henrietta Maria—*Queen to Charles I*

Charles Stuart, second of that name—*Prince of Wales, and after King of England, Scotland, France, and Ireland*

Catherine of Braganza—*Queen to Charles II*

James Stuart—*Duke of York, and brother to Charles II*

James Stuart—*late King of England, Scotland, France, and Ireland, and father to Charles I*

Mary Stuart—*late Queen of Scots, and mother to King James*

The House of Lords

William Laud—*Archbishop of Canterbury*

Thomas Wentworth—*Lord Deputy of Ireland, created Earl of Strafford*

Thomas Grey—*Lord Grey of Groby*

John Mordaunt—*Viscount Mordaunt of Avalon, and a Royalist conspirator*

Edward Hyde—*later Earl of Clarendon, and a Royalist conspirator*

William Craven—*Earl of Craven*

Maxwell—*Gentleman Usher of the Black Rod*

The House of Commons

John Glanville—*Speaker of the House of Commons*

William Lenthall—*Speaker of the House of Commons*

Sir Antony Ware }

Thomas Soame } —*aldermen and members for London*

Isaac Penington }

John Pym—*a Parliamentary leader*

John Hampden   }
Denzil Holles   }   *—allies of John Pym*
Arthur Hesilrige   }
William Strode   }
Sir Francis Seymour—*a knight and member of Parliament*
William Prynne—*a member of Parliament*

The New Model Army

Oliver Cromwell—*a general and member of Parliament, and later Lord Protector of England*
Henry Ireton—*a general and member of Parliament*
Thomas Fairfax—*Lord Fairfax of Cameron, likewise a general*
Thomas Pride—*a colonel*
Edmund Ludlow—*an officer*
Richard Cromwell—*son of Oliver Cromwell, and second Lord Protector*
George Monck—*general of the Army in Scotland*

Londoners

Sir Morris Abbot   }
Thomas Alleyn   }   *—Lord Mayors of London*
Sir Thomas Bludworth   }
Sir William Turner—*an alderman of London*
Katherine Ware—*wife to Sir Antony Ware*
Burnett—*manservant to Sir Antony Ware*
Thomas Farynor—*a baker*
Humphrey Taylor—*a Puritan*
Benjamin Hipley—*a spymaster*
John Lilburne—*leader of the Leveller movement*
Marchamont Nedham—*a printer of news*
John Bradshaw—*Lord President of the High Court of Justice*
Elizabeth Murray—*suo jure Countess of Dysart, and a Royalist conspirator*
John Ellin—*a doctor*
Samuel Pepys—*a diarist*
Robert Hubert—*a traitor*
Sir Michael Deven—*a mortal man, now dead*

The Onyx Court

Lune—*Queen of the Onyx Court*
Valentin Aspell—*Lord Keeper*
Amadea Shirrell—*Lady Chamberlain*

Nianna Chrysanthe—*Mistress of the Robes*
Sir Prigurd Nellt—*a giant, and Captain of the Onyx Guard*
Sir Cerenel }
Sir Essain }
Sir Mellehan } —*knights of the Onyx Guard*
Sir Peregrin Thorne }
Dame Segraine }
Gertrude Goodemeade—*a brownie of Islington*
Rosamund Goodemeade—*her sister, and likewise a brownie*
Sir Leslic—*an elf-knight*
Lewan Erle—*an elf-lord*
Carline—*an elf-lady*
Angrisla—*a nightmare*
Tom Toggin—*a hob*
Bonecruncher—*a barguest*
Blacktooth Meg—*the hag of the River Fleet*

Foreigners, exiles, and deceased fae

Fiacha }
Nuada } —*Ard-Rithe, High Kings of Ireland*
The Dagda }
Conchobar—*King of Ulster*
Eochu Airt—*ollamh and ambassador from Temair*
Ailill—*King of Connacht*
Medb—*Queen of Connacht*
Feidelm of the Far-Seeing Eye—*poet and ambassador from Temair*
Nicneven—*the Gyre-Carling of Fife*
Kentigern Nellt—*an exiled giant, and brother to Sir Prigurd Nellt*
Halgresta Nellt—*their sister, likewise a giant, now dead*
Cunobel—*an exiled knight, and brother to Sir Cerenel*
Ifarren Vidar—*an exiled lord*
Orgat—*a powrie of the Border*
Cailleach Bheur—*the Blue Hag of Winter*
Wayland Smith—*King of the Vale of the White Horse*
Irrith—*a sprite of Berkshire*
Invidiana—*late Queen of the Onyx Court*

PROLOGUE
THE SPARK

PUDDING LANE, LONDON
Sunday, 2 September 1666

The bakery lay silent and dark in the small hours of the morning, lit only by the faint glow of embers from the hearth. Faggots of wood sat under the beehive dome of the oven, awaiting the morning's burden: loaves of bread, pots of baked meat. Sunday was a day of rest, but not of fasting, and so the baker must to work.

The embers flared and subsided. By law, a baker must extinguish his oven and hearth every night, for in a city of timber, fire was an ever-present threat. But kindling the flames anew each morning was a tedious chore, and so most let their ovens fall cold in the night, but banked the coals of the hearth for easy revival.

A cherry-red fragment collapsed with a sigh, and sparks leapt free.

In the house above, Thomas Farynor slept soundly. Business was good; he supplied ship's biscuit to the King's navy, and in these times of war with the Dutch he did not lack for work. He and his daughter Hanna had both a maid and a manservant to look after them and help with the running of the bakery.

Sparks had escaped the hearth before. They died soon after, reduced to black cinders that stained the rafters, the walls, and the brick-laid floor. But tonight one drifted farther than most, dancing on the invisible currents of the air, until it found a resting place on the fuel piled in the oven.

A tiny flame kindled on a splinter of wood.

Afterward, Farynor would claim he banked his fire safely when the day's business was done. He raked his oven clean, swept the bricks of the floor—and so he had, but sloppily. His daughter Hanna, inspecting the kitchen before she retired at midnight, saw nothing to fear.

But now, an hour later, the room glowed with new light.

Smoke wreathed the sooty beams of the ceiling. The Farynors' manservant, asleep on the ground floor, frowned and tossed beneath his blanket. His breathing grew ragged; he coughed once, then again, until at last he waked to the danger.

With a hoarse shout, he tore his way free of the bedclothes. The kitchen was well alight by now, hearth and oven blazing merrily, the debris on the floor, the piles of ready wood. The wall timbers, dried by a long summer of drought, smoked and were hot to the touch. He stumbled his way by reflex toward the stairs, barely able to see in the choking gloom.

The cloud pursued him upward. Crying out, the manservant pounded on his master's door. "Fire! In God's name, wake—the house is alight!"

The door swung open. Farynor, scraping sleep from his eyes, did not seem to understand. But when he went to the head of the stairs and saw for himself the scene below, all drowsiness fled. "God Almighty," he whispered, and ran back through his room to the adjoining door.

Hanna woke but slowly, and her maid more slowly still. Once up, they hurried on their shoes, while Farynor lent his man a pair. But as fast as they moved, they tarried too long: the flames had claimed the foot of the stairs.

The maid screamed and clutched at her mistress, gagging on the thick air. "We must try," Hanna cried, and gathered up the skirt of her shift. With one sleeve over her face to filter the air, she forced her way against the punishing heat, down into the hell below.

"Hanna!" Her father plunged after her. Already she was lost in the blinding smoke, but an instant later he heard a scream. A lurching body crashed into him, fire leaping up the side of her shift; they fell hard against the wooden steps, and his hands flew without thinking, beating out the flames. Hanna wept with pain as he dragged her bodily upward again, into the illusory safety of the chamber above.

"The window," his manservant said, while Hanna's legs collapsed beneath her. "We must try to climb out."

On an ordinary night, Farynor would have called it lunacy. But when the only alternative was death—"We cannot climb down, though."

His man was already unlatching the window. "Then

we go across. Onto the roof—if you go first, I will help your daughter."

Expansions years ago had jettied the upper floor outward so that it overhung the street. Farynor gasped in the fresher air, then forced his aging body through the narrow opening, clawing for the eaves above. His grip slipped, almost sending him to the street below, but his manservant caught his foot and gave him the push needed to lift him safely over the edge. Hanna was next, biting through her lip when the manservant gripped her blistered legs.

"Help!" she cried, as soon as she had her voice again. "Fire! Wake, rouse yourselves—fire in Pudding Lane!" Movement flickered in other windows. Theirs was not the only house whose upper stories overreached the boundary of its plot; she could almost touch the windows across the way, where faces pressed briefly against the glass, then vanished.

Pain and smoke set her to coughing, but by then Farynor had the cry. So Hanna was the one to see their manservant haul himself up over the edge of the roof—but where was the maid?

"She will not come," he said, eyes wild and bleak. "She fears the height too much. I tried—"

Hanna bent and shouted toward the open window, but there was no reply.

They could not stay. Moving carefully, the three eased their way along the edge of the roof to the neighbour's shutters. Farynor kicked against these, bellowing. Figures had begun to appear in the street below, most in their nightshirts, some with breeches and boots on. They knew what would be needed.

The shutters opened abruptly, scraping Farynor's bare leg. Reaching hands eased his daughter through into safety; then the baker, then his man. Heat radiated from the wall between the dwellings, but as yet there was no fire, and the house's leather buckets had been brought already, to soak the beams and the plaster in between.

In Pudding Lane, the parishioners of St Margaret's Fish Street rose to their duty, arranging bucket lines, flinging soil and dung, pails of milk, anything that came to hand. On this, the Lord's day of rest, they settled themselves for battle, to save themselves and their homes from fire.

PART ONE

TRUST IN PRINCES
1639–1642

"Consider seriously whither the beginning
of the happinesse of a people should be written
in letters of blood..."

THOMAS WENTWORTH,
FIRST EARL OF STRAFFORD
12 MAY 1641

THE ROYAL EXCHANGE, LONDON
3 June 1639

The beating heart of London's commerce sweltered like an oven in the early heat, dampening undershirts and linen collars, and subduing the voices that echoed off the walls. In the open stone of the courtyard, the sun hammered down on the hats and caps of the finely dressed merchants and customers who met to conduct business or exchange news. Some took refuge in the gallery ringing the space, where shade offered a relative degree of relief.

Upstairs, in the tiny enclosed shops, the air was stiflingly close. Sir Antony Ware fanned uselessly at his dripping face with a sheaf of papers—a petition foisted on him by a man outside. He might read it later, but for now, it served a better purpose. The fingers of his free hand trailed over a bottle of cobalt glass, while from behind the table the shopkeeper beamed encouragement at him. Those who patronised the Royal Exchange tended to be the better class of men, but even so, for this fellow to claim a baronet and alderman of London as a customer would give him a touch of prestige.

For his own part, Antony was more concerned with the question of whether Kate would like the bottle, or whether she would laugh at being presented with yet another gift. Pondering that, he heard too late the voice calling his name. The man trying to press through a knot of people outside stumbled and fell into him. Antony caught himself against the edge of the table, dropping the petition and setting the bottles to rocking dangerously.

He twisted to curse the man who made him stagger, but swallowed it at the last moment. "Sorry," Thomas Soame said, recovering his balance. "God's blood—everyone and his brother is packing in here. My foot snagged another fellow's, I fear."

"No harm done," Antony said, reassuring the glass merchant with a calming hand. "I did not see you."

"Nor hear me, it seems. Come, let's away, before someone else jostles me and disaster ensues. What is that?"

Antony sighed as he collected the scattered sheets, marked with damp patches where he had clutched them in his sweating hand. "A petition."

"For what?"

"No idea; I have not read it yet."

"Might be wiser to keep it that way. We could paper the walls of the Guildhall with the petitions that get shoved at us." Soame wasted no time, but turned and bulled his way carefully through the corridor outside. Following in his broad-shouldered wake, Antony hoped his friend did not mean to stand out in the courtyard and converse.

He did not. They descended the staircase, and so out into the clamour of Cornhill. Soame paused to let a keg-laden cart rumble past, and Antony catch up to him. Settling his hat more comfortably on his head, Antony asked the younger man, "Where do you lead me?"

"An alehouse," Soame said feelingly. "Out of this accursed sun, and into a place where I can tell you the news."

News? Antony's attention sharpened. A tavern would offer shade, drink—and a degree of privacy not to be found in the gossiping atmosphere of the Exchange. They went down the sloping mire of Cornhill and onward to Cheapside, where stood the Nag's Head, Soame's favourite tippling house. His friend planted a familiar kiss on a serving-wench and got them a table in a cool corner, with cups of sack to wet their throats. "Best watch your wife doesn't learn of that, Tom," Antony said, with a smile to cushion the warning; Mary Soame was a Puritan sort, and not likely to turn a blind eye to philandering.

Soame dismissed it with a wave of his hand. "A harmless buss on the cheek, is all; nothing to it."

On the lips, rather, but the younger man's behaviour was his own problem. Antony let it pass. "What brought you after me? This is hot weather for considering anything of import."

The broad features darkened. "And likely to get hotter," Soame said, not meaning the weather. "Have you heard Abbot's latest woe? *Our* woe, I should say."

Which made it political, not personal. Soame was an alderman for Vintry Ward, as Antony was for Langbourn, and while the list of things that might bring trouble to the Lord Mayor of London and his Court of Aldermen was long, Antony felt unpleasantly capable of narrowing it down. "Don't drag it out, man; just say."

"A loan."

"*Again?*"

"Are you surprised? The King pisses away money as his father did—though at least he has the decency to piss it on war instead of drunkenness and catamites."

Antony winced at the blunt words. "Watch your tongue! If you haven't a care for yourself, at least think of me; I'll be hanged for hearing your sedition, as you'll be hanged for speaking it."

Soame grinned, pulling out a roll of tobacco and his pipe. "I do no more than quote our Lord Mayor. But very well; I'll spare your tender sensibilities. Returning to the point: it seems the five thousand pounds the Common Council gave our good King Charles in March—"

"Were an insult at the time, and not one I imagine he's forgotten." Antony pinched the bridge of his nose and reached for his wine. "What has he asked for?"

"A hundred thousand."

Coughing on the wine, Antony fumbled for his handkerchief to wipe the spittle from his beard. "God in Heaven. Not again."

"You're quoting Abbot, too." Soame lit a spill from the candle and touched it to his pipe, drawing until the tobacco smouldered to his satisfaction. Exhaling the fragrant smoke, he went on. "We are the King's chamber, after all, are we not? The jewel in his crown, the preeminent city of his realm. For which distinction we pay handsomely—and pay, and pay again."

With compensation, to be sure—but only when they could squeeze it out of the royal purse. Which was not often enough for anyone's peace of mind. The Crown was chronically short of money, and slow to repay its debts. "Are the securities any good?"

"They're pig swill. But we've a war on our back step; unless we want to be buggered up the arse by the Scots, his Majesty will need money."

Antony sighed. "And to think—one sovereign on both thrones was supposed to *solve* that problem."

"Just like it did with the Irish, eh?" Soame sank back on the settle, wedging his shoulders into the corner of the walls. "Must be like trying to drive a team of three horses, all of them trying to bite each other."

An apt analogy. Old James, Charles's father, had dreamt of uniting his realms under a single crown, making himself not three Kings in one, but one King, ruling over one conjoined land. Or at least of Scotland and England conjoined; Antony was not certain whether he had meant to include Ireland in that happy harmony. At any rate, it had never come about; the English were fractious about a Scotsman ascending their throne in the first place, and not liable to agree to any such change.

With separate realms, though, came a host of inevitable problems, and Charles showed little delicacy in handling them—as this morass with the Scottish Covenanters demonstrated. Antony had some sympathy for their refusal to adopt the Anglican prayer book; the King's attempt to force it upon the Presbyterians up north had been as badly conceived and executed as this entire damn war. When they ejected the Anglican bishops, however, it only hardened the King against them.

Antony began to place his fingers one by one on the table's stained surface, mapping out the political landscape in his mind. The aldermen of London rarely refused the Crown, but the Common Council had grown more recalcitrant of late. *Their* response was certain: they had baulked against a loan in March, and would do so again.

Could the City raise the money? No doubt. Many aldermen and wealthy citizens were connected with the East India Company, the Providence Company, and other great trading ventures. Antony himself was an East India man, as was the Lord Mayor Abbot. The companies had loaned money to the Crown before. Their resentment was growing, though, as more and more of those loans went unpaid.

And religion played its role in the south, too. London harboured more than a few men sympathetic to the Presbyterian cause in Scotland; Antony knew full well that many of his fellow aldermen would gladly see the Church of England discard bishops and other popish trappings. They would not look kindly on the attempt to squelch the Scottish dissent.

Which was stronger: religion or nation? Ideology or economy?

"How fares the army?" he asked. "Is the King's need legitimate?"

In response, Soame beckoned for more wine, and waited until it came before he answered. "I drink to the poor souls up at Berwick," he said, and toasted the absent soldiers solemnly. "Half can't tell their right foot from their left, and from what I hear they're armed with pitchforks and profanity. Starvation, smallpox, an infestation of lice... I would not be there for all the wenches in Christendom."

"And no chance of peace?" Antony waved away his own question before Soame could answer it. "Always a chance, yes, I know. But it requires diplomacy his Majesty may not be inclined to exercise." If by *diplomacy* he meant a willingness to bend. And Charles was not renowned for his cooperative nature, especially in the twin matters of religion and royal prerogative. The Scots had stepped on both, with hobnailed boots.

Soame drew again on his pipe, staring mournfully down into the bowl. "Be of good cheer. The King's Majesty has not chosen to sell another monopoly—beg pardon, *patent*—or find another three-hundred-year-old tax to re-impose on us instead. At least a loan *might* be repaid."

"God willing," Antony muttered. "Peace may be likelier. Do you think these Covenanters in Scotland will accept it if the King promises them a Parliament?"

"When he hasn't given *us* one these ten years? What chance of that?"

"A delaying tactic," Antony said. "It allows the King

to disband the army, at least for now, and prepare more thoroughly for his next move."

The other man pondered it, chin propped on his fist. "It might serve. But if he calls a Parliament there, you *know* people will demand one here. That is a Pandora's box he will not wish to open."

True enough. Parliaments convened at the King's will, and Charles had made it abundantly clear ten years ago that he was done with them. They argued with him too much, and so he would rule England personally, without recourse to that fractious body. It was his right, but that did not make it popular—or, for that matter, successful.

Soame quirked his eyebrow at Antony's pensive face. "You've had a thought."

Not one Antony wished to share. He drained the last of his wine and shook his head. "The war with Scotland is not our problem to solve. Thank you for the warning; I shall sound out the common councilmen and our fellows, and see if opinions have changed since March. Will you join us tonight? Kate has recovered enough to go out; she wishes to ride into Covent Garden for dinner, and she would enjoy the company."

"Perhaps. I will call at your house this evening, at least."

Smiling, Antony stood and took his leave. But once outside the Nag's Head, his steps did not lead north, to the Guildhall and the chambers of London's government. If he was to effect any change, he would have to do it from elsewhere.

* * *

THE ONYX HALL, LONDON
3 June 1639

The lesser presence chamber might have been a portrait of well-bred courtiers at leisure. A gentleman flirted with a lady in the corner; others sat at a small table, playing cards. But the lady wore a farthingale that had not been fashionable since the days of old Elizabeth, while her paramour seemed formed of living stone; at the card table, the stakes at hazard were the forgotten memories of a silversmith and a midwife, a carpenter and a maidservant. The only mortal in the chamber was all but ignored, a musician whose flute struggled to be heard above the chatter of the faerie courtiers.

His melody went up, and up again, its tone increasingly piercing. Seated in her chair of estate a little distance away, Lune hid a wince behind her fan. *This will not do.*

She raised one hand, rings winking in the cool light. The flutist did not notice, but a nearby lord, eager to serve, hastened over and stopped him with little attempt at tact.

"We have had enough of music," Lune said, more diplomatically than she intended. The man's face had bunched in anger at the interruption, but at her words it faded to disappointment. "We thank you for your time. Sir Cerenel, if you would lead him out?" Not Lewan Erle, who had silenced him; that would see the mortal player dropped unceremoniously on the streets of London, lost and bewildered after his time among the fae. The man had played well—until the end. "With suitable reward for his service."

The knight she'd named bowed, one hand over his heart, and escorted the musician from the chamber. In his wake, the chatter of courtiers and ladies rose again.

Lune sighed and laid her fan against her lips to conceal her boredom. In truth, the player should not be faulted. She was discontented today, and small things grated.

From the door to the chamber, the sprite serving as usher announced, "Lord Eochu Airt!"

Or large ones.

The three who entered stood out vividly from the courtiers filling the chamber. Where the fae of her realm mostly followed the fashions of the human court, with such alterations as they saw fit, the Irish dressed in barbaric style. The warriors heeling the ambassador from Temair wore vivid blue cloaks clasped at one shoulder, but their chests were bare beneath, with bronze cuffs around their weapon arms. Eochu Airt himself wore a splendid robe decked with feathers and small, glittering medallions, and bore a golden branch in his hand.

"My lord," Lune greeted him, rising from her chair of estate and descending to meet the sidhe.

"Your Majesty." Eochu Airt answered her with a formal bow and a kiss of her hand, while behind him his bodyguards knelt. "I hope I find you well?"

"Idle. How liked you the play?"

The Irish elf scowled. His strawberry hair, long as a woman's but uncurled, fell over one eye as he straightened from his bow. He might be an ollamh, the highest rank of poet, but the Irish expected their poets to be warriors, too. The scowl was fierce. "Very little. The art of mortals is fine enough, and we give it favour as it deserves. But art, madam, is not what interests me."

Had she expected him to answer otherwise? Eochu Airt had arrived at the Onyx Court not long after All Hallows' Eve, replacing an ambassador who had been among them for years—a sure sign that Fiacha of Temair intended change. If she could endure until November, she might be rid of the newcomer; the yearly cycle of High Kings in Ireland meant change could be ephemeral.

But not always. This impatience had been growing for years. Should Eochu Airt be replaced, she might find someone worse in his place.

If there was to be an argument, Lune would rather not have it in the more public space of the presence chamber. "Come, my lord ollamh," she said, taking him by the arm. Feathers tickled her wrist, but she concealed the irritation they sparked. "Let us retire and speak of this more."

The elf-knights on the far door swept the panels open for the two of them to pass through, leaving the Irish warriors behind. Several of her ladies made to follow, until Lune gestured them back with a flick of her fingertips. She did not want them standing at attention over the conversation, but if they sat at their ease with embroidery or cards, Eochu Airt invariably felt she was not considering his points as seriously as she should.

Faerie lights flared into wakefulness around the privy

chamber, and some prescient hob had set out two chairs on the figured Turkish carpet. Lune indicated that the sidhe should take one. "You seem to have perceived your afternoon as an insult," she said, settling herself in the other. "I assure you, I intended no such offence. I merely thought you, as a poet, would appreciate the artistry."

"It was well-written," he grudged, and laid the golden branch of his rank aside in this atmosphere of lesser formality. "But the journey reeked of distraction."

Which it had been—or at least that was the idea. Lune had hoped he might become enamoured of the playhouses, and spend more of his time there. It would mean supplying him with protection against the iron and faith of the mortal world, but she would account it well spent, to have him out of her chambers.

She frowned at him. "I would not belittle your intelligence in such a fashion, to think you so easily led astray. I know you treat your duties here with all the reverence and dedication they deserve."

"Pretty words, madam. Need I remind you, though—I did not come here for words. I came for action. The 'thorough' policy of your Wentworth is an outrage."

Not my *Wentworth,* she wanted to say. *I had nothing to do with his appointment as Lord Deputy of Ireland.* But that would only play into Eochu Airt's hands, raising the very point she was trying to dodge. "Some of Wentworth's notions for governing Ireland could be beneficial to you, did you but acknowledge it. Catholic rituals hold a great deal of power against our kind. Their passing may be a good thing. The hotter sort of Protestantism poses its own danger, true—but what Wentworth would institute is no more than lukewarm." In truth it was half-popish, as the Scots kept screaming. But not in ways that mattered overmuch to fae.

Eochu Airt's expression darkened. "What he institutes is *plantation*." He spat the word like the obscenity he no doubt considered it to be.

Had she really expected to divert him from that issue? Lune rose from her chair and rang a bell. "Some wine, I think, would lubricate this discussion." The door opened, and her Lady Chamberlain Amadea Shirrell came in with platter, decanter, and goblets. *Efficient as always.* Lune waved her away, pouring the wine herself, and waited until the door had shut again, closing out the low rumble of the presence chamber. "I do understand your concern. The New English—"

"New English, Old English—they are all the same to me. They are *English,* in Ireland." Eochu Airt accepted the wine from her hand, but paced angrily as he spoke. "They claim our lands for their own, driving off those whose families have dwelt there since we fae lived outside our hills. Our hobs weep without ceasing, to see their ancient service brought to an ignominious end."

The ollamh's voice flowed melodically, even spurred by anger. Lune answered him evenly, trying not to show her own. "I cannot undo England's conquest of Ireland, my lord ambassador."

"But you *could* act against Wentworth and his allies.

Put a stop to this rape of our land."

The figures chased in silver around the outside of the wine cup dug into Lune's fingers. "I *have* acted. Charles confirmed the Earl of Clanricarde's title against Wentworth's challenge. His estates will not be planted with settlers."

It only gained her a scowl. "Which helps Galway. But what of the rest of Ireland, madam, that still suffers beneath the English yoke?" He was an Ulsterman himself; she had chosen her defence poorly. With a visible effort, the sidhe moderated his tone. "We do not demand assistance for free. All of the Ard-Ríthe, and any of the lesser kings beneath them, would be glad to grant concessions in return. We have information you would find most useful."

Neither of them had taken a sip of the wine. So much for lubrication. Setting hers down, Lune suppressed a sigh, and folded her hands across the front of her skirt. "What you desire is more direct manipulation, and that is not the policy of this court."

"Once it was."

She went very still. Here it came at last: the overt reminder. She had been wondering how long it would take, ever since his arrival after All Hallows' Eve. This ambassador was willing to use more weapons than his predecessor had been. "Never under our rule. We will thank you to remember that."

The formal shift to the plural pronoun hit him like a slap. Eochu Airt smoothed the hair out of his face, then set down his own wine and crossed back to the chairs, where he retrieved his golden branch of office. "As you wish, madam. But I fear the Ard-Rí will not be glad to hear it."

"Tell our cousin Fiacha," Lune said, "that we are not averse to cooperation. But I will not wrap strings around the mortal court and dance it like my puppet. I work for the harmony of humans and fae by more subtle means."

"Your Highness." Eochu Airt answered her with a stiff bow and exited, leaving her alone in the privy chamber.

Lune placed one hand against the silver-gilt leather covering the wall and gritted her teeth. Not well handled. Not well at all. But what could she do? The Irish were probably the only fae in Europe who missed the days when her predecessor ruled, when the Queen of the Onyx Court did not baulk at manipulating anyone, mortal or otherwise.

No, not the only ones. But the most vexatious.

She had some sympathy for their desires. If her own land were overrun by foreigners, ousting those with ancestral claim, she, too, would fight tooth and claw to defend it. But this was not her fight, and she would not compromise her principles to win it for the Irish. Mortals were not pawns, to be shuffled about the board at will.

Lune composed her expression and went back out into the presence chamber. Her courtiers murmured amongst themselves; no one would have overlooked the departure of Eochu Airt and his warriors. Some of them had even accepted gifts to solicit her on behalf of the Irish. Nianna, the silly fool, was flirting with a ganconer the ambassador had the audacity to bring, trading on her position as

Mistress of the Robes. If Lune gave them half a chance, they would all be seeking her ear.

She had no patience for it, not now. There were bathing chambers in the Onyx Hall, their waters heated by salamanders; perhaps she would go rest in one of those, and try to think of a way to mollify the High Court at Temair.

But she did not move quickly enough. While she hesitated next to her chair, the door opened again, revealing a man more out of place than even the Irish. Sandy-haired, solid of build, ordinary as brown bread—and wearing a determined expression entirely at odds with the blithe amusements of the chamber. The usher raised his voice again. "The Prince of the Stone!"

LONDON ABOVE AND BELOW
3 June 1639

Threadneedle Street was an unmoving snarl of carts, coaches, horses, and men afoot, so Antony turned south, seeking a path through the lesser crowds of Walbrook Street, and then the much smaller Cloak Lane, where the jettied upper storeys of houses overhung the mud of the roadway. In the shadow of the Cutlers' Hall, he placed one hand on the thick, pitch-coated beam that separated two houses, and splayed his fingers wide.

Behind him, the people of London continued on their way, taking no notice of him—nor of the shadowed gap that appeared where none had been before, squeezing itself into the non-existent space between the houses. Into this narrow aperture Antony stepped, turning sideways so his shoulders would not scrape the walls.

When it closed behind him, he stood at the head of an equally narrow staircase spiralling downward, with only faint illumination to guide him. Antony descended, careful of his footing on the steps—not slate, nor limestone, nor Kentish ragstone, but a slick blackness found nowhere in the ordinary structures of London.

For the realm he entered was no ordinary structure. It felt like another world, and so, in a sense, it was: London's shadow, taken shape within the earth, and sheltering in its myriad of chambers and passages an entire faerie court, unseen and unsuspected.

Except by a few.

A vaulted gallery led out from the bottom of the staircase. Cool lights shone down from among the ribs that supported the ceiling, some wandering gently of their own will, so that the shadows shifted and danced. This place reflected the world above, but not directly; the Threadneedle entrance lay not far from him, though a goodly distance away as he had walked it. If Antony's guess was right, he was near the place—and the person—he sought.

A liveried sprite stood at a nearby door, confirming his guess. The creature bowed deeply, threw the door open, and announced in a voice far larger than his body, "The Prince of the Stone!"

The sight that greeted him inside the chamber was a blinding one, an array of jewel-bright silks and fantastical bodies, sitting or standing at carefully-posed leisure. Long use had accustomed him to the splendour—but not to its centrepiece, the axis around which it all revolved.

Lune stood by her chair of estate, with the alert, arrested posture of a deer. The elaborate curls of her silver hair still trembled against her cheek, for she had turned her head sharply just before the usher's cry. They outshone the cloth-of-silver of her petticoat, and made the lute-string silk of her bodice and looped-up overskirt a richer midnight by comparison. Sapphires winked in her circlet, each one worth a lord's ransom.

Their eyes met; then he blinked, breaking the spell. A faerie queen was a powerful sight, however often one saw it. And he had been some time away.

Lune came forward to greet him. A small furrow marred the line of her brow; she must be concealing a much larger frustration. "Antony," the Queen said. Her voice rang purely, after the harsh clamour of the streets above, and she smiled to see him, but it did not reach her unsettled eyes. "I am glad for your return. Will you walk with me in the garden?"

It suited his purpose well. Antony made his bow, then offered her his arm. Together they left the chamber, a small flock of her closest ladies trailing behind.

The fae they passed along the way bowed out of their paths, deference offered to both the Queen and her mortal

Prince. Antony had never grown entirely accustomed to it. His wealthy father had purchased a baronetcy when old King James created the rank and sold titles to prop up the Crown's sagging finances, but a hereditary knighthood did not merit the kinds of courtesies offered to a prince. He had long practice at shifting between the two, but never quite ceased to find the honours strange.

They came through a delicate arch into the night garden. Here, against all nature, greenery thrived; the efforts of dedicated faerie gardeners produced fantastical sprays of blossoms, and fruit out of season. Its proximity was one reason Lune preferred the lesser presence chamber to its more imposing counterpart, where her throne stood. She walked often along the winding paths, in company or alone, listening to musicians or the liquid melodies of the Walbrook. Antony himself found regrettably little time to enjoy it.

A current eddied the stars above them as they stepped out into the cool, fragrant air; the constellation of faerie lights regrouped themselves into a tight mass, a counterfeit moon. "I take it something troubles you," Antony said, and felt Lune's fingers tighten on his arm.

"Not something—some*one*. Would you care to guess?"

He smiled wryly. "There are but two likely suspects. I shall guess Nicneven."

"I almost wish it were."

The sour response surprised him. Faerie Scotland was not a single kingdom, no more than faerie England was, and

Lune had occasional trouble with the monarchs up north. The Gyre-Carling of Fife, however, was a constant thorn in her side. Nicneven made no secret of her hatred for this court and everything it stood for, the close harmony of mortals and fae. She had on more than one occasion threatened to kill Antony, or curse his family for nine generations.

On the whole, his preference was for Irish trouble. "I can guess the substance of it, then," he said.

Lune released his arm, going to the side of the path, where a lily bloomed in an urn. Its pristine white petals darkened into a bloody throat, and she stroked them with a fingertip. "One day some clever lad over there will get it into his head to murder Wentworth."

"They know better than that," Antony said, alarmed. "If the King's deputy in Ireland dies, it will go much harder for them."

"Oh, indeed—*some* of them know it. But all it needs is one hot-headed warrior, one goblin out to make mischief…" Behind them, the flock of ladies hovered, like birds in jewelled feathers and elegant little masks. Lune sighed and continued down the path to a fountain, where she arranged herself on a bench, and her ladies perched themselves near enough to listen discreetly. "Eochu Airt said his masters at Temair had information I would desire. I shall have to find something else he wants in exchange."

Antony leaned against the lip of the fountain, palms flat to the cool marble. The water flecked his back, but his rose-coloured doublet was of plain serge; it could survive a wetting. He had not dressed for elegance. "Wentworth isn't popular at court. His relationship with the King is uneven; Charles does not entirely trust him, but still supports him, for he is one of the few effective men serving the Crown. There has even been talk of his making Wentworth a peer. But the Lord Deputy has enemies in plenty, not just in Ireland but in England, who do not like his influence over the King. His downfall might not be far away."

"Will that change anything for Ireland?" Lune's question was clearly rhetorical. She scowled at the embroidered toe of her slipper for a moment, then fixed her attention back on Antony. "So what has brought you below? When last you were here, you said you wished to spend more time with Lady Ware and your new son. How fares he? Is he growing quickly?"

Her distraction was charming. Children came so rarely to fae; they found the young of mortals fascinating. "Robin grows healthy and strong—no doubt thanks to your blessing." Three children, and none of them lost to childhood illness. Antony knew more godly sorts would say he had sold his soul for those blessings, consorting with fae as he did. Seeing his family thrive, he thought it a worthy price.

Lune's eyes narrowed. "But you, it seems, did not come to talk about your son. What, then? You walked into the presence chamber with a purpose."

"An opportunity," Antony admitted. "One that may sweeten your mood."

The ladies leaned closer to hear as he went on. "The war with Scotland does not go well. Charles has marched an army up there to suppress the Covenanters, but that army is falling apart at the seams, for want of money to hold it together. And so he has asked the City for a loan."

"Again?" Lune said, echoing his own response to Soame. "This begging has become habit, and unfitting to a king." He couldn't argue the truth of that. "But why bring you this to me? It won't help matters to pay the loan in faerie gold."

"Of course not. My intent is not to pay it at all."

The Queen stared at him, silver eyes unblinking. Her entire image might have been cast from silver, and draped in darkest lapis. He waited while she weighed the repercussions. "I am sure you have your reasons," she said at last, the statue coming to life once more. "You know the finances of the City better than I. But see the larger picture: failure to crush the Covenanters now will mean their stronger presence in the future. Too much of London is sympathetic to them already, and *they* are hostile to *us*."

Us had many possible meanings, depending on the occasion. Sometimes it was the royal pronoun. Sometimes it meant Londoners, above and below. This time, it was unmistakably the meaning in between: the fae of the Onyx Court. Nowhere in the world, that Antony knew of, was there a faerie city alongside a mortal one; the other kingdoms of the fae held their seats in places remote from human habitation.

The Onyx Hall made it possible. That great structure,

encompassing within itself chambers and passages as London did buildings and streets, sheltered them from the church bells and iron of the world above. But its inhabitants ventured above, too, and preferred to find the world they visited, if not friendly, then at least neutral.

The hotter Protestants—Presbyterians and the independent-minded "godly", whose enemies called them Puritan—were far from neutral. To such people, all fae were devils, and Scotland under their rule was a harsh and austere place. If their influence in England were to grow, the fae would suffer for it.

Antony said, "I am aware. There is, however, another consideration.

"The King is desperate for money. Already his judges and his lawyers have found every loophole, every obscure and unenforced statute that might afford him some revenue—ship money, distraint of knighthood; he even continues to collect tonnage and poundage, without the legal right. And still it is not enough."

Lune's chin came up, and he wondered if she saw where he aimed. Though her face showed no identifiable age, she had reigned longer than he had been alive, and had been at the game of politics longer than that.

"If he cannot get money from the City," Antony said, "then he will be forced to convene Parliament."

A nightingale sang in a nearby willow tree. The ladies were too well bred to whisper amongst themselves while their Queen sat in silent thought, but they exchanged glances. Lune kept no one about her who did not understand at least the basics of mortal politics.

At last she said, "Why bring this to me?"

"For aid," Antony said. She had not rejected the notion out of hand; it encouraged him. "When I said my intent was not to pay it, I spoke of the outcome I hope to see. But I think it will be a close decision. The Common Council will vote against it, but I should like to ensure the aldermen likewise decide against the King. Penington and others have little love for this war."

"Then arrange it yourself." Lune rapped the words out like the crack of an unfolding fan. "Surely you have the means to convince your fellows."

Her sharp rejoinder took him aback. Straightening from his ease against the fountain, Antony said in mild tones, "If I had sufficient time, perhaps. But I cannot be both quick and subtle, and the King is not above imprisoning those who defy him."

Lune, too, rose from her seat on the bench. "You ask this of me—by influencing their dreams, I presume?" It was the most gentle method of persuasion, but Antony had no chance to say so before she went on. "For the sake of a refusal they might not otherwise give. But I am not convinced of your course."

Why did she resist it so unthinking? Fear of the Covenanters and their religion could not explain it all. Lune was protective of her fae subjects, yes, but she was also protective of England—

Ah. Of England, and of the monarchy. Which she had once sworn to defend, many years ago, when an Englishwoman still sat upon the throne. Such rebellion to the will of the Crown would not sit well with her. But Lune was not fond of the man who wore that crown; she knew Charles's flaws as well as Antony did. What she overlooked was how reluctance would serve England better than obedience would. "For ten years now, Charles has ruled without the advice of Parliament," he reminded her.

A sniff came from the cluster of listeners. Boldly, Lady Nianna said, "Her Majesty rules without need of a Parliament."

"Her Majesty rules a realm with fewer subjects than my ward," Antony snapped back, angered at the interruption. Grimacing, he made a quick bow of apology to Lune. "England has many thousands of inhabitants—hundreds of thousands in the vicinity of London alone. One man, even advised by councillors, cannot fairly oversee so much. And Parliament, the House of Commons especially, has long been the means by which the people may speak, and make their needs known to their sovereign. But he discarded that tradition when it became inconvenient to him."

The Queen had stiffened at his reply to Nianna; now she watched him impassively. Antony hesitated, then played a dangerous card. "He would rule as your predecessor did— his will absolute, with none to gainsay him."

Anger flared in those silver eyes. "Do not make comparisons where you are ignorant," Lune said, her voice cold. "You know nothing of this court in those times."

"I know what you have told me," Antony said, meeting her without flinching. "And I know why you asked me to rule at your side, bestowed upon me the title I bear. So that we could work together for the benefit of all, both mortal and fae. Very well: I come before you, as Prince of the Stone, and tell you that London needs this. *England* needs this."

It was easy to be overawed in the presence of a faerie queen. The Prince was the Queen's consort, though, and bore his own authority in this court. They had gone to loggerheads before, when Antony felt his duty demanded it; Lune had chosen him for that reason, because he would stubbornly defend the mortal concerns she might otherwise forget. Because she could trust him to do so only when necessary.

He met her gaze, and did not back down.

A faint shadow appeared along her jaw where a muscle tightened and then released. This confrontation might have been inevitable, but he could at least have arranged for privacy. It felt too much like coercion, asserting his rank before her ladies, forcing her to acknowledge his right to ask this favour. He would apologise for that later.

"Very well," Lune said at last, through her teeth. "We will see to it that those who waver are swayed against the loan."

The royal *we,* or the faerie one? Either way, he had what he wanted, though not gracefully. Antony offered her a sincere bow. "My thanks. In exchange, I will likewise do what I can to turn opinion against the Covenanters."

There was a gleam in Lune's eye he could not interpret—

anger given way to something like amusement. "Indeed you will. If this goes as you hope, and Charles summons a new Parliament, then we expect you to be there."

He blinked. "In Parliament?"

"You are not a peer, and you have few connections in the countryside; you will have to fight for one of London's seats in the Commons. But that is fitting: you will sit for London's faerie inhabitants, as the others sit for the mortals."

Antony had not thought that far. There was, admittedly, no reason he could not do as she asked. Except that the long delay since the last Parliament left him with little sense of that world—how to get into it, and what to do once he was there.

It could not be so different from the Court of Aldermen. And although he was used to thinking of himself as the envoy of mortals to the fae, he could cross that boundary in the other direction as well. It was the sort of thing the Prince of the Stone *should* do.

He gave Lune a second bow. "As you command, madam."

KETTON STREET, LONDON
2 April 1640

The man forced to his knees on the cellar floor in front of Lune was securely gagged, and his hands bound behind him. Above the silencing rag, the mortal's eyes burned with hatred that would sear her to ash if it could.

Had he his tongue to speak, he could not burn her, but he could cause great harm. She was protected, of course; Lune never came above without consuming milk or bread tithed to the fae, which shielded them against faith, iron, and other inimical charms. Strong enough faith, though, could overcome much, like an axe crashing through armour.

She did not want to test this man's faith. He could glare at her all he wished, so long as he did not invoke divine names, and the gag was the gentlest means of silencing him.

"Where did you find him?" she asked Sir Prigurd Nellt.

The giant towered behind the kneeling man, even though the glamour concealing his nature reduced him to something like human size. The Captain of the Onyx Guard was uncomfortable with such disguises, and wore them badly. "Near Aldersgate," he rumbled, his deep voice vibrating in her body. "Piling tinder at the base of the tree, with flint and steel in his hand."

Lune concealed her shiver. Prigurd was steadfast in the execution of his duty to protect her; if she showed how much this man frightened her, the giant might just crack his head and be done with it.

What could his fire have done? She honestly did not know. The Onyx Hall was a familiar presence in her mind, like a second skin, laid over her flesh when she claimed sovereignty. But she had not uncovered all its secrets, and could only speculate what would happen if someone tried to destroy one of the hidden entrances that joined the faerie palace to the mortal fabric of London.

It was a question worth investigating, but not now. "Who is he?"

The prisoner jerked against his bonds. Behind him, Prigurd's fingers twitched, and a low growl betrayed the giant's leashed temper.

The man who stepped forward to answer her fit better in their mean surroundings than either Lune or Prigurd. He dressed as a common labourer—even though his education, if not his birth, entitled him to better—and knew places like the tavern above their heads well enough to secure this cellar for the interrogation, when Lune decided not to risk bringing the prisoner into the Onyx Hall. Were it not for the undisguised sprite perched on his shoulder, holding a quill and a horn of ink, he might have been any ordinary, forgettable man.

Which suited him perfectly for his role. A spymaster should not be memorable.

Mortals who had dealings with the Onyx Court and knew it were still few in number, despite efforts by both Lune and Antony. They had over a dozen now, which was an improvement, but the ever-present threat of the godly and the necessity of keeping the Onyx Hall secure made bringing in strangers a chancy proposition at best. Most were there because they had ties to some courtier—a lover, usually, or the artistic client of a faerie patron. Of them all, only Benjamin Hipley had risen to a position of influence, carrying out certain underhand tasks Antony could not or would not handle.

"Humphrey Taylor," he said, reading from a scrap of paper the sprite handed down to him. "His parish is St Botolph Aldersgate, outside the wall, where he's been known to preach a Puritan sermon or twelve."

She was not surprised in the least. Humphrey Taylor's torn and scuffed clothes were severe in cloth, colour, and cut, a statement against the vainglory of the royal court. Those would have identified him, if the zeal in his eyes had not.

Lune wished she could take the gag from his mouth and question him herself. But even if she could trick him into accepting faerie wine, thus stopping the godliness of his tongue, Lune did not want the man crawling about for the rest of his life, pining after the faerie world he'd lost.

No. A fellow such as this would not pine. He would commit suicide, accepting that damnation to escape this one; or he would find some way to martyr himself trying to obliterate her court.

Much like this first attempt.

"You say he was trying to burn the alder tree," she said, circling her prisoner, just far enough away that her skirts would not brush him. Prigurd shifted, clearly not pleased to see his Queen approach the man so closely, but let her pass unhindered. "How did he learn of it? Did he know what it was he sought to destroy?"

Hipley gave the paper back to the sprite and shooed it off its shoulder perch. "He had at least some notion it was connected with the fae. How much beyond that, I can't say for sure. But he learned of it through dreams."

"Dreams?" Lune halted in her pacing. "From whom?"

Her mortal spymaster shrugged apologetically. "What's in a man's head cannot be tracked, more's the pity. But I asked questions of his neighbours—no family in London—and learned that his dreams started after a visit from a Scottish Presbyterian this winter."

"A real one?"

"If I could find the Scotsman," Hipley replied, "I might be able to say. Taylor certainly thought he was real."

Lune pinched the bridge of her nose, then made herself lower her hand. Whether the Presbyterian had been a disguised faerie or not, he linked this attack to Scotland—and the court of Nicneven, the Gyre-Carling of Fife.

It was no use to protest that Nicneven's hatred of her was misdirected. Lune had no part in the intrigues that had killed the mortal Queen of Scots fifty years before, but that did not matter; Onyx Court interference had contributed to the execution of Mary Stuart. Most Scottish fae had forgotten it—such human things quickly passed from their minds—but Nicneven yet harboured a grudge.

Until now, though, the Gyre-Carling's opposition had been a subtle thing. A sizable faction in Lune's court, encouraged by Nicneven's allies and agents, believed fae superior to mortals. Humans were playthings at best; at worst, they weakened the fae, diminished them from the great beings they once were, in the distant past no one could remember clearly. Cooperation with them—the harmony Lune advocated—could only be to the detriment of the fae.

The Onyx Hall was the instrument of that cooperation, the shelter that allowed their coexistence. It seemed that Nicneven, impatient with her progress, had decided to strike more directly.

Even with Taylor stopped, there might still be danger. Lune roused herself and addressed Hipley once more. "What has he said to his neighbours?"

He saw the real question. "They think him deranged. A fever of the brain, perhaps—though the man who shares his lodgings thinks it some cryptic protest against the corruption of the court. Some kind of metaphor. He asked if I was an agent of the privy council. I think he hoped for a reward."

Then they were safe—for now. When the only mortals brought into the Onyx Hall were the pets and pawns of courtiers, discarded after they broke, concealment had been easier. But with the rising tide of Puritan faith, she would have to take more care. If anyone ever came to believe there were faeries beneath London—anyone hostile...

"Track the Scotsman," she said. "Do you have his name? Find out who sent him, whether some power in Scotland, or another working through ruses." The Cour du Lys in France bore her no love, after some tangled dealings in the past. And French connections to Scotland were still strong enough that they might find it a useful cover for their actions.

Taylor lurched to his feet without warning and lunged for the door to the tavern above. The sprite was there before the rest of them could react, tripping the prisoner and sending him headlong into the dirt floor. Prigurd wrestled the man back to his knees, and this time held him there with one heavy hand. Hipley moved to the stairs, to see if the noise had brought any undue attention; when all was quiet, he turned back to Lune. "What would you like done with him, madam?"

Humphrey Taylor knew one entrance to the Onyx Hall. With that information in his keeping, he could not be permitted to go back to his parish, nor to communicate with those pulling his strings. Even if they blurred his memory, it would be too risky, given the strength of his faith.

"He is Lord Antony's to dispose of," Lune reminded Hipley. Anything pertaining to mortals required the Prince's consent. "You may tell him it is our recommendation that a manikin be left somewhere discoverable, so enchanted and fortified that it may be taken for his body and buried. The man himself…"

She looked down at Humphrey Taylor and his burning, hate-filled eyes. It would be easiest to kill him—easiest, but wrong. The Onyx Court did not behave thus anymore. What she would send him to, though, might amount to the same thing in the end.

"Put him on a ship for the colonies," she said. "Let him make a new life for himself there, where he cannot threaten us."

GUILDHALL, LONDON
14 April 1640

Despite the headache and sour stomach that were mementos of the previous night's celebration, a smile kept warming Antony's face as he approached the soot-stained front of London's Guildhall. Soame and other friends had dined with his family last night, and together they drank to the opening of Charles's fourth Parliament. It had taken longer than Antony expected, but the House of Lords and House of Commons once again met in their chambers in Westminster Palace.

In fact, the Commons was sitting at that very moment, and Antony regretted his absence. When he and Lune agreed he should secure one of the four seats for London, he had not realised how much time it was likely to consume. A foolish oversight on his part; it would run him ragged, he feared, juggling his responsibilities in City government with those of Parliament, and trying to maintain his trade interests as well.

Not to mention, his guilty conscience whispered, *your duties down below.*

But he could do little enough to address Lune's problems, especially since Eochu Airt cordially detested him. Antony had little or nothing to do with London's contracts to plant Ireland with English settlers—many of those agreements were formed when he was a child not yet in breeches—but as far as the sidhe was concerned, his place in the City's government tarnished him with that guilt.

Parliament, however, was a different battlefield entirely, and one where he had great hopes of victory. Now that Charles had retreated from his declaration of personal rule, the old balance could be restored. Antony hurried through the doors, hoping he could dispose of this business quickly and get himself to Westminster. The chamber where the Commons met was too small; he would likely find no seat at this hour. But even if it meant standing, he was eager to attend.

Inside, the Great Hall teemed like an anthill with councilmen, clerks, petitioners, and more. He should have chosen a better hour, when men with grievances were less likely to be lying in wait. Antony ducked his head, letting the brim of his hat conceal his face, and slipped through the crowd, hurrying through the hall and upstairs.

Once free of the press, he discovered he was not the only person absent from the Commons that morning. Isaac Penington greeted him with a degree of cheer not warranted by their usual relationship. The alderman for Bridge Without was a much more vehement soul than Antony in matters of both politics and religion, and they had clashed on several occasions.

"Not in Westminster?" the other man said, deliberately jovial. "I hope you haven't tired of Parliament already."

Antony donned an equally deliberate smile. "Not at all. Merely addressing some business."

"Good, good! We have some grand designs for these next few weeks, you know. I would not want you to miss them."

Grand designs? That sounded ominous. And Antony suspected that *we* had a rather more specific meaning than the Commons as a whole. He sorted hastily through the names in his head, trying to remember who out of the hundreds of members might be in alliance with Penington. Antony's own father had sat in Charles's last Parliament, and though most of the leaders from that age had died or moved on, at least one was back again. The man had led the attempt to impeach the King's old chief councillor, the Duke of Buckingham, and his political ambitions did not stop there. "Yourself and John Pym?" Antony hazarded.

Penington's smile grew more genuine. "More than just us. Hampden, Holles—quite a few, really. We finally have an opportunity to make a stand against the King's offences, and we shall not waste it."

Antony's unease deepened. Hidden in the King's opening speech the day before was the very real concern of an impending second war with the Scots. Charles had buried it in a morass of platitudes about the zealous and humble affection the Commons no doubt felt for their sovereign, but the simple fact was that he had called them because he needed money to put down the rebellious Covenanters, as he had failed to do the previous year. "Which offences?"

"Why, all of them, man!" Penington laughed. "Religion first, I should think—Archbishop Laud's popish changes to the Church, surplices, altar rails, all those Romish abominations. We will have the bishops out before we are done, I vow. Or this policy of friendship to Rome's minions; bad enough to have a Catholic Queen, but the King tolerates priests even beyond her household. He would sell England to Spain if it would gain him some advantage. Or perhaps another approach; we may speak first of his offences against the liberties of Parliament."

"The King," Antony said, choosing his words carefully, "will no doubt be more inclined to consider those matters once the venture against Scotland is provided for."

Now the smile had a wolfish cast. "Oh, the King will have his subsidies—but not until we have had our voice."

That was in direct contravention of Charles's instructions. Antony caught those words before they left his mouth, though. Penington could hardly have forgotten that speech. He flouted it knowingly.

To some extent, he could see the man's point. Once Charles had his money, there was a very real risk the King would feel free to ignore his Parliament, or even to dissolve it entirely, considering its business done. Those subsidies were the only advantage they held.

And the offences, he had to admit, were real. Ten years without a Parliament—more like eleven, by now—were only an outward sign of the problem. The real contention was Charles's philosophy, supported by his judges and councillors, that the sole foundation of all law was the royal will and pleasure, and by no means did that law bind that will. Unjust taxation and all the rest followed from that, for how could it be unjust if the King decreed it necessary?

Penington was watching him closely. "We shall make

time for you to speak, if you like," he said. "There must needs be some debate, though we hope to have bills prepared for voting before much longer. They will stall in the Lords, of course, but it's a start."

The unspoken words hung behind the spoken, with more than a little menace: *You are with us, are you not?*

Antony did not know. He was no lapdog to the King, but what he knew of Pym and the others Penington had named worried him. Puritan zealots, most of them, and far too eager to undermine the King in pursuit of their own ends. Ends that were not necessarily Antony's own. Fortunately, over Penington's shoulder he saw the clerk he needed to speak to. With false humour, he said, "If I do not finish my work here, I shall never make it to Westminster in time to do anything. If you will pardon me?"

"Of course," Penington said, and let him by—but Antony felt the man's gaze on his back as he went.

THE ANGEL INN. ISLINGTON
23 April 1640

Accepting a cup of mead with a grateful smile, Lune said, "I know you two keep yourselves informed. No doubt you can guess what has brought me here today."

Rosamund Goodemeade blinked innocent eyes at her and said, curtsying, "Why, your Majesty, we thought you just wished our company!"

"And our mead," her sister Gertrude added. "And our food, I suspect—we've bread fresh from the oven, some excellent cherries, and roast pheasant, if you fancy a bite to eat." She scarcely even waited for Lune's answering nod, but bustled off to gather it, and no doubt more besides.

As much as Lune loved her hidden palace, she had to admit that no part of it equalled the comfort and warmth of the Goodemeades' home. Concealed beneath the Angel, a coaching inn north of the City, it was a favoured sanctuary for courtiers needing a respite from the Onyx Hall and its intrigues. The brownie sisters who maintained it always had a ready meal and a readier smile for any friend stopping in, and they counted as friends more fae than Lune would have believed possible.

Rosamund tucked a honey-brown curl up inside her linen cap and settled herself in one of the child-size chairs they kept for themselves and other small guests. Any formality between them had long since melted away, at least in private; she needed no permission to sit, even from her Queen. "I'm guessing it's Nicneven," she said, returning to the purpose of this visit.

Lune sighed. As much as she would have liked to spend her afternoon merely enjoying the Goodemeades' company, she could not spare the time. As Rosamund had clearly deduced. "You came originally from the Border, I know. I do not suppose it was the Scottish side?"

She was unsurprised when the brownie shook her head. "And the folk in Fife are different yet from Border folk, even on the Scots side," Rosamund said. "We shall help you in any way we can, of course, but we know little of the Gyre-Carling and her people."

Gertrude had returned, balancing a tray almost as large as she was, piled high with more food than Lune could possibly eat. Judging by the way Gertrude nibbled at the cherries while setting out dishes, though, she and Rosamund intended to share. "What were you hoping for?" she asked, licking her fingers clean of juice.

"Some sort of agent," Lune admitted. "A friend you might have in Fife, or someone you know in one of the other Scottish courts, who could go there and not seem out of place. My courtiers are almost all English fae, or more foreign than that."

"A spy?" Rosamund said.

As Ben Hipley conducted the Onyx Hall's covert work among mortals, so did Valentin Aspell, her Lord Keeper, handle that which dealt with fae. But for certain matters— more delicate ones—the Goodemeades were Lune's best, and least suspected, resource. She said, "You know of the attack on the alder tree. As much as I wish I could believe Taylor was sent on his errand by a traitor in my own court— as strange as it is to wish for such a thing—I have reason to believe Nicneven is behind it. Which means something has changed in the North. I must find out what."

Gertrude gestured, admonishing her to eat, and obediently Lune began to butter a hunk of fresh bread. *This plainer food might appeal to Eochu Airt,* she thought, remembering his disdainful comments about the more elaborate meals of her court. The Irish, as she understood it, feasted in simpler fashion. *I may try this, and see if it sweetens his mood.*

She was allowing herself to become distracted; the problem at hand was Scotland, not Ireland. Communicating through glances and the occasional half-finished word, the Goodemeades had already carried out an entire conversation. Now Rosamund said, "It might not be the Gyre-Carling. You know who's at her court."

The bread caught in Lune's throat; she washed it down with mead. "Yes," she said, heavily. "Kentigern Nellt. And yes, I have considered that this may be nothing more or less than revenge for Halgresta."

The giant had not loved his sister; Lune sincerely doubted him capable of love. But Kentigern had taken deep offence when Halgresta died in battle, and he had cause to blame Lune, for that battle was her doing. She had exiled him precisely to avoid any attempt at vengeance; had he tried, she would have been forced to execute him, and that she would not do. But exiled, he had gone back to his old home in the North, and found a place serving the Unseely Queen of Fife.

Leaving behind his brother Prigurd. Who alone, among the brutal Nellt siblings, served out of loyalty instead of rapacious ambition, and was willing to bestow that loyalty upon Lune. Some had argued that she should not trust him, at least not so far as to award him Halgresta's old position as captain—but the Onyx Guard was all Prigurd knew. And though he was not bright, he was at least faithful in his duty.

"If it's revenge," Gertrude said, "then it *might* be cleared away if you sent Prigurd north."

Rosamund and Lune both frankly stared at her. "Prigurd as a diplomat?" the other brownie said, disbelieving. "Mab love him, but he hasn't three thoughts in his head to call his own. Kentigern would skin him, joint him, and serve him to Nicneven raw."

"I doubt anyone could dissuade him from revenge by words alone," Lune said. Gertrude's sweet disposition was admirable, but sometimes it resulted in naïveté. "But I also doubt that this is simply Kentigern's doing. Left to his own devices, he would storm the Onyx Hall one night, axe in hand, seeking my blood. If anything, Nicneven is restraining him, not being driven by him."

Kentigern was not the only courtier who departed at her accession, nor even the only one who had found a home in Fife. The others, though, had left peaceably—or else had fled so far she no longer feared them. And—

Lune groaned out loud as a thought came to her. The sisters gave her matched looks of startlement. "Eochu Airt," she said. "He claims to have some information of use to me. There have been dealings between Ulster and Scotland before. It may be King Conchobar, or another in Ulster, knows something of this new malevolence from Nicneven."

"What do they want in return?" Gertrude asked.

Ireland free of all English settlers, with no English King over her.

"The removal of Wentworth," Lune said. "Which I have no graceful way to accomplish. I have offered him everything I can, but none of it suffices. I *must* find a way to get my own agent into Fife."

The brownies exchanged dubious glances. "We shall try," Rosamund said, without much hope. "We have a few friends along the Border, who might be of use."

"I would be most grateful," Lune replied.

"Good," Gertrude said. "Now *I* would be grateful if you don't let this pheasant go to waste. Tuck in, your most sovereign Majesty; you cannot solve all the island's ills if you do not eat."

ST STEPHEN'S CHAPEL, WESTMINSTER
5 May 1640

Three weeks of this chaos, and nothing to show for it.

The refrain echoed incessantly in Antony's mind as he crossed the lobby outside St Stephen's Chapel, where the House of Commons sat. Three weeks of increasingly contentious argument, Pym and his supporters holding firm even though hostilities with Scotland had opened once more. From religion to control of the militia, the list of changes they sought kept growing.

Antony was not without resources, but they only went

so far. Lune's faerie spies and Ben Hipley's mortal agents kept their fingers on the pulse of the House of Lords and Charles's privy council, but he had no control over those bodies; he only knew the general tenor of their discussions. And what he heard did not bode well. Charles believed, as he ever did, that the opposition in the Commons was the work of a few malcontented individuals, while the majority held a more tractable stance. But this was the same man who invariably expected matters to go according to his wishes, regardless of circumstances; the same man who closed his ears to any indication the reality might be worse than he thought. His advisers were weak men, and those few who were strong—Wentworth and Archbishop Laud— were also hated. The rottenness in England's government went far beyond one man.

Even at this early hour, the lobby was well filled with clerks, servants, and men with business they hoped to place before the Commons. It was worse than the Guildhall; Antony had to fend off petitioners from three different counties before he passed the bar that marked the entrance into the chapel. Complaints about ship money, all three of them, and no surprise there. It was the most hated tax in all of England.

The problem—his thoughts kept returning to the Commons—was lack of leadership. Wentworth, who had been one of the most able men in the House eleven years ago, was recently created the Earl of Strafford, and as such had his seat in the Lords. In his own way the man was as blind as Charles, and far more adept at making enemies, but at least he was effective. In his absence, the King's men floundered, while John Pym and his fellows organised a strong opposition.

Antony's reservations about Pym had grown from niggling suspicion into outright distrust. It would be bad enough if the man were simply a champion of the godly reformers, but his ambitions did not stop there. Pym seemed to view Parliament, not as the King's support, but as his leash. He wanted control of matters that were manifestly the prerogative of the King, and that Antony could not support.

Which left him caught in the middle. Standing on the floor of the chapel, with the tiers of seats rising around him in a horseshoe, Antony felt briefly like a bear staked out for baiting. Then he took his seat with the other members for London, near to the Speaker's chair. He felt no allegiance with them: Penington and Craddock were firmly in Pym's camp, and Soame was increasingly of their mind. But Sir Francis Seymour sat behind them—an old friend of Antony's father, allied with him in the last Parliament, and a comforting presence in this maze Antony had not yet learned to thread.

As he slid onto the bench in front of the knight, murmuring a greeting, Antony marshalled his resolve. *It has only been three weeks. I* will *master this dance.* Neither for the King's demands, nor for Pym's turbulent reforms, but for a moderate course between the two. It would not be easy, but given time, it could be done.

Then an oddity caught his eye. "Where is Glanville?" he whispered into Seymour's ear. The Speaker's chair stood empty, even though it was nearly time for the opening prayers to begin.

Seymour shook his head. "I do not know. Nor do I like the look of it."

Neither did Antony. Glanville had spoken with some force the previous day, which could not have won him favour with the King. Would Charles go so far as to depose the Speaker of the House of Commons? Pym was overfond of declaring everything a breach of the privileges of Parliament, but on this point Antony would have no choice but to agree with him. Surely the King would not give such flagrant offence—not when the House was already at odds with him. It would destroy any hope of conciliation.

He worried about it as he bowed his head for the prayers. What would happen, if Glanville had been removed? Speakers, he knew, had met bad ends before; there was a reason the chosen man was traditionally dragged to his chair. But Antony had thought that all in the distant past.

"Amen," the assembled members said, some with more fervency than others. And then, without warning, the doors to the chapel swung open.

A man bearing a black rod of office entered and positioned himself before the Speaker's table. The clerks who sat at one end paused, pens in the air, staring in surprise. Maxwell, Gentleman Usher of the Black Rod for the House of Lords, had the duty of summoning the Commons to attend any full meetings of the entire Parliament. Given Glanville's absence, it was not a promising sign.

In a loud voice, Maxwell declared, "It is his Majesty's pleasure that you knights, citizens, and burgesses of his House of Commons come up presently to his Majesty, to sit in assembly with the House of Lords."

Antony's own oath was drowned out by louder ones around him. A few men stood, shouting questions, but Maxwell ignored them all; he simply waited, impassive, to guide them to the greater chamber where the Lords met.

"You have more experience of this than I," Antony said to Seymour, under the cover of the shouting. "Tell me—is there any good cause for which his Majesty might summon us now?"

The older man's face had sagged into weary lines, and his eyes held the bleak cast of hopes on the verge of death. "If you mean good for us... unlikely. A terrible defeat in Scotland, perhaps. Or rebellion in Ireland; these plans to arm the Irish against the Scots may be reaping their expected reward. Or some other disaster."

And that is the best *we can hope for.* Antony gritted his teeth, then raised his voice over the clamour. "It does us no good to argue it here! We are summoned to the Lords; our answers lie with them. Let us go and be done."

Still muttering in confusion and anger, they formed up and let Black Rod lead them through the Palace of Westminster. Antony's blood ran cold when he entered the Lords' chamber and saw Glanville at the far end. The dark circles under the Speaker's eyes stood out like bruises.

Near him, in a richly upholstered chair, sat Charles Stuart, first of his name, by the Grace of God, King of England, Scotland, France and Ireland, Defender of the Faith, et cetera. The dais on which the chair sat elevated him to a position of prominence, but could not disguise the King's low stature. Antony sometimes wondered if some of his obstinacy were not born of that deficiency, which put him at perpetual disadvantage against taller, stronger men.

Certainly obstinacy was writ large in his expression. The members of the House of Lords were in their seats; filing in, the Commons stood on the floor between the peers and the bishops. Antony had a poor view, blocked by the men who had crowded in front of him, but by shifting his weight onto his left foot he could just see the King's face. Behind his luxuriant moustache and pointed beard, Charles's lips were pressed into a thin, impatient line.

When the doors closed behind the last man, the King spoke.

"There can no occasion of coming to this House," he said, delivering the words in a measured cadence designed to minimise his unfortunate stammer, "be so unpleasant to me as this at this time."

Antony's stomach clenched. And the sickness in it only grew as Charles continued to speak, thanking the Lords of the higher house for their good endeavours. "If there had been any means to have had a happy end of this Parliament," the King said, "it was not your lordships' fault that it was not so."

Whatever hope old Seymour might have clung to, that they were called forth to be told the Irish were revolting and the Scots had overrun the North and the Dutch had sunk all their ships and Charles had sold England to Spain, it must have died in that moment. For his own part, Antony was not surprised. Not since he had seen Glanville.

Glanville, who led the House on which Charles was squarely placing the blame.

Oh, the King made a passing nod, as he went on, to the Lords' part in presenting grievances. "Out of Parliament," the King added, most unconvincingly, "I shall be as ready—if not *more* willing—to hear any, and to redress just grievances, as in Parliament."

No, you will not, Antony thought, fury and disappointed rage boiling in his gut. *If you were, we would never have come to this pass.*

Charles could claim all he liked that he would preserve the purity of religion now established in the Church of England; he could remind them that delay in supplying his war was more dangerous than refusing. None of it mattered a rush, for everyone heard the words, even before Charles commanded the Lord Keeper to speak them.

The words that burnt to black cinders all Antony's victories, and all his hopes for the future.

"It is his Majesty's pleasure," the Lord Keeper said, his words echoing from the walls of the chamber, where less than a month before they had conducted the opening ceremonies, "that this Parliament be dissolved; and he giveth licence to all knights, citizens, and burgesses to depart at their pleasure. And so, God save the King!"

THE ONYX HALL, LONDON
5 May 1640

Lune tapped her fan against the arm of her chair in time to the beat of the allemande, watching the fae of her court swirl past in their finery. The music this time came from an entire consort of mortals, which rumour said had been snatched from one of the fine houses along the Strand, where some peer or other had contracted them for his own amusement.

But the musicians did not look unhappy to be here, and so she let the matter pass. So long as no one was mistreated, the occasional temporary theft did not bother her. They would be returned no worse for the wear, and in time might even come to frequent this court. That would please her immensely.

Which her courtiers knew. She was therefore not surprised to see the black head of Sir Cerenel coming her way, with a man in tow behind him. The stranger, a human in ragged clothing, gaped open-mouthed at everything around him, devoting his attention impartially to goblins and shoes, her ivory chair and the sharply arched ceiling of the hall in which the fae danced. Cerenel had him firmly but not unkindly in hand, and with gentle pressure convinced the man to kneel with him before Lune.

"Your Majesty," the knight said, "I beg your indulgence to bring a guest to this occasion."

In Antony's absence, Lune glanced around and gestured for Benjamin Hipley to approach. "Who is he?"

Cerenel glanced sideways at the unwashed stranger, then up at her. "I found him in London, madam, where I had gone to call upon a lady. Though I was well masked in a glamour, and protected against its failure, this fellow saw my true face through that concealment."

"A lunatic," she said, straightening in her chair. No one had brought such a mortal below for quite some time, though they used to be fashionable. "Escaped from Bedlam?"

"More likely he was permitted to leave," Hipley said, when she looked to him for clarification. With her permission he approached the man, who flinched back, but did not run. "The violent ones are chained, and not likely to escape. Did he have a small bowl?" That last was directed to Cerenel, who nodded. "Licensed to beg, then."

He did not look happy at the madman's presence in the Onyx Hall, but whether it was because of the stranger's mean status, or Cerenel's notion of entertainment, Lune could not say. She herself was not fond of lunatics; she remembered too well how this court had once abused them. But this one would not be mistreated now—and it might be useful to welcome him. Let her subjects see that she favoured those who dealt kindly with the mad. "Has he a name?" she asked.

"None I can get from him," Cerenel said. She believed him, too. He had not always been concerned with mortals as people, but he was one of Lune's better converts; over the years since her accession, Cerenel had come more or less to share her way of thinking. Not quite with such fervency, but she counted it a victory.

The allemande had drawn to a close, the musicians playing out their final measures long after most of the dancers had ceased to move. Courtiers jostled for position, trying to see the stranger.

"He is welcome among us," Lune declared, loud enough for all to hear. "As an honoured guest. Food and wine for him, from Lord Antony's store." Addressing the madman, she said, "Be of good cheer. Tonight, you need not beg for your supper."

She did not need to tell Hipley to watch after the man. Nor, she was glad to see, did he do so alone; while several ladies flirted with Cerenel, feeding on the minor status he had just won, Lady Amadea devoted her attentions to the lunatic, keeping him safe from the more predatory of courtiers. As for the madman, he gorged happily enough on the sweetmeats and candied fruit brought for him, though he watched the room through skittish eyes.

Her supervision was interrupted when the usher at the door announced the Prince of the Stone. Everyone paused in their places, bowing to Antony as he entered, but no one approached him; the black look on his face forbade it.

He came straight for Lune and spoke before she could even ask what was wrong. "He has dissolved Parliament."

It struck like a blow, less for her own disappointment

and frustration than his. Antony had struggled so hard to achieve this, and now it was taken from him, after a few short, wasted weeks. "We passed acts concerning the pointing of needles," he said through his teeth, "while Pym and his men forced us toward business they *knew* would alienate the King. Indeed, they *wished* it! The Puritans among them have no desire to see the Covenanters suppressed."

The notion that they would deliberately undermine the King was disturbing. "That," Lune said, "is just shy of treason."

"Or past it." Antony dropped without looking into the chair a hobthrush hurried to place behind him, and glared away the fae who were unabashedly eavesdropping.

Lune recognised the bleak hardness in his eyes. It had grown over the years she'd known him, from his first arrival in this court as a young man with scarcely enough whiskers to call a beard. She made him her consort because she needed his stubborn loyalty to the mortal world; he accepted because he dreamed of changing that world for the better, with faerie aid. But he was a single man, whatever aid he had, and all too often his efforts ended in failure.

It saddened her to see him thus, growing older and grimmer, year by year. How old was he now? How much longer would he last?

I will lose him some day. As I lost the man before him.

She smiled, a practised mask to conceal the inevitable grief. "There will be another opportunity," she said. "Charles is not the ruler his father was; he has no skill at playing factions off one another. I have no doubt that circumstances will force him to convene Parliament again."

"But how long will that take?" Antony muttered, and lapsed into silence.

She left him to it, recognising the need to let a mood pass. Her own subdued spirits demanded distraction, not contemplation. After the next dance was done, she left the dais and went to join an energetic courante, her slippers flickering along the marble floor. All around her was a mass of paned sleeves and flying curls, courtiers moving flawlessly through the quick, running steps of the dance. For a few moments, she was able to lay her thoughts aside.

Until a chill sharper than winter's breath gripped her bones.

Without warning, the dancers faltered. They staggered against one another, weak and nauseous, and Lune's foot caught the hem of her skirts; she stumbled and almost fell.

Pain stabbed through her shoulder, locking her entire body in paralysis, so she could not even cry out.

A roar came from behind her, and then the transfixing spike ripped free, leaving her to crumple in a boneless heap to the floor. Rolling, weeping in agony and shock, Lune saw her attacker.

He, too, was on the floor, pinned under the weight of the elf-knight who had thrown him down. The madman laughed in unintelligible triumph even as the knight smashed his hand against the marble, shattering bones and knocking free his blood-stained iron knife.

And then the laughter stopped, lost in a wet gurgle when the knight plunged his own dagger through the mortal's throat.

Antony slammed through the nauseated fae an instant later, interposing himself between Lune and the dead man. "What the devil is going on?"

Followed by another, earthier curse, as Antony saw the iron blade. He didn't hesitate; with the knights of the Onyx Guard closing in to protect their Queen, he snatched up the weapon and tossed it to Hipley, who ran for the door. Lune breathed more easily with every step he took, though she would feel its presence until he removed it from the Onyx Hall entirely.

Even then, the taint would remain, poisoning her body. Had she not stumbled... Lune wavered to her feet, trying not to lean too obviously against Antony for support. "I will fetch a physician," he murmured in her ear.

"No," she whispered in reply, and forced her back straight. He was right: the poison must be drawn, and soon. But that would take time, and since she was not dead, it was imperative that she first deal with the situation. She dared not show her weakness.

Her rescuer had likewise risen, behind the protecting wall of her bodyguard. The golden-haired elf was not of their number; his name was Sir Leslic, come perhaps five years ago to her court, and up until this point she had taken little notice of him. Blood spattered his face and darkened the sapphire of his doublet. He was wiping his skin clean when he saw her and went instantly to his knee. Space had cleared for a good three paces around them, excepting the bodyguards who ringed her. "Your Majesty. I beg your forgiveness, for drawing a weapon in your presence."

She would hardly punish him for that offence, when he had saved her life. "What happened?" she asked, and managed to sound authoritative instead of shaken.

"I saw it as the dance brought me near. He seemed to join in our sport, but then he broke without warning for your Grace's person, and pulled forth that knife. Had I been but a moment faster, I—I might have stopped him in time."

Shame broke his voice. Lune said, "You have done well, Sir Leslic." With one hand she prodded her bodyguards aside, giving her a clear view of her would-be killer. He was a pathetic thing, filthy and ragged on the marble. The lustre of the stone was dimmed where the knife had fallen, and smeared with her blood.

The knight moved suddenly, stepping forward and then checking himself as her guards twitched. Antony half-dropped his buttressing grip on Lune's arms, but restored it as she swayed. Leslic's attention flew past Lune's shoulder like an arrow. "*You,*" he said, spitting the word. "You brought this murderer here."

Sir Cerenel stood trembling just behind her and to the right, mouth open in sick horror. Leslic's snarl brought him up with a snap. "Do you accuse me of conspiracy?"

Lune's own thoughts had not yet gotten that far. Clutching to her bleeding shoulder the fold of cloth Amadea provided, she went cold with sudden fear. Had she so misjudged him? Could Cerenel be playing at agreement with her ideals, all the while paying heed to Nicneven's agents?

The knights' anger was evenly matched, and rising. Leslic said, "I would not so impugn her Majesty's judgement as to imagine she would take such a traitor into her bosom. But you found this man; you brought him here. Are you not of the Onyx Guard? Is it not your duty to protect your Queen from harm? What measures did you take to ensure her safety?"

Cerenel went pale. "Upon my oath, you will withdraw that insult to my honour, sir."

"For the insult to our gracious sovereign," Leslic said, "I stand by my words. Prove your honour, sir, or prove it lost." He spun to face Lune. "Madam, this *knight* has given the lie to my words. I beg your leave to face him in combat."

It was too much, too quickly. Lune's head spun, and blackness feathered the edges of her vision. *I should have withdrawn.*

Antony's hands tightened on her arms, and his answer struck both knights into silence. "You would make demands of your Queen? On the heels of such an outrage? Your *honour,* sirs, is not worth a brass thimble!"

But if she had gone, they would still have had this confrontation. At least now she had some hope of controlling it. Lune had never forbidden duelling, for her people rarely fought to the death, and a little bloodshed for the sake of honour was understandable enough. But for this, a private duel would not serve; it touched too closely on *her* royal honour. The settlement of the question must be public.

Cerenel was still pale, and he looked at Lune with desperate eyes. That he had not planned this, she was certain. But his honour and reputation *were* damaged, and he must be given leave to defend them.

Not tonight. "This matter shall be settled in honourable fashion," she said, holding on to strength with her fingernails. "When we are recovered, we shall oversee it in person. Until such time, we forbid you to visit violence upon one another, nor even to speak; nor to allow any of your allies to do the same, save to arrange the terms of the duel." She glared both knights down as if she could stop them by will alone. Which she hoped she could. "Do not think to disobey us."

THE ONYX HALL, LONDON
5 May 1640

Later, Antony went to her bedchamber, where she had dismissed all of her ladies and sprites and sat gazing at a candle flame. "What of the blade?" she asked, without turning to face him.

She sounded far calmer than he would have expected, though he could see the bulk of a bandage altering the line of her shoulder. "Safely gone," he replied. "It was a cheap Sheffield knife, such as any man might own. Nothing to learn from it. We found a sheath in his clothing, though—made of hawthorn, to mask its presence. Someone prepared this." Nicneven, without a doubt. She had threatened violence before.

But always against him. Never Lune. Anger such as he rarely felt heated Antony's blood. Murder was a foul thing; regicide, far fouler.

Lune did not comment on the sheath, though he knew she had heard him. Antony swallowed down his anger and cleared his throat. "Will you..." He hesitated to give the question tongue. No one had been wounded with iron during his time here; he realised now that he did not know what would happen. "Will you recover?"

"In part." Lune's breath hissed between her teeth before she continued. "The poison has been drawn. But wounds so given never fully heal."

And she was immortal. Never would last a very long time for her.

The ensuing silence persisted long enough that he opened his mouth to take his leave. She needed to rest, and might do so if he were gone. But then she spoke again. "Did you mark how Leslic leapt on the man?"

He had watched the incident from the dais—all of it over too fast for him to see much. Or so he thought. But now, recalling the scene, he noted what he had overlooked in the moment. How had Lune, bleeding on the floor, seen such a small thing?

Easily. She knew far better than he how the presence of iron felt. "He did not flinch."

"No," Lune said.

Another silence, this time as they both considered the implications. Antony stayed by the door, suspecting she did not want a companion in her weakness. She rarely did. Instead he asked, "Do you wish me to find out where he got the bread?"

She shook her head, then stopped as if the movement hurt her shoulder. "The trade in it is so brisk, I doubt you could trace it. The better question is why he had eaten of it so recently, and was so conveniently protected against the iron."

He did not know the golden-haired knight well, but he remembered the company in which Leslic had been seen. Fae who sneered at mortals as lesser beings, and rarely set foot outside the Onyx Hall. What bread they had was generally bartered for political favours, not kept for their own use.

Antony said, "I will look for the answer."

"No," Lune said, turning to look at him at last. "You have concerns enough of your own. I have others who can find out more efficiently."

Concerns. Trade, and his family, and the day-to-day governance of his ward. He would get plenty of rest, now that he need not concern himself with Parliament. But Lune was right; there were others who could do that work better. "Then let them have a care for their safety, too," he said. "Those who would kill you would not hesitate to murder others."

* * *

THE ONYX HALL, LONDON
11 May 1640

Wiping his mouth with a napkin, Eochu Airt said, "I am glad to see you so rapidly recovered, madam. Please accept as well the sympathies of the Ard-Rí, who is most outraged over such a foul, dishonourable offence."

Lune was not quite so recovered as she took pains to appear, but the wound from that knife had already incapacitated her for nearly a week; she could not afford a longer absence from the field. She was at least glad to see that her thought about Eochu Airt had borne fruit. He was much more agreeable when given venison and boar to tear into, rather than pickled lampreys. The quiet meal they shared now was still not the rowdy public banquets hosted by the kings and queens of his land, but it helped, and was a bargain at the price.

She sipped from a cup of wine well fortified with strengthening herbs and said, "The offender answered with his life."

The ambassador smiled in a way that said he recognised the opportunity she gave him. Lune's body might still be weak, but she had not missed the implication of his phrasing: that the lunatic's attack was more than an unfortunate accident. "But what of the one behind him?"

Lune replied with nothing more than politely raised eyebrows, waiting to see how he would continue.

"You may recall, madam," he said, fingering a bone on

his plate, "that nearly a year ago, I offered you information. I assure you, its value has not fallen with time."

"But has its price? What you offer, my lord ollamh, may not be so valuable as you think. No doubt you offer me some intelligence concerning the Gyre-Carling of Fife. Oh, yes," Lune said, "I am not ignorant of the pattern here. This is the only attempt so direct against my person, but there have been other attacks, and I know their source. True, I do not yet know their cause—what has changed in Fife, thus changing Nicneven's tactics. But you are hardly my only means of learning *that*, my lord."

"Aye, you have other ways—but how long will they take you? And how many more threats will there be in the meantime?" The sidhe had abandoned the last pretence of casual conversation; now he studied her with a frankness that stopped just shy of insult. "You know our price. It has not changed. Bring down Wentworth, and you shall have the name, and more besides."

Behind him, the door opened to admit Sir Peregrin, who bowed and waited. "We shall bear that in mind, my lord," Lune said, rising and extending her hand. "In the meantime, I am afraid obligations call me away. You are welcome to attend, if you so desire."

"Thank you, madam. I may at that." Eochu Airt kissed her hand and departed.

Left with the lieutenant of her guard, Lune said, "I will come presently."

"If it please your Majesty," he replied, "the Goodemeade

sisters beg a moment of your time."

"Show them in." The brownies dropped into respectful curtsies, straightening as soon as Peregrin was gone. "I am due in the amphitheatre," Lune said. "Please say you have something for me."

Rosamund answered briskly, incongruous in someone who still, despite years of association with the court, appeared so very country. The Goodemeades almost never changed into fine clothes for their visits to the Onyx Hall. "Sir Leslic hasn't gone above since March, and as near as we can tell, he had no plans to do so."

Confirming her suspicions. What to do about it depended on what happened tonight. "Thank you," Lune said, checking the pins that held up her elaborate curls. "I may have need of you soon. Will you stay for the duel?"

Gertrude wrinkled her round face in distaste, but nodded. Lune touched her shoulder briefly in thanks, then went forth from the chamber.

The amphitheatre lay in one of the more distant corners of the Onyx Hall. Its ancient, crumbling stones dated back to the Romans; long since buried beneath the changing face of the city, it thus found itself incorporated into the faerie palace below. When the space was quiet, one could still hear the faint shouts and screams of the men and beasts who had died within its ring.

But it was far from quiet now. Lune strode out onto the white sand to find what looked like every member of her court settled onto the risers, with cushions and cups of wine, ready for entertainment. A canopy of estate covered the box where she took her seat, just behind the low wall ringing the sand. When she nodded, two trumpeters blew fanfares from the entrances, and Sir Cerenel and Sir Leslic entered, followed by their seconds.

The black-haired knight and the gold. If she weighed their hearts aright, they stood opposite one another, when it came to mortal kind. This duel would be seen as a fight between those two perspectives, and unfortunately, she could do nothing to prevent that.

They made their bows before her, and Lune pitched her voice to carry. "Sir Leslic. Upon what grounds do you come here today, in defence of your honour?"

Challenging Cerenel had been his right, even though the offence was his to begin with, because Cerenel's defence called into question the truth of Leslic's words, and therefore his honesty. According to the forms of such things, this had nothing to do with the attempt on Lune's life; it was entirely a question of whether Leslic had spoken rightly in calling Cerenel negligent. The golden-haired knight recounted the tale with simple but effective phrasing, as if there might be a mouse in the corner that had *not* already heard the gossip.

"Sir Cerenel," Lune said when he was done. "As the challenged, what weapons do you choose for this duel?"

He bowed again. "If it please your Majesty, rapier and dagger."

"We approve this choice." A formality; the entire

question had been settled by their seconds the day before.

As accuser, Leslic took the oath first, then Cerenel, both of them upon their knees in the sand. "In the name of most ancient Mab, and before your Grace's sovereign throne, I hereby swear that I have this day neither eaten nor drank, nor have upon me, neither bone, stone, nor grass, nor any enchantment, sorcery, or witchcraft, whereby the honour of Faerie may be abased, nor dishonour exalted."

But when Cerenel was done, Leslic remained kneeling. "Madam," he said, "though I fight to defend my honour, I do so for your own glory, and never my own. May I beg you to grant me your favour?"

Lune bit back a curse. Of course he asked; she should have expected it. He was, after all, her saviour, the knight most of her court had come to cheer on. For her to refuse him would betray her suspicions. Yet it galled her to show affection to such a viper.

It was the only way to find out what he sought to gain, and who was pulling his strings. For now, she must play his game. Lune pulled off her glove of black lace, and bent to hand it down. Leslic pinned it to his snow-white sleeve, and the crowd applauded him.

Then, at last, they took their places on the hard-packed sand, silver rapiers and daggers glinting in their hands. The amphitheatre fell silent.

"Begin," Lune said.

Cerenel barely waited for the word to leave her mouth. Quick as a snake, he leapt forward, and Leslic recoiled. With a rapid flurry of blows, they crossed the sand, Leslic dodging aside from a thrust to keep from being trapped against the low wall. No question of it: Cerenel was a fine swordsman.

But Leslic had for the last year been tutored by Il Veloce, an Italian faun resident in the Onyx Hall. He had a clever dagger hand, and was quick to use Cerenel's momentum against him. First once, then again, the dark knight found his accuser unexpectedly within his guard, and saved himself only with a desperate twist away.

The silence that had marked their beginning was long since broken, fae shouting out encouragement to the one they favoured. Cerenel's name sounded but rarely. Leslic was the hero of the moment, but that was not all; listening, Lune identified more of his allies, more fae who shared his views on mortals. Their approval did not stop at one dead murderer.

Below, the blades continued their glittering dance. Whether above or below, the point of a duel was to show oneself willing to defend one's honour; the outcome was almost immaterial. Almost, but not quite: in the final accounting, Cerenel *had* been negligent. Leslic's words were true. And so while the audience came hoping for a good show, everyone knew how it would end.

Leslic beat his opponent back to the wall and trapped his sword against it; the swift thrust of his dagger would have maimed Cerenel's hand, had the other knight not abandoned his sword and pulled away. But however desperately he retreated, twisting and leaping, he could not defend himself long with only a knife, and Leslic closed in for the kill.

"Hold!" Lune called out, just before the blade would have slid home.

Cerenel had fallen to his knees; the tip of Leslic's rapier stopped a mere finger's-breadth from his throat. Duels rarely went to the death, but in a matter touching so closely on the Queen's honour, no one would have faulted Leslic. Too proud to cry craven and thus save his life, Cerenel would have died.

But Lune had other plans for him.

"To shed the blood of a fae is an abominable thing," she said. "Such a fate, we must reserve for true traitors to our realm. The negligence of Cerenel has been proved. Let his punishment be thus: that for a year and a day, he be exiled from the Onyx Court and all its dominions, and his place in our guard revoked. But when that time ends, he will be welcomed back in our halls, and may in time regain the honours he formerly held."

Did she imagine the brief flash of anger in Leslic's eyes? It was quickly hidden, regardless; he sheathed his rapier and dagger and said, "Your Majesty's wisdom and mercy is a great gift to this realm."

Looking across the sand, Lune caught the gazes of the Goodemeades, who nodded minutely.

"Go," she said to Cerenel, where he still knelt in the sand. "Your exile begins at once."

* * *

THE ANGEL INN, ISLINGTON
11 May 1640

"Would you like more privacy, madam?"

"No," Lune said. "That will not be necessary."

She *hoped* it would not. If matters had come to such a pass that she needed to take elaborate measures to protect her secrets, she was in a worse state than she believed. But Lune doubted anyone would be following her movements closely enough to eavesdrop on the comfortable chamber in which she now sat.

Not yet, at least.

Cerenel stood rigid by the hearth, hands locked behind his back. He had accepted the Goodemeades' offer of shelter; their home lay within the bounds of Lune's realm, but Rosamund had assured him the Queen would not take it amiss if he tarried there a single night. Lune had watched his face settle into hard, understanding lines when she came down the staircase and threw back the hood of her concealing cloak.

She came out in secret, not even informing Sir Prigurd of her departure. It was easy enough to ensure she would not be disturbed in her chamber—all it took was a protest of exhaustion, after the excitement of the duel—and wearing a crown had not made her forget how to sneak about.

Lune arrayed herself in the chair Gertrude provided, and judged whether or not to offer Cerenel a seat. No; he was too stiff with anger, and might refuse.

"I will be brief," she said. "For I suspect you wish not to see me just now."

A shift in the tendons of his neck was her only reply, as he clenched his jaw.

"You were negligent," she went on, and saw him flinch. "It was obvious before the duel, and proven with it. But I tell you now what is *not* obvious: that the mortal you brought below was bait, for a trap you unwittingly sprung."

Cerenel was far from the stupidest of her knights. He paled in anger and spoke for the first time since he knelt at her arrival. *"Leslic."* His hands came free from behind his back and flexed, wishing for the hilt of the sword he had laid aside. "Madam, let me but stay a moment to challenge him—"

Lune cut him off. "You may not. Did I wish Leslic exposed, I had done it myself. There is no proof, nothing direct. And though you could fight him again, this time with right on your side, that would simply remove him from play, with nothing gained. I am not concerned with Leslic. I am concerned with those who gave him his orders.

"This murderer was part of a pattern. There have been attacks on the Onyx Hall—subtle ones, not those of armies. Subtle enough that I have, until now, kept them secret. I must know more of their source." She held his gaze. "The Unseely Court of Fife."

The knight's body stilled. Lune watched his face, trying to read his expression through the shadows that flickered over it, cast by the fire's wavering light. He licked his lips before speaking. "You suspect my brother?"

A wry smile tugged at the corner of her mouth, born of bitter amusement. "No more than others in the Gyre-Carling's court. Cunobel holds no love for me, I know. But he left here in peace—which I cannot say of another who once called this court home. Presumably he has told you that Kentigern Nellt is there as well."

He said, with a touch of bitterness, "Another exile. Like me."

"Not like you." Rosamund's voice came from the corner; by the twitch of Cerenel's shoulders, he had forgotten the Goodemeades were listening, quiet as mice. "Her Grace exiled him permanently."

"And for better cause," Lune added. "You made a mistake, Cerenel—a foolish one, for which you are duly shamed. But I do not consider you my enemy."

His relief spoke plainly. "Then you suspect Kentigern."

Lune laughed. "Of subtlety and intrigue? He is no more capable of it than a thunderstorm. No. Someone else is the architect of these new troubles.

"Ever since the coalition in the North dissolved, Nicneven has lacked the military might to strike directly at us, and she has never had the subtlety for more insidious attacks. The worst she could do was to encourage the baser elements of my court—fae such as Leslic. I believe someone else must have come to her, someone with both the mind and the will to craft this new malignance. I wish to know who."

Only a blind man would not see where she aimed. "You wish me to spy."

"You have the justification you need. Exiled from London, disaffected with our court—who is to say you would not journey north to Fife, and throw your lot in with Nicneven and your brother?"

Cerenel's eyes glittered in the firelight. He said quietly, "How do you know I would not?"

Because you ask that question. Lune stood from her chair and took one of his hands in her own. His fingers were very cold. "I know you nearly followed your brother," she said. "You stayed because you wished to see what manner of Queen I would be, and in time you came to believe in my ideals. I do not doubt your honour, and when the year and a day has passed, we shall welcome you back with open arms. If you can bring us the information we need... you will be richly rewarded."

He knelt and pressed his lips to her hand. "I shall do as you bid, your Majesty."

Excellent. Cerenel was not the tool Lune would have chosen for the task, but he had the pretext she needed, to get someone close to the Gyre-Carling. Still, she must be cautious.

Laying her free hand on his head, she said, "Then swear it."

His fingers tightened involuntarily on hers. The dim light darkened his eyes to deepest amethyst; in that instant, they were guileless, speaking eloquently of his surprise.

"If you swear it," Lune said, "then I need not fear a misstep on your part. You will let slip no accidental word that might endanger you, or us here in London. Give me your vow, and I will know for certain we are safe."

Surprise gave way to anger, mounting with her every word. Lune had known it would offend him, but she could not afford to do otherwise. Cerenel was no practised spy, and though she was confident he would not turn traitor *now*, she could not trust what would happen after a year and a day spent among those with cause to hate her.

For him to refuse would cast his loyalty into doubt. He could imagine for himself the consequences of that. She watched him struggle with it, swallowing his fury down, and did not move.

At last the knight bowed his head, and repeated in a dead voice the words she proposed. "I swear to you, in ancient Mab's name, that I will seek out the malignance in Fife that sets itself against the Onyx Court, and neither by speech nor by action betray to another my purpose in being there." His fingers never once relaxed their stone-hard grip on her hand.

"Learn what you can," Lune said when he was done, her tone as gentle as she could make it. "Then return to us for your reward."

ST STEPHEN'S CHAPEL, WESTMINSTER
11 November 1640

If there was one decision that could have made the dissolution of Parliament in May seem an even graver error, it was the choice to summon it again six months later.

There was little joy this time, except of a fierce and battle-ready sort. All over England, supporters of the Crown went down in resounding defeat. And although Antony did not consider himself a King's man, he was not godly enough, and not sympathetic enough to Pym's cause, to win re-election easily. Publicly, he said he regained his seat through the grace of God; in truth, he owed it to the fae. Lune had not said one word of complaint when he asked her for aid. It was the only way to keep the Onyx Court represented in the Commons.

So in the bleak days of November, they gathered once more in Westminster Palace, to fight over the governance of England. Damply unpleasant winds blew in through the broken windows of the chapel, causing the men who gathered within to shiver and wrap their cloaks more firmly about their shoulders. The windows had been as badly off the previous spring—victims of the long years when the Commons was disbanded—but no one had minded them then. Now, in the chill grip of an early winter, they added a grim touch to grimmer proceedings.

Arrayed along one wall were the King's opponents, with their officers all in a row. Antony doubted anyone did not see John Pym as a general in this political war, leading Hampden, St John, Strode and Holles, Hesilrige and Secretary Vane's fanatical son, against the Crown's own disorganised forces. They would cripple the King if they could, paring away slivers of his power until it all rested in their own hands; indeed, they had already begun. Now they prepared for their next move.

Antony watched Pym unblinking from the moment the opening prayers concluded. *Without question, he knows what has happened. His intelligence is at least as good as mine.*

And if Antony had learned anything about Pym in the three and a half disastrous weeks last spring, it was that the man was a master of timing. Unlike his subordinates, he never let the passion of his beliefs carry him out of the course of effective action. Though Penington was chafing at the bit to attack the bishops and destroy the episcopacy, root and branch, Pym held him back, lest such Puritan zeal alienate more moderate members of the House. But when his time came...

Antony, not attending in the slightest to the debate currently under way, saw Pym receive a message and rise with his hat off.

He must have taken his seat.

Thomas Wentworth, the Earl of Strafford, had arrived in London the previous night. Parliament was nearly a week into its new sitting, but Pym delayed his attack, waiting for his enemy to arrive and take his place in the House of Lords. Now, at last, Pym could move against the King's "evil councillor"—the man he would make a whipping boy for all the troubles in Scotland and Ireland both, and England, too. Pym could not strike directly at Charles, but he could harry the King like a dog at a bear, inflicting a hundred small wounds to bleed and weaken him of his power.

Lenthall, the weak-willed man who had succeeded Glanville as Speaker, gave Pym permission to speak. "I have something of gravest import to say," Pym told them all, "and so I call upon the sergeant-at-arms to clear the antechamber, and to bar all doors from this House." He waited while this was done, while the rumours ran up and down the benches, and then commenced his assault.

From tyranny to sexual misdeeds, he laid a whole series of crimes at Strafford's feet. Nor was he alone: his minion Clotworthy succeeded him with another speech, far less coherent but far more inflammatory, and then more after him. All riding hard toward the same end: the impeachment of the Earl of Strafford, on the charge of treason.

Pym had tried it years ago, with the Duke of Buckingham; Charles had dissolved Parliament rather than let his chief councillor of the time suffer attack. Now the leader of Parliament took aim again, when Charles could not evade it. This time, he might strike home.

But first, a committee; hardly anything was done anymore without a committee to chew it over first. The composition of that body was no surprise, either. Pym had planned for this, as he planned for everything, and the committee returned in remarkably quick time, opening the general debate. Antony seized his own opportunity to speak.

"Of a certainty, Lord Strafford has taken many actions both here and in Ireland that bear closer scrutiny," he said, meeting the eyes of his fellow members. "Whether those actions constitute treason is a matter for the law to decide.

But we must not let them pass unremarked, for fear that others might then try to press that liberty beyond the bounds of what is just and right. By all means, gentlemen—let us send to the Lords a message of impeachment."

He took perverse pleasure in seeing the astonishment on Pym's face as he sat once more. *You think I support you and your junto. But I do not do this for you; I do it for Lune.*

They had no word yet from Cerenel, though they knew he had arrived in Fife. And while no madmen with iron knives had shown up again, the disturbances at court had not ended. They needed the information Eochu Airt had—and that meant getting rid of Thomas Wentworth, the Earl of Strafford.

For once, Antony was glad of Pym's attack. He still despised the man's junto, and many of the things it fought for, but in this one matter, they stood as temporary allies.

The message summoned Antony out into the Old Palace Yard, where he found Ben Hipley waiting for him on the cobblestones.

"Have they impeached the earl?" the other man asked, hardly even pausing to make his greeting.

"Yes," Antony said. "They have taken the message in to the Lords—Pym and the others."

Hipley swore sulphurously. "And Strafford just came back. He left this morning for Whitehall, to talk to the King, but I saw him return not five minutes ago. Damnation!"

The curses were drawing far too much attention. They were hardly the only people in the yard; Parliament scarcely sat but there were mobs outside, thronging the streets of Westminster. These were the same apprentices and labourers, mariners and dockhands who had attacked Archbishop Laud's palace earlier in the year. Riots had become a common feature of London life, no doubt encouraged by Pym and the others. Antony drew Hipley to one side and lowered his voice. "Temair wants him gone. Lune has told me to do it if I can. Why baulk now?"

"Because Strafford was going to impeach Pym and the others," his spymaster said through his teeth. "For treasonous dealings with the Covenanters. He might have broken their strength—so they are determined to break his first."

It set Antony back on his heels. That Pym was deep in alliance with the Covenanters, he did not doubt. But he had not realised such a good opportunity existed to curb the opposition's power.

He spun without a word and hurried back into the palace, Ben close behind, but even as he neared the Lords' chamber the roar of the crowd there told him he was too late—even supposing he could have done anything to stop it. He could just glimpse Strafford exiting the chamber; gems glinted in the light as the earl removed his sword and surrendered it to Maxwell.

Illness had ravaged Wentworth; his complexion was sallow, his skin sagging in loose curves. He hardly looked the terrible figure popular opinion made him out to be.

But the watching masses showed no respect; Antony heard many cutting remarks, and did not see a single man doff his cap to the bare-headed earl.

"What's the matter?" a jeering voice cried out, as Strafford wearily faced the gauntlet he must run.

Strafford answered as confidently as he could, but his voice was weak and hoarse. "A small matter, I warrant you."

"Yes, indeed," someone else shouted. "High treason is a small matter!"

Under the cover of the ensuing laughter, Antony said to Ben, "The charges are weak. It may well be that he can defeat them."

"I hope so," his companion replied, watching the crowd dog Strafford's heels as he crossed to the outer door. "For the sake of us all. Pym's power worries me."

And me, Antony admitted privately. He had hoped to do some good for Lune, but it appeared the good of England would have to come first.

THE ONYX HALL, LONDON
28 December 1640

Of all the practices fae had adopted from mortals, the giving of Christmas gifts puzzled Lune the most. They were never called by such name, of course, but midwinter exchanges had become common, and served a particular purpose in courtly life.

As she was reminded of, cynically, when Sir Leslic appeared one day with a hound following at his heels.

The creature was a paragon of its kind, with a long, sleek, cream-furred body, and ears of russet. A faerie hound, not a faerie in the form of a hound, and a breed raised by the Tylwyth Teg of Wales, if she did not miss her guess. She wondered what he had given up to gain it.

Leslic bowed, sweeping his hat wide, drawing every eye in the chamber. Naturally he picked a moment of leisure, and one well attended by Lune's idle courtiers. "Your radiant Grace—I cannot sleep at nights, fearful as I am for your safety. I beg you to allow me to make this poor gift to you, a faithful companion to watch over your rest."

Lune did not miss the annoyance among some of her courtiers. Leslic's one failing, in his pursuit of her favour, was an over-ready will to invoke the rescue that had catapulted him from relative obscurity to a place in the Onyx Guard, and therefore close by her side. But he redeemed the error quickly enough; peeking slyly up from his bow, he added, "Or at least to pursue the fox for you, when next you ride to the hunt."

He had a charming smile, she granted him that. Lune made herself return one equally charming, or rather charmed. When she extended her hand, the dog came without prompting; there was no need for leashes and beatings, such as humans used to train their beasts. The animal sniffed her fingers delicately, then bent his head into her friendly scratch behind his ears.

Leslic sighed grandly and pressed one hand over his heart. "Fortunate hound, that comes home to his mistress's touch. I shall sleep in envy instead of fear tonight, wishing I might have his place at the foot of your bed."

They had gathered a small audience, the courtiers who flocked to his rising star. Not all of them, certainly; fae were capable of great oceans of jealous resentment. Lewan Erle pouted incessantly, feeling himself slighted. Lune was disappointed to see Valentin Aspell drifting near. She wished she could believe her faerie spymaster was simply keeping close watch on the knight, but the truth was that he found Leslic's opinions congenial.

What to do with the hound? She was not at all certain she could trust the beast at the foot of her bed. Not out of fear for her safety; if Leslic wanted her dead, he could simply have let the lunatic kill her. Far as he had risen, there was much farther to go, and he needed her alive for that. But the hounds of the Tylwyth Teg were intelligent creatures, capable of much more than a normal dog. The gift was to curry favour; all these midwinter presents were simply another path to advantage at court. That did not, however, mean Leslic had no other purpose for it.

She had to draw him out. "Wouldst sleep at the foot of my bed, then?" she said teasingly, arching one eyebrow. "Is that your desired place?"

"I would account the cold stone there a finer bed than any that stood farther from your presence," he answered, less in jest than before. A trace of longing threaded his answer, taut in the air between them.

Lune let him come closer; heeding that cue, the watchers faded back, returning to their diversions. They had the illusion of privacy, at least. "But you dream of a warmer bed."

"What man would not?"

There was no possibility of deluding herself. The hunger in Leslic's heart was not for her. In body, perhaps a little, but none for her spirit; it was power he sought, and a closer place in her counsel. All else was merely a pretext, a mask for the truth.

Every breath of their encounters was a sham. Amadea had made so bold as to ask Lune why she showed such favour to a knight who made no secret of his disdain for mortals; Lune excused his behaviour as concern for the threat they posed, though she knew it went far deeper and fouler than that. The fae who scorned mortals as lesser creatures were calling themselves Ascendants now, and looked to Leslic as their captain. As the godly became more vocal above, the Ascendants became more common below.

Yet the true root of that threat lay, not here, but in Scotland. Lune could not tell her Lady Chamberlain the truth: that clasping this viper to her breast would teach her more of his aims. The closer she brought him, the more she learned of his connections to Nicneven.

Giving Leslic what he desired might gain her a great deal. Men said things over a pillow they might not let slip otherwise.

But bile rose in her throat at the thought. She had loved once, with her heart as well as her body, and once given, a faerie's love did not fade. Now, though she took the occasional gentleman to her bed, they were rare, and never from her own court; the favour thus granted would upset the delicate balance she strove to maintain. And if she were to break that prohibition, it would not be for this golden-haired devil, this smiling traitor, who would betray her to her death if it suited his ambition.

Not even for the safety of her crown and her court would she take Leslic into her bed.

Her hesitation had gone on too long. Lune forced a smile onto her face, forced promise to hide behind that smile. "You are no man, but an elfin knight. Yet dreams come to our kind, even in our waking hours, and some dreams, they say, are prophecy."

He took her hand and kissed it, feather-light; she fought not to shudder at his touch. "I shall petition the Fates to make me a seer, then, and until that day, live in hope."

ST STEPHEN'S CHAPEL, WESTMINSTER
21 April 1641

"Consider the law," Antony said, endeavouring to sound stronger and more confident than he felt. "For weeks, we have seen the Earl of Strafford defend himself upon the charges laid against him. He has established beyond doubt that, however much we may dispute the choices he has made, the actions he has taken, they have *not* crossed the line into treason.

"What are the strongest pieces of evidence against him?" A rhetorical question, but he had come to learn some of the theatrics of oration. Though he could not match the eloquence of Strode or Holles, he had to try. Antony raised a sheet of paper. "A copy of a copy of a note, made against Secretary Vane's knowledge." On a bench across the way, Vane's son glared, not in the least embarrassed by his theft. "And Secretary Vane's statement regarding the privy council meeting at which that note was made. The same piece of evidence, rendered twice, does not become twice as strong.

"Lord Strafford suggested the Irish army be used to reduce 'this kingdom'. Had he meant England, that would be treason indeed—but he did not say England. Others present at that meeting have no doubt he meant Scotland, which was, after all, the rebellious land then under debate. There is no treason here."

He tossed down the paper, contemptuously, and locked his hands behind his back to conceal their trembling. "The charge of impeachment has failed. This bill of attainder seeks to circumvent that failure—to declare that Strafford *intended* to subvert the laws of this land, and that such intent, unproved and not acted upon, yet constitutes treason. In effect, the bill declares that Strafford must die for the good of England, *because we say it is so*."

A pause, to let that sink in. But the benches around him were far too empty; where were the men who should have packed into the aisles for such an important vote? Scarcely half of the Commons had come today, despite the penalties for absence. They were afraid to commit themselves.

Afraid to put themselves in the path of Pym's relentless assault, which struck not only at this one man, but the roots of sovereignty itself. Laud was in the Tower with Strafford; other servants of the Crown had fled abroad. Parliament—which was to say, the Commons—asserted the right to question and oversee the King's councillors, to alter the Church as it saw fit, to control the revenues of the state; they wanted authority over the militia given into their hands. The only thing yet passed into law was a bill to call Parliament not less often than every three years—but if Antony lost this chance to thwart the opposition, who knew where the avalanche would end?

"Let us not make ourselves into a tyrannous mob," he said, quietly, into the watchful silence. "The law has rendered Strafford innocent of treason. We must heed its voice."

Then he sat down, before his knees could give out.

"The question," said Speaker Lenthall, "is the bill of attainder for Thomas Wentworth, Earl of Strafford. The House will divide."

The lobby to the chapel was cleared of all its usual rabble. Sir Gilbert Gerard and Sir Thomas Barrington stood by the door, ready to mark down the names of those voting against the bill.

Antony was the first to rise and pass outside the bar. In that moment, he hated this arrangement, which encouraged the lazy and the fearful to remain in their seats, while those who stood against were forced to walk out, under the eyes of their enemies.

Even before he turned around in the lobby, he knew it would not be enough.

A score. Two score. Watching, praying, he ended his count at fifty-nine. The dissenters recalled into the chamber, Lenthall read out the division: the yeas had gathered two hundred and four.

There was still a chance. The Lords had not yet passed the bill, and the King had not assented. And Charles had promised Strafford repeatedly that he would suffer no such ungrateful reward for his service.

But whatever the outcome for Wentworth's life, the earl was defeated; Pym had won.

TOWER HILL, LONDON
12 May 1641

The sea of people stretched as far as the eye could see in all directions: on rooftops, hanging out windows, flooding Petty Wales and Tower Street and Woodroffe Lane, packing into the open spaces of Tower Hill until there was scarcely room to draw breath. *How many are there?* Antony wondered.

How many thousands have come to see him die?

Katherine was not one of them. Antony had asked that morning, tentatively, whether she wished to accompany him. Other wives stood with his fellow aldermen, just as eager as their husbands to see Black Tom Tyrant meet his end. But while Kate had as strong a heart as any for most things, she could not abide blood; she had gone into Covent Garden for the day, far from the thousand-headed monster that now waited with unholy glee.

That monster frankly scared Antony. He'd already fled one angry mob a few days after the vote in the Commons, discovering only then that the divisions had been published, and that he was tarred as a Straffordian. And as bad as the riots had been lately, the celebration tonight would be worse. London had become a beast that answered to no man's command.

Noon was nearly upon them. Sunlight gilded the tops of the White Tower, and the scaffold where the headsman waited. The wind off the river was cool, but with so many bodies pressed so close, the air sweltered and stank. Despite that, hawkers wandered tirelessly through the crowd, selling beer and onions and cheese. A few enterprising souls seemed even to have brought chamber pots, so they need not risk losing their places.

Antony prayed for it to be over soon, and was answered with an animal roar. Mail and pike heads glittered along the Tower wall: they were bringing Strafford out.

Thomas Wentworth, born of a wealthy Yorkshire family, bore himself as proudly as any duke. Illness and imprisonment had weakened his body, but his spirit was yet strong; he had even written to the King, telling him to sign the bill of attainder, for the good of England. Antony suspected it a political gambit on Strafford's part, a ploy to gain sympathy from the Lords by his noble self-sacrifice, but if so, it had failed signally. All it had bought him was death.

Movement flickered in a window of the fortress: craning his neck, Antony saw Laud, looking out from his own cell. The archbishop raised his hands in blessing as his friend passed; then he staggered, weeping, and crumpled out of sight.

Having mounted the steps to the scaffold, Wentworth composed himself and addressed the crowd. Only fitful snatches of the man's final speech reached Antony's ears. "I do freely forgive all the world—"

Even his King, Antony thought, and shifted uncomfortably. All Charles's promises to Strafford had come to naught. The King had even made one last, frantic attempt to free the earl by force, dispatching soldiers to break him from the Tower of London, but it accomplished nothing. No, something more, and worse: it had fed the hysterical rumours of gunpowder plots and invasion from abroad, and strengthened Pym's position. Who could trust the King now?

His speech concluded, Wentworth was praying. The rumble of the crowd subsided, waiting for the moment. And in that hush, Antony heard a voice, hissing venomous words.

"Put not your trust in princes, nor in the sons of men, for in them there is no salvation."

He thought at first it was one of his fellow aldermen. But they were all watching the scaffold, where Strafford refused a blindfold. Scarcely breathing, Antony cast his eyes about, trying to find the source of the voice. All about him were merchants and gentlemen, common councillors—

There. A man he did not know, standing a little distance in front and to the left of him. Respectably dressed, with nothing about him to draw attention—save some indefinable quality in how he held himself, some feral touch in his bearing, that most would not remark. But Antony had seen it before.

Wentworth knelt and stretched out his arms.

Disturbance was spreading around the stranger, ugly muttering, men scowling in anger and hate. The executioner raised his axe, and as it fell home, the stranger's lips curved in a wicked smile.

Antony was moving almost before the roar began, well before the severed head was lifted for all to see. Not toward the stranger; anything he tried to do in this crowd would get him killed. He was a known Straffordian, and the howls coming from that knot of men sounded more like the cries of wolves than civilised Englishmen. It *would* be a riot, if he did anything to provoke it.

It might become one regardless.

Hoof beats at the far verges of the crowd, men riding to bring the glad news to the rest of the country. Elbows jostled Antony, almost knocking him from his feet. *If I fall, I will be trampled.* He caught the sleeve of a nearby man and regained his balance while the fellow spat a curse in his face. *I must get out of here!*

Free air, finally, as he broke through into more open space. The fringes of the crowd, packed into the farthest reaches of the streets that still had some view of the scaffold, were roiling away now, shouting, singing joyous melodies. Antony joined their movement, but not their song, and headed for the realm below.

THE ONYX HALL, LONDON
12 May 1641

"It has been a year and a day," Lune said to Gertrude, pacing the small, painted chamber in a back corner of the Onyx Hall. Someone had decorated it decades ago for their mortal lover; now it lay empty, unused, forgotten. Which made it very suitable for private audiences. "Where is he?"

"Well," the little brownie said philosophically, "times aren't what they used to be. Can't just go flying through the air on a bit of straw anymore; someone might see. Perhaps the roads were bad."

Perhaps. Lune fretted, though. Had the oath been enough? Or had the knight found some way to betray her?

Or been discovered and killed.

She worried without cause. Scotland was far away; Cerenel might, as Gertrude suggested, have misjudged how long the journey would take. Or perhaps he could not slip away so easily. They were assuming, regardless, that he would go first to the Angel, and from there Rosamund would guide him. Cerenel might be planning a more public return, testing before the court Lune's promise that he would be welcomed back.

A year and a day. A year and a day of the Ascendants rising in power, and brawls between courtiers about the proper relations of mortals and fae. No attacks as obvious as the murderer or Taylor's attempt on the alder tree, but one of her more idealistic knights—one come to the Onyx Court after her accession, drawn by her rhetoric of harmony—was found dead in the streets, while wandering in mortal guise. Chance accident? Or a deliberate weakening of her support?

She hoped to find out today. Lune breathed more easily when the door opened, and Rosamund bowed Sir Cerenel into the room.

He was just as he had been; they were not mortals, to be aged and worn by their trials. True, he wore barbarous fashion—a loose, belted tunic laced at the neck and sleeves with leather thongs—but then, he had taken nothing with him in his exile save the clothes and sword he wore. Studying him, though, Lune saw stiffness in his posture. Whatever else happened, this banishment had forever changed how he would serve her.

I hope it was not in vain.

Cerenel knelt, the curtain of his black hair falling forward. When Lune offered her hand, he kissed it with dry lips. "Rise," she said. "And tell us what you have learned."

She settled into her chair as he began, hands clasped behind his back. "As commanded, your Majesty, I have been to the Gyre-Carling's court in Fife. You have weighed her heart to an ounce: her animosity to you and yours is unequalled."

Sun and Moon knew where the Goodemeades had vanished to, though Lune was sure they would be ready to hand if she needed them. Cerenel had not appreciated their presence before.

"All of this is known," Lune said, trying not to show her impatience too obviously. "Who is the architect of our troubles?"

"I suspect one they call the Lord of Shadows," Cerenel said. Lune's mouth twitched at the ostentatious title. "He is newly come to Nicneven, though his arrival there seems to have preceded the attacks by some span."

Hardly an argument against him. Unless Nicneven were a fool—and would that she were—she would weigh the merits of any newcomer before deciding to follow his advice.

"How stands he in the court? Who are his allies?"

"Kentigern Nellt," Cerenel replied, not at all to Lune's surprise. "The giant rails against the subtlety and slow progress counselled by the Lord of Shadows, but their goals are in accord. My brother keeps more free of him, wishing to be rid of all politics in his life. But others fled from this court are there, and many declare themselves his followers."

Lune curled her fingers into the point that edged her cuffs. Was Cerenel understating his brother's involvement to protect him? It hardly mattered. If she could remove the head of the snake, the body, if not dead, would at least be robbed of its fangs. "And what can you tell me of him? His name, where he came from—"

But Cerenel was already shaking his head. "Madam,

I know not. He is never seen at court. Nicneven has many grottoes and glens that form her realm; some are her private retreat alone, and there she keeps him. Her closest advisers have been to see him—Sir Kentigern now commands her guard—but she has claimed him for her own, and leashes him tightly."

"Is he her lover?"

"The only one she keeps, at present."

Another reason for her to hate me, when I rob her of him. But how to do it? Lune could not simply invade Fife; her military strength might top Nicneven's, but first she would have to get it there. And anyone subtle enough to send hired knives after her would be on guard for the same.

She was interrupted in this planning by Rosamund suddenly throwing open the door. "Madam," she said, "The Pr—"

The hob didn't manage to get the title out before Antony was past her. "Who of your people went above, to watch the execution?" he demanded.

Lune was on her feet, startled. Out of the corner of her eye, she glimpsed Cerenel concealing a knife in his sleeve once more. He had come armed, and was nervous enough to draw when surprised: both worried her. But first, Antony. "I do not know," she said. "No doubt several, but they were not forbidden to attend. Why?"

"I know a glamoured faerie when I see one," Antony said. His breath came fast, and the chain of his office had been knocked askew. "One was in the crowd, speaking sedition."

"*Sedition?*"

"Strafford's own words, when he heard Charles had signed for his death. '*Put not your trust in princes, nor in the sons of men, for in them there is no salvation.*' " Antony spat the words out.

Lune's blood ran cold. Men said such things, yes, from time to time—but not in public. What a man condemned to the scaffold might say, a man on the street could not. Or *should* not. "Are you certain it was a fae?"

Antony paced the small room restlessly. He was speaking more freely than she might have wished, given Cerenel's presence, but whatever idea had possessed him would not let him go, and to send the knight away would only offend him. "I had a thought," her consort said. "These mobs, this controversy and bloodthirst that fuels the strife against the King—what if it is no accident?"

Alarmed, Lune said, "No one could possibly have created it all."

"No," he said, mouth twisting. "Our grievances are our own, born from a history of ill-usage and divided opinion. But what need is there to create them? All it takes is a spark. Someone to help them along. A bit of muttered sedition here; an accusation of papistry there. Rumours spread, or encouraged in their spread, to sow chaos and discord throughout the City. I thought it Pym's doing, and perhaps it was—but not alone."

Cerenel shifted his weight. Lune rounded on him, skirts flaring. "Did you know of this?"

"Madam," he said, holding his hands out in placation, "I was coming to that. I—"

"Does this Lord of Shadows strike against London, as well as the Onyx Court?"

He flinched from her hard voice. "I think it likely, yes. But it was rumour only; I cannot be certain."

She should have suspected. But Lune was accustomed to thinking of her own court as the only one that worked in two worlds at once. This was precisely the kind of interference Nicneven hated, when it cost the Queen of Scots her life. She had assumed that meant the Gyre-Carling would eschew it herself.

And perhaps she did. But the Lord of Shadows did not.

If Nicneven wanted to hurt Lune, then she could hurt London—and through it, all of England. Charles Stuart crippled by his own Parliament, in vengeance for Mary Stuart's death. They were halfway there already.

"Who is the Lord of Shadows?" Antony asked. Confusion distracted him briefly from his own anger.

Lune was more grateful than ever for the oath, now. It would make this easier, if not more palatable. "I do not yet know. But Sir Cerenel will be returning north, to find out."

The knight stepped back, violet eyes wide. "Madam— my exile is done."

"But you went into Nicneven's court on the pretence of disaffection here. They will not be surprised if you return."

"They sent me back to spy on *you!*"

Silence followed, ringing in the aftermath of his shout. Everyone in the room stood frozen, like statues, until

Cerenel went to his knees, white as a ghost. "Your Grace—Lord Antony—the command came to me from Nicneven herself. She bade me return to your court and pass along what I learned here."

Antony moved up to stand at Lune's side. "By what means? How will you communicate?"

The knight shook his head. "She said a messenger would come. I know nothing more."

To catch that messenger, they would have to keep Cerenel here. Exchanging a quick glance with Antony, Lune said, "No. I have no doubt that your orders began with this Lord of Shadows. To stop him, we must learn more of him, and that can only be done in Fife. Tell Nicneven I was suspicious of you, or that my favour has moved on; tell her whatever you wish. But you *will* go back."

Tears jewelled Cerenel's lashes, that he was too proud to shed. "Madam," he whispered, from where he knelt before her, "this is my *home*."

"Then help us preserve it," Lune said. "Find us this Lord of Shadows."

GUILDHALL, LONDON
3 January 1642

"They've overstepped," Antony said, angry satisfaction tingeing his words. "It nearly came to blows in the Commons, when they first proposed to print the Grand

Remonstrance. Bad enough to present to the King a list of grievances long enough to pass for the fifth gospel of the Bible, but publishing it for all to read..."

He did not exaggerate. The days when Parliament debated issues quietly and members dozed on their benches were long past; scarcely a man there had not drawn his sword in the end. It needed no faerie interference to spark their anger—assuming a fae could get within twenty feet of those godly zealots—their own bad blood was enough. They could pass motions to deal with the tumults outside their chamber, but what of those within?

Yet that victory, the public declaration of the Commons' war against its own sovereign, had misfired exactly as Antony hoped. Printed just before Christmas, the Grand Remonstrance—God be thanked—had put loyalist mobs in the street, fighting the Puritans and Levellers and other fanatic malcontents who supported Parliament's leaders. Pym and his friends had become drunk on their own power and ideals, and would reap the consequences.

Not before time, either. Ireland was in open rebellion, fighting to throw off the English yoke entirely. And Eochu Airt, furious at Antony's reversal of position on Strafford, showed no willingness to halt the bloodshed. It was time for England to put its own house in order, and stop this internal fighting that threatened to gut all its strength.

But Ben Hipley did not seem to share his cheerful outlook. "I fear the King is about to lose what goodwill he has earned."

"What? How?"

The ancient stones of the Guildhall echoed their every word to the would-be eavesdropper, and with City sentiment having swung fiercely to the Puritan, Antony had cause to fear it. He should have known Ben did not bear good news, though; the spymaster would not have come to him here unless the cause was urgent.

Hipley stepped in closer and lowered his voice. "Pym and the others have attacked the King's advisers, and met with success. Now they aim their bolts at the Queen."

Henrietta Maria. Hardly popular in England, for she was both French and Catholic, the latter a constant source of discord. "But to strike at her—that will only turn people even more against them. We may not love her, but who would see her dragged through the mud, as Strafford was?"

"The King would not," Hipley said. "He's sent Sir Edward Herbert to the Lords this morning, to impeach Lord Mandeville, and five from the Commons. Pym, Hampden, Holles, Hesilrige, and Strode."

Antony's heart stopped. "Will the Lords—"

Ben shook his head. "I don't know. But you should get to Westminster."

ST STEPHEN'S CHAPEL, WESTMINSTER
4 January 1642

He got to Westminster, for all the good it did. Pym already knew what was coming. The King's creatures should have moved for the immediate imprisonment of the accused men, but they let the moment slip. Antony, who might have done it for them, was not prepared; he arrived only just in time to hear the impeachment read. And so nothing came of it, not yet, save a meaningless resolution that the Commons would consider the matter.

Whatever happens now, he thought on his way back to Westminster late the following morning, *the damage has been done. If you threaten your enemies, you must follow through, and win. The King has done neither.*

Only after the noon recess did he realise the disaster was not yet complete.

The sergeant-at-arms threw wide the doors of the chapel and bellowed in a loud voice, "The King!"

A hideous silence fell. Browne had been reporting on a delegation sent to the Inns of Court; he trailed off midsentence and stood staring. Lenthall gaped from the Speaker's chair. Antony, in the midst of scribbling a note, sat paralysed as ink dripped and blotted his page.

Into that silence came Charles. Sweeping his hat off with an elegant gesture, he advanced down the floor of the chapel, while around him the members of the Commons came to their feet in a ragged wave, snatching their own hats from their heads. Charles's nephew trailed a pace behind him, their paired steps deliberate in the quiet.

The man behind Antony whispered, "Sweet swiving Jesus."

"Mr Speaker," the King said, his tone mild, "I must for

a time make bold with your chair."

Lenthall staggered belatedly out of the way. Once arranged in his seat, Charles surveyed the chapel and its occupants with a curious eye. As well he might: no monarch of England had ever intruded on the deliberations of the Commons. They were—or had been—inviolate.

Charles had dressed with great splendour for his intrusion, in a doublet of well-tailored taffeta, a broad collar of finest lawn edged with point. They gave his body bulk, but not height, and he looked small in Lenthall's chair.

But his presence was larger than he. "No person," he said into the silence, "has privileges, when charged with treason. I am come among you to know if any of those so accused are in attendance." He waited, but no one spoke. "Is Mr Pym here?"

Not a soul breathed in reply.

Irritated, he turned to Lenthall. "Are any of those persons in the house, who stand accused of treason? Do you see them here? Show them to me!"

The Speaker lacked a spine of his own; he was a creature of the strongest authority about him. In that moment, he showed how truly the winds had changed. Swallowing convulsively, Lenthall fell to his knees. "May it please your Majesty, I have neither eyes to see nor tongue to speak in this place, but as the House is pleased to direct me, whose servant I am here; and humbly beg your Majesty's pardon that I cannot give any other answer than this is, to what your Majesty is pleased to demand of me."

A few men gasped. A few more chuckled in malicious pleasure. Antony did neither. Having come late, he sat near the chapel entrance; now, hearing sounds in the lobby, he turned and looked into the gap between the benches. The Earl of Roxburgh lounged in the entrance, propping the doors open, so that Antony and anyone else who cared to could see what awaited them.

Armed men filled the lobby. Elegant courtiers, many of them the Queen's men, but not a one of their number less than skilled in the use of the pistols they held. One met Antony's gaze and grinned insolently, cocking his weapon and aiming it toward him—saying, clear and cold, *I wait only for the King's word.*

His blood ran with ice, and for the first time, it occurred to him to fear, not the dissolution of Parliament, but its massacre.

"'Tis no matter," the King said, his light tone belying the venom that backed it. "I think my eyes are as good as another's."

He lifted his chin and scanned the ranks of standing men. Antony squeezed his own eyes shut. He did not have to look. A messenger had come for Pym not ten minutes before, after which he obtained leave for himself and the others to depart. Lenthall had not detained them, though the Commons agreed the day before that the accused members should present themselves to answer the charges. Only Strode had caused any delay, insisting he wished to stay for the confrontation. Pym and the others dragged him out of the chapel by his cloak.

The only thing worse than arresting members of Parliament was coming to arrest them, and failing.

"I see all my birds have flown," Charles said at last. The satisfied grandeur with which he had entered was gone; in its place reigned discontented anger. "I cannot do what I came for." And with a snarl, he rose from the Speaker's chair and stormed from the House, followed by rising voices crying the offended privileges of Parliament.

THE ONYX HALL, LONDON
10 January 1642

Lune's heavy skirts flared every time she reached the end of her pacing and pivoted to retrace her steps. The Onyx Hall was a goodly palace, with many chambers and galleries, entertainments aplenty to amuse her, but for all that it was a cage; she missed the sun and breeze on her face.

London was not safe, though. Mortal bread might shield her against the prayers and invocations of the Puritan mobs in its streets, but it would do nothing to save her from a rock to the head. The barricades of benches torn from taverns, put up by the apprentices before their Christmas holiday ended on Twelfth Night, had been cleared away, but in their place were the Trained Bands of London. They placed cannon on the corners and stretched chains across the streets, all in preparation for the attack they feared would come.

She dared not go above; she wished Antony would not. He had struggled since that abortive Parliament two years ago to maintain an impossible balance: fighting for moderation while never trusting the King, opposing Pym's junto while never alienating them too obviously. They branded him a Straffordian for voting against the attainder, and could do worse. Members of Parliament had been ousted from their seats for their opposition. Some had been sent to the Tower.

But Antony sat even now in the Guildhall with the House of Commons, which had exiled itself from Westminster for its own safety. At his request, she had sent out a few of her more reliable goblins, and learned the five treasonous members were hiding in Coleman Street, but what good did that do? The King could not strike them now. He had already suffered the failure he could not afford, and outraged the populace beyond endurance.

And Lune, who had vowed to protect England from such troubles, could only wait for a message: the name and nature of the Lord of Shadows, who fed this violence against the King on Nicneven's behalf.

The flapping of wings halted her pacing. A falcon arrowed through the open latticework of the chamber wall and perched on the back of a chair. It shook its wings, then again, and with the third shake stretched upward and down until a sharp-faced powrie stood gripping the chair in his bony fingers. Where he had gotten the falcon cloak from, Lune never asked; it was not the common raiment of goblinkind. But it made him useful.

He had no cap to take off, no clothing save the cloak, which he swept around himself as he knelt. Lune offered her hand perfunctorily, bade him rise, and said, "What word?"

Orgat was no Onyx Courtier; his home was a disused peel tower along the Border. But the Goodemeades knew him from their time in the North, ages ago, and they had contracted him to bear messages from Cerenel. She was grateful now for her decision to leave Valentin Aspell out of those plans; he was too much in company with the Ascendants, these days.

"Got it here," the powrie said, and began rooting around in the feathers of his cloak with one hand, the other clutching it in front of his groin for a modicum of decency. "Nimble little bastard—hope you can make sense of it, yer Grace—come *on,* now—ah! Didn't even squish him."

The spy triumphantly produced something small and wiggling. That Cerenel would not send a written message, or even a verbal one, Lune expected; it was not safe. But— "A spider?"

"Told me to fetch it meself," Orgat said. "From me tower, he is. That there's a cupboard spider, as we call them. Was real particular that it had to be a male." He dropped it in the hand Lune reflexively held up; she shuddered as its legs scrabbled against her skin. "Careful with him, now. Supposed to be alive, too."

A spider. A living, male cupboard spider, from Orgat's peel tower.

This was the message Cerenel had sent her.

Find me this Lord of Shadows.

She knew someone, once, who called to mind images of spiders. Her heartless, twisted predecessor, the Queen of the Onyx Court. Invidiana.

But Invidiana was dead.

A living, *male* spider.

Lune whispered, "Ifarren Vidar."

THREE CRANES WHARF, LONDON
11 January 1642

Drumbeats echoed off the warehouses that lined the north bank of the Thames, overmastered only by the shouts of the crowd. The Trained Bands kept order, but in good cheer; they were not there to prevent violence—for there was none—but to keep the masses from overrunning the group that stood on the wharf.

The barge was drawn up to its moorings and steadied by the same lightermen who the day before had marched in the streets, offering their lives in defence of Parliament. Now they offered their hands to the five men who waited to board.

John Pym stood in the cold air, his eyes raised to God, his prayer of thanksgiving drowned out by the noise of the onlookers. Then he stepped aboard, followed by Hampden, Holles, Hesilrige, and Strode. No more concealment for them: they waved to their supporters, and received cheers and prayers in return.

The rest of the House of Commons made their way onto the barge. Antony placed himself in the middle, a false smile on his face. At this moment, of all moments, he could not afford to show his horror at the news.

The King was fled. For the royal family to retire to Hampton Court was common enough; for them to depart in the night, with no warning to the palace that they were coming, was not. But it was only an admission of the obvious: that Charles's attempt to take the leaders of Parliament under arrest had irrevocably lost him the goodwill of his City.

London had feared attack, and prepared itself for such. Instead it won, without a fight.

Casting off the ropes, the lightermen put the barge to the river. They made slow progress up the Thames, surrounded on all sides by gaily decorated vessels, packed to their gunwales with celebrating men. From the Strand, Antony could hear the Trained Bands, paralleling their journey with drums and song, and the mocking calls they made as they passed the deserted Palace of Whitehall.

"Where is the King and his Cavaliers?"

Holding on to his smile for his life, Antony thought, *They are gone to prepare for war.*

SUNDAY
2 SEPTEMBER 1666

THE BATTLE FOR THE RIVER

"A quay of fire ran all along the shore,
And lighten'd all the river with the blaze:
The waken' d tides began again to roar,
And wondering fish in shining waters gaze.
Old father Thames raised up his reverend head,
But fear'd the fate of Simois would return:
Deep in his ooze he sought his sedgy bed,
And shrunk his waters back into his urn."

JOHN DRYDEN
ANNUS MIRABILIS

T**he baker's house burns** like a candle, a pillar of flame in the narrow, night-dark street. The people of Pudding Lane have awakened, roused from their beds by the muffled peal of the parish bell, signalling fire. The leather buckets have been fetched from the church, their contents flung in useless doses: water, ale, even urine or sand—anything that might quench the blaze.

But onward it burns, stubbornly fed by a strange wind blowing from the east. Sparks dance in the breeze, a graceful courante in the dark, until one adventures westward, to the Star Inn on Fish Street Hill. The galleried inn, backing onto the baker's own property, keeps hay in its yard.

A single spark is enough.

Men shout in the street, their neighbours' rest be damned. Anyone still sleeping ought to be woken. While those nearest take the precaution of hurrying their possessions out-of-doors, north or south to safety, the more charitable bellow for the fire-hooks, to pull the adjoining buildings down before they too can catch.

But the landlords who own those buildings are not here.

Those who live on Pudding Lane are poorer sorts, renting from their betters. And so, fearing the consequences should he destroy such property, the Lord Mayor of London, hauled from his bed to answer this threat, dismisses it before going back home.

"*Pish—a woman might piss it out.*"

London has survived fires before.

THE ONYX HALL, LONDON
five o'clock in the morning

The breath of the Cailleach Bheur howled through the stone galleries, the high-vaulting latticework of the chamber ceilings, leaving no corner in peace. Three days it had blown, above ground and below, the latest assault from the Gyre-Carling of Fife—and the worst. Spies could be driven out; warriors could be fought. The Cailleach was unstoppable.

And the fae of the Onyx Court were wild-eyed and hollow-cheeked beneath her touch. For the wind brought more than the Blue Hag's icy chill: ghosting on its wings were voices, inaudible whispers of winter's promise. Age. Mortality. Death.

Small wonder we are going mad.

Lune shivered inside her fur-lined cloak. Years of struggle against Nicneven—decades, since that first attempt to burn the alder tree—and all she had to show for it was war.

No. This was not war. Lune had fought wars, on her journey to this point. This was something different: not clean confrontation in battle, nor even the underhand knife-work of spying and betrayal. The Cailleach could kill them all, without ever exposing herself to attack. What Nicneven had done to gain such aid, Lune could not even guess; the Blue Hag was something older and more powerful than any of them. But after all her attempts and all her failures, the Unseely Queen of Fife had finally found something powerful enough to truly threaten the Onyx Court.

Such fears only played into the Cailleach's power. Lune gritted her teeth and bent over the rough map she had constructed from the objects to hand. Lady Amadea's fan served as a model for London, its sweeping edge representing the City wall, its outside sticks marking the line of the river in the south. On the left sat a silver tobacco box—St Paul's Cathedral—and on the right, a jet brooch, for the Tower of London. A long pin fixed the fan to the table below, in approximation of the London Stone.

She tapped her gloved finger on the fan's top edge. "The Cailleach Bheur is the Hag of Winter; her power therefore comes from the north. But here we are protected; the wall guards us not just above, but also below. It blocks entry into our realm. And so she veers east."

"Why not west?" Sir Peregrin Thorne asked. The Captain of the Onyx Guard did not have too much dignity to stuff his hands beneath his arms, warming his fingers and hiding their tremble. Lune had sent him above earlier in the night; the wind blew outside as well, but in the mortal realm it became nothing more than air. That brief respite was already failing him, though, and his haunted eyes flicked restlessly over the map. "West is death—also the Cailleach's domain."

"Because of this." Lune's finger moved southeast, to the jet brooch. "The Tower is our weak point. The entrance to our realm lies in the keep at the centre, true—but you must consider the fortress as a whole. With the City wall joining its eastern defences, that entrance may be said to lie on a border. And that renders it vulnerable."

"You *have* closed that pit, yes?"

The question came from Irrith, and so Lune forgave its insolent lack of deference. The slender sprite had done her many a good service these past years, and had been rewarded for it with knighthood, but she was ill-practised in her courtesies; the court of her Berkshire home was a far rougher one, with less ceremony, and Irrith had not been among Lune's people long. Besides, she was more ignorant of mortality than any of them, and held up poorly under the insidious terrors of the wind.

Not that Lune herself fared much better. She suffered not just on her own behalf, but that of the faerie palace, which grew colder and more brittle with every passing hour. "Of course," she said, struggling not to betray the frayed state of her own nerves. *How do mortals* live *like this—knowing every moment brings death one step closer?* "It is closed, and as sealed as I can make it—but that is not enough."

"What about—" Irrith persisted, but the question ended in a yelp as the door to the council chamber slammed open. They could not keep doors closed anymore; everything blew open, sooner or later, scaring everyone out of their wits.

But this time the movement had a human cause. Jack Ellin hauled at the door's edge, struggling futilely to close it, before swearing and giving up. Lune's councillors flinched away from the tall man as he came up to the table; the presence of a mortal echoed the wind's promises. Lune had to hold herself still as he reached out and laid one hand on her cheek.

The gesture was dispassionate, a physician's touch. They had discovered this by accident, when a chance brush of his fingers lifted some of the darkness from Lune's spirit. For Jack Ellin, as for any mortal, the promises of the Cailleach were inevitable nature. He bore without thinking a weight that threatened to crush Lune. And thanks to the bond that connected them, she could share that weight with him, and gain some measure of clarity for herself.

She allowed herself a grateful look but no smile as the Prince of the Stone dropped his hand, leaving her to stand on her own. It was a temporary reprieve, nothing more. But it gave her hope.

Then Jack said, in a deceptively light tone, "Madam—were you aware that your roof is on fire?"

Lune's attention went upward before she could stop it, accompanied by the shameful thought that she might almost welcome the Onyx Hall bursting into flame, if only to end the unbearable cold. But the stone was frost-rimed and black.

"Pudding Lane," Jack said, kindly ignoring her foolish impulse. "And now Fish Street Hill as well."

Warmth. Light. She had to work to remind herself

that he was speaking of destruction, not salvation. "Fires happen, Jack." And she had an abundance of other matters to concern her.

"So you will let it burn?"

His expression said everything his voice left unspoken. The wry eyebrows had risen in surprise, and a cynical twist shaped his lips. *He came here expecting us to help.*

As he had every right to. And Lune had an obligation to answer the Prince's call.

In Mab's name, I swear to you that I will do everything I can to preserve London and its people from disaster—and let fear hinder me no more.

Her own words echoed in her ears, spoken a bare year before. This was the very purpose for which she had chosen Jack; the physician was no courtier, but he was devoted to the safety and wellbeing of London. She could hardly ask him to champion that cause, then ignore him when he did so. Even *without* an oath to bind her.

The part of her mind that cowered like a mouse before a hawk protested shrilly that it was not fear hindering her, but cold calculation; what help could she spare Jack, with the Cailleach howling death in their ears?

A great deal. Lune had already confiscated all the bread in the Onyx Hall, once she realised her people were likely to flee before the onslaught. That was what Nicneven wanted, why she had sent the Blue Hag against them: to empty the palace, leaving it unguarded against a physical assault. But Lune could give some of her people a respite, and send them to aid Jack.

She extended her senses upward, feeling the heat scorching the stone and earth of those two streets. No comfort there; her whole body shuddered, caught between fire and ice. But now she had the shape of it, and the direction.

"Billingsgate is clear," she said. "Take any half-dozen you feel will be useful—any you can trust not to leave. More if you need them. You have the bread." Casting her eye around the table, she settled on Irrith. The Berkshire sprite did not know London well at all, but much more of this wind and she would break. "Go with the Prince. Be our messenger, in case he needs aught else."

Irrith bowed to her and to Jack. He smiled reassuringly at the sprite, but did not reach out; without the tie that bound him to Lune, Prince to Queen, his touch did more harm than good. Amadea had screamed when he tried before, weeping that she felt the decay in his flesh.

"I'll do what I can," he promised, before hurrying out the door. "Perhaps we can turn this to our advantage against the Hag."

RIVER THAMES, LONDON
six o'clock in the morning

Jack Ellin was no greybeard doctor, but he had worked through fever and plague, in the face of fell death itself. He knew the value of a comforting lie. Belief in a hopeful future, no matter how unfounded, could give a patient strength, and Lune needed strength right now.

But the truth was that he had no idea how to turn the heat above to combat the cold below. Jack was a curious man, always hungry for knowledge; when it became apparent that the unnatural wind was the breath of the Cailleach Bheur, he began asking questions about the Scottish hag. His curiosity went mostly unfed: the London fae knew hardly anything of her, and were too distracted by unfamiliar thoughts of death. It gave him little to work with.

I'm more inclined to take it the other way, he admitted ruefully as he hoisted himself out of a shaft into the tiny courtyard of a Billingsgate house. If he could strangle the fire with cold, he would; conflagrations were terrifying things, in a City built so largely of timber. And with the summer so dry...

Up here, however, the wind bore no particular chill, for all that it blew from the east, against the habit of the region. *All those fine gentlemen in their Covent Garden houses will be smelling the City's stink,* he thought, blinking in the morning twilight. It did not amuse him as much as he hoped.

Behind him, his troop of faerie helpers followed him out of the entrance. Jack hoped they would do some good; he still was not entirely certain what fae were capable of. Surely their arts would have use, though. And he had bypassed the courtiers, seeking out Lune's humbler subjects; the goblins and hobs he chose were tougher and more used to physical labour. Fighting fires was hard, grinding, filthy physical labour indeed—even, he imagined, with magic to help.

Three goblins, two hobs, and one sprite, all covered by concealing glamours. They did not have to look hard to spot the fire; its sullen glow made a false dawn above the rooftops to the northwest, not far away at all. "To the river," Jack told his companions, after a moment's consideration.

"We can't go that way?" Mungle demanded, pointing toward the smoke. Judging by the filth that caked his body, the bogle had not gone within arm's-length of water for longer than Jack had been alive. "My lord," he added, as an afterthought.

"Not quickly," Jack answered the goblin. "And I'm not 'my lord' here, nor Prince of the Stone. We shall have enough to do without someone asking when I was ennobled, and whether I can help them at court. As to your question: the fire is tending south and west; we'll be more use on the other side. But the streets are packed with people moving their belongings out of harm's way, so we shall get a wherry and come at it from the river."

With only a little grumbling—Mungle wanted a fight, and did not seem to understand that his opponent was not one to be met with fists—they sought out the nearest river stair. Plenty of wherrymen floated within hailing distance; most were gaping at the smoke, and the rest were rowing passengers who gaped on their behalf. Jack got a boat large enough for them all, and gave instructions for their man to take them through the races of the bridge, landing them on the other side.

Where they would do... something. *Fire-fighting was not what I expected, when I joined a faerie court.* But it would be a fine opportunity to see what fae were capable of.

The tide was low, and at slack water, so the wherry ventured forth into the river. The oarsman had to thread his way through the other boats, though, so their progress was slow. And before they reached the stone piers of the bridge, a sudden flare of light brought all their heads around as one.

With a roar like a terrible beast, one of the many warehouses lining the river's bank burst into orange and gold. Heat seared their faces, and Irrith flinched hard enough to almost go over the gunwale. The wherryman, a member of the London class most renowned for its command of profanity, put all his foul words to use, staring at the sudden expansion of the fire.

"Pitch and tar," the hob Tom Toggin said when the wherryman was done. He was not swearing, Jack realised after a moment. "Or oil. Or hemp. Prob'ly pitch, it going up like that."

And then it was Jack's turn to curse. Seizing the oarsman's shoulder, he said, "You know the wharves well, yes? How many of the warehouses contain such material?"

The man seemed to have lost the ability to blink. "Er— don't rightly know—"

"How many?"

The boat drifted aimlessly on the current as the man shrugged. "Most of 'em?"

Another roar, another wash of heat. The next

warehouse in the row had caught.

And in the heart of the flames, something stirred. It might have been nothing more than a curling tongue of light, a ripple of fire along the collapsing line of a roof. But the fae in the boat saw with different eyes than a mortal might, and Tom Toggin grabbed Jack's sleeve, pointing with a finger that shook from pure terror.

Salamanders, Jack thought, curious despite his concern. There were a few in the Onyx Hall, creatures of elemental fire; he kept meaning to study them. But from what he knew, they were hardly a thing to inspire such fear.

Then he looked more closely, and his eyes widened.

He had seen such a thing before, yes—but much, much smaller.

In the hottest part of the blaze, a sinuous shape uncoiled, flexing its newfound power. Not a salamander, a mere lizard born of fire's light. Conceived in the inferno's womb and fed by the combustible treasures of London's wharves, it was far larger, far stronger, and worthy of a greater name.

Christ, Jack thought, staring in abject horror. *It's huge.*

The Dragon of the Fire roared.

THE ONYX HALL, LONDON
eight o'clock in the morning

Word spread through the Onyx Hall, faster than the flames above. *A Dragon has been born.*

A Dragon. Such had not been seen in England for many a forgotten age.

It was a source of great excitement, almost enough to distract the fae from the Cailleach Bheur. These were not the deep reaches of Faerie, far removed from the mortal world; few creatures of such power still existed here, and those few that did mostly slept. When they thought of the Dragon, they saw only the grandeur of it, and did not think of London.

But Lune did, even before Irrith came to tell her that another church was in flames.

"I forget the name," the sprite said, wiping soot from her face, left behind when the icy wind had dried all the sweat. "At the north end of the bridge. Jack—Lord John, that is—says it had a water tower."

Even through the leaden weariness inflicted by the Cailleach, the exhaustion of decrepit age, Lune knew what she meant. The church of St Magnus the Martyr, at the foot of London Bridge.

Where, thanks to the innovation of a clever Dutchman, waterwheels in the northernmost races churned the Thames upward, through leaden pipes that arched over the steeple of the church, from whence they fell with sufficient force to propel water through a goodly portion of the City's riverside district. Thus were houses supplied—and the men fighting the Fire.

"It knows," she whispered, and pressed the heels of her hands into her eyes. *The Dragon knows how we oppose it, and fights back.*

We. But the Onyx Court was already engaged in one

battle, against the Cailleach Bheur—if battle it could be called, when her scouts could not find the Hag's location, nor her advisers craft any means of blocking the deathly wind. How could they fight a second in the streets above? Fear gibbered at the edges of her vision, a hundred variants of death braiding into one terrifying whole. Death by fire, by ice, by the withering of age or the putrefaction of plague, creeping closer with every moment that passed—

No. Lune snarled it away. This was her oath, and her burden. She could no more abandon mortal London to the Fire than she could leave her court to the Hag. If Jack was brave enough to face a Dragon, she must give him all possible aid.

She forced herself to think. The church was under attack; the Bridge itself would not long be safe. The stones could not burn, but houses and shops had crowded its length for centuries, choking the roadway with timber and plaster. And where people travelled, so too could the Fire: down the Bridge to the crowded suburb of Southwark. Then they would lose all hope of controlling its spread.

Her fingernails had dug deeply enough into her palms to cut. Lune pried them free, wincing, and said, "Find Dame Segraine. Tell her to call out every water nymph, every asrai and draca in this court, and marshal them at the Queenhithe entrance. If a fae can *swim*, send him out to fight. We must keep the Dragon from crossing the river."

* * *

CANNON STREET, LONDON
eleven o'clock in the morning

Nearly a quarter mile of the riverfront was alight now, by Jack's best estimate, the cheap weather-boarded tenements that crowded about the wharves going up like dry tinder. The conflagration had roared through Stockfishmonger Row, Churchyard Alley, Red Cross Alley; men stood in lines, slinging full buckets up from the river, empty ones back down, but they might as well have pissed on the blaze, for all the good it did. The city's few fire-carts could not even make it into those warrens, nor close enough to the river to fill their tanks. The Clerkenwell engine had fallen in.

He sagged back against a shop on Cannon Street, breathing mercifully clean air. The road was filled wall-to-wall with carts and men on foot; what belongings could be evacuated had been brought here. The livery companies were rescuing records and plate from their company halls, while the poorer folk of the Coldharbour tenements ran with what they could carry on their backs, unable to afford the rising price of a wherry or cart.

Not everyone out there was a dockside labourer, though. One finely dressed gentleman, holding a kerchief over his nose to filter out the drifting smoke, stopped at Jack's side. "Where is the Lord Mayor?"

Jack wiped his streaming eyes and straightened, taking advantage of his height to crane over the shouting masses. "I think I see him—here, let me lead you."

The fellow kept hard at Jack's heels, forcing between two stopped carts whose drivers swore uselessly at each other. Sir Thomas Bludworth, when they came upon him, was a wretched sight; the Lord Mayor of London mopped at his face with the kerchief around his neck, staring and lost, trying ineffectually to direct the men around him.

"My lord," the gentleman said, loudly enough to get Bludworth's attention, "I have carried word to his Majesty at Whitehall of the troubles here, and he bids me tell you to spare no houses, but to pull them down before the fire in every direction."

It was the only thing that might work. They had no hope of quenching the flames; but if they could create wide enough breaks, too wide to leap, then they might at least contain it. Bludworth blinked, seeming not to understand the words, nor to recognise the man before him. "Samuel Pepys," the gentleman said, in the tone of one reminding a fellow he has always thought an idiot. "My Lord Mayor, the King commands—"

Bludworth jerked, as if coming awake. "Lord," he cried, "what can I do? I am spent. People will not obey me. I have been pulling down houses, but the fire overtakes us faster than we can do it."

Pepys bowed—hiding, Jack thought, an unsympathetic expression. He then stepped closer to the Lord Mayor, so he need not cry his next news to the world. "His Majesty has given orders to send in his Life Guards, or perhaps some of the Coldstream; the Duke of York also, and Lord Arlington.

You are to notify them at once if you need more soldiers, for the keeping of the peace, and carrying out the demolitions."

"Oh, no, no," Bludworth said immediately, flapping his hands. "I need no more soldiers, no, we have the Trained Bands—but for myself, I must go and refresh myself; I have been up all night." Still babbling, he slipped away, leaving Pepys staring.

"He has *not* been pulling houses down," Jack said in his wake. "He fears to do so, without the permission of the men who own them—and there's no chance of getting that in time. But I'll help you spread the word." *It should have begun hours ago. Before a simple fire turned into a God-damned Dragon.*

Once, he would have been delighted for the chance to see a dragon, to observe its characteristics and perhaps learn something of its nature. Not anymore. The creature was destruction; that was all he cared to know. That, and how to stop it.

Pepys did not see the Dragon, no more than any man fighting the Fire did. They spoke of it as if it had a will, as if it hungered and schemed and sought to overcome their defences, but they did not realise the truth of those words. Nevertheless, the gentleman had enough wit to see that decisive action was necessary. He gripped Jack's hand in thanks. "There is a contingent of the Life Guards in Cornhill; will you go to them?"

Nodding, Jack gathered in his breath and set off as quickly as he could down a side lane. He did not get a dozen paces off Cannon Street, though, before a wild-eyed man grabbed him by the sleeve, with the hand *not* waving a rusted sword. "Arm yourself, man!"

"Arm myself? For what?"

"They've fired St Laurence Pountney!"

"They?" His sword-bearing friend had other friends, pounding up behind him, all equally ill armed. Jack, carrying only an eating knife, began to think about losing himself once more in the Cannon masses.

One of the men said, "The papists, of course! Thousands of them! French papists are firing houses and churches—one of them threw a fire-ball into the steeple of St Laurence!"

The last thing Jack felt like doing was laughing, but he made his best effort at light derision. "A good arm he must have, then; it's one of the tallest steeples in town. I saw the church go, my friends; it was nothing more than a spark, that melted through the leading into the timber underneath." A spark flung with intent. But not by anything human, nor anything their swords could touch.

"But the papists—"

"*There are no papists.* All you'll find here are men throwing themselves, body and soul, into *stopping* the Fire." Men, and fae; Christ, he was supposed to be waiting in Cannon Street for Irrith to find him, with word on the efforts of the river fae. He fought the urge to shake the clowns facing him. "If you want to be of use, put down those weapons, and go fetch a fire-hook from your parish church. The King has given orders; the houses are to be pulled down."

They stared. Jack was no commander of men, but he had used his last ounce of patience, and the raw force left behind sufficed. *"Go!"*

They went.

THE ONYX HALL, LONDON

noon

At Jack's renewed touch, the worst of the Cailleach's chill receded, leaving Lune drained and shaking. *Sun and Moon. This, then, is the consequence of being connected to one's realm; I suffer as it does. And worse than my subjects do.*

"The King is at Queenhithe," he said, once she had caught her breath, "with the Duke of York, to give heart to the people. They hope to stop the Fire at Three Cranes Wharf in the west, and St Botolph's Wharf in the east. There's great fear that it will reach the Tower, and the munitions stored there."

The mere thought chilled her as badly as the wind. No doubt the work of emptying the Tower had already begun, but how long would it take to clear the fortress of all its powder? Such an explosion could destroy the City.

Jack was white underneath the filth that marred his face, and he had long since stripped to his linen shirt against the heat of the Fire; now he shivered madly, despite the cloak that wrapped him. "The wind is checking the spread eastward, of course, but that's not much blessing, for it also feeds the flames west. Our efforts slow the Fire's progress, but don't stop it. When we made a gap, we were driven back before we could clear the debris. We might as well have laid a path for the damned thing. If—"

He hesitated, looking down at her, then completed the thought. "If we did not have to contend with the wind, we might stand a chance."

She had all morning to think of that. A wind did not have a wellspring, not as a river did; the Cailleach was not crouched outside the eastern wall, puffing away at London. But Lune had tried another method of stopping her. "I sent a messenger, asking for a brief truce," she said. "Nicneven's quarrel is with me and my court, not the mortals of London."

"And?"

Jack read the answer in her eyes, sparing her from having to say it. He gritted his teeth, took a deep breath, and said, "She doesn't care."

Or at least her commander here did not. There was an encampment of Scottish fae somewhere outside the City, awaiting their chance to attack. Once the court was weakened enough, or fled, they would move in and claim what they had come for.

As if he could read her thoughts, Jack said, "Why not give it to her?"

Lune turned away, wrapping her own cloak more tightly. "No. I am not giving Nicneven Ifarren Vidar."

Faint noises told her Jack started and stopped three replies before he spoke clearly. "So you've said, and I'm sure you have your reasons—and perhaps when we have a little leisure, you'll see fit to share them with me. But Lune... what will that mean for London?"

The Fire still scorched her mind, spreading ever outward. The City had not seen a disaster this great in ages, and it showed no sign of ending. But the true problem was not Nicneven and the Cailleach Bheur, not for the people above; for them, the Cailleach's breath was mere wind. The problem was the Dragon, the elemental, ravening force that devoured all in its path. *That* was what they must strike at.

But what power could stand against it, with half the riverside its domain?

The river.

"Come with me," Lune said, and swept from the room without looking to see if Jack would follow.

The Onyx Hall seemed half-empty; some of her people had fled, even without protection. Others cowered in futile defence against the wind. Nianna staggered through a crossing ahead of Lune, tearing her hair out in clumps; they withered to grey in her hands, and the lady whimpered in horror. Lune seized her and snapped, "Go above. Do not worry about bread. Come below again when the bells drive you, but Sun and Moon, *get yourself out of here.*"

Nianna stared; Lune was not sure the lady even heard her. But she could not spare the time to make certain. She went on through her half-deserted palace, seeking out an entrance she never used.

Water lapped at the stone in a neat square, in a chamber otherwise unadorned. This was not a part of the Onyx Hall anyone dwelt in, and few of her subjects came here; its use was small for anyone not born of water. But it was the one place in her entire realm where the palace connected directly to the Thames, through the tiny harbour of Queenhithe.

Lune knelt at the water's edge, and beckoned for Jack to do the same. "The King is very nearly above your head," he told her, craning his neck.

"It is not the King I seek to contact. We need Father Thames."

He blinked. When she did not tell him it was a jest, his jaw came loose. "You talk to the river?"

"On occasion." *Once. Ages ago.* Father Thames little concerned himself with the politics of the Onyx Hall. Even those fae who were his children almost never heard his voice. One of the nymphs told Lune she thought the great river spirit slept, borne down by the weight of the city upon his shores.

If ever there was a time for him to wake, it had come.

Lune extended her left hand to Jack, who was still gaping. "He may answer us, if we call him together." *Or he may not.* She had not the leisure for the sort of ritual she had engaged in before. But she was tied to London, and Jack with her; she hoped that would count for something. The river had answered to mortal and faerie voices before.

"I have no idea how to do this," he warned her as he took her hand.

"Simply call him," she said, reaching their joined fingers down into the water. "Bid him wake, and fight the Dragon who roars along his bank. Else it will cross to Southwark ere long, and consume more of London besides. A Great Fire has been born in our City; only a Great River may quench it."

Her words were spoken as much to the water as to the Prince. His eyes had drifted shut, listening to the cadence; when she faltered, he continued on, in his own less than formal way. "We hope you do not mind the, er, theft of your waters—I'm sure you understand the need. But however many buckets we throw, they are not enough; we need *you*. Help your children against this threat."

Lune's left hand was chilled to the bone, but not from the Cailleach's wind. Gripped hard by Jack, she was for the moment safe from that attack; what she felt instead was an immensity, stretching from the headwaters far west to the sea far east, washing to and fro in the tides of the moon. Old Father Thames was, ages before London was dreamt, and would be long after they were gone. Measured against him, even fae were young.

And that great, aged immensity slept, letting the years ebb away unmarked.

"*Wake,*" she whispered—or Jack did, or both of them, with one voice. "*Wake, Old Father, to battle.*"

RIVER THAMES, LONDON
one o'clock in the afternoon

From Southwark, the City seemed a wall of fire and smoke, choking clouds obscuring the forest of steeples, the parts as yet unburnt. Half the northern bank was consumed, and despite the frantic efforts of men, the blaze marched down the Bridge, a phalanx of flame no defences could halt.

The Bridge had burned scarce thirty years before, its northern end consumed, the remainder saved only by a gap in the houses too wide for the sparks to cross. Now the Fire stood once more at that breach, straining to overleap it, to seek out and ravage the untouched expanses of Southwark. Smoke wreathed the severed heads of traitors and regicides that spiked the southern end, like fingers feeling for a hold.

With a shuddering crack, one towering, tottering building collapsed, half its substance tumbling into the roadway of the Bridge, a hellish tunnel no creature could traverse. The other half plummeted into the flood, hissing where it met the waters, smoking debris joining the clutter already floating there, the belongings hurled into the water by those unable to transport them more safely. The wreckage of London would be washing ashore downriver for days to come.

An asrai surfaced, having thrown herself frantically clear when the timbers came crashing down. The river to either side of the Bridge was choked with wherries and barges, carrying people and their goods to Westminster or across to Southwark, but all focus was on the City; no one attended to the lithe shapes slipping through the murk, lending their aid where they could. If droplets of water occasionally arced skyward, snuffing embers as they floated through the air, it was hardly worth noticing, when horror so great demanded the eye.

But these little children of the river could not stand against the beast that now gathered its strength in the raging inferno of the Bridge. The Dragon was all the Fire, from the leaping sparks of Three Cranes Wharf to the tongues licking stubbornly eastward against the wind, but its malevolence was here, preparing to conquer the defences of London Bridge, and claim a second victim to the south.

Beneath its glare, amidst the turbulent waters of the races, another power gathered.

Had anyone been able to approach the northernmost arches, they would have seen a true wonder. A face formed in the flood's high tide, shifting and grey. One pier hollowed out its mouth, thrusting down into the soft river mud; its eyes were two whirlpools, on either side of the span. Debris vanished beneath it, leaving the features focused and clear.

A voice too deep to hear said, *"Come to me, my children."*

And the fae of the river responded. Leaping, wriggling, slipping like quicksilver through the wherries and the wreckage, they came from upstream and down, flocking like a ragged school of fish to the call of their Old Father. Around his face they swam, in and out of the piers of the Bridge, flicking up against the wooden starlings that protected the stone, sending spray into the air.

It hissed angrily into steam as it met the Fire's heat. No mere water could stop the Dragon. But the true battle, though invisible to the eye, was far more striking, and the children of the Thames felt it in their souls. They *were* their Father, as leaves are the tree that gives them forth, and in them was his strength. He hoarded it now, and sent it upward against their enemy.

Fire and water. Dry heat against cold wetness, alchemical and elemental opposites. The air shimmered and split where they met. The stones of the Bridge shifted in their ancient seats, expanding and contracting, losing stability under the strain—but they held. London Bridge was not so fragile a thing.

The Dragon roared, flames leaping into the sky. Silently, inexorably, Father Thames answered it. Their strength was matched, here in this place, and the river spoke forth its will, that the Fire could not deny. *Here you will not pass.*

Snarling, its fury baulked, the Dragon retreated. Still the houses blazed, sending their ruins tumbling down, but the gap itself held, blocking the passage of the sparks. The rest of the Bridge, and Southwark that it defended, were safe.

Exhausted, his power spent, Father Thames sank back. The waters recoiled from the northern shore, leaving mud to be baked dry by the rage of the Fire. Men bailed them frantically upwards, filling barrels and tanks to be carried closer in, that the battle might continue.

The Fire could not pass the river—but north lay all the City, that Father Thames could not defend.

* * *

*A*s night falls, men watching from the walls of the Tower see the shape of the beast they battle. In the east it moves but slowly, fighting for every inch of ground it takes. In the west, it has claimed half the bank already. But the wind, veering first north, then south, has driven the flames up from the wharves, into virgin territory far from the water.

A great arch of fire reaches across the City, eclipsing the moon with its brightness. Behind its advancing front, a glowing, malevolent heart: the shattered ruins of churches, houses, company halls. Hundreds burnt, and thousands displaced.

And no sign of ending.

The Dragon snarls its pleasure, flexing across the darkened lanes. In the untouched parts of the City, candles and lanterns yet burn, obedient to laws that decree certain streets should be lit at night, for the safety and comfort of citizens. Those tiny flames speak a promise to the beast, that soon they, too, shall join its power, and feed its fury onward.

For the more it consumes, the more it hungers—and the stronger it ever grows.

PART TWO

THAT MAN OF BLOOD
1648–1649

The King. *Shew me that Jurisdiction where
Reason is not to be heard.*
Lord President. *Sir, we shew it you here,
the Commons of England.*

"KING CHARLS HIS TRYAL AT THE
HIGH COURT OF JUSTICE"

THE ONYX HALL, LONDON
3 October 1648

Throughout the night garden, the only sound was the quiet trickle of the Walbrook—a river long buried and half forgotten by the City of London, now a part of the Onyx Hall.

No lords and ladies walked the path, conversing quietly. No musicians played. The faerie lights that lit the garden formed a river of stars above, as if guiding Lune to her destination.

She needed no guide. This was a path she had walked many times before, every year upon this day.

She wore a simple, loose gown, a relic of an earlier age. The white fabric was rich samite, but unadorned by jewels or embroidery, and she stepped barefoot on the grassy paths. Tonight, the garden was hers alone. No one would disturb her.

The place she sought stood, not in the centre of the garden, but in a sheltered corner. Lune had no illusions. No one in her court mourned as she did, for faerie hearts were fickle things—most of the time.

Once given, though, their passion never faded.

The obelisk stood beneath a canopy of ever-blooming apple trees, their petals carpeting the grass around its base. She could have had a statue carved, but it would have been one knife too many. His face would never fade from her memory.

Lune knelt at the grave of Michael Deven, the mortal man she had once loved—and did still.

She kissed her fingertips, then laid them against the cool marble. Pain rose up from a well deep inside. She rarely dipped into it, or let herself think of its existence; to do otherwise was to reduce herself to this, a shell containing nothing but sorrow. Her grief was as sharp now as the night he died. It was the price she paid for choosing to love him.

"I miss you, my heart," she whispered to the stone—a refrain repeated far too many times. "There are nights I think I might give anything to see you again... to hear your voice. To feel your touch."

Her skin ached with the loss. No more to have his arms around her, his warmth at her side. And he could never be replaced: Antony was not and never would be Michael Deven. She had known it, when she first vowed always to keep a mortal at her side, ruling the Onyx Court with her. She created the title Prince of the Stone to cushion the blow of change, so that she might think of it as a political position, an office any man might fill. Not her consort, with all that implied.

Antony understood. As had Michael; he knew he could not live forever. Dwelling too long among the fae would break even the strongest mind. The time her Princes spent in the Onyx Hall, the touch of enchantment they bore, slowed life for them; Antony, at forty, looked a decade younger.

But despite that, inevitably, they aged and died.

The grass pricked through the fabric of her gown, and she dug her fingers into the cool soil. "We needed more time," she murmured. "Time to map the path I stumble blindly down now. 'Tis a fine thing, to say this place stands for the harmony of mortals and fae, the possibility of bridging those worlds. But *how*? How may I aid them, without taking from them their choices? How may *they* aid *us,* when they do not even know we are here?"

It had been easier, when couched in terms of *use* instead of *aid*. That notion still thrived too strongly in her court, and not only because of Nicneven's interference. Lune herself still struggled to effect change, without crossing that line.

And she had failed.

Six years of civil war. Royalist Cavaliers against Parliamentarian Roundheads, conflict reaching into every corner of the realm. Brother against brother. Father against son. Scotland at war with England, Ireland in raging revolt. The King imprisoned, sold by his own subjects to the Parliamentary armies for thirty pieces of silver. The land she had sworn to defend had torn itself apart... and she was powerless to heal it.

"We took Mary Stuart from them," she said, tasting the bitterness in the words. "So they have taken her grandson from us."

Nicneven's grudge, given scope and power by Ifarren Vidar: an old enemy, and one Lune should have suspected from the start. But intelligence had put him in France, at the

Cour du Lys, after he found no faerie kingdom in England would welcome him. Lune thought him safely gone. Nicneven, however, had given him a home. There was bitter irony in that; Vidar, at Invidiana's command, had helped the Queen of Scots along her path to the headsman. Lune had no proof, though, and Nicneven would not believe her without it.

So now Lune reaped the consequences of letting him escape when she ascended her throne.

The years pressed down upon her, a weight she rarely felt. But by her bond of love, she tasted mortality, and at moments like this it threatened to crush her. The weariness of ages sapped her strength, and yet her mind would not rest; even now, here, she dragged the chains of her duty and her failures.

She had to lay it aside. For this one night, every year, she was not the Queen of the Onyx Court; she was simply Lune, and free to grieve, not for England, but for a single man.

Curling her legs underneath her, she leaned against the stone that marked Michael Deven's grave, and gave herself over to sorrow.

LOMBARD STREET, LONDON
4 October 1648

The house showed no physical scars of six long years of struggle. The defences built for London had faced no army, let alone been breached. But the marks were there, albeit more subtly: in the absence of tapestries, candlesticks, much of the silver plate. The continual levies for the maintenance of the Parliamentary armies, the repeated loans from the City, had stripped Antony of funds, while the Royalist forces in Oxfordshire had so beggared his estate there that he was forced to sell it.

This is the price of moderation.

It could have been worse. Rightly suspecting his dedication to the Parliamentary cause, the commissioners appointed to gather the money had assessed him more highly than most, but at least they had not driven him from his home. And when things were at their tightest, carefully managed gifts of faerie gold had kept him from losing all.

Antony sat at the table, hands flat on its surface, gazing sightlessly at the wood between his fingers. The house was quiet. His sons and daughter had been sent to live with a cousin of Kate's in Norfolk—a man of neutrality so inoffensive that he had managed to preserve himself relatively unscathed through a conflict that had brought not only all of England, but Scotland and Ireland, too, into battle. Antony's manservant, inspired by sectarian zeal, had joined Fairfax's New Model Army, fighting for Parliament against the King, and had not come back. The cook, finding herself with much less work to do, drank—but at least she was quiet about it.

He heard a door open, footsteps on the stairs. A light step, and so Antony did not bestir himself. Soon enough Kate came into the room, and stopped when she saw him.

She finished unwinding the scarf that had protected her against the chilly air, and laid it at the other end of the table. "Coal is dear," she said, "but not so bad as it has been. We shall have more tomorrow."

"Thank you," Antony said, rising to take his wife's hands. She had suffered more than he through the bitter winters of the war, when the King or the Scots controlled Newcastle and little coal came to London. That had been the other reason for sending the children away: the cousin had wood and turf to burn for warming his house.

She gripped his fingers, chin sunk down; then made an unreadable noise and turned away. "What is it?" he asked, baffled by her sudden aversion.

Kate pulled off the modest linen cap that covered her hair and twisted it before facing him, as abruptly as she had fled. "Do you think I don't see the ink stains on your fingers? Do you think I don't know what they mean?"

Antony stared at his hands. He had not given it much thought. His attention was elsewhere—a thousand other elsewheres. More than he could handle.

"Tell me," she said bitterly, "do you work with Lilburne? Or someone else? What ideas do you put about, that are so subversive they must be printed in secret? Do not tell me those are from a quill; I know those marks from these."

Her tirade left him speechless. Could she honestly believe he sided with Lilburne's outrageous Levellers, those men who wished England to be ruled by the common mob? Lilburne spoke honestly about the corruption of

Parliament, its leaders gone mad with their newfound power, but Antony's agreement with the man ended there.

Except that was not Kate's point. If she objected to the ideas he championed, she would argue them with him. This was something else.

She objected to secrets.

"Not Lilburne," he admitted quietly, lowering his hands. "But yes—there is a printing press."

Kate's jaw tensed before she replied. "And what is it you deem so important, that you would risk being dragged to the Tower, or pilloried in the street?"

Antony sighed and went back to his chair. After a stiff hesitation, she joined him. "What else have you known me to promote? Moderation, and the hope of peace. Revelations of what goes on inside the House of Commons, what the Army plans, that their leaders would prefer the people not to know."

The words came easily, hiding a world of confusion beneath. Moderation, yes—but how? There were not two sides, and a clear course between them; the world had come to such a disordered pass that he could see no sure path back to sanity, let alone herd anyone else down it.

His wife absorbed this quietly. She had not forgiven him; he had just openly admitted to endangering himself and his family, in these most dangerous times. But the initial flare of her anger had settled back to a smouldering heat. "When they published those incomplete reports from General Cromwell," she said. "Was it your doing, that the full texts also came out?"

"One. The other was a mistake—sincere or contrived—on the part of the Lords."

Kate still had her cap in her fists; she smoothed out the creases and laid it on the table. "Antony... they know you for what you are. Do you think you have fooled them, by cutting your hair like a Roundhead?" He put one hand self-consciously to his barely covered collar. "How many members of the Commons have been driven out for opposing them? If they do not learn of this secret press of yours, they will hound you into the Tower for your politics, and the one makes it more likely that they will discover the other."

She did not—need not—know how close he had already come. The fae were cautious of their aid these days; London was plagued with men convinced they could enact the godly Reformation they had come so near, and missed, in the days of old Elizabeth. It made an uncomfortable world for those who lived below. But they had stepped in when he had need of them, to keep him free of the Tower.

"Antony," Kate said, her voice barely more than a whisper, "will you not consider leaving?"

He flinched. That pleading note... she was no coward, his Kate. But she saw little profit to remaining in the City, and much danger. Nor was she wrong.

But Lune asked him to stay.

Openly, he had little use in the Commons. If he spoke his mind, he would be out before he could finish. But he watched, and reported, and worked covertly to tip the balance when he could. Even now, commissioners sat in the King's prison on the Isle of Wight, struggling to achieve a treaty that might yet restore England to some semblance of ordinary life.

He reached out and took Kate's hands again, resting them atop the linen cap. "I cannot back away," he said. "The Army has too many supporters in Parliament for anyone's peace of mind. We are a hair's-breadth from it declaring itself the master of England, and the rule of law giving way to the rule of the sword."

"Have we not been there six years?" she said, bitter once more.

"Not so badly as we might be. There are some yet in the Commons who fear the Army's leaders, and want to see our old ways restored, with the King on his throne instead of in prison. But the hotter minded among them would cast aside all the structures and precepts by which God meant men to be governed, and leave us at the mercy of a Parliament with no foundation but what armed might makes."

They walked that edge already, starting with Pym's old nonsensical arguments: that the King's authority was separate from the person of the King, and that such authority rested with Parliament so long as Charles did not do as he should—in other words, as Parliament wished. Yet for all he despised such sophistry, such justifications for these wars against the Crown, Antony wished Pym were still alive. The man had at least been a politician, not a bloody-minded revolutionary. The men who had succeeded him were worse.

His wife took a deep breath and stood, towering over him in his seat. "Antony," she said, "I will not let you destroy this family."

His heart stuttered. "Kate—"

"They know how you speak; they know how you write. If not that, then someone will see you going to this press of yours." She straightened her skirts, unnecessarily. "Henceforth I shall handle these pamphlets of yours."

Now he was on his feet, with no recollection of having moved. "Kate—"

"Do you think me any happier with this world than you?" she demanded, blazing up. "Scottish forces brought onto English soil to fight the King of them both, then selling that King to his enemies—this 'New Model Army' of Parliament's holding the country to ransom—all the bonds of courtesy and respect that once held us together broken, perhaps beyond repair—" She cut herself off, breathing heavily. Mastering her rage with an effort, Kate said in a low growl, "I can write as well as you. I do not know what to put in them, but you can tell me that."

His tongue seemed to have fled. When it came back, Antony said the first thing that came into his mind—which was far from the most important objection. "But I cannot send you to print them."

"Why not?"

Because the press lies in the Onyx Hall. He had gotten himself into this disaster by expiating the sin of keeping one secret; now he brought her hard up against another.

And this one, he could *not* confess.

"If they saw you," he said, "do not think they would hesitate to administer punishment because you're a woman."

Kate sniffed. "If you must so shelter me—surely you do not work alone? No. Send some man or boy, then, to collect the papers from our house. That will be less suspicious than you forever running off to the thing you don't want them to find."

Against his will, he found himself considering it. The messenger could be a fae, and disguised under a variety of glamours to prevent suspicion. And it would be one less thing for him to exhaust himself over—

"I know that look," Kate said dryly. "You just thought of agreeing, then wondered in horror how you could possibly consider such a thing. If it salves your conscience at all, tell yourself this is safer than letting me find my own means of being useful. Else you'll find me sailing about the countryside with as many armed men as I can raise, calling myself 'Her She Majesty Generalissima' like the Queen."

Laughter snorted out of him despite himself. She would do it, too; plenty of noble and gentry women had maintained their homes against sieges during the war, or smuggled messages through enemy lines. Kate chafed under the austere life of London nowadays, with no plays or frivolity on Sundays.

Truth be told, he chafed, too. And *he* had the outlet of the Onyx Hall, which bit its thumb at Puritan piety.

"I shall take your silence as a 'yes'," Kate said, more

cheerful than she had sounded in days. "Fear not—you may read over what I write, and tell me if it's up to standard. Now, let us go wake the cook from her stupor, and have some supper."

THE ONYX HALL, LONDON
8 October 1648

An assortment of fae ringed the room, whispering amongst themselves, from elf-kind to goblins, pucks, and hobs. They had come to see for themselves if the rumours were true.

From behind the figured velvet curtains circling the bed came harsh, panicked breathing. Lune gestured, and a sprite whisked them aside.

Lady Carline flinched at the movement. Her lovely, voluptuous face gleamed with the sweat that soaked the bedclothes, and her pale fingers clutched convulsively in the fabric.

"What happened?"

The lady struggled upright. "Majesty—the man sang—"

"Stop. Begin earlier." Worry sharpened the command; Lune schooled herself to a softer tone. "Why had you gone above?"

"To—to visit a man."

She need not have bothered asking. As far as Carline was concerned, bed play was the purpose for which mortal men had been put on earth. Men of any kind, really. "Who?"

Carline brushed damp strands out of her face, a reflexive gesture, as if being questioned about her lover made her realise her dishevelled and unattractive state, and the onlookers there to witness it. "A Cavalier," she said. "One who took arms for the King, and fought at Naseby. He lives in secret, in a friend's cellar, and I—I keep him company."

The faintest exhalation from Leslic, at Lune's left shoulder—sardonic amusement at the delicate phrasing. Or perhaps irritation that, after all these years, he had gained the office of Master of Hounds, but not the royal bed. Lune ignored him. "Go on. Leave out nothing."

The beauty patch of star-shaped taffeta Carline had applied to her cheekbone was peeling off. Its loose edge danced as she swallowed hard and said, "I went above—by way of the well in Threadneedle Street. With a glamour, of course. He's in Finch Lane. It wasn't far. But as I was turning the corner, a man—I don't know who he was—he began to sing a psalm—"

Whispers ran around the walls. Scowling, Lune gestured sharply; Amadea began herding, and soon the Lady Chamberlain had cleared the room of everyone except Lune, Carline, Leslic, and herself.

Carline turned her tear-streaked face up to Lune. "Your Majesty—my glamour fell."

So Lune had heard. The lady was a fool, venturing forth on a Sunday for an afternoon's dalliance. What others turned into the stuff of rumour and fear, though, Lune credited to a more ordinary source. "You had eaten bread?" Carline nodded. "How long before?"

"Scarce half an hour, madam."

Which should have been safe. A single bite protected for a day. Lune's gaze fell upon an intricate casket, grown instead of carved out of intertwining birch twigs. When she lifted the lid, she found easily two weeks' worth of bread inside, torn into suitable pieces. She wondered what favours Carline had been trading, to have so much on hand. Three bad harvests in a row had made bread scarce for everyone, and mortals did not tithe to fae when they could barely feed their own.

She lifted a piece: coarse-ground wheat, a little burnt on the bottom. "Is this what you ate?"

"No, madam. It was oat bread I had."

Oat bread. Poor stuff, but not surprising; the wealthy of London were much more strongly Puritan than their lessers, and spared little thought for the fae, except to term them devils in disguise. If the pattern continued, she would have to find other solutions to this chronic shortage.

From behind her, Carline whispered, "Your Grace— what if it no longer works?"

Lune turned back to see the lady on her feet, dark hair tumbled around her face in a cloud, framing her dead white skin. "What—what if their faith has grown so strong—"

"I doubt it," Lune said coolly, cutting her off before she could go further. Before she could give strength to the fears already spreading outside the chamber door. "More likely an error on the part of whatever goodwife placed it out.

Perhaps the local minister came by and blessed the house. Lady Amadea—" Her chamberlain curtsied. "Ask among the court; find who else has that bread, and confiscate it."

"They will complain, madam."

And if she did *not* confiscate it, they would complain she failed to protect them. "Replace it from my own stores. And bring me what you find."

Leslic stood attentive at the foot of Carline's bed. Not putting himself forward, not offering his aid; he had learned that pushing gained him little. But always ready to help, yes.

That was why Lune had given the task to Amadea.

I have nothing but instinct—yet it has served me well enough in the past. And instinct tells me this trouble is his doing.

Certainly other troubles were. Lune resisted the urge to press one hand over her shoulder, where the iron wound ached. Still not fully healed, and it never would be. The pain was a useful reminder.

Unfortunately, she could not ignore Leslic entirely; the slight would be all over court before the next meal. Drawing him aside, she murmured, "Stay with Carline, and give her comfort. Else she will dwell on this incident, and worry herself sick."

The knight bowed his shining head. *Comfort* would probably involve the bed Carline once more swooned upon, but so much the better. It might blunt his advances toward Lune herself, at least for a while.

She could not put any warmth into her countenance as Leslic went gallantly to Carline's side. His Ascendants had disrupted Puritan conventicles, in such a manner as to direct the blame toward Royalist sympathisers; they found it great sport, to watch the mortals fight amongst themselves. Lune kept watch on all the entrances to the Onyx Hall, forestalling any repeats of Taylor's attempted destruction, and had Antony more closely guarded than the Prince knew, but some of Leslic's schemes she allowed to play out, cringing at the need, because they revealed the threads of the web in which he sat.

But perhaps it was time to end it. She knew his allies, his resources, his methods of communicating with Nicneven and Vidar. They were preparing for some final move, she had no doubt, to hamstring the treaty with Charles; civil war was not enough, when they could depose the King entirely. Leslic's troublemakers would be crucial to their plans. What profit remained in keeping him at her side?

Very little. Perhaps none. And that meant that, at long last, the time had come to dispose of the golden Sir Leslic.

THE ANGEL INN, ISLINGTON
11 October 1648

Antony's shoulders ached with tension as he rode north out of the City. Peace stood so close he could taste it; all they needed was this treaty with the King, restoring him to his proper place. But if the Army and its Leveller supporters staged some rebellion, it might all yet fall apart again.

To forestall that, he worked with one hand in each world. During the day, he ate, breathed, and slept Parliamentary affairs, struggling alongside others to maintain a strong enough alliance to oppose the Army's officers in the Commons: Henry Ireton, Oliver Cromwell, and all the rest.

At night, he turned to the faerie folk for help. And tonight, that meant riding to Islington.

On horseback, it took mere minutes to reach the Angel Inn. He had to bribe a guard to let him through Cripplegate; the curfew on the City was much more stringent than usual. Come daylight, though, he would need to be back in Westminster. He was missing a debate regardless, as once again the Commons ran late into the night.

His destination was not the Angel, but an enormous, tangled rosebush that stood behind it, resisting even the thought of being trimmed back. Antony concealed his horse in a stand of trees and crossed to the bush, which offered up one stubborn blossom, despite the dreary autumn chill. "Antony Ware," he murmured into it, and reached into the leather purse he wore over his shoulder.

While he pulled a cloth bundle out, the branches shifted and wove themself into a thorn-studded archway over a set of battered steps leading downward. Treading carefully in the hollows worn by untold feet before his, Antony descended into the Goodemeades' home.

Rosamund was waiting for him in the comfortable chamber below. "We heard your pigeon, my lord," she said, offering him a curtsy. "I'd be happy to look at what you have."

Fae had several advantages over mortals when it came to secret communication, among them the usefulness of pigeons. Antony had no need to tie a message to its leg; the sisters conversed with birds as easily as with him.

He unwrapped his bundle and held a small hunk of rye bread out to Rosamund. She had put on a glamour, making herself the height of a short woman, instead of a child. The brownie pinched off a bite and chewed it thoughtfully. "Hard to say," she told him once she had swallowed, "but I fear you may be right. Shall we test it?"

Not in the house, certainly. They went back to the open air, and for safety's sake into the trees, where his horse dozed—a more sensible creature than him. Rosamund folded her hands expectantly. Antony hesitated. "If our suspicions are correct—"

"I've lived through worse," Rosamund told him stoutly. "Sing away, my lord."

He would not sing; the brownie had offered herself up for enough without suffering his inability to carry a tune. Instead he spoke softly.

Once, right after he bound himself to the Onyx Court as Prince of the Stone, the words had fled his tongue, silenced by a faerie touch. Even now they did not come as naturally as they had in his boyhood. He had to exert his will to say, "Glory be to the Father, and to the Son, and to the Holy Ghost. As it was in the beginning, is now and ever shall be, world without end. Amen."

Rosamund was ready for it, and so she did not cry out. But she stiffened, and her entire body shook; and when it was done shaking, she was the size of a child again, and swaying on her feet. Antony caught her and lowered her gently to the cold dirt. His cloak, flung around her shoulders, made her look even tinier, but Rosamund gripped it gratefully.

"No," she said in a valiant imitation of a light tone, "I don't think it's working."

His prayer was a common one in the Church of England, nothing drawn from a more Puritan faith. But they did not have to look to such arcane causes for an explanation. "That bread," he said grimly, "was passed on to Lewan Erle from one of Sir Leslic's closest followers."

The little hob's normally pink cheeks were pale from more than moonlight. "She will never just throw him out. You've not been at court, my lord—too many people admire him, since he saved the Queen. Lune dares not be thought capricious, casting him down when he's enjoyed so much favour. And she hesitates to scheme against him; it reminds her too much of Invidiana."

The old Queen. Lune rarely spoke of her, but at times Antony felt as if her black shadow still darkened the court and all its doings. Even Lune herself—simply by her resolution not to be like her predecessor. "She will have to do *something*," Antony said. "Others have seen their protections fail; they fear to go into the streets at all. Nicneven may have at last found a way to destroy everything the Onyx Court stands for."

"Not just Nicneven," Rosamund corrected him. "Vidar."

"Yes, this 'Lord of Shadows.'" The name twisted in his mouth, warped by anger for the damage the creature had done. Not just to the Onyx Court, but to the world above it; Antony would never know if civil war might have been avoided, had Vidar not taken every opportunity to deepen the bitterness and rancour that divided England from itself. "Lune speaks but little of him. Why such hatred between them?"

"I will tell you," Rosamund said, "but not here."

Reflexively, Antony glanced about, searching the night-time woods. "Is someone watching?"

The brownie grinned with more of her usual cheer. "No, but I'm freezing my rump off. Come inside."

He helped her to her feet, glad to see that smile return, and they went back down into the sheltering warmth. Gertrude was attending Lune at court, and so they had the comfortable home to themselves. Rosamund returned Antony's cloak with thanks and stood warming her hands at the fire. "Vidar," she told him, "was a lord in the old court."

"One faithful to Invidiana?"

"Not in the least! He was ever searching for ways to sell her out to her enemies, and claim the throne for himself."

Antony pulled off his gloves and rubbed his hands over his shortened hair. "So he envies her for doing what he could not."

Rosamund frowned. "That, but also other things. We, er—used him at the end, when the overthrow came. And it made him very unwelcome among the other faerie Kings of England. Last we heard, he'd gone across the Channel and found a place in the Cour du Lys, where they do not love Lune either."

But now he was in Scotland, and helping to destroy what he could not have. Always Scotland: the clashes there had precipitated Charles's crisis nearly a decade ago, and now the Army was rabid to prevent the Presbyterian terms the Scots wanted in the treaty with the King. Though Ireland, to be fair, was an equally fruitful source of trouble.

Sighing, Antony rose and said, "And this trick with the bread is his latest treachery, by way of Sir Leslic. Clever. I can only hope that when I confirm it to Lune, she will rid herself of that snake, before he can harm us further."

"Oh, don't you worry; I'll send her a mouse." Rosamund eyed him critically. "You look about done in, my lord. Sit down, and have a restorative draught before you go."

The *restorative draught* would be mead—it was always mead, whatever ailed a man—but Antony did not object. "Thank you," he said. He would take his rest where and when he could find it.

THE ONYX HALL, LONDON
31 October 1648

The group that gathered in the antechamber was not a merry one. It rarely was, even in happier times; All Hallows' Eve did not evoke laughter or the casual flirtation that occupied many fae. But this year of all years it was grim, for London was filled with godly zeal, and the traditional protections seemed to be failing.

Which made it all the more vital to go out. The old practices of the night had largely died at the Reformation, but faerie-kind kept their own ceremonies. Those souls who lingered after death, rather than fleeing to Heaven or Hell, occupied a realm not far removed from that of the fae, and on this night each year the two worlds touched. Forgoing the rituals of the night would only encourage fear.

Thirteen stood in the chamber, ranging in rank from Lune and her knight-protectors of the Onyx Guard down to a trio of tough-minded goblins—a mara, a hobyah, and a fetch. *They* showed no apprehension, and grinned at those who did. Goblins were far from the most elegant of fae, and so were often scorned at court, but at least Lune was sure of their loyalty.

As she was sure of the disloyalty of others.

She felt a shiver in her bones as the churches of the City above rang out the midnight hour, the peals of their bells washing harmlessly over the charms that kept the palace safe. At one end of the chamber loomed the dark archway that would take them to a courtyard off Fish Street. Some of her more timid courtiers cast frightened glances in its direction.

Serenely, as if she had no fears in all the world, Lune said, "Come, Sir Leslic. The bells have rung."

The golden-haired knight bowed and took up a coffer of faceted amethyst. Kneeling, he presented it to Lune, lifting the lid to reveal the carefully portioned pieces of bread within.

The bells had faded; all was silent, inside and out. Lune reached forth and took a piece. But she did not lift it to her lips; instead she looked at it curiously, then transferred her attention to the still kneeling knight. "Tell me, Sir Leslic," she said. "Is the plan merely for us to suffer the consequences of walking unmasked in the mortal realm—or do you plot something more? Do Puritan preachers wait above, to strike our souls to dust?" Her voice hardened and rang out from the chamber's barrel-vaulted ceiling. "For what purpose do you offer us untithed bread?"

He almost dropped the coffer. Leslic's head came up with a jerk, and for the barest of instants she saw his eyes unguarded. There lived the truth she had guessed at all this time, and her stomach tightened with sudden terror. If he acted upon it—

But Leslic was nothing if not a practised dissembler. "Untithed bread, your Majesty? What—" Now the coffer did go down, cracking hard against the stone as he surged to his feet. One hand gripped his sword, but he kept his head well enough not to draw in her presence—not without better cause than he had. "Guards! Someone has attempted to deceive the Queen's Grace!"

Lune stopped the knights with a sharp flick of her hand. "You speak it well," she said, "and we might even believe you—had we not proof. *You* are the author of this deceit, Leslic. We have evidence in abundance. And, not content with the fears you have spread among our subjects, now you strike at our very heart."

A snap of her fingers, and the goblins were there. The mara had the belt from around Leslic's waist before he even knew it, his still sheathed sword clutched in her bony fingers, and the fetch grinned maliciously into his eyes. It was only a death omen for mortals, but even a fae might shudder to see such a smile.

They had their orders from her the day before. Lune brought the goblins because her guard could not be trusted; she could not risk them hesitating in their arrest. Even now the knights hovered in confusion, on the balls of their feet, wanting to move but not knowing to what end. Leslic drew himself up nobly. "Majesty," he swore, "I had no intention of giving you untithed bread."

Which was true, as his earlier protest had not been. Leslic might seed the court with ordinary bread, never offered as a gift to the fae, but he was not foolish enough to give it to the Queen. Some of his followers, on the other hand, needed little to encourage them in their folly. Lune refused to contrive a false incident for Leslic's downfall, however richly he deserved it; but she could and would tangle him in the fringes of his own schemes. And she needed this, an open offence, something appalling enough that her people would repudiate Leslic of their own accord, robbing him and all his faction of the influence they enjoyed.

"If you wish it," she said, exquisite in her courtesy, "you may defend yourself in wager of battle. If you are guiltless of changing tithed bread for untithed so as to spread fear and dissension, then by all means, sir—prove it with your blade."

A flush crept upward from his collar. That was an accusation he could not defeat; just as Cerenel's negligence had ensured his loss in the duel of honour, so Leslic's guilt would damn him if he fought for his innocence. They were not mortals, to rise or fall by their skill with a blade.

She broke her gaze from his at last to survey the antechamber. Her knights, courtiers, and ladies were all suitably shocked—even those who had spoken fair to Leslic in the past. "He stands silent," she said, as if it needed pointing out. "And we have abundant evidence of his guilt. His... and others'."

Rooting out the Ascendants in their entirety would cripple her court, but she didn't need to. The four chief malignants would suffice; without them, the rest would crumble back into line. Even now, the other three should be in the custody of her loyalists.

Gesturing at the goblins who still held Leslic, she said, "Take him to the Tower. We shall question him there about the masters he serves—once we have fulfilled our duties tonight." At another snap of her fingers, a spriggan came out of the shadows, bearing safe bread. "Come. All Hallows' Eve awaits us."

* * *

THE ROYAL EXCHANGE. LONDON
7 November 1648

"You're sending me *away*?"

The courtyard of the Royal Exchange was a poor place for a private conversation, but Benjamin Hipley had sought Antony out there, and did not look minded to hold his peace. Glancing around, Antony pulled him into the corner of the arcade, where a stretch of the bench that ringed it sat empty. "You speak as though you are the first to be asked to serve the Onyx Court elsewhere."

Ben's native discretion did not fail him; he kept his voice low, though intense. "It's not a matter of leaving London. I cannot leave *you*. Not at such a time."

The damp chill of the air stifled business, leaving the courtyard only half full of its usual gentry. The flowerlike array of colours that once prevailed had given way to the sad hues favoured by the godly; though the fabrics were still rich, a dull green was the brightest thing in sight. For all the fae reflected the tastes of the world above, sometimes they did so by inversion. Court nowadays was enough to make a man's eyes bleed.

Antony gestured at his own staid murrey doublet. "I am a respectable baronet, an alderman, and a member of Parliament. By the skin of my teeth, but it suffices. I will be safe."

Ben shook his head. "You need me here. The machinations in Parliament, over this treaty with the King—"

"I need you more *there*. I can watch Parliament on my

own, but I cannot keep one eye on Westminster and one on Hertfordshire. Henry Ireton has called a 'General Council of the Army' at St Albans, and it has the potential to destroy everything. He hates the treaty like poison. His idea of peace is to see the King punished like any other man."

The blood drained from Hipley's face. "He goes that far?"

It was the logical extension of all that had gone before, yet it still had power to appal. Pym had undermined the foundations of sovereignty itself, until men like Ireton could look at the King and see a common criminal.

But not everyone felt that way, God be thanked. "You're not the only one to flinch," Antony said grimly. "General Cromwell is delaying in the North; I think he hesitates to oppose a fellow officer openly, but he would see us follow a different course. Fairfax argues against it as well. Those two are greatly loved in the Army, and without them, Ireton may achieve nothing—but I cannot afford to let him go unwatched."

The truth was that they needed agents within the Army, men or disguised fae placed close enough to the generals and lower officers that they could supply both intelligence and action as needed. But the Army was beyond their reach: forged out of the disastrous chaos of Parliament's early armies, it had become a finely honed weapon that crushed the Royalists at every turn. And between their common soldiers, who liked the Leveller arguments that *they* should rule England, and their fiercely Puritan officers, there had never been any good chance to position such agents. Antony had sat in Westminster through all those years of war, exerting what force he could in Parliament, but the sieges and battles, the capture of prisoners and the smuggling of information, had gone on in a hundred locations across the kingdom, miles away from the men who thought the power was still in their hands.

Until they reached this point. A General Council of the Army at St Albans, and Henry Ireton their self-appointed champion, preparing to tear England's wounds yet wider.

Scowling, Ben rose and moved a few steps away, pausing with his back to Antony. At last the intelligencer asked, "Will the treaty conclude in time?"

The question every man in Parliament would give his fortune to answer. They had already extended the deadline for the negotiations once. England wanted *peace*; it wanted an end to the chaos and upheaval caused by the disruption of government and the forced quartering of soldiers and the lack of uniformity in religion.

Some of England did. But not all.

"We stand at a precipice," Antony said, just loudly enough for Ben to hear. "The King is poised to retake all he had, making no concessions he cannot squirm out of once power is his again. Those who sue for peace tie hope over their eyes like a blindfold, telling themselves he can be trusted. But our alternative is the Army, and the Levellers, and Independency in religion. We know it; our treaty commissioners know it. Charles knows it, and so he sits in his prison on the Isle of Wight and waits."

Ben turned back, his hands curled at his sides, not quite fists. "You haven't answered my question."

Antony offered him a baring of teeth that might stand in for a smile. "Whether or not it concludes in time depends on what Ireton and the Army do. Get to St Albans—tell me what you find there—and I will answer your question then."

THE ONYX HALL, LONDON
20 November 1648

The greater presence chamber had never been Lune's favourite part of the Onyx Hall, being too grand, too chill—too full of the memory of Invidiana. For formal state occasions, however, she could not avoid it. Anything less would be an insult to the dignitaries who gathered for this ceremony.

So she sat upon her silver throne, and a selection of her courtiers waited in bright array across the black-and-white *pietra dura* floor. Eochu Airt stood to one side, in the full splendour of what passed for court dress among the Irish, with gold torcs banding his neck and arms.

He made a poisonously polite nod to the empty seat next to hers on the dais. "I see your Prince could not be here today."

Lune pressed her lips together. Antony's reply to her messenger had been brusque to the point of rudeness: he was at Westminster, and could not leave. The General Council of the Army had presented a Remonstrance to the Commons, a listing of their grievances, like the one the Commons had once presented to the King. Lune did not know their demands; her messenger had not tarried, but come back with stinging ears to relay Antony's words. He did say, though, that the Remonstrance had already been two hours in the reading, and showed no signs of ending soon.

Antony's refusal vexed her, but perhaps it was just as well. "He sends his regrets, my lord, and wishes you all good speed."

A snort answered that. "At Parliament, I see. Voting again to gut my land and hang it out to dry?"

Her ladies whispered behind their fans. Only their eyes showed, glinting like jewels in the masks they had adopted and elaborated from mortal fashion; even Lune could not read their expressions from that alone. "My lord ambassador, nothing happens in isolation. Lord Antony wishes the Army disbanded as much as you do. With the soldiers owed arrears of pay, however, and fearing reprisals for their wartime actions, setting them loose would threaten stability here."

"And so he votes to send them to Ireland. Where England sends all of its refuse."

Now it was not lips but teeth she was pressing together. "Had the mortals of your land not risen in rebellion—"

"Had they not done so, we would not now have a free Ireland!"

"You will not have it for long." Try as she might to be

angry with Eochu Airt, in truth, Lune felt sadness; the Irish, mortal and fae alike, were so blinded by success and the hope it brought that they did not see the hammer poised above them.

She tried to find the words to make at least this one sidhe see. "Had they settled with Charles during the war, they might have won something." *And brought the King to victory in the bargain.* "But the Vatican's ambassador encouraged them to overreach, and now, wanting the whole of their freedom, they will instead lose the whole. Their Catholic Confederation will survive only so long as England's attention is divided. Once we have peace here, *someone*—Charles or Parliament—will crush them."

"With the very Army your Prince voted to send. Just as he voted to save Strafford's life."

Against Lune's wishes, in both cases. If she could have persuaded the Prince to vote against sending regiments across, it might have gone some way to healing that injury. But Antony—understandably, damn him—was more concerned with England's well-being than Ireland's. In the end the proposal had failed by a single vote... but not his.

"The hammer has not yet fallen upon you," Lune said, doing what little she could to mollify the sidhe. "I will do everything in my power to stay it."

Whatever response Eochu Airt might have made, he swallowed it when the great doors at the other end of the chamber swung open. Lune's Lord Herald spoke in a voice that echoed from the high ceiling. "From the Court of

Temair in Ireland, the ambassador of Nuada Ard-Rí, Lady Feidelm of the Far-Seeing Eye!"

An imposing sidhe woman appeared in the opening. Her green silk tunic, clasped at the shoulders with silver and gold, was stiff with red-gold embroidery; her cloak, thrown back, revealed strong white shoulders. The branch she held, however, was mere silver, compared to Eochu Airt's gold. She knelt briefly, then rose and advanced until she came to the foot of the dais, where she knelt again.

"Lady Feidelm," Lune said, "we welcome you to the Onyx Court, and tender our thanks to our royal cousin Nuada."

The new ambassador's voice was rich and finely trained. "His Majesty sends his greetings, and begs your kind pardon for calling away Lord Eochu Airt, whose services are needed in Emain Macha, serving King Conchobar of Ulster."

Lune smiled pleasantly at the old ambassador, who stood mute and unreadable. "We shall sorely miss his presence at court, for he has been an unfailing advocate on Temair's behalf, and an ornament to our days, with poetry and song."

A lovely mask of courteous speech, laid over the simple truth that Eochu Airt had asked to go. He could not be quit of them soon enough. What remained to be seen was what Feidelm's appointment signalled. If the lady were amenable, Lune hoped to negotiate for aid against Nicneven.

But that would have to wait. Lune beckoned to Lord Valentin, who came forward with a parchment already prepared. When the revocation of Eochu Airt's diplomatic status was done, and Feidelm proclaimed in his place—*then* she would see the dance Temair followed now.

THE ONYX HALL, LONDON
21 November 1648

The feasting and presentation of gifts ran through the night, with music and dancing and a contest of poetry between the old and new ambassadors. Eochu Airt begged leave to retire when it was done, though, and soon after Lune withdrew to walk with Feidelm in the garden.

The sidhe hailed from Connacht, and spoke as openly of King Ailill and Queen Medb as she did of the High Kings of Temair. The different perspective was useful to Lune, after years of Eochu Airt's Ulster-bred sentiments. More useful still was the lack of hostility; Feidelm might not be an ally, but she clearly intended to form her own opinion of Lune, rather than adopting her predecessor's. It was as close to a tabula rasa as Lune would get, and with Nicneven temporarily set back by the removal of Sir Leslic, Lune had the leisure to try and mend her relations with Temair.

"Lady Feidelm," she said as they wandered the paths, "I know from the branch you bear that you are a poetess. Yet for you to be called 'the Far-Seeing Eye'—are not such matters the province of your druids?"

"The *imbas forosnai* is the province of poets," the sidhe replied in her rich lilt, trailing her fingers over the flank of a marble stag that stood along the path. "For my skill at that, I am so named."

"We have no seer at this court," Lune said, and did not have to feign the regret in her voice. "And we live in most unpredictable times, when all the world seems upside-down. Might I prevail upon you to see on our behalf, and give some sense of what lies ahead?"

Feidelm pursed her sculpted lips. "Madam, visions do not come at a simple command. It needs something to call them, to bid the gates of time open."

She had heard that the Irish hedged their divination about with barbaric rituals. "What do you need?"

The answer made Lune wonder if this were some malicious prank perpetrated on her as petty revenge for her soured relations with Temair. But Feidelm's attendants did not seem at all surprised when their mistress called for a bull to be slaughtered. In the end Lune sent a pair of goblins to steal one from a garden above, with Sir Prigurd to carry it back down, and to leave payment for the missing beast. Then the Irish set to work, and soon presented the ambassadress with meat and broth and a stinking, bloody hide. There in the night garden, without any embarrassment, Feidelm stripped off her finery and wrapped herself in the hide, then lay down beneath a hazel tree.

The attendants bowed and retired, leaving Lune alone with the poetess.

She had no idea what to expect, except that Feidelm had promised her answers to three questions. Lune pondered her choices while the sidhe lay silent in the trance of the *imbas forosnai*. When the faerie's emerald eyes snapped open, she twitched in surprise.

Feidelm said, "Speak."

The words stumbled out, despite her preparation; the strange atmosphere of this entire affair had Lune off balance. "What—what do you see for my people?"

"I see them bloody; I see them red."

Her heart skipped a beat. Warfare, or murder. Were the precautions she had taken not enough? Killing Leslic and his allies was too drastic a move; fae bred so rarely. Sending them back to Vidar was not an option. So she had placed them in cells beneath the Tower of London—but perhaps she must do more.

Vowing to double their guard as soon as she left the garden, Lune tried again. "What of my home?"

"I see it ashen, I see it gold."

Less clear—unless the men who insisted the rule of their Christ would begin in eighteen years were right, and London to rise as the new Jerusalem, the fifth monarchy of Heaven. But would he cast down the City first? Feidelm's answers were maddeningly cryptic, and far too brief.

Her third question came the hardest of all. This was the answer Antony wanted, the answer she feared to obtain for him. "What do you see for England?"

Feidelm took a slow, wavering breath; then the words flowed from her like a river, as if this one question released all the eloquence dammed up before. "I see a broad-shouldered man who takes the head and becomes the head, though he crushes the crown beneath his boot. In his hands he holds the ink that brings death: both for them who wrote it, and him it is written for. I see the churches cast down and raised up, and the people weep for sorrow and joy. Many are the wounds this land has suffered, and will suffer, and yet will go forward; I see it endure, and yet I see its end, that lies both near and far. The Kingdom of England will die twice ere long, and you will see those deaths."

Hope and fear warred in Lune's heart, and fear had the advantage. Nothing endured forever, not even fae; they could be slain, or become weary of life and fade away. The great empire of Rome had spanned the world, but where was it now? Fragmented and gone, its Italian heartland languishing under Spanish rule. She knew, if she was honest, that some day England, too, would pass. But when? What was *soon* to a faerie?

Feidelm shuddered, and Lune thought the trance ended. But the sidhe's gaze shifted to Lune, unfocused yet piercing, as if seeing through her flesh to the spirit beneath, and her voice still held the resonance of the *imbas forosnai*. "What is a king, or a queen? For whom does one such rule, and by what right? What shall be the fate of sovereignty? These are the questions the land asks, the people, the heart. But you have not asked, and so you must answer them yourself."

Her eyelids sagged, pale lashes brushing her skin. When Feidelm opened her eyes once more, the fog of her trance had lifted from them, but she seemed to have no awareness of the words she had just spoken. For a moment, Lune met that emerald gaze, and wondered.

Did she invent her answers, as a subterfuge to gain some advantage?

She might wish it so, but she thought not. The Irish seer had spoken truly.

What lay hidden in her words—that, Lune would have to discover for herself.

PALACE YARD, WESTMINSTER
5 December 1648

The sun crept above the horizon, hidden behind a veil of thick clouds and blustering winds. The only sign of its presence was a muted brightening, a grey pallor replacing the blackness of night.

The doors to Westminster Hall swung open, and out filed a line of weary men: the two-hundred-odd members of Parliament who had doggedly persevered, in a session that lasted all day and all through the night, to surmount the obstacles of acrimony and fear, and to answer the question put to them.

The men agitating for the Army's outrageous wishes had wanted that question put thus: whether the King's answers to the treaty, brought to them at long last, were satisfactory. But every man partisan enough to the Royalist cause to say yes had long since been driven from the Commons; that vote was designed to fail, and so those who sought peace had diverted it away. Satisfaction was not needed. After the long struggles, the near misses and dashed hopes for reconciliation, all the Commons wanted to know was this: whether the King's concessions were enough to be going on with.

The question passed without a division. They would accept the treaty, and move on to restoring peace in England. The wars were done at last.

Antony ignored the abusive language flung by the Army officers who pursued the members down the stairs and out through Westminster Hall; he could barely hear them through his jaw-cracking yawn. Soame, at his side, had declared that walking normally was not worth the effort; he staggered as if drunk. "Somewhere in Hell," the younger man said, ramming the heels of his hands into his eyes, "there is a circle where men are forced to listen to Prynne go on for three hours without pause. And when I am sent thither, I'll tell the Devil I have been there already, and ask for something new."

It sparked a weary laugh, tinged with exhausted relief. "And in Heaven is a feather mattress, well fluffed and warm. I'm for home," Antony said. "I will see you tomorrow."

WESTMINSTER PALACE, WESTMINSTER
6 December 1648

He fell asleep like a man who has been clubbed over the head, and woke only for supper. "It passed?" Kate asked;

she had waited the whole night for him, knowing they debated England's fate. And Antony said, "Pray God we will find some peace now."

The race that preceded the vote had drained him as badly as the unending debate. From St Albans the Army had marched, drawing nearer every day, into Westminster itself, until the fear that Ireton and his soldiers would forcibly dissolve Parliament had frayed every man's nerves. To do so would destroy the Houses' last shreds of tattered credibility; anything after that would have no claim to legitimacy. But they might have done it.

Falling prey to his relief would be easy. Their vote yesterday, however, had not sent their problems up in smoke; the Army was still quartered all over Westminster, still capable of trouble. Antony had not heard from Ben Hipley in days, not since the soldiers left St Albans. He went by coach the next morning, and heard the measured beat of boots on cobblestones. Lifting the curtain, he saw soldiers patrolling the streets—not the Trained Bands of the City, but New Model men, loyal to Henry Ireton.

Then he descended from his coach in the Palace Yard, and saw it was worse.

Two companies, one of horse, one of foot, were stationed around the edges of the courtyard. They stood at attention, not menacing anyone—but again, where were the Trained Bands, whose task it was to guard this place? Antony stood, staring, unblinking, until from above he heard a whisper from his coachman. "Sir…"

Glancing up, he saw fear in the man's eyes. "Go," he said, as if there were nothing amiss. "I will be well."

Or if I be not, you can do nothing to help me.

With his coach rattling away behind him, he settled his cloak and advanced. The soldiers let him pass without comment, and he breathed more easily—but did not release his fear. Their presence must portend *something* ill. He worried at the question as he hurried through the vaulted, crowded space of Westminster Hall, past the legal courts that met there, into the Court of Wards that lay in a set of chambers off its southern end. He was almost at the stairs leading up to the lobby of the Commons when he heard a disturbance.

"Mr Prynne," an unfamiliar voice said, "you must not go into the House, but must go along with me."

Heedless of the looks from men carrying on their business around him, Antony stopped just shy of the doorway and listened.

From the stairs came William Prynne's defiant tones. "I am a member of the House, and am going into it to discharge my duty."

Footsteps, then a sudden scuffle. Despite his better judgement, Antony peered around the corner—and what he saw turned his blood to ice.

Soldiers, more New Model men, blocked the stairs to the Commons. Antony recognised one fellow, a grinning dwarf of a man called Lord Grey of Groby; but the rest were unfamiliar, and among them was a colonel who directed his men to drag the struggling Prynne bodily back down the steps. Prynne fought them, his ugly, scarred face red with effort, but he stood no chance. Recognising that, he employed his favourite weapon, that had served him so loyally during the debate. "This is a *high* breach of the privileges of Parliament! And an affront to the House of Commons, whose servant I am!" Antony leapt back as the soldiers hauled the man through the doorway. All pretence of business in the Court of Wards had stopped, and Prynne's bellows rang from the walls; he knew how to use his voice. "These men, being more and stronger than I, and all armed, may forcibly carry me where they please— but stir from here of my own accord I *will not!*"

His own accord mattered not a whit; will he, nil he, they forced him through into the Court of Requests, and came out a moment later, breathing hard, but some of the men laughing.

By then Antony had faded back amongst the bystanders, where they might not see him. He could taste his own pulse, so strongly was his heart pounding. What criteria formed that list, he didn't know, but by any standards the Army might use, he would not be allowed through.

If the Commons will not vote against the King, as the Army wishes it to—why, then, they will purge it until it does.

He had known for months—years—that the power in England had shifted once again, into the hands of the Army's officers, both in and out of Parliament. But he had never imagined they would exert it so nakedly, against all the laws and traditions of the land.

Fear curdled the blood in his veins.

So long as the contrary members did not sit, that might satisfy them; it might be enough for him to return home, and not try to enter the Commons. But what if it were not? If they came after him...

They were arresting members of Parliament. They might do *anything*.

He could flee to the safety of the Onyx Hall, had he warning enough, and no soldier would find him there.

But he could not take Kate with him.

Whether Lune would allow her in was not the question. Antony could not so suddenly reveal to his wife the secrets of all these years. But—*Hell,* he snarled inwardly, and cursed his wandering thoughts, which flinched from the real question: whether he should advance or retreat.

Advance, and he would find himself held in the Court of Requests with Prynne—and, no doubt, others from the Commons. Retreat...

Antony thought of Kate. The hard set of her jaw when she insisted she be permitted to lend her aid in the writing of secret pamphlets. Her disdain for his sober clothes and trimmed hair, disguising his body as he disguised his principles—all to maintain his position in the Commons and Guildhall, where he might do some good.

But I haven't, he realised. *Not enough. Not to prevent this catastrophe.*

A clerk stood nearby, still gaping. With scarcely a word, Antony claimed a pen and scrap of paper from the man and scribbled a quick note, spattering ink in his haste. The clerk handed over sealing wax without being asked, and after Antony had pressed his signet into the soft mass, he gave the paper back, followed by the first coin that came into his hand—a shilling, and more than enough. "Take this note to Lombard Street—the house under the sign of the White Hart. Do you understand me?" The clerk nodded. "Go."

With the man gone, Antony took a moment to straighten his doublet and settle his cloak on his shoulders, before he turned and ascended the steps.

Groby whispered in the colonel's ear, pointing at the list. When Antony reached them, the officer swept his hat off and greeted him with hypocritical courtesy. "Sir Antony Ware. I am Colonel Thomas Pride, and my orders are not to permit you within the House, but to take you into custody."

Antony met his eyes, then Groby's, willing some doubt to be there. But he found none. "You have no authority save that which your swords and pistols make. By barring me from my rightful place, you trample upon the very liberties you swore to protect."

Groby said, "We are liberating Parliament from a self-interested and corrupt faction that impedes the faithful and trustworthy in the conduct of their duties."

He sounded almost as if he believed it, and perhaps he did. If there was one thing Antony knew from all these struggles, it was that men could come to believe in anything, no matter how absurd.

Pride said merely, "Do you refuse to go?"

The eager-handed soldiers wanted another fight, but Antony would not give them one. He would be ruled by choice, not by the sword. "You will not need your weapons," he said. "Under protest, I will go."

THE ONYX HALL, LONDON
6 December 1648

Lune was playing cards with her ladies when Ben Hipley slammed through the door, trailing an offended usher. "They've taken him."

She stared at the man. Where had he been for the last week? She had quarrelled with Antony over sending Hipley to St Albans; she had another use for their mortal spymaster. But she had been willing to accept it so long as Hipley was sending useful information. For days, though, nothing—and now he showed up utterly without warning, unwashed and bristling with unshaved stubble.

Then his words sank in. "What? Who?"

"Antony," Hipley said, confirming the fear already forming in her mind. "The Army. They were waiting at Westminster. They've taken Antony to Hell."

The cards slipped from Lune's nerveless fingers and fluttered to the carpet; she had stood without realising. Her body felt very far away. All she could hear was that final word, echoing like thunder.

"It's an eating house!" Hipley exclaimed, putting his

hands up. Lune returned to herself with the crack of a bone popping back into its socket. "In Westminster. There's three of them—Heaven, Purgatory, and Hell. Someone with a twisted sense of humour put them in Hell. Lord Antony, and about forty others."

Nianna fluttered at Lune's side, fan in hand as if she thought her Queen would faint. Lune gestured her away, irritable now that the fear was gone—or at least reduced. Her trembling, she hoped, was hardly noticeable. "Members of Parliament?"

He nodded. "Anybody with a record of voting against the Army's desires has been excluded from the Commons; the worst offenders are arrested. But there's more, madam. They've moved the King to Hurst Castle, under strict guard. They're going to try him."

Hence the arrest of those in opposition. Even with the open Royalists driven out these past years, and recruiters elected to fill their places, the full Commons would not vote for the Army's desired aims—not to the extent of putting their anointed sovereign on trial like a common criminal.

And what sentence would they pass?

That was a concern, but not the first one. Lune had no immediate way to stop this coup; she had to focus on getting Antony out. She cursed the choice of Westminster. The Onyx Hall did not extend beyond the walls of the City. But the Army had already occupied London once, during the later part of the war, creating much ill will; they would not be so stupid as to imprison their opponents among their enemies.

The cards were long forgotten; all her ladies were on their feet, hovering uselessly. *I let myself be caught here, idle, while outside the world changed irrevocably.* "Get out!" Lune spat, flinging her fury at them; as one, they curtsied and fled.

Leaving just her and Hipley. Lune paced the chamber, fingers curled under the point of her bodice. "Can you get in to see him?"

The plan taking shape in her mind collapsed when he shook his head. "I've already been caught asking too many questions around St Albans."

He made no explanation beyond that, but the mystery of his absence was solved. Small wonder they had no warning of this beforehand. Snarling, Lune spun back to the nearest table and grabbed a mask Nianna had left behind, intending to hurl it across the room. Then she paused.

"You can still go," she said, fingering the mask, and gave Hipley a thin smile. "You only need a different face."

HELL AND WHITEHALL, WESTMINSTER
7 December 1648

"Wallingford House, my lily-white arse."

Soame muttered the words under his breath, a profane counterpoint to the psalms some of the other men were singing. The holy music grated on Antony's nerves, but there was little else to do; more than two score men were crammed into a pair of upstairs chambers, with nowhere to sleep but benches or the floor. A few read, by the light of what candles they had been grudgingly allotted; others talked in low voices in the corners. Prynne was pacing, threading his way carefully amongst those trying to rest.

Antony wondered if it was a misunderstanding or a deliberate lie that made Hugh Peter promise they were to be taken from Westminster Hall to suitable lodgings at Wallingford. Instead the coaches deposited them scarcely a street away, at the aptly named Hell. A handful of the prisoners had been offered their parole and leave to go home, but to a man they had refused. He was not the only one taking a martyr's pleasure in facing this outrage.

Morning light peeped through the shutters, lending slivers of brightness to the otherwise gloomy chamber. Light-headed from lack of food and sleep, Antony nevertheless crossed the room and threw open the door.

The pair of soldiers outside jerked around, hands on their pistols as if eager to strike. Antony carefully stayed inside the threshold, making no threatening move. "You have been holding us since yesterday morning with no food, and little to drink. Unless it is your officers' intention to starve us, we need breakfast."

"And if it *is* your intention to starve us, at least have the decency to admit it, so we can begin trapping pigeons and rats." Thomas Soame had come up behind his right shoulder, and his stomach rumbled loudly in accompaniment.

The soldiers merely glared. "Get back inside."

The hostility was nothing new. Who spread the rumour, Antony did not know, but their guards believed them to have pocketed the coin that should have covered the Army's arrears of pay. *I can no longer even tell what might be faerie interference, and what is simply the madness of our own world.*

"Some of these men are ill," Antony said. As if to demonstrate, Sir Robert Harley sneezed miserably, huddled on his bench. He was one who could have gone home, but refused. "I do not imagine your Provost-Marshal would be glad to hear that anyone came to great harm while under your watch."

One soldier sneered, but the other said, "We'll ask," and slammed the door shut.

The Provost-Marshal agreed to request food, but was gone for hours, and when he returned it was not to give them breakfast. Instead the arrested members were shoved back into the coaches and taken to Whitehall. Nor was there anything waiting for them on the other end but a cold room without a fire, where they waited for hours longer. Supposedly the General Council intended to interview them, but Antony suspected that message was nothing more than a delaying tactic, something to give hope to the men who still believed that if they just protested the illegality of their treatment loudly enough, the officers would come to their senses.

At last a man came in with burnt wine and biscuits. The prisoners fell to as if it were a feast, scattering around the chamber with their food, like dogs protecting the bones they gnawed upon. Antony waited, letting others take their share first, until at last the man came around to him.

"Lord Antony," the fellow said in an undertone, "her Majesty sent me. I am to try and get you out."

Antony blinked. He'd never seen the soldier before, but that meant nothing; he simply could not believe she would risk sending a faerie into the Puritan teeth of the Army.

And so she hadn't. "Ben," the man whispered, jerking his thumb surreptitiously toward himself.

There was no reason one couldn't put a glamour on a mortal; Antony had just never thought to do so. He cast a swift glance around. Only one guard was looking his way, but that was already too many; they could not talk for long. "We've been kept in Hell."

"I know."

"Too closely guarded there and here. You'll never manage a rescue. Do it politically."

That was all he dared say; Ben had to move on with his wine jug. Antony spoke in hope; he didn't know if there was any way to free him through legitimate efforts. But any attempt to do so by more arcane means would attract too much attention, if only by his sudden absence.

So he sat in the room with his fellow prisoners until long after the sun had set and an officer came in to say the General Council was too busy to see them until the morrow. "Back to Hell we go," Soame muttered, but no; a troop of musketeers took them into custody and marched them to the Strand. Antony suffered himself to be hauled along by the arm, ignored the insults of the soldiers, and thought, *Very well. I am a prisoner, as I chose. But what can I accomplish from here?*

I can speak my mind.

THE ONYX HALL, LONDON
11 December 1648

"What is he *doing?*" Lune exploded, hurling down the papers she held.

Benjamin Hipley wisely waited until the fluttering pages had settled before he said, "Making a point, madam."

"He does us *no good* there. Cromwell has his minions running about, planning who knows *what* against Ireton—certainly *I* do not know. And why not? Because Sir Antony Ware, who *should* be helping me, chose to go to prison!"

It was unfair to shout at Hipley, who was doing everything he could. But the man was the son of a cooper; his contacts were apprentices and labourers and dockhands on the streets of London, not the gentry and officers who would decide the fate of the kingdom. Antony was her eyes and ears when it came to such matters, and he was under guard in the King's Head, one of two inns to which the secluded members of Parliament had been moved.

Hipley coughed discreetly and, bowing, offered her a slender sheaf of papers.

She regarded them with deep suspicion. "What are these?"

"What the good Lord Antony is doing," Hipley said. "Not alone; I'm given to understand one William Prynne did much of the scribing. But the Prince wishes it published, as soon as may be."

Lune accepted the sheaf. Across the top, in a bold hand she did not recognise, was a title: *A Solemn Protestation of the Imprisoned and Secluded Members*. The rest was less clear to the eye, but she glanced over it, and marked many calls for action against the Army, which had sinned so gravely against the liberties of Parliament.

"Will it do any good?" she asked, half to herself.

Hipley paused before answering, unsure whether she addressed him. "It may, madam. Short of an armed revolt at the King's Head, or a bald-faced theft of him by faerie magic, I see little else we can do."

Stir up anger against the Army. It *might* work. The officers were losing the support of the men beneath them, who wanted outrageous reforms even Ireton baulked at, and the common people hated them, even before the purge of the Commons. General Fairfax, the beloved hero of the New Model Army, was no fool; he had done what he could to quarter his soldiers in warehouses and other empty places. But nothing could hide that London was under martial occupation. There were even troops inside St Paul's itself. Lune had little care for the houses of the Almighty, but the cathedral was a sorry sight, shorn of its grandeur, its choir stalls and panelling reduced to firewood for the soldiers.

Opponents of the Army were plentiful; what they

were *not* was unified. If they could be joined to this cause, though, however briefly—

It might at least free Antony. And Lune needed that, if she were to do anything about the rest of it.

Lune handed the *Solemn Protestation* back to Hipley. "Have a fair copy made; then take those to Lady Ware. This protestation should be printed above, where people can hear of it. And talk to Marchamont Nedham. His *Mercurius Pragmaticus* is too Parliamentarian for my taste, but it's the most effective news-sheet in London; we may as well make use of it."

Hipley bowed. "And for Lord Antony?"

She gritted her teeth. "If his voice is all he has left himself, then bid him use it well."

WESTMINSTER AND LONDON
25 December 1648

The guarded rooms in the Swan and the King's Head made a more tolerable prison than Hell even when they had over forty men crammed into them; now, with half that number freed, they almost passed for comfortable.

Prynne sat at the table, scratching away at yet another lawyerly condemnation of the Army's actions. "What other word can I use than *villainous?*" he asked, frowning at his page.

"Working still?" Antony said, sitting with one boot

propped against the wall. "Today is Christmas, you know."

"What of it?"

Antony sighed. *Why must so many Puritan Independents follow a vision of God that has no room in it for beauty or celebration?*

Prynne chewed on the battered end of his quill, then scribbled a few more words. "It is madness," he muttered to himself, as if it had not been said a thousand times before, by every man here. "If they had simply dissolved Parliament—"

"It would still have been an outrage." Antony took down his boot and shook his head. "Parliament cannot be dissolved except by its own consent; we created that law years ago." But Prynne was right: it would have had some savour of legitimacy about it, with a new Parliament elected to replace it. Arresting the dissenting members was possibly the worst course of action Ireton could have followed, comparable to Charles's smaller, failed attempt before the outbreak of war.

An uneasy thought came, lifting him to his feet. "Prynne— you hear things, as I do. Did Ireton intend this purge?"

"What?" Prynne blinked up at him. The firelight was not kind to him, highlighting the scars where his ears had been, the brand on his cheek. Before he devoted his energies to arguing against the Army, it had been the Presbyterians, and before that the godly Independents he later joined, but it was his opposition to the King that had earned him repeated sentences from the Court of Star Chamber. "No, he wanted a new Parliament. Edmund Ludlow insisted on the purge."

And where had Ludlow gotten that notion? Antony did not realise he had said it out loud until Prynne shrugged and said, "Villainy, no matter who its author. But I keep using that word; surely there must be others. For variety, you see."

"Try Harley downstairs," Antony said, distracted. "He has a talent for words."

Prynne grunted and stood, gathering up his papers and pen. Antony paced as he left, scratching at his overgrown beard.

Purging the Commons: the most outrageous, divisive, *destructive* thing the Army could have done, short of declaring itself the sole authority over England, defying King, Commons, and all. And while Antony did not doubt Ludlow and the others mad enough to do it...

Evil thoughts, whispered into the right ears at the right time, had nurtured violence in London before.

Had Ifarren Vidar's minions visited that council at St Albans?

He and Lune had expected the next move to come through Sir Leslic's Ascendants, who had seemed to be positioning themselves to create more anger against the Royalists, which would help the Army's cause. But what if Vidar had gone directly for the Army itself? The Commons had voted to restore the King; a new House, if the old were dissolved, might well do the same. This purge was the only way to ensure a Commons composed solely of men who would act against Charles Stuart.

Which would please Nicneven very well.

And Antony's own arrest would distract Lune, at this most crucial of times.

Movement in the shadows made him leap nearly out of his skin. But the figure Antony saw was familiar to him, and would hardly welcome the arrival of his Puritan fellow captives. He swallowed the cry just in time.

The mara Angrisla was not much prettier than Prynne, being a nightmare personified. But Antony had seen Lune's secret messengers before, chosen more for their stealth than their social graces. "Lord Antony," the mara said perfunctorily. "You'll be out today. Her Majesty sent me to tell you."

So much for his great martyrdom. But Antony had let his guilt over previous failures drive him into a greater one: he let himself be taken from Lune's side, when she needed him most. And perhaps Vidar had predicted that, too.

Certainly Antony had not done here what he hoped. The surprise of the arrests had, in the end, come to nothing much; the prisoners were being released a few at a time, with little fanfare, while some troublesome few were moved to closer confinement in St James' Palace. Those still held here could do little more than write pamphlet after pamphlet, from the *Solemn Protestation* onward—most of which might as well be flung into the void, for all Antony knew of their effect.

He might not do much good outside, either. He would not swear his dissent from the treaty vote on the fifth—the vote overturned by the purged Commons a week later—and so would not be readmitted to his seat. But he might yet do some good in Guildhall. And if his suspicions were correct, he needed to be in the Onyx Hall, pursuing the question of Vidar. "Bear my thanks to her Majesty," he told the mara, and resumed his pacing, worrying at his thoughts like a dog with a bone.

Soon enough a messenger came to take him and a few others to Whitehall. Fairfax, of course, was "too busy" to see them; Antony imagined the man was busy indeed, trying to check the excesses of his brethren in arms. In time, however, a lesser officer told them they were free to go.

Exiting into the frosty street, Antony found a familiar carriage waiting for him. The coachman opened the door, and a voice called out, "How long did they keep you waiting?"

Antony climbed in and sat across from Thomas Soame. The other man had been freed five days before, with many of their companions, and looked worlds more cheerful. "A few hours."

"About what I expected. I passed the time by drinking." Soame leaned out the window and called to the coachman, "Lombard Street."

Home. And Kate. But Antony said, "No—take me to the Guildhall."

Soame shook his head. "You don't want to go there. Haven't you heard?" At Antony's alarmed look, he explained, "The Common Council elections were four days ago. Parliament passed an ordinance debarring anyone who favoured the treaty with the King. We may have a Royalist Lord Mayor right now, but his councilmen are a pack of frothing Levellers."

Even allowing for Soame's tendency to exaggeration, it was appalling news. "Are *we* disabled?"

"You may be." Soame fished around the coach floor and produced a small jug from behind his feet. Antony accepted a swig, expecting wine, and choked on aqua vitae. "Depends on whether they know you helped write the *Solemn Protestation*."

Which was to say, another damnable ordinance. Word of it had reached them in prison, of course: no one involved with the *Protestation* could ever hold public office or a seat in Parliament again. "They don't have the slightest shred of authority backing it," Antony said. Anger warmed his body against the icy air. "To call the Commons a free and representative body, after what they did to us—"

"Not to mention they can barely manage a quorum most days," Soame agreed. "Hell, even Vane isn't attending, and he's been the Independents' leader for how long now? Some men are afraid to show their faces; others stay away in protest. The Lords muster six on a good day. It's a farce."

"I'm not laughing," Antony said, more sharply than Soame deserved. "So tell me, then—what reply is planned?"

His friend blinked owlishly above the furred edge of his cloak. "Reply?"

"What protest? You cannot tell me the people are taking this in silence."

"Oh, they're not. I've seen a few petitions—not that the Commons or the General Council will even receive them—and enough argumentative pamphlets to paper over St Paul's. Publishing is the latest fashion, you know."

Indeed. What was well and good for men in prison,

though, was hardly enough for men who had their freedom. "What *action*?" Antony demanded in frustration.

The bitter humour faded from Soame's face. "None that I've seen."

None? It was inconceivable. "But the London Presbyterians hate the Army."

"And preach against them at every opportunity. More words. It's all words, Antony, from the Thames to the City wall."

He shook his head, curling fingers numb with cold into fists at his sides. "Then I will change that."

"How? Man, there's artillery at Blackfriars, and soldiers quartered three doors down from your house. The Army lets people talk, but anyone who moves will be crushed like an ant."

"Are you telling me the citizens of London are afraid to defend their liberty?"

"I'm telling you they're *tired*," Soame answered bluntly. "Six years of unrest, civil war from one end of the land to the other—trade is decaying, we've had three bad harvests in a row, and there's ice on the Thames already. They're minded to hold on to what they have, rather than risk losing the rest."

And so by their indifference, they will lose that rest. Except that Antony knew, even as he thought it, that he was wrong. The Army would make a mockery of their liberties, gut Parliament, force the King to the indignity of trial, and otherwise destroy half of the things the war had supposedly been fought to defend, but the average man could still expect to work at his trade and go home to his family at night. And so long as he had that, it was possible to overlook the things he had lost.

Those lost things mattered. But if pamphlets and preachers could not move men to action, what could? When would the people of London stand up?

The coach had rattled down the frosted streets while he and Soame argued, over the Fleet ditch, through Ludgate, and across the City to his home. Now it rolled to a stop, and a moment later the coachman opened the door for him. Soame reached over before Antony could move and gripped his arm. "I understand," his fellow alderman and erstwhile member of Parliament said, quietly serious. "But I think they mean this trial to frighten the King into real concessions. Once that is done, we will have sanity again."

"I hope you are right," Antony replied. "But I will not trust only to hope."

Then he descended from the carriage and turned to face his house. Kate stood in the door, well-muffled in a cloak, but she threw its edges wide to envelop him in a tight embrace. "Welcome home," she said into his shoulder, "and merry Christmas."

THE ONYX HALL, LONDON
9 January 1649

"Six trumpeters," Antony said through his teeth, "and two troops of horse to keep Dendy safe while he read the proclamation. The *Act* they passed three days ago was no bluff." He spat the word out, contemptuous of its pretended authority. Acts were things passed by King, Lords, and Commons—not Commons in the absence of Lords or King.

Not Commons *against* the King.

"So they will do it," Lune murmured, warming her hands at the fire. "They will put him on trial."

"They will play at it, like mummers. This so-called High Court of Justice is nothing more than a pack of rogues and self-interested knaves. None of their original Chief Justices would have anything to do with it—a tiny show of principles and reason. The Commons has no jurisdiction to try the King."

No one did. Lune knew little of the common law of England, but she knew that much. A sovereign monarch *was* authority. Mortals derived it from the Almighty; fae based it in the very realm itself, which answered only to its rightful master. Neither source allowed for subjects to declare their own pre-eminence, then use it against those set to rule them.

She recognised the touch of hypocrisy in her own thoughts. Invidiana had not designated Lune her heir and passed the crown to her; the change of Queens was born of rebellion. An accidental one, in some ways—Lune had not meant to claim the throne—and one could argue the illegitimacy of Invidiana's own power. But in a very real sense, Lune was more guilty of treason than the fae now imprisoned beneath the Tower.

Perhaps that made her, of all people, qualified to recognise it in others.

Turning from the fire, she lowered herself into a chair. Antony needed no permission to sit, but he stood by choice, caged fury driving him to pace before he checked himself into stillness. This anger had burned brightly in him ever since Hipley confirmed his suspicion: there *had* been troublemakers at St Albans, particularly around Edmund Ludlow, who argued for the purge. Lune had no messages from Cerenel since he fulfilled her final command, discovering Vidar's presence in Fife, but it was easy enough to imagine what Nicneven had commanded her Lord of Shadows to do. Charles was humiliated; now he must be deposed.

Lune wondered how long it had been since Antony slept a full night through. But she could not reassure him into resting; there was no reassurance to be had. "Jurisdiction or not, they will do it," she said. "I think you are right: this is no bluff. And they will find him guilty."

"No, they will not." Antony ground the words out. "We will stop them."

"How?" She could not but pity the frustration that raged in him. "We have tried to move the people of London, to no avail. Their fear is too great, and their exhaustion."

"Then we'll try something else!" he shouted, whirling on her as if on an enemy. "You're a faerie, God damn it; use your arts!"

The oath hit her like a blow to the gut, driving the wind from her lungs, the light from her eyes. The fire flickered low, and a tremor rocked the walls. Only a faint one; it was but a single word, and spoken in blasphemous anger, not prayer.

But it shook her to the bone.

When Lune's vision cleared, she saw Antony's white face mere inches away. He had her by the shoulders, steadying her. The iron wound throbbed under his hand. Then the door slammed open and a pair of attendants rushed in, wild and ready to fight off some assailant. Finding only the Prince, they faltered.

Marshalling her wits, Lune held up a shaking hand. "Be at ease—it was a slip of the tongue only. You need not be alarmed."

They retired, uncertainly, and left her with Antony. "Forgive me," he breathed. "I forgot myself."

That he had done so showed the depth of his distress. Lune took his hands from her shoulders and held them in her own, looking down at him where he crouched on the carpet before her. "You are right," she said, her voice coming to her ears as from a great distance. "I could save the King."

His eyes widened. The velvet across his shoulders tightened, and he gripped her fingers hard. "I could," Lune went on, "claim every piece of bread in the Onyx Hall, and arm a force of fae against the world above. I could send them to the King's prison at Windsor Castle. They could mask themselves, beguile the guards, and spirit Charles away. With a friendly captain, we might get him to France. And then more charms might end the current chaos there and help Henrietta Maria persuade the French court to grant him the soldiers they refused before, which—with sufficient help at sea—might get through to England and make a third rising, more successful than his first two. And so the Army and this false Commons would be overthrown, and Charles restored to his throne.

"And if you ask it of me, I will do it."

Her words hung in the quiet air.

Antony was staring, lips parted in shock. This was not how it went: they argued, each advocating for their own kind, resisting compromise but eventually finding it. *That* was how they ruled, as Queen and Prince.

Never had she offered him such a choice.

"It is not mine to decide," Antony said, barely audible.

"It *is*," Lune told him. "You are the Prince of the Stone. Yours is to say when the fae of this land can be of aid. Such things are, and always should be, your decision. I have forgotten that on occasion, but not now. If you wish the King rescued, then say so."

She spoke it more easily than it came. Even as the possibilities rolled out, her mind filled in the consequences. But principles adhered to only when they were easy were no principles at all.

If the well-being of mortal England depended on this, then she would do it.

Antony rose, pulling his hands from her grasp, and moved back a few steps, the toes of his boots feeling for the floor as if leading a blind man. "If we had acted but a little more strongly, years ago," he said, "we might have averted this by less extreme measures."

Lune nodded, gut twisting with regret. "Had we

foreseen where it would end. But I do not think anyone—perhaps not even a seer—could have predicted then that the innumerable branching paths of our choices would lead us to this pass."

Our choices in the broadest sense. She and Antony were hardly the only ones who mattered, or even the most important. Pym had not anticipated this end, when he began his troublemaking in Parliament years ago. Nor had Charles, when he belittled the threat so posed; nor the Army officers who now roared for a trial. No one person, mortal or fae, had created the disaster that faced them now. They had done it together. And now only violent action would end it.

Her consort had closed his eyes in thought. "Your subjects," Antony began, then corrected himself. "*Our* subjects would resent the forcible taxation of their scarce bread. And the Cour du Lys would scream in outrage at such trespass in France."

Lune said nothing.

"Such conspicuous interference would threaten your safety as well," he went on. "For you cannot charm so many men so entirely without it being marked. It might draw attention to this very Hall, and even if not, accusations of witchcraft would dog the King to the end of his days."

Then he opened his eyes, and she saw the agony he had tried to conceal from her. "And in the end," he said, "it would only confirm Charles's invincible certainty that

218

Heaven is on his side. The Almighty, not the people of England, has made him King, and no lesser force may deny him. He believes his failure in war is Heaven's punishment for acceding to Strafford's death, against his own sworn word. Last-minute salvation of such supernatural kind would be a sign that his penance is done. Once restored, he would thereafter reign in the absolute assurance that his power is divinely ordained. And he would be worse than ever."

Laying her hands in stillness on her skirt, Lune said, "What is your wish?"

It surprised a bitter laugh from him. "My wish? For sanity and reason to return to this land. A King who heeds those below him, as well as the One above. And these past six years erased, as if they had never been. But you cannot offer me that; you can only offer this. And as generous as it is…" His breath came out in an anguished grunt. "No. We cannot rescue the King."

Tears pricked her eyes unexpectedly. It was the sensible choice, the realistic one; the cost of acting would be too high. But some part of Antony had died when he made that decision, and she suspected it was the dreamer in him, the man who believed that working with the fae would help him transform his own world for the better.

They did not always rule in harmony, but she called him friend—and she grieved to see him change.

She rose from her chair and would have reached for his hands again, but he stepped away, armouring himself in stoicism. "We will continue to watch," she said. "If a chance offers itself..."

"Indeed," Antony said, but there was not much hope in his voice. "If it does, we shall be ready."

WESTMINSTER HALL, WESTMINSTER
20 January 1649

They could have held it at Windsor Castle, in far greater safety. But men who believed they enacted God's will would not be satisfied with a circumspect execution of justice, out of the public eye; instead, they brought the grand delinquent of the kingdom to the very seat of his power. In the knife-edged cold of a Saturday morning, Antony, Kate, and Soame took a coach upriver to Westminster Hall, to witness the trial of the King.

Soldiers stood watch on the rooftops, repelling those who would have climbed up to peer through or even break the windows. A great mass of people waited for access to the floor of the hall, but Antony directed his coachman to a house abutting the eastern side. There he paid for the three of them to pass through onto one of the hastily constructed galleries inside the hall itself.

On the floor of the chamber, they had knocked down the partitions customarily separating the various courts that met there. Instead of claiming the middle of the hall, this great affair was wedged into the southern end, normally occupied by the Court of King's Bench and the Court of Chancery. It weakened the spectacle—the common folk crowding in behind the wooden barriers would hear little and see less—but Antony, alert to possible dangers, understood. Ireton's men had eschewed the safety of Windsor, but controlled what they could here. Few galleries meant fewer opportunities to shoot the participants.

Yet no one seemed to be weighing that threat today. The soldiers certainly knew where the gallery entrances were, but they made no move to search those who passed through. *I could smuggle a pistol up here—even a musket— and no one would be the wiser.*

If he believed it would do any good, he might have brought one.

They had come early, to ensure a place; now they waited, through the morning and into the afternoon. Kate, white-faced, made little conversation. Soame's attempts at jests fell flat. Antony, for his own part, found himself praying—but for what, he did not know. Inarticulate pleas filled his mind.

The bells had just rung two when at last the doors were flung wide, admitting twenty halberdiers and officers bearing the ceremonial sword and mace. Behind them...

Scarcely half of the Commissioners had even come. Antony counted sixty-eight in total, though it was hard to be certain. They arrayed themselves on benches beneath the great south window, and one, in a black barrister's gown, took the Lord President's raised chair in the front row. "Bradshaw," Soame muttered, and Antony nodded in recognition. The man used to be a judge in London, but he was hardly one of the great lights of English law. Every detail spoke the low character of this trial.

He hardly listened as the opening rituals were observed. While the halberdiers went to fetch the King, one of the clerks rose and droned through the roll call of Commissioners. Those who were present stood. But when the man called out, "Thomas Fairfax, Lord Fairfax of Cameron," movement came, not from the Commissioners' benches, but from the gallery in which Antony sat. A masked lady rose and shouted back in a furious voice, "He has more wit than to be here!"

Shocked murmurs rippled outward. On the floor, it seemed she had scarcely been heard; the clerk went on with the names. The lady shoved her way free of the crowd and vanished. "Lady Newburgh, I think," Soame said in an undertone.

Antony shook his head. Lady Newburgh was an unabashed Royalist, true, but he knew that voice; he had approached her two weeks before, hoping through her to persuade her husband to denounce the actions of his Army. The speaker was Lady Fairfax, the general's wife.

And then the hall fell silent—as silent as such a crowd could be—for the entrance of the King.

He did not come the length of the hall; they brought him through a side door, safely behind the barriers. From above, Antony could see little more than his black cloak and hat, and the radiant star that was the badge of the

Garter. A red velvet chair had been set out for him, which he took with calm dignity, baring his face to his accusers and the spectators in the galleries.

The years of strife had been no kinder to Charles than anyone else. His hair and beard were solidly grey, and his eyes bore the shadows of a man who has not slept. But he showed no weariness as Bradshaw read his self-consciously formal statement. "Charles Stuart, King of England: the Commons of England, assembled in Parliament, being sensible of the great calamities that have been brought upon this nation and of the innocent blood that hath been shed in this nation, which are referred to you as the author if it; and according to that duty which they owe to God, to the nation, and to themselves, and according to that power and fundamental trust that is reposed in them by the people, have constituted this High Court of Justice before which you are now brought, and you are to hear your charge upon which the court will proceed."

At Antony's side, Kate shivered. He moved to put his arm around her, but she shrugged it off with stiff pride.

Below, they read out the charges. Charles was a tyrant and a murderer, and had subverted the fundamental laws of the realm; he had committed treason against his own people, all to glorify and exert his own will.

To which the King of England merely laughed.

His cause for humour was plain enough. When they finally gave him leave to speak, he replied clearly, without any hint of the stammer that normally impeded him. And with his first words, he cut straight to the heart of the matter. "I would know by what power I am called hither," he said. "I would know by what authority—I mean *lawful*. There are many unlawful authorities in the world, thieves and robbers by the highway…"

What he said after that, Antony could not catch; there was noise and movement in the hall below. His heart leapt into his mouth, and he realised for the first time just how frightened he was. It seemed impossible that such events as these could proceed without dissolving into sheer anarchy and bloodshed.

But this was no hot-headed attempt to rescue or kill the King. Cries of "Justice!" arose in the crowd, as if by chance. "They planned that," Antony murmured in Soame's ear, and his friend grunted in agreement. The Puritans despised theatre, but what was this if not a staged play?

The King, however, refused to follow the script. Batting aside Bradshaw's weak counters, he hammered the point again and again, questioning the authority of the court, and asserting his right to ask that question.

Tom scowled. "Why does he not plead?" he demanded in an undertone. "Every time Bradshaw asks for his answer, he deflects it with more arguments—but a man who does not plead is assumed to be guilty!"

"Because to plead innocence *or* guilt is to grant legitimacy to this court," Antony said.

"But it seals his fate. He could win on points of law, if only he would defend himself!"

Kate's bitter laugh answered him, from Antony's other side. "Do you think these men are concerned with the law?

They answer to God, and none other. No defence would save him."

Soame's answering noise was pure, inarticulate frustration. "At least it would show how nonsensical these charges are!"

Nothing Antony had seen that day brought home the injustice of the trial more than hearing Soame—no friend to the King—condemn its conduct. Much of the behaviour they named, Charles was guilty of, though perhaps not to such exaggerated extent. Yet it could not be termed criminal under the structure of English law; in prosecuting his transgressions, these men committed their own.

Kate was right: it had little or nothing to do with the law. "The people would not understand," Antony said. "If Charles pleads his innocence, they will spend the next three days describing all his sins in exquisite detail. *That* is what the crowd would remember. He will not give them that opportunity."

What they would remember, instead, was the King's unflappable eloquence, not in his own defence, but in demolition of those who faced him. When Bradshaw called him "elected King", Charles reminded him of the inheritance of English monarchy; when he asserted the authority of the Commons, the King pointed out the absence of the Lords, who were essential to the constitution of a Parliament. "You have shown no lawful authority to satisfy any reasonable man," he said, and it was true.

A tight knot formed in Antony's throat as he watched.

He saw Charles with clear eyes; the events of the war had established all too clearly the man's duplicity and arrogance. When he claimed to defend the liberties of the people, it was laughable—and yet, he might lay a greater claim to that defence than the men who now held England at the point of a blade. A tiny spark of respect flared in Antony's heart, and he despised himself for it. But there it was: the man faced his judges, overriding their attempts to interrupt and silence him, with all the unshakable confidence of the martyr resigned to his fate.

He will not avert it, Antony realised, as Bradshaw finally lost his patience and ordered the soldiers to remove the King. *And he knows it. But he will sell himself dearly, with words alone.*

With the prisoner gone, the day's work was ended; people began to depart. Kate stood unmoving at his side, her lips pressed tightly together, her eyes blazing with rage. "It's a disgrace," she said, when she saw Antony's eyes on her.

"Yes," he agreed, and took her arm gently. "And more disgrace to us, that we have fallen to such a state."

THE ONYX HALL, LONDON
26 January 1649

Dejection weighed down Lune's spirit like iron shackles, dragging at her steps as she paced restlessly from one side of the library to the other. The fae who frequented this room—

scholarly sorts, uninterested in the active amusements of most courtiers—had been startled to see their Queen appear, and had ceded the chamber to her without pause. Lune herself rarely came here, and that was why she sought it now: for the unfamiliarity, for surroundings bare of all her usual comfort.

I have failed.

Failed Antony, failed England. Failed the promise made to an old woman decades ago. Not a vow, sworn on an ancient name of Faerie, but Lune had tried to behave as if it were. Yet it was just as well she had not so sworn: she could not defend England from itself. From a King so unworthy of his people; from subjects so unworthy of their land. Or from the faerie enemies who found and exploited those cracks, hammering at them until the whole of the state shattered.

In nearly sixty years on her throne, she had never faced a test such as this. And now that it had come, she failed.

So she came here, to keep company with her guilt. She could not share it with Antony, who bore so great a burden himself. Michael Deven, who would have comforted her, was dead—and a part of her was grateful he was not here to see this fall.

A knock at the door brought a snarl to her lips. Fae did not weary as mortals did; she'd shunned all attempts to bring her food, to make her sleep, until her ladies and her advisers understood that all she wished for was solitude. "Leave me be!"

Despite her command, the heavy oaken door swung

open, admitting Lord Valentin Aspell and Sir Prigurd Nellt. They both went to their knees immediately, and her Lord Keeper said, "Your Grace, I most humbly beg your forgiveness for this disturbance."

"You shall not have it," she snapped, dashing wetness from her cheeks before it could be seen. "We wish to be left alone."

"Madam, it concerns the safety of your realm."

It might have been a leash, pulling tight about her neck. Lune's body jerked, caught between a desire to strike him and an impulse to flee. To go somewhere they could not find her and burden her with such news.

But duty was a bridle she had put on herself; she could not cast it off. Digging her nails into her palms, Lune said, "Tell me."

Aspell visibly inhaled with relief. "An Islington lubberkin has brought word from an oak man north of the City. There were fae in his grove last night—foreigners. Perhaps as many as a dozen."

Chilling as the words were, they concentrated her mind wonderfully. "The Scots."

"I do not think so, madam. The oak man said they wore red armour."

"*All* of them?"

"Yes, madam."

Faerie knights painted and lacquered their armour, but according to their own tastes—usually. Red armour, in a group, pointed unerringly to one source. "Knights of the Red Branch," Lune whispered.

Not Scots, but Irish. Ulstermen. The elite of King Conchobar's warriors, as the Onyx Guard were of Lune's. Ulster—the place to which Eochu Airt had returned so suddenly, not long ago. She doubted the two were unconnected.

But what purpose did they aim at? Lune's eyes had been so firmly fixed on Scotland, she'd given Ireland little thought of late. Could it be—

Her heart leapt for one brief, foolish instant. *Could it be they come to rescue the King?*

Charles had been willing to promise the mortal Irish many things, in order to gain their aid in war. How much more might he give, in gratitude for his liberation?

But common sense asserted its leaden weight, reminding her of the obstacles that blocked the Red Branch, even as they blocked her. And surely Conchobar knew as well as she how little the King's promises could be trusted. And—

And you have put the hounds in front of their prey, running madly off to nowhere. She had no reason to believe their intentions good, and more than enough caution to fear otherwise.

Aspell and Prigurd waited silently, breathing more easily now that she had not lashed out in anger. Strangely, her misery had subsided; it waited for her, too, but could not compete with the thoughts now racing through her mind. *I must try to discover what the Red Branch intends in London—and in the meanwhile, prepare for the worst.* "Lord Valentin," she said. "Bid Lady Feidelm attend me in my privy chamber. Do not, however, say anything to her of the oak man's message. Sir Prigurd—" The giant twitched, head still down. "Make certain that all entrances are under guard, by knights you can trust. If the Red Branch plans some assault or infiltration of our realm, we shall defend if necessary. But do not offer battle first. We may yet settle this peaceably."

Peace was unlikely when the Ulster fae came in secret, not informing Temair's ambassadress of their approach. But Conchobar was not Nicneven, and Lune would avoid having two such enemies if she could.

WESTMINSTER HALL, WESTMINSTER
27 January 1649

Sunday was a day of rest; Monday and Tuesday were more of the same mockery as before. Bradshaw, it seemed, could not bring himself to believe that Charles would cling so stubbornly to his position, refusing, as always, to plead. Time and again they removed him forcibly from the hall, and with every repetition it proved the King's point more: that their only authority lay in force of arms.

Antony's words to Soame proved prophetic. On Wednesday the High Court summoned witnesses to testify before a committee, enumerating all the King's sins, and the following day their statements were made public—but in the Painted Chamber, where the Commission met to debate, not in Westminster Hall. They could not conduct the trial *as* a trial. The King had barred that door.

Kate did not go with Antony to hear the session in the Painted Chamber. *I should never have given her access to the printing press,* he thought ruefully; in a few short months she had become a more prolific author of pamphlets than ever he was. London seemed snowed under by the competing publications, many of them openly against the trial. Yet it was still nothing more than words, and they held no more force than the ink used to print them.

On Saturday the High Court convened again, to pass sentence on the unrepentant King.

Antony saw Lady Fairfax slip into the gallery, masked once again, with a friend at her side. The declaration made against disturbances on the second day did not seem to have deterred her. When Bradshaw claimed once again to speak in the name of the people of England, she cried out once more: "Not half, not a *quarter* of the people of England. Oliver Cromwell is a traitor!"

"Down!" Antony snapped to Kate, almost before he registered the sudden move of the soldiers; half the gallery quailed as the Army men brought their muskets to bear. Half-crouching himself, he forced his way to the speaker's side. "Lady Fairfax—"

She snarled a curse that never should have fouled the mouth of a lady, and, desperate, he took her by the arm. "They *will* shoot!"

Lady Fairfax went with him, but not willingly. Outside,

she lifted her chin and insisted, "I care not for their guns—but I would not endanger those around me."

"I would your husband had your principles and courage," Antony said, meeting her eyes, blazing like fire in her mask. "Had England more like you, she would rest far easier at night."

The lady's mouth wavered. "My husband is a good man."

But rendered powerless by forces that had escaped all control. The Army no longer answered to him. Antony had no comfort to offer Lady Fairfax, and none for himself.

Back inside, he found confusion. The Commissioners were filing out, in less order than was their custom, and the people were muttering amongst themselves. "What's going on?"

Tom shrugged. "The King requested a hearing before the Lords and Commons. Claimed he had something that might bring peace. Bradshaw refused it, and then the Commissioners began arguing; Cromwell himself went after the man who started it. Didn't hear what they said, though. And now Bradshaw has called for a withdrawal."

It lasted half an hour—an uneasy span of time. Antony had some experience of Oliver Cromwell in the Commons; the man was good at intimidation. And while he had not joined Ireton in purging the House, once Cromwell agreed to participate in this trial, his support had been steadfast. Whatever objection his fellow Commissioner might have raised, Antony doubted it would survive the confrontation now going on in private.

He was right. When the assembly returned, Tom

muttered that the dissenter was missing, and Bradshaw denied Charles's request for the hearing.

His address to the prisoner went on interminably, through a thicket of legal arguments and historical examples, most of which Antony could have dismantled in a heartbeat. Only one thing Bradshaw said struck him.

"There is a contract and a bargain made between a King and his people," the red-robed Commissioner said. "The one tie, the one bond, is the bond of protection that is due from the sovereign; the other is the bond of subjection that is due from the subject. Sir, if this bond be once broken, farewell sovereignty!"

Such a world once existed, Antony thought sadly. *But it is broken indeed.*

Charles tried to interrupt, to respond, to answer the charges Bradshaw laid. After three painful days of his attacks, though, Bradshaw was not going to repeat the mistake of letting the King gain any footing. Rushing through his final points, he declared the prisoner guilty, and a clerk rose to read the sentence from a paper already prepared.

"The said Charles Stuart, as a tyrant, traitor, murderer, and a public enemy, shall be put to death, by the severing of his head from his body."

In a solemn wave, the Commissioners rose, silently declaring their assent.

The words fell into Antony's heart like drops of lead. *Not deposition. Not imprisonment.*

They will execute him.

From his seat on the floor of the hall, the King of England said mildly, "Will you hear me a word, sir?"

But Bradshaw would not. Sentenced to death, Charles was already dead, in the eyes of the law. A dead man could not speak. Heartsick, Antony saw the growing dismay on the King's face as he realised his miscalculation. He had not understood; he had expected to have one more chance—not to change his sentence, but to give one last statement. His voice rose, higher and more desperate, as the guards closed around him like an iron gauntlet, as the Commissioners ignored his cries.

Grim in this, his ignominious defeat, Charles had his final word. "I am not suffered for to speak: expect what justice other people will have."

THE ONYX COURT, LONDON
30 January 1649

"You cannot go," Antony said, his voice flat and weary. "You *cannot.*"

Lune's ladies were utterly silent as they carried out the task of dressing their mistress. They were not all needed— not for the plain gown Lune had ordered them to clothe her in—but they all stayed, the better to radiate their disapproval in harmony with the Prince. "Your authority, Lord Antony, extends to mortal affairs—not those of fae. Where we choose to go is our own concern."

She should not have addressed him so formally, but her own temper was frayed beyond any chance of courtesy. As was his own, no doubt. Antony said through his teeth, "I give no commands, madam. I merely advise you that to leave your realm and go into such danger is unwise in the extreme."

"I was once accounted quite good at this," she said with some asperity, trying to make light of it. "You need not fear I will be found out."

"Good or not, you propose to expose yourself to that which is anathema to you, with *nothing* to gain for it!"

A spark of rage flared in her heart. Did he think her entirely motivated by gain? Incapable of concerns beyond the betterment of her court? Amadea entered the room, bearing a crystalline coffer, but recoiled from the glare Lune laid on her. Free for the moment from her attendants, Lune turned to face her consort.

"I promised," she said, forming each word precisely, "to protect England. Instead I have let her fall into the hands of a militant faction who discard her well-being in pursuit of their own interests. And so today they will cut the head from her King—a *reigning monarch*, tried and put to death by his own subjects." Words were insufficient to contain her horror. Kings and queens had died before—deposed, abdicated, murdered without warning—but never like this. Never while on their thrones, under pretence of law.

Disguising what she felt was impossible; instead she used it as a weapon, letting Antony see. "I will not let this pass unwitnessed."

*He argues to preserve this realm—out of fear that
something may befall me, and so both realms will crumble into
chaos together.* Robbed of his seat in Parliament, his position
as alderman, his influence in his own world, Antony fought
all the harder to preserve his other sovereign. She understood.

But I must do this.

At last Antony bowed his head. "Then come. The time
grows short."

WHITEHALL PALACE, WESTMINSTER
30 January 1649

Silence reigned over King Street. Here and there a tearful,
murmured prayer rose from hesitant lips, but the hundreds
of people packing the road, leaning out of windows,
perching on the roof, waited in grim and unnatural silence.

The Italianate expanse of the Banqueting House formed
the background of the scene, a classical limestone island in the
midst of Tudor brick. Black cloth draped the railings of the
platform in front, concealing from those in the street the low
block at its centre, and the staples hammered into the boards
around it. Should it prove necessary, they would chain the
King to his scaffold, like a dog.

Tower Hill and Tyburn were both too large and open,
too difficult to control. A vast mob had gathered to gloat
over Strafford's death; the men who now held England's
reins could not risk a similar mob turning against them.

The confines of Whitehall Palace could be controlled, with the Banqueting House marking one side of King Street, the Tilt-yard the other, and Holbein Gate capping the southern end. An artillery platform left over from the wars, wedged in the corner by the scaffold, kept black watch over the street, and mounted soldiers ringed the scaffold, armoured and armed. They would kill Charles outside his monument to beauty, Inigo Jones's elegant architecture and Rubens's transcendent ceiling within: an added twist of the knife.

The spare, ascetic woman at Antony's side showed her years in her grey hairs and the worn lines of her face, and a hint of stiffness in her joints betrayed the encroachment of age. Lune had not exaggerated; she counterfeited humanity so well, he could not have told her for a fae. The three who accompanied her were easier to identify: Sir Prigurd Nellt was the enormous fellow with shoulders as wide as an axe handle, and the other two served in the Onyx Guard. Even now, dressed as humble tradesmen, they stood like knights—and faerie knights at that. The sober, Puritan dress they all wore was a thin mask. But no one's eye would be on them today.

Kate had called Antony monstrous for attending, as if the grisly spectacle were his reason. The truth was that he could not let Lune come alone.

It was easy to think the elfin woman careless, even heartless. Together they had played the game of politics for so long he had lost sight of the truth: that Lune *did* care, as deeply as he. And this day might even hurt her more, for her dedication to the monarchy was born in a time when the monarch deserved the love of her servants.

Now, they might not have even an undeserving monarch. Earlier, one of Ben Hipley's beggar-children informants had found Antony where he and the others waited on the steeply gabled roof above the artillery platform, overlooking the scaffold. The execution was delayed because the Commons was rushing a bill through, rendering it illegal for anyone to proclaim a new king. It was a defensive tactic, a futile attempt to protect themselves against Charles, the Prince of Wales, who was young, energetic, not hated as his father was, and roaming free on the Continent. But Antony feared they intended something more permanent.

Movement drew his eye. Men were filing out onto the scaffold: soldiers, a couple of fellows with inkhorns and paper, and the executioner, who along with his assistant was heavily disguised. The noble windows of the Banqueting House had mostly been blocked up, but one in the annex on the north side had been torn out and enlarged, and it was through this they came.

Whispers ran through the crowd, rippling the deadly tension. And then a gasp, as the King stepped into view.

He dressed plainly, his only jewel the George, the insignia of the Order of the Garter. He seemed composed, but asked one of the soldiers something with a nod toward the block. Though the crowd was fearfully quiet, a sharp wind blew, bringing winter's bite and carrying Charles's voice away. Even from his nearby position, Antony could only catch stray words; the rest of the onlookers, held back by the thick ring of mounted troops, would fare little better. When Charles drew a small paper from his pocket, he addressed his final speech to the men on the scaffold, the only ones who could hear him. But the men with the inkhorns took notes, and it would not be long before the King's last words were published all over London.

I must get their notes, Antony thought, biting his lip. *If they censor anything out—the people must have the truth.*

With the help of the bishop who had accompanied him out of the Banqueting House, Charles donned a nightcap and tucked his hair inside, leaving his neck bare. What the bishop said to Charles was inaudible, but the King's reply came in a stronger voice, carrying to the now almost perfectly silent crowd. "I go from a corruptible to an incorruptible crown, where no disturbance can be—no disturbance in the world."

Antony's stomach twisted in agony as the King removed the George and handed it to the bishop. "Remember," Charles said, and Antony thought, *Yes. I will remember forever this moment—when a man convinced that God has ordained his authority is murdered by men convinced that God has ordained theirs.*

Always they laid it at the feet of the Almighty. Charles believed his defeat proof of God's punishment. Parliament's leaders believed their victory proof of God's favour.

Or was it simply proof of Cromwell's military genius, and the effectiveness of the New Model Army? What if all of this, every bit of it, was the work of men alone— their choices and mistakes, their dreams and ideals—and

God watched it all play out, letting them rise and fall with neither aid nor hindrance?

Someone had to be wrong; God could not be on both sides. And watching Charles remove his doublet and cloak, watching him raise his hands in prayer and then lay himself flat with his head over the low block, Antony felt with cold certainty that *both* were wrong. God watched, nothing more. His hand was nowhere in this day—nor any other.

This is the doing of men.

A frozen, silent instant—then Charles stretched out his arms.

The axe flashed through the air, and a groan wrenched free of the crowd, horror too great for words.

The disguised executioner lifted up the severed head of the King by his hair, the nightcap tumbling to the boards. Weeping and praying filled the air as the soldiers dragged the body clear and loaded it into a coffin draped with black velvet.

Before they were even finished, a clatter broke the grief. Horsemen advanced from the far end of King Street and the interior side of Holbein Gate, not too fast, but with enough deliberate menace to achieve their aim: the people broke ranks and scattered as best they could. Some brave few dodged beneath the scaffold to dip their handkerchiefs in the blood—a few even dared the soldiers by vaulting the railings—but most began to flee.

Even the rooftops were not safe. Shouts arose from the

gate; turning, Antony saw soldiers climbing over the leads. They paid little notice to the people around them, though, instead moving forward with purpose.

His hand moved without him thinking, closing around Lune's arm like steel. Then he realised she was looking the other way, toward the buildings that fronted the Privy Garden behind them—toward a second troop of soldiers, approaching from the other direction. And they, like the others, caught his eye in a way he had come to recognise.

Even before one of them pointed and called to his men, Antony knew their target.

"They—" Lune began to say, but he cut her off.

"Run."

The Banqueting House rose to their right, but that would only trap them on the roofs. Discarding propriety and her pretence of age, Lune kilted up her skirts and leapt forward. Antony didn't let himself think; he just followed her. For an instant he felt weightless; then the artillery platform below rushed up with terrible speed. White heat flared through his right knee as he hit and rolled to the side. It was more by accident than design that his momentum carried him off the boards and onto the street before the soldiers could recover from their surprise.

Lune heard his cry of pain and moved to help him. Antony shoved her forward. "Go!" She needed no second encouragement. Around the base of the scaffold, through the scattering crowds—a horse blocked their path and they dodged right, into the arch of the Court Gate and the Palace Court beyond it.

"Sir Prigurd—" Lune said, twisting to look back.

"Will buy time for us to get away. Those were fae, Lune, and I do not think they were yours."

The Palace Court wasn't empty. Nor were he and Lune the first to come through; ahead they saw other onlookers being wrestled aside by the soldiers stationed there. Antony swore a blistering oath and hurled himself left, into a narrow passageway that ran past the Comptroller's rooms. Whitehall Palace was a God-forsaken maze; when the passage ended, they had to go right, into another courtyard.

One glance at Lune told him it had been too long since she came here; she was more lost than he. Praying his own memory served him correctly, Antony went left again, through an even narrower passage that twisted almost back on itself before ending in yet another courtyard.

But this one opened back onto King Street. They were far enough from the scaffold now that the soldiers paid them little mind, and the convolutions of Whitehall did them one service; their faerie pursuers had lost them for the moment.

He would not count them safe, though, until they reached the Onyx Hall. "The river," Antony said.

Lune shook her head. "A wherry would make us easy targets. They'll watch for that. Can you continue?"

"I will," Antony said grimly, and limped toward Charing Cross.

WESTMINSTER AND LONDON
30 January 1649

Something ached beneath Lune's breastbone, deeper than grief or despair. She felt as if the ground beneath her might fall away at any moment, as if the world had lost some fundamental solidity.

The King is dead.

She hurried through the streets with Antony at her side and her eyes burned, dry and unblinking.

The King is dead.

It shivered through her marrow. *The King is dead; long live the King*—But no. By decree of Parliament, young Charles did not yet succeed to his father's place. The throne was empty. It had sat empty before, between the death of one sovereign and the coronation of another, but that was a different suspension—the hesitation between one breath and the next. This was purgatory, without a promised end.

It meant nothing. The news would reach the Prince, the new King, soon enough; people would declare him regardless. He was King by the grace of God, not Parliament. Their law meant nothing.

And yet it meant far too much.

England had no King. And on some deep level, the spiritual bedrock of the land, that absence rang like a terrible brazen bell.

She could not afford to think on it, not until they reached safety, and they were not there yet. Despite the fierce cold, sweat stood out in beads on Antony's face. She hadn't stopped to think when she leapt from the roof; he was human, and no longer young. His limp worsened with every furlong, but he forced himself onward—now that she had made it clear she would not leave him behind.

The closest entrance was the only one to breach the City's boundaries; the tunnel opened inside the wall, but gave out into the filth of the River Fleet. Even were she willing to brave that sewer, the hag of the Fleet might not let them pass. They would have to go through Ludgate to the Fish Street arch—

No. Feidelm had been unable to guess the purpose for which the Red Branch was sent to London, but it seemed clear they intended to strike at either Lune or Antony. Or both. Which meant, if they were clever, they would place a force at Ludgate, where the Queen and Prince would be most likely to pass.

How many knights had Conchobar sent? There had been eight at King Street. But the oak man might have seen only one group; there could be more. Surely, though, they could not be enough to guard all the entrances, or the gates into the City.

They were already on Fleet Street; she had to make a decision. Glancing at Antony, seeing his clenched jaw, Lune knew he could not make it to Islington and the Goodemeades. They would have to risk it.

"Follow me," she said, and turned north on Fetter Lane. Passing the lesser Inns of Court, they crossed the Fleet at

Turnagain Lane and came in through Newgate. The skin between her shoulder blades crawled, expecting an arrow at any moment, but none came. They reached the butchers' shambles, and Lune helped Antony down the steps into a cellar that ceased to be a cellar as they traversed it.

Her breath came back in a great, relieved gasp when they reached the safety of home. The iron wound stabbed with new pain, and she had snapped the busk of her bodice in her landing; its broken ends ground into her stomach. Antony sagged against the wall, dead white save for the hectic flush in his cheeks, and did not even manage to straighten when the door banged open and admitted two armed knights.

Lune leapt in front of him, dropping her mortal guise. The pair who faced her stared in astonishment; she spoke before they could overcome it. "Come. Lord Antony needs help, and we are under attack."

She blessed Valentin Aspell for disturbing her with news of the Red Branch; the Onyx Guard was prepared. These two, Essain and Mellehan, were newly recruited to its ranks, but they responded with alacrity. Mellehan helped Antony upright, supporting the mortal man's bad side. "We've heard disturbances, your Majesty," Essain said. "Your knights are gathering in your greater presence chamber—"

Lune swore foully. "Not at their posts? I gave orders to guard the entrances! Sir Prigurd is still outside—" They were a ragged procession, hurrying through the maze of galleries that led to her throne room, but it mattered little;

there were no courtiers out to see. Ahead were the double doors, open for her already. "I do not know what our pursuers intend—"

The answer awaited her inside.

"Hello, Lune," Ifarren Vidar said, from his comfortable seat on her throne.

THE ONYX HALL, LONDON
30 January 1649

The bony, long-limbed fae looked like a spider, one arm and one leg draped over opposite sides of the silver throne. He sat without the cold grace of its former occupant, but his pale skin and black hair were all too similar; for one wrenching instant, Lune saw Invidiana.

She could not control her flinch, and it widened Vidar's smile. Laughter came from the faerie lord's right hand, breaking the spell; Lune realised Sir Leslic was standing with drawn sword, displaying a smile more like a snarl. Antony's seat had been knocked down and shoved to one side, its cushion slashed in half. Leslic's fellow prisoners also stood free, ranged about the dais.

That much Lune saw before she spun. But the doors were already swinging shut, and Essain was there, his sword levelled at her breast. "Do not, your Majesty."

Mellehan still supported Antony, but with a dagger at his throat, while a goblin knotted a gag across his mouth.

Lune met the Prince's eyes briefly, and saw the confusion and horrified disbelief there. She could not answer him. Instead she pivoted back to face Ifarren Vidar.

Doing so, she marked for the first time the fae who stood along the walls of the presence chamber, beneath the silver filigree and crystal panels of the vaulted ceiling. Some—too many—were knights of her own Onyx Guard. But others...

Vidar's narrow face split into a merciless smile. "Did you think the Scots my only allies? You have disappointed the Irish terribly, Lune. So many broken promises, so many missed opportunities. They desire an Onyx Court that will not hesitate to use every tool at its disposal."

Nicneven lacked the might to attack. But others did not. Red Branch knights: Ulstermen, led by Eochu Airt. The former ambassador was there, standing well back from the drawn swords, out of possible danger. Now she understood why he had left her court. This had been planned for at least two months, and likely longer than that. But by Temair itself, or only King Conchobar of Ulster?

Surrounded by swords, and yet politics are all I can think of. Because they were the only weapon she had. Drawing herself up as if she cared not a rush for the blades all around her, Lune made herself meet Vidar's gaze.

She had never known where he came from. Lune was not certain if he was even English. But the rumour was that he fled his original court after his ambition earned him the wrath of his lord, and she believed it. Ifarren Vidar would do anything to gain power. This was only the latest attempt—and, she feared, the most well laid.

"Is that what you have promised Ireland?" Lune asked. "That you will pressure me into greater support?" Her lip curled. "Of course not. You want what you have always wanted: the throne upon which you now sit. But you are not Invidiana, Vidar. You will never have the control she did."

He was unperturbed. "I will do better than you, who cannot even control your own court."

The doors swung open again. Lune did not turn; she would not show that fear. But she felt the tremors as heavy boots thudded against the marble behind her, and then all her attention went to a shadowed corner to Vidar's left, where an enormous figure straightened and came forward into the light.

Kentigern Nellt, his giant form only barely constrained enough to fit into the presence chamber, halted with a vicious smile spreading over his ugly face. "Well done, brother."

A pause—and then Sir Prigurd continued on past Lune, to stand at his brother's side.

Pain lanced through her heart. Fully a dozen of her knights stood alongside the Scots and Irish, turncoats showing their true colours at last, but none of those grieved her like this one, which explained them all. New recruits, gathered over the decades since she took the throne, and all of them brought in by their captain, Sir Prigurd Nellt.

I should never have trusted him.

The giant she had thought loyal would not meet her eye; he stared shamefacedly at the black and white patterns of the floor. But he stood alongside his brother, and Lune did not know whether she wanted to weep or tear his throat out in rage.

She would have no chance to do either. "Kentigern wants blood," Vidar said casually, standing. He had discarded the human fashions that curried favour in the Onyx Court, but not the black and silver he aped during Invidiana's reign. One glittering, long-fingered hand smoothed the velvet of his tunic. "And he shall have it—starting with that mortal pet at your side. We have not yet decided what to do with you. It may be that her most gracious Majesty, the Gyre-Carling of Fife, will claim the right of your disposal. One English sovereign has died today; she may develop a taste for it. But all that shall wait until we have fully secured this palace. For now…" Vidar paused, ostentatiously savouring the words. "Take them both to the Tower."

While Prigurd tied Lune's hands behind her outside the presence chamber, Kentigern studied Antony with a cold, calculating eye. "He's injured."

"They escaped us at Whitehall," Prigurd said, his voice a softer, higher bass than his brother's. "Jumped off the roof."

Antony stared fixedly past Kentigern, eyes hard over the gag muffling his mouth. If he felt fear, he did not show it. "Maybe we'll wait," Kentigern said. "Until he heals. No sport, otherwise."

The amphitheatre. It had seen bloody entertainments

in Roman times, and would again. Antony would not last one pass against the giant—but Lune had no intention of letting that battle occur. *They're taking us to the Tower. How well do they know it?* If their captors took them the right way—if she could buy even a moment's freedom for herself and Antony—

She caught the bleak look in his eye, and shook her head minutely. A year ago, she never would have feared rash action on his part; Antony was not a rash man. Something had changed in him, though. Parts of him had broken, and more than just his old dreams. *I cannot predict what he'll do.*

Whether he recognised her warning, let alone accepted it, she could not tell.

Vidar called from inside the presence chamber, and Kentigern grunted. Clapping his brother on the shoulder, he went back inside, leaving Prigurd, Essain, and Mellehan to escort the prisoners to the cells underneath the Tower of London. Bound and outnumbered, with Antony wounded and Lune no warrior, they were little enough threat—but still, the meagre escort told her something. Vidar might have Scots from Nicneven's court and Red Branch knights from Conchobar's, but he did not have enough to spare Prigurd a larger guard.

The giant knew it, and wasted no time. Lune's skirts tangled her legs as she hurried to keep up, since she could not lift them out of her way. Essain's rapier pricked the small of her back every time she stumbled. Antony, favouring his hurt knee, fared worse. Even if she *could* break free of this guard—

The gallery they were traversing fronted onto one of the lesser gardens, where some courtier was fostering a splendid array of tulips. From the brilliant, many-coloured froth of their petals came a voice, singing tunelessly but with strength, in a voice that made the walls tremble and the tulips wither in their urns. "Plead my cause, O Lord, with them that strive with me: fight against them that fight against me. Take hold of shield and buckler, and stand up for mine help."

The psalm broke harmlessly over Lune, deflected by the tithe, but the other fae cried out. Whirling, she saw Mellehan drop his rapier, and Essain staggered. Lune thrust her hip beneath his, and sent him stumbling into his companion. Benjamin Hipley, still singing, appeared from behind a dying bush. "Draw out also the spear, and stop the way against them that persecute me..." He had no patience for the tactics of gentlemen; his hilt-weighted fist cracked Mellehan's head, and then he disarmed Essain and clubbed him in the neck with the pommel of his own blade.

A basso growl brought Lune desperately around. Prigurd had collapsed to his knees, one broad hand planted on a pillar, but before he could struggle up again, Antony was there. Supporting his weight somehow on his bad leg, he kicked out, with enough force to knock the giant sideways, then staggered forward and slammed the same boot down.

His knee gave out from under him, but the work was done; Prigurd lay senseless on the floor. Hipley cut short his psalm. "Your Majesty—Lord Antony—"

"Help him," Lune said, jerking her chin at the fallen

man, and Hipley rushed to unbind his hands and mouth. Only now did her heartbeat catch up to the sudden excitement, pounding hard enough to make her shake. *I should kill these knights.*

It was a thought worthy of Invidiana. Vidar forced her back into those dark habits, the days when bloody ruthlessness was the only way to survive at court. Lune flung the notion from herself in revulsion. But half the Onyx Hall would have felt the force of Ben's holy song; they had to move quickly.

Hipley came to untie her hands. Antony, supporting himself against the pillar, met Lune's eyes again. More then twenty years they had reigned together; there were many things they need not say. "Go," Lune told him. "Before they think to."

"What of you?" Antony asked.

Her hands came free, and she chafed life back into her fingers. "Will you stay with me?" she asked their mortal spymaster, and Hipley nodded. "Vidar intends to take the Onyx Hall for himself. We must make certain he cannot."

LOMBARD STREET, LONDON
30 January 1649

Antony's sweat-soaked clothing froze against his skin the moment he levered himself up out of the flagstone-capped pit. He thanked God—or rather, the power of Faerie—for the charms that concealed anyone entering or exiting one of the passages from the Onyx Hall, replaced the flagstone, and staggered grimly away from the Billingsgate house, toward Lombard Street.

With the Queen and the Prince captured, would Vidar still spare a force to patrol the streets in disguise? Perhaps, depending on how many more he needed to subdue. And if he guessed their escape, then definitely.

He limped faster.

O Lord, Almighty Father—I beg of You, protect those I love. If that usurper struck at more than the Onyx Hall—if they harmed her while I was gone—

The house was quiet, with candles burning against the early winter night. Antony heaved himself through the clerks' office on the ground floor and up the stairs, gasping. "Kate? Kate!"

No answer. His breath coming faster, Antony made for the next floor. *She could be out—*

"Antony?"

Her clear, bright voice came from the top of the stairs. Then a sudden clatter as she rushed down them, slipping under his arm and supporting his weight. "What happened? I've been waiting—"

"Kate," he said, pulling free of her so he could take her face in his numb hands. "We must leave. *Now.*"

She went perfectly silent and still. A hundred questions shouted in her eyes—what was wrong? Who was coming for them? What had he done? But her mind worked fast enough to recognise that if they were in danger, staying to ask why would only increase it. He loved his wife intensely for the good sense that made her say only, "Do I have time to prepare?"

I do not know. But a modicum of practicality won through; if they fled without any preparation, the bitter January night would kill them as surely as the fae. "Essentials only. Warm clothing, and coin. We'll return for the rest later."

I only pray we can.

THE ONYX HALL, LONDON
30 January 1649

Shouts and the occasional feminine scream echoed through the stone reaches of the Onyx Hall. Perversely, they gave Lune hope. How many of her court remained loyal, she did not know, but it sounded as if Vidar was having to subdue more than a few.

Which meant he did not yet have the leisure to enjoy the spoils of his conquest.

She knew the faerie palace like she knew her own body, every passage and hidden door as familiar as her hands. Hipley, judging by the small noises that escaped him, never suspected the existence of half the paths they took. But otherwise he followed in silence, until Lune paused at what seemed to be a dead end.

She listened intently, but heard nothing from the other side. *Empty? Or a trap?*

Waiting would not improve her chances. Holding her

breath, Lune pressed against the wall, and it slid aside, silent as only charmed stone could be.

The chamber beyond already glowed with faerie lights, illuminating the gathered treasures of the Onyx Court. Jewels and boxes and stranger things, most of them gifted during Invidiana's reign, half of them unknown to Lune. Reluctant to touch them, she had never taken the time to discover their various purposes. But she had no eyes for them now; all she saw was the figure in the centre of the room, clasping something to her body.

Amadea Shirrell gaped at the sight of her Queen, standing in the opening of the secret door. She had time for only one undignified squawk before Hipley was there, one hand clamped over her mouth; the other controlled the hilt of the sword she cradled in her arms.

The main door to this, the innermost treasury chamber, was already shut. Lune, coming forward, kept her voice low. "Lady Amadea. Do tell us—what did you intend with the London Sword?"

Warily, Hipley unclamped his hand. The Lady Chamberlain gulped and whispered, "Your Grace—they are saying the Scots have overrun the Onyx Hall. If it be so—I could not let this fall into their hands!"

She slipped free of Hipley's grasp and knelt, offering the blade to Lune, gripping it by the sheath. Amadea offered no resistance when Lune took it from her. Hipley's eyes were full of doubt, but Lune knew Vidar as he did not. Amadea was not his chosen kind of pawn.

"Get yourself to safety," she told her Lady Chamberlain. "The Onyx Hall is not safe at present—but we will rectify that, never fear."

Amadea rose, curtsied, and fled through the opening by which they had come, closing it behind her.

"Was that wise?" Hipley asked, then added as an afterthought, "Madam."

"Guard the door," was all Lune said, and turned to the case from which Amadea had taken the sword.

The weapon rested ordinarily in a glass-fronted box on the wall, nestled in blue velvet. Showing none of the care she had before, Lune dropped the blade she held, and ran her fingers along the oaken sides of the case, whispering under her breath the key.

The whole structure swung outward, glass, velvet, and all, revealing a niche carved into the stone behind. In that recess hung another sword: the exact duplicate, in every respect, of the one Amadea had come to rescue.

Lune breathed in relief, and lifted the true London Sword from its concealment.

The Onyx Court had other crown jewels, but none of equal significance. This was the blade that, drawn from the London Stone, had made her Queen; with it in her hands, some of the terrible uncertainty she had felt ever since Charles's death receded. *The Onyx Hall is still mine.* Whether simple possession of the Sword would grant Vidar sovereignty, Lune didn't know, but she did not intend to find out. Let him take the decoy, and think himself the victor.

I will take that from him soon enough.

Belted over her dress, the Sword looked less than dignified, but it would be too easy to snatch from her hands. With it secured, she swung the case back into position, then replaced the false blade in its velvet nest.

Behind her, she heard a faint, choking gurgle.

Nothing more. No sound of the door, no cry from Hipley. But when Lune turned, she found Sir Leslic standing over the threshold, pinning the intelligencer to the wall by a knife through his throat.

"My hat is off to you, madam," the golden-haired elf-knight said ironically, not so much as touching his velvet cap. "I move quickly, but it seems you have me bested." He pulled the dagger free, and Hipley crumpled to the floor. "Two swords? Very clever. Perhaps I shall let Vidar have the one on the wall, and keep the one you hold for myself."

He would be on her before she could reach the secret door, let alone close it behind her. Hipley twitched, choking on his own blood; she would find no second salvation there.

Drawing the London Sword, Lune said, "You know what that requires."

"Oh yes." Leslic unsheathed his own rapier, and smiled murder at her. Pain flared from the iron wound. "Believe me, madam—it will be my pleasure."

Then a foot of bloody silver punched through the front of his doublet. "No," Cerenel said from behind him, "It will not. This, *cur,* is for the humiliation you forced upon me."

Leslic opened his mouth—to reply, to scream—but never had a chance. Cerenel's dagger hand flashed around, and blood cascaded from the traitor's throat.

The tip of the London Sword threatened to waver as the knight pulled his rapier free and let Leslic's corpse drop. Lune had no more notion of how to fence than she did of how to conduct a Catholic Mass: she had seen it done, but had no capacity for it herself. *Perhaps it's time I learned.*

No goodwill warmed Cerenel's eyes when he looked up. The oath bound him, but it could not command his heart. *I should not have forced him,* Lune thought. *I have made of him an enemy, too—though one who must fight on my behalf.*

She wanted to apologise for the necessity that had trapped him in Scotland these long years. She wanted to release him from his oath. But the latter would free him to turn on her; she could not afford such mercy. And the former, on its own, would be a mockery.

"You should go, madam," he said with cold formality. "Vidar's forces are moving to control the entrances; soon you will not be able to leave."

Only those he knows of. Lune prayed she was right, that three remained a secret known only to a few. Regardless, she should hurry.

Stepping past Cerenel, she put her fingers to Hipley's neck, but knew the answer before she did. "One more favour I will ask of you," she said to the oath-bound knight. She didn't want to command him, but he was the only tool available to her now. "See to it that this man receives proper burial. Do not let Vidar's people have him."

"As you command, your Grace." He bit the words off.

She would not force his loyalty any further. Lune waited until he was gone with Hipley's body, then slipped back into the secret passage, the London Sword at her side.

THE ANGEL INN, ISLINGTON
31 January 1649

The group that gathered in front of the hearth was a small one, and dismal. Lady Ware waited upstairs, unaware that her husband sat in a faerie house below. The necessary tales had been told; now Lune sat, exhausted and blank, realising the enormity of the disaster.

Charles dead. Herself dethroned. The two should not be connected; that bond was severed back in Elizabeth's day. But the execution of the King cut far deeper than any faerie pact, into the heart of England itself. She could only guess at the consequences.

Guess, and try to find a way forward. But her mind refused to stir.

"There will be others," Rosamund predicted, after a painfully long silence. "Loyal to you, that is, not—" She paused, blinking away tears for Ben Hipley, then went on. "Lady Amadea, for one. They'll know to come here, as you did."

"All the worse," Antony said. His voice was harsh from weariness and suppressed grief. "Everyone knows this is a place of safety. It will not be long before Vidar thinks to look here."

"We can turn him away—"

Lune shook her head, finding the energy to speak once more. "No, Rosamund. Your pretence of innocence will not be enough, not this time. Even if Vidar believes you outside of court politics, he knows my people will come to you. The only safety is for him to find no one here."

Silence again. Even the crackling of the fire seemed subdued. Gertrude twisted her hands in her apron and said, "We can hide you—but that isn't what you mean, is it?"

Lune stared into the flames. The London Sword lay across her knees, a heavy reminder. *It must not fall into Vidar's hands.*

She'd been thinking in immediate terms since she fled Westminster. Evade pursuit; escape Vidar's trap; protect the London Sword. But the immediate moment was past, and she could no longer avoid the truth.

"Whatever courtiers escape," she said, "whoever is still loyal—they will not be enough. As we are... we cannot retake the Onyx Hall."

Retake. Cold acknowledgment: she had lost the palace.

Gertrude's breath caught. In her peripheral vision, Lune saw Rosamund touch her sister's hand. There was nothing they could say. In one disastrous day, she had lost a war on two fronts; she had failed in every way as a Queen. She could protect no one, not Charles, not her subjects—not even her Prince.

Against her will, she lifted her gaze to meet Antony's.

The strain showed on him, not just of this night, but of the years that brought them to it. What mortal wars and Army arrest could not manage, the faerie invasion had accomplished in a single night: it had driven Antony from his home. And it had very nearly killed him.

Once, Lune would have staked her life on his loyalty. But now...

If he leaves, I will not stop him.

He took a deep breath, and she saw him force weariness aside, taking up the duty that lay before him. "Then we must find you allies."

Monday 3 September 1666

THE BATTLE FOR THE STONE

"All things of beauty, shatter'd lost and gone,
Little of London whole but London-Stone."

JOHN CROUCH
LONDINENSES LACRYMAE: LONDON'S SECOND TEARS
MINGLED WITH HER ASHES

All through the night, London's riverside has lain under the glow of a false dawn. Drifting smoke obscures the stars, and hides for a time the sun's true approach to the horizon. But the day at last blooms gloriously bright, the firmament arching perfect blue over the Hell below.

At Queenhithe, men scurry like ants, frantically clearing the market square that sits at the harbour's northern edge. Their defence at Three Cranes failed in the night, but now they have a second hope. Here, they need not tear down houses to make space; here, they may be able to check the Fire's progress.

The Dragon watches their efforts and laughs.

It has children now, a hundred thousand sons and daughters, salamanders that race up the walls as they burn. They crawl under the roof tiles of houses, seeking out the tinder-dry timbers beneath, and latch onto the pitched gables. They burrow into cellars, creating nurseries of coal in which their siblings are born. The men of London fight not one beast, but many, all driven by the *same corporate purpose. They are legion.*

Now the Fire gathers its children for the assault.

Blazing flakes dance on the unceasing wind. Most die, but not all. And twenty houses distant, down the length of Thames Street as yet unburned, another building sends up a finger of smoke.

The men weep in despair as the Queenhithe gap is bridged, and the Dragon roars in triumph.

THE ONYX HALL, LONDON
ten o'clock in the morning

Wrapped in her cloak, with red flannel petticoats bulking out her skirt like a London goodwife's in winter, Lune gathered her lieutenants for their commands.

"In one sense only," she said, trying to keep her teeth from chattering, "this Fire may prove a blessing. Even Nicneven's people cannot walk through the inferno." *Sun and Moon, I hope they cannot.* "If it continues to spread—as we must assume it will—then the entrances it overtakes will not need to be guarded."

Sir Peregrin's elegant features had lost much of their handsome cast to haggard wear, but the knight had strength at his core; he bore up under the Cailleach's assault better than Lune expected. He was still alert enough to foresee a problem. "When it reaches those points—what then? Will it break through to us below?"

That very fear had paralysed Lune in the night, before the Fire itself delivered the answer. "Cloak Lane is gone already," she said. Along with the Cutlers' Hall, the Post Office, and everything else in its vicinity. The downfall of churches was another disguised blessing for the fae, but not one she rejoiced over. "You see, Sir Peregrin, that we are still here."

Her advisers breathed more easily. Lune herself was not so easy; would the entrance still function when the buildings that had comprised it were replaced? The men above were slowing the Dragon's progress, but she feared the Onyx Hall would lose more doors before the Fire was quenched.

"We must keep every entrance under watch," she reiterated, trying not to dwell on the last time she gave such an order. If she could not trust her guard now, then she truly was doomed. "From below. My previous orders stand." There was little bread to steal regardless, but desperation flooded the palace. If she did not find some means of protecting her people, they would soon flee, church bells, iron, and Fire be damned.

The captain bowed and left at a run. "Amadea," Lune said, and her chamberlain jerked upright. Where Peregrin withstood the cold and terror, the gentle lady did not. She had passed beyond merely haggard, now resembling an ambulant corpse. "Gather everyone together. I leave it to you as to where; some place large enough to hold everyone. But not the greater presence chamber." They would offer some resistance if Nicneven's people did penetrate the Hall, but Lune refused to go that far. *If it comes to such a pass, I will give the Gyre-Carling what she desires, no matter the consequences for myself, or even the Onyx Hall. I will not throw all my subjects' lives away.*

"To what end, madam?" Amadea asked, an indistinct mumble from lips that quivered with fear. Lune blinked in surprise. She had thought it obvious—but not, clearly, to the Lady Chamberlain. Not in her state.

"For warmth," Lune said gently. "It should help some. We do ourselves no favours, scattering about the palace as we do." Letting them dwell on thoughts of dying, alone.

A silent tear rolled down the lady's cheek. "It will not save us."

No, it will not. But Lune could hardly admit the truth: that it was a tactical delay, something to keep her people's minds off death while she searched in desperation for a way to stop the Cailleach and the Dragon both.

Gentleness was not what Amadea needed. Lune glared until she had the Lady Chamberlain's attention; then she bit off her command, not blinking. "We did not ask for your opinion, and the giving of it wastes our time—which should be better employed in carrying out our next plans. *Gather them.* We shall see to the defeat of our enemy."

It got the lady on her feet and out the door, which was enough; that Amadea had forgotten to curtsy was an insolence Lune believed unintended. Amadea's shoes scraped along the floor in leaving, as if she could barely muster the will to lift them. *I would rather she obey than spend her strength in courtesies.*

She disposed of her remaining advisers, giving more commands of little use. They were distractions, nothing more—not just for them, but for herself.

Lune did not want to face the possibility of flight.

The Onyx Hall was her blood and bone, the second skin her spirit wore. She'd fled it once, and the bitter memory would gall her until the end of her days.

I will not run a second time.

Lune extended her senses into the palace, not flinching from the crippling cold. Frost rimed the stones, and the arching ribs of the ceilings grew teeth of ice. The floor ached under her feet. There must be *some* way to protect the palace, to close it off such that even the Cailleach's breath could not penetrate, and they could wait out Nicneven's patience. This was a siege—one where the resource to be hoarded was not food or clean water, but warmth.

There was warmth in plenty above. Too much. The inescapable heat of the Fire, grinding its way down Cannon Street—

A spike of transcendent agony pierced her soul.

When her vision cleared, she was running, staggering into the icy walls like a drunkard, feet tangling in her layered petticoats. She fell and bruised her hands, but was up again before the pain registered, weeping, gasping, desperate to reach her target in time.

I am a fool.

Down the length of the great presence chamber, forcing

her throne aside with a strength she did not know she had, hurling herself into the alcove behind it, and then her hand struck the rough surface of the London Stone.

All the fury of the Fire roared into her body. She smelled scorching flesh, but the seared skin of her palm was a tiny cry against the scream of the Onyx Hall.

The Dragon could burn the entrances and it wouldn't matter, because they were secondary things, insignificant to the Hall itself. But this, the London Stone, standing amidst flames in Cannon Street above—this was the axis, the palace's heart, the key to all that lay below.

Stone could not burn. But it could crack and crumble, and it could convey heat from one world into the other. That was its *purpose:* as above, so below.

Locking her teeth tight against her scream, Lune held on.

ALDERSGATE, LONDON
eleven o'clock in the morning

Half-blind with exhaustion and heat, Jack lurched around a cart that had stopped in the middle of St Martin's Lane to be loaded with a frightened tradesman's worldly possessions. *Damned fool. The Fire is not yet here.* But perhaps the man was simply more prudent than most. The snarl of London's streets had stopped practically all movement dead; it might take the cart half the day to move the short distance to Aldersgate, the rest of the day to pass through. By then, who knew where the Fire would be?

Moving into the middle of the street, he tripped over an obstruction, keeping his feet only because there was no space to fall. Jack swore and looked down to discover that someone had torn up the kennel at the centre of the lane, exposing the elm wood of the water pipe beneath. Exposing—and cutting into.

"God's rot! Lack-brained whoreson cullies—the Fire is nowhere *near you!*" Jack bellowed, to no one in particular. Whatever panicked knave had cut open the pipe, no doubt to douse his own shop in protection, the ass had probably long since fled. No wonder there was so little water coming to the conduits farther down in the City. Jack had no doubt this same crime had been repeated elsewhere. Between that and the drought that had withered the City's wells, they had scarcely any water at all.

He tried to master his rage. All was not lost. The King had come to support his people again, and left behind his brother the Duke of York to take command of their efforts. Under that generalship, a semblance of order was coming to the war.

The fire-post up ahead was one of the duke's creations, and a beacon of sanity amidst the howling chaos of the gate. Jack forced his way over to it; the soldiers let him pass, recognising him for one of the men assembled by the parish constables. Beyond, he collapsed without dignity against a wall, and soon someone pressed a pewter tankard into his hand. Looking up, Jack found himself at the feet of the Earl of Craven.

He scrambled upright again, or tried to; the earl pressed

him down. "Take your rest, lad," Craven advised him. "You need it."

I'm twenty-six, Jack wanted to say, but one did not argue with a peer, especially one to whom he *was* a lad. Instead, he stayed obediently where he was, and choked on his first sip of beer. *I know that taste.* It seemed the Angel Inn was supplying at least one fire-post. Strength spread through his tired body, from his gut outward; the Goodemeades knew what they were about.

From where he sat, the Fire did not look like much. A thick pall of smoke streamed eastward under the impetus of the wind, but beneath it, there was scarcely a glow. God, in His irony, had given them a perfectly clear day, the sun dwarfing all the Fire's rage.

Jack was not fooled, and neither was any other man with enough wit to breathe. The riverside blaze had been bad enough, but it kept expanding northward. And with every yard it shifted in that direction, it gave itself a broader front: more territory for them to contest, and more edge on which the wind could find purchase. For every yard northward, the Fire would claim three to the west. God alone knew how much of London it would devour before it was done.

If only we did not have the wind...

How far dared he push Lune? He knew the gist of what Ifarren Vidar had done; the faerie lord was undoubtedly the Queen's enemy. Yet she insisted on keeping him from the Gyre-Carling, even in the teeth of the Cailleach Bheur. She must have *some* reason for it.

That much, Jack understood. What he did not understand was what reason could be worth sacrificing London for.

He became aware of voices to his right, saying something about Lombard Street. Jack drained the last of the Goodemeades' beer and pushed himself up. *Didn't even need the wall to help me.* How long the strength from that draught would last, he didn't know, but for now it would do. "My lord," he said, approaching the earl and a pair of other men, "can I be of service?"

Craven studied him. "The Fire is moving up through St Clement's, Nicholas, and Abchurch Lanes," he said at last. "One arm of it, at least."

Toward Lombard, and the houses owned by wealthy merchants and bankers. Who would not appreciate their homes burning down, but would be equally angered to hear of their deliberate destruction. It would be easy to believe, after the fact, that the Fire might have been stopped short of that point, and their belongings saved. Jack raked one filthy hand through his hair and thought. With the wind as it was... "My lord," he said, "I don't think we could halt it there regardless. But there are two stone churches on the south side of Cornhill, that might serve as a bulwark; if we create a break there, we might have a chance."

One of the others said, "That would permit the Fire too close to the Exchange."

"Permit?" Craven said, with a breath that wasn't quite a laugh. "When we have the power to command this blaze, then we may speak of permitting it things. For now... Dr

Ellin is right. Send word to the duke, but I think we must make our defence at Cornhill."

Jack startled at the sound of his name. To Craven's weary smile, he said, "I didn't think you would remember me, my lord."

"I remember all men who stand up in defence of London's people," the earl said. Which sounded noble, even if it were exaggeration. Craven had been one of the few peers who didn't flee before the plague last year, instead staying to manage the efforts against it. If he'd earned Jack's eternal gratitude and respect then, it was confirmed now, as the old man placed himself once more in the path of disaster.

Craven clapped him on the shoulder. "Do not overreach yourself," he said, with a wry twist that said he also remembered how faint a mark such advice left on Jack. "We have hours more to fight before we can think of victory, and we need every man we can muster."

Jack nodded, but Craven was scarcely out of sight before the physician took to his heels. If the Cornhill break were to be created in time, they would need every hand they could get.

THE ONYX HALL, LONDON

noon

Real heat would have burned Lune's body to ash by now. She was aware of that much, even if she did not know how much time had passed. As it was, the power of the Fire struck, not at her physical flesh, but at her spirit, which struggled to contain it: to keep it from spilling over into the Onyx Hall. Caught between shattering cold and melting flame, the palace would be destroyed.

The bitter irony of it choked her, in the one tiny portion of her mind that could think of anything other than forcing back the heat. The Dragon was not Nicneven's creature, but in its quest to devour the City, it would do the Gyre-Carling's work.

Unless she stopped it. With her hand on the keystone of the Onyx Hall, Lune could keep the devastation above from passing below. But for how long? Could she hold until Cannon Street was reduced to cinders, with nothing left to burn? The creeping demise of age the Cailleach whispered in her heart was drowned out, transformed into a raging death, a swift immolation no less dreadful for its speed. She'd put herself in its path; now she could not back away, and it might kill her.

No. Lune's joints ached from the strain, but she held. Dying would save no one; it was her life they needed. Her presence here, with her hand on the Stone, holding back the inferno. Whatever it cost her in pain and blood, she would pay it. *I would give my life for my realm. I can give this, too.*

It was nothing more than nature, simple flame, the London Stone above standing like an altar in a cathedral of coals. The flames, Lune could hold back.

But even as the Fire's edge moved onward, something shifted in its heart, and a terrible awareness fell upon Lune.

She choked on her own breath, quailing beneath that hellish gaze. Until now, the Dragon's attention had flickered here and there, diverted by each fresh victim, each challenge mustered by the City's defenders. It saw only what it devoured, and what yet lay in its path.

It had not looked below.

The cataclysmic power turned inward. Even as tongues of flame licked out, the inexorable progress slowed by men's efforts but never halted, the Dragon itself cast a curious eye upon the London Stone. That unassuming limestone block held something different, something *more,* that the beast had not noticed when it took Cannon Street into its maw.

Lune's rigid body jerked. She strove desperately to conceal herself somehow, and with her, the Onyx Hall. It could not be done. A probing tendril of awareness snaked down through the Stone, and found her in its path.

Curiosity became avarice, and all-consuming hunger.

Here was a prize more glorious than the one Father Thames had barred, a mirror to the realm already under the Fire's claws. Here was a place of power. If the pitch and oil of London's wharves had given birth to the Dragon, the enchantments of the Onyx Hall could make of it a god, against which all the efforts of mere humans would be as nothing.

In a molten voice that boiled all the blood in Lune's veins, the Fire snarled, *This will be mine.*

Its claws flexed within her gut, and it began to pull.

THE ONYX HALL, LONDON
one o'clock in the afternoon

Irrith hesitated outside the Fish Street arch for several minutes before forcing herself through. Familiarity did not make the Cailleach's icy touch any easier to bear; she dreaded it more with every encounter. Perhaps some of the London fae helping Jack Ellin were there because they loved their City; all Irrith cared about was escape.

But that wasn't true. She gave it the lie the moment she passed through the blackness of the arch, as she did every time she bore a message between the Queen and the Prince, every time she turned her thoughts and efforts to battling the Fire instead of fleeing back home to Berkshire. She dared not examine her reasons too closely, for fear they would dissolve into senseless panic, but they propelled her onward nonetheless.

Still, she gasped in horror as the Hag's cold breath penetrated her flesh. All the vital spark of her immortal life dimmed, becoming something fragile and vulnerable. She thought of the disaster above: collapsing houses, choking smoke, stampeding mortals running like rats to save their tiny lives. A thousand and one ways to die. Fast or slow, in pain or in black unconsciousness, it didn't matter; in the end, she would be snuffed out, as easily as a candle.

Irrith tasted blood. She had stifled her scream with a fist, and bit down so hard she broke the skin. Spitting, she made herself straighten from her instinctive crouch. The fae above—more than six of them, now; others had come to join the fight, or at least to escape the wind—needed instruction from the Queen. Angrisla was frightening people from their houses, when they would stay past the point of safety; Tom Toggin was shepherding children separated from their parents; they were all helping in their own ways. But it was like carrying water in a sieve: the few drops that shifted made scant difference against the whole.

The sprite put her head down and drove herself onward. Much of the Onyx Hall was still a maze to her, a labyrinth full of dark secrets, but she knew the major ways well enough to keep her path without having to look. Arriving in the council chamber, however, she found it echoing and empty, holding only the pierced arc of Amadea's fan. Irrith stared dully at the makeshift map, trying not to imagine her own body pierced by a blade; there were roving bands of women in the streets above, some of them armed, seeking out anyone who wore strange dress or spoke English badly. Foreigners had been attacked all over. A few were in prison now. Others were dead.

Death came so easily, with so little warning.

Breath ragged in her chest, Irrith dug her broken nails into her scalp. "Stop it," she whispered, teeth grating until her jaw ached. "Find the Queen."

Not only could she not find Lune; she could not find *anyone*. The Onyx Hall might have been an unpopulated grave. Had they all fled, without telling her? Fury at that thought gave Irrith a little defence against the cold—so long as she did not think of dying here, alone. She tried the Queen's bedchamber, without luck, and the night garden. All the flowers there had shivered into black, brittle stalks, and dead leaves carpeted the ground. It was the one place that had felt like home to Irrith, and she ran from it, weeping.

Her shoulder slammed into a wall, checking her flight. She was near the greater presence chamber now, and still no sight of anyone. But she heard a strangled cry.

Irrith's heart leapt. Company, any company, would be a blessing, a minute consolation that all the world had not perished. Shivering, she ducked through the great doors.

The chamber was empty, and its black heights gave no solace. The crystal panes stretching between the arches of the ceiling gleamed opaque with ice. Frost coated the silver throne at the far end, and so it took a moment for Irrith to realise the great chair had been shifted askew.

She crossed the patterned floor on feet gone numb, now dreading what she might find. The sounds coming from behind the throne hurt just to hear. She had to look, though; she had to know.

Curling her fingers around the freezing metal, Irrith peeked into the space beyond.

Hope surged at the sight of Lune. Why the Queen was here, hidden behind her throne, standing on some kind of platform with one hand on a pitted block of limestone, Irrith couldn't begin to guess, but at least she was *here*. Not everyone was gone.

Then she felt the heat flooding the alcove.

There was no comfort in it. Earlier that morning, Irrith had found herself caught between two horns of the Fire, trapped between a pair of burning houses, the hot air searing her lungs. This was worse. This destruction had *awareness*.

Another broken groan escaped Lune, and her fingers whitened on the stone. Her silver hair hung lank about her face, all the curls blasted out, and her head sagged as if she could not keep it up. Something fell from behind that curtain, sizzling where it struck the wooden planks, leaving a scorch mark on their surface.

She was weeping tears of fire.

A new sound reached Irrith's ears: a high-pitched moan, a wordless cry of terror. Only when Lune twitched did the sprite realise it came from her own throat. The Queen's other hand jerked upward, searching blindly; she knew someone else was there. Irrith almost reached for her, then held herself back. The power suffusing Lune would destroy anyone who touched her.

"What can I do?" she whimpered, fighting not to flee.

The reply came out in a parched whisper, torn from the depths of Lune's body.

"Find. Jack."

LOMBARD STREET, LONDON
two o'clock in the afternoon

His own coughing woke him. Ash coated Jack's mouth and throat; he hacked, body convulsing, to expel it and draw clean air.

But clean air was nowhere to be found. More ash and smoke came in with every breath, and desiccating heat seared his lungs. The dirt beneath him was baked dry, cobbles like a griddle on which he roasted. Jack heaved himself upward, but made it only halfway before his elbows and knees gave out, dropping him once more. The effort advanced him a foot or two, though, and so he kept trying, lurching by this crippled means away from the danger that threatened him.

For he had woken in a narrow alley between two houses, both of them alight. When Jack made it to the dubious safety of the street, he found that much of Lombard was in flames, its defenders fled. The signs marking the houses of the wealthy burnt like witches on their pyres: the Golden Fleece, the Fox, the White Hart. Jack might have been in a painting of Judgement Day, showing the fate of worldly riches.

A fate that would soon be his, if he didn't move. Fear and the occasional gust of cooler air helped him gain his feet, and he staggered at a half-run toward the untouched part of the street. How had he come to be in that alley? His searching fingers found a lump on his head. Attacked? No—he had fallen, he remembered his knees giving out...

Despite the fire all around, he found himself shivering. Plague-high fever gripped his body; he had just enough wit left to recognise that. His vision swam. Exhaustion from the heat—Craven was right, he overreached himself. To the point of collapse. He had to reach a fire-post—Cripplegate was nearest—take some rest, away from the battle. He hadn't slept the previous night, and unconsciousness didn't count.

A flicker of movement. A slender body arrowed through the smoke, ghostlike and low. Jack recognised Lune's hound by its red ears. A faerie hound, here in the City, and undisguised; and judging by its behaviour, looking for him.

The dog ran a swift circuit around the Prince. Turning to follow its path, Jack almost collapsed again. *I'm delirious. Or dead, and the hound has come to take me to Hell.* Then it was gone, leaving him sure it had never been there at all.

"My lord!" The cry came from ahead. That, he did not imagine; a lithe figure darted his way, shouting his fae title for all the world to hear. Irrith made a strange-looking boy, but she could hardly run about as a girl, and God in Heaven, the hound was leading her.

Can't even think straight. Jack tried to clear his mind, and the effort distracted him from his feet. He would have measured his length on the cobbles if Irrith hadn't caught him.

"Where have you *been*?" the sprite demanded, still shouting, as if she were not six inches from his ear. "I've been searching—"

The fever wracked his whole body in a shudder. *More than exhaustion. I cannot have the plague, can I?* The thought terrified him. But surely he would have noticed the other signs—would he not? Some other illness, perhaps, though few came on so quickly…

"Jack!" His name brought him back to his senses. Irrith gripped him by the jaw, forcing him to look at her. "You have to come. It may already be too late."

"Too late?" Barely even a whisper. How long had he lain there, while the Fire drew ever closer?

"It's the Queen," Irrith said. "She needs you. *Now*."

THE ONYX HALL, LONDON
two o'clock in the afternoon

The well in Threadneedle Street was mobbed, walled in by carts and constantly in use by the men fighting the fire; Jack and Irrith had to fight their way to Ketton Street instead, and the entrance there. The cold hit him like a hammer as he passed below, and for the first time he grasped some measure of its horror for the fae. The Cailleach's merest touch reminded him how close he'd come to death, and it set off a paroxysm of shivering that nearly dropped him. "No *time* for that!" Irrith insisted, dragging him along bodily. Now they were once more within the Hag's reach, she avoided touching his skin, but she was no less effective for that. "It's already been too long—I couldn't find you; if it weren't for the Queen's hound—"

"Lune," Jack managed, through his chattering teeth. "What?"

"I don't know. But she told me to get you."

The sprite pulled him into the great presence chamber. Jack guessed where they were going even before he saw the throne knocked from its place; Cannon Street had fallen to the Fire hours ago. And now that he turned his thoughts to the London Stone—

"*Up!*" Irrith screamed at him. Ice seared his cheek with cold; he'd collapsed to the floor. *Not a fever. Not from illness.* It was Lune. They were bound to one another, through the Stone, and though she held back everything she could to protect his fragile mortality, it spilled over. Even as the Dragon forced itself downward, it also was draining her, draining the Onyx Hall itself, feeding on the power it found there, and her strength to battle it was fading fast.

Irrith didn't have to pull him up. Jack sought Lune as unerringly as the hound sought him—and what he found stopped him dead on the threshold.

The very air crackled and spat sparks. Her hair floated in a radiant nimbus about her body, drifting on the heated currents, its silver burning gold. Flames danced along the hem of her skirts, up the panes of her sleeves. He could not approach within two steps; the inferno she contained drove him back.

"Lune," he whispered, and her head snapped up.

The silver eyes were molten flame, windows to the fire within. Any mortal creature would have been annihilated by the power she held; even immortal flesh could not withstand it forever. "Jack," she answered him, and her mouth might have been the entrance to a forge, with Hell's coals inside.

He almost prayed, and choked it down in time.

"The power," she said, her voice cracking and spitting. Each gust of air tried to drive him back, out of the alcove containing the Stone. He couldn't even see her hand, buried in incandescent light surrounding the rock above. "The

Dragon's. In me. It must… be sent… elsewhere."

God Almighty, *yes*. Before it destroyed her. Jack didn't let himself consider the possibility that he was already too late for that.

But where? Not the City above; that was where it *came* from. He didn't think they could force the power into the areas already consumed, and if they tried, it might just explode outward to the parts still untouched. And with the Tower so close—they hadn't yet cleared all the gunpowder out. That *would* destroy the City.

Nowhere that people lived. The Thames? The river's spirit was already exhausted. Throwing the power there could well boil all the waters away, and once again it would make their situation worse, rather than better.

He wished it were possible to fling the Fire's heat all the way to the sea, where English ships still battled the Dutch, ignorant of the disaster at home. But even if he could, he would not; the Dutch didn't deserve to be obliterated without warning, simply for the crime of contending with the English over shipping.

Lune cried out, and the air blazed white. The tendons stood out in her neck as she clenched her jaw and fought it down. The very sight hurt Jack, his own fevered body aching in response.

"Hurry," Irrith breathed, from where she crouched by his feet.

Think! Jack pressed his hands against his head, as if they could hold his mind together through the delirium that crippled it. Fire. Heat. Destruction. There was no safe outlet for such a thing.

But fire is more than that.

The fever carried him onward. Fire. Promethean, illuminative. Generative. Fire was the spark of life, as well as the immolation of death. *There is something there, I know it—*

If we could just transmute it.

Jack had never been more than a brief dabbler in alchemy. And this was no place nor time for arcane experiments with *prima materia* and alembics; he needed something simpler. Some way to transform the fire in Lune to a safer form.

He couldn't even come near her. If he touched her, he might well go up in flames on the spot.

But he had only the one idea, and doubted he had time to think of another. The tips of Lune's hair were smouldering. It was either try his idea and die, or stand around a moment longer and die.

"I hope this works," Jack muttered, and leapt up onto the platform with Lune.

Fire went out of Lune in a rush, draining away with terrifying speed to someone else, then reflecting back into her like the sudden inflow of the tide. As if lightning-struck, her body went rigid.

Sun and Moon—

Passion the likes of which Lune had not known for

decades flared through her body, making her gasp. Pain receded, and in its wake came desire.

Her skin ached with it, flooding all her senses. No lover had woken her so strongly, not since Michael Deven had died. Lune wept, remembering the treasured hands, lost to her forever. Her sense of self threatened to dissolve into the drowning wave of grief. So easy to let go, to release herself into oblivion... and that was what the Cailleach and the Dragon wanted her to do. To die. To end at last the long immortality of her existence, and let herself be destroyed.

But no. Forced down into the core of her soul by the twin assaults, she found a cool stillness there, free from fire and the Hag's wintry cold. *This is who I am.* Child of the moon, timeless and serene. She lost that serenity so easily now, caught up in politics, imitating humans so fervently in their intrigues. But she was more than that—more than just spying and plotting and passing the time in frivolous pursuits.

Leslic's Ascendants were right. Fae *had* once been more, but those who dwelt in the cracks of the mortal world forgot it in their fascination with humans. For this one eternal moment, Lune was as she had been.

Then, rising with newfound strength, she surfaced to find herself answered by the brief, bright heat of another. Not the Fire: a mortal flicker. A lively mind, an intellect driven by curiosity and compassion, the desire to gain knowledge and then turn it to useful ends. *This is who he is.* Sun to her Moon. Opposite, but not opposed. Alchemical complements, joined into a single, transcendent whole, burning with the fire of life instead of death.

Thought vanished into ecstasy that went beyond mere flesh.

They came to their senses once more to find the power transformed, obedient to their shaping wills. Still too strong, too much for safety; it would crush them if they held on. It had to go somewhere else.

Together, they reached out into their second body. The Onyx Hall, frozen under the cold of the Cailleach Bheur. Most parts lay empty, but there—in the amphitheatre, crouching together on the white sand, the withering remnants of their court.

Gently, Lune whispered, and she and Jack breathed life into the fae.

Heads rose from their exhausted droops. Eyes brightened. Shoulders straightened. Slowly, carefully, the Queen and the Prince filled their people with life-giving fire, armouring them against the Cailleach's chill. A glow spread through the amphitheatre, casting sharp-edged shadows from the stone seats. The sand baked as if warmed by the sun it had not seen for centuries. Still haggard, but with newfound strength, the fae of the Onyx Court rose to their feet, ready to fight for their home.

For the Dragon's power was all stolen. From the flames' humble origins in Thomas Farynor's bakery to the birth of the Dragon in the mighty conflagration of the wharves, the Fire was composed of stolen London, timber and plaster rendered into flame. Now that essence, safely transmuted, brought the faerie folk of the City alive—and ready to face their enemy above.

The inferno that would scour the Onyx Hall to its farthest corners had vanished, but the Dragon was still there, draining power from the palace to feed its raging flames. The Hall was a fathomless well, from which it had drunk only the first drops. Already it was stronger.

Lune had not been able to close the portal against it, for the Stone did not answer to faerie touch alone. But now Jack's hand joined hers on the rough surface, and together they gathered the last of the fire, that they had kept for themselves.

Not here, they said, and sealed the London Stone, leaving the Dragon to roar its frustration in the street above.

Sensation returned to Lune's flesh, and for the first time in who knew how long, it was all her own.

The cool stillness in her heart was fading, that perfect sense of who she was. Not gone—but she had made her choice, ages past, to forgo what she had been, what she might still be if she left the mortal world behind, instead of dwelling in this place. She made that choice when she first came to London, and again when she became Queen; she made it every day she remained here, living an imitation of mortal life.

It was not a choice Lune regretted. And the time had come to return.

Her eyes blinked open, and she found herself staring at Jack's ear.

The Prince of the Stone startled and pulled back from the kiss. His free arm was still around her waist; the platform beneath the Stone was small enough that they could barely fit, otherwise. "I," he said, and stopped as if he had no idea what he was going to say. "Er."

The memory of passion still warmed Lune's body, the incandescent pleasure that had inundated them both. It was a strange thing, a catalyst to transmute the Dragon's power from death to life, but now the purpose for which it had been created was done. *Do I desire him still?*

No. What they had shared—the power they had tamed—did not constrain her heart. Lune no more loved the man before her now than she had yesterday. But she would carry the remembrance of that transforming fire for ages to come.

As would he, she suspected. He was actually *blushing*. Jack disentangled his arm and stepped back, not meeting her eyes. Lune caught his sleeve with her own free hand and said, "You saved my life. You have nothing to apologise for."

Jack met her gaze sheepishly—a look that flashed to instant concern as she brought her other hand down.

The skin of Lune's palm and fingers was blistered and charred. Her hand had cramped into the position it held on the Stone, but she felt no pain; she felt nothing at all, as Jack took it in his own, cradling it with a physician's delicacy. The flesh might have belonged to another.

"Lune," he whispered, but she cut him off.

"Bind it if you must; it will make little difference. The

scars will remain." An ordinary burn might answer to treatment, but not one inflicted by the Dragon.

He gave her a horrified look. Lune pulled her numb hand from his grasp and descended toward the door, where Irrith gaped at them both. The Cailleach had begun as a threat to the world below, and the Dragon to that above, but both now breached those bounds. What touched one world touched the other, and it would take mortals and fae to answer them both.

"Come," Lune said. "We have a City to defend."

*A*t Leadenhall, they have their first victory.

The day has been one of mounting losses. The statues of England's sovereigns that lined the Royal Exchange have toppled to the ground; the pepper and spices stored below now cloy the smoke. The grocers and apothecaries along Bucklersbury have added their drugs to the choking air. Baynard's Castle has caught, the City's old fortress burning like a torch in the night sky, the western foot of a blazing arch stretching from Blackfriars to Threadneedle, and down again to Billingsgate.

But at Leadenhall, the Fire is stopped. Someone with the appearance of an alderman throws coins in the street, promising them to any man who stays to fight. The western front is damaged, but the interior, holding the fabulous wealth of the East India Company, survives unscathed.

The Dragon snarls, robbed of its prey.

But now it has sampled the riches below. The power stolen from London's shadow fuels its flames, and it craves more. The little openings it consumes are too strait and narrow to grant more than the most tantalising taste, but it senses two others, both great and vulnerable. One lies to the west.

It will ride the wind to that place, and make its conquest complete.

PART THREE

WHEN THE KING ENJOYS HIS OWN AGAIN
1658–1660

"I wonder indeed, how the major part of the
Council of Officers *can take themselves to be*
honest, who first Declared against A Single Person:
Then routed the Parliament: *Then set up a* Mock-
Parliament; *Then pulled it down: Then made their*
General Protector *for life; Then made him to beget*
a Protector: *Then broke this Government: Then*
suffered the Parliament *to sit again: Now have broke*
them again. What comes next? That which they will
break again ere long."

THE GRAND CONCERNMENTS OF ENGLAND ENSURED:
TO THE ARMY, THE SUPREAM AUTHORITY OF ENGLAND

VALE OF THE WHITE HORSE, BERKSHIRE
23 June 1658

The night wind whipping across the crest of the hill was fierce enough to make even the tall Midsummer bonfire bow, twist, and then fight back. The earthworks, known to the locals as Uffington Castle even though no castle stood there, gave only a suggestion of shelter, but the fae dancing about the flames paid the wind little heed. Most of them had lived in Berkshire since before they could remember, and to them, the gusts were old friends.

For the few strangers, the wind was merely one more reminder that this place was not their home. Nine years since they were driven from London; as much as seven, for some of them, since they came here to the Vale, where at last they found a faerie court that would give them shelter. Others had followed later, falling once more into the orbit of their exiled star.

Tonight, however, that star had slipped their watch, and now stood a small distance away, atop a second hill. Less impressive than its earthwork-crowned sibling, the hill's suspiciously flat crest was marked by a bare patch of chalk that gleamed in the waning moonlight. Legend said a dragon had been slain there, its blood poisoning the ground so that nothing would grow. It suited Lune's melancholy mood.

They would have been dancing in Moor Fields that night, had they been in London, luring mortals out to join their revelry. Lune wondered if Vidar bothered, and what welcome those mortals might find if he did. Fae were not always kind. Those serving him, rarely so.

The wind wrapped her skirts around her legs and carried them off to one side, tugging constantly at her, so that she had to brace her feet apart or risk being knocked off balance. Behind her, the ground fell into a broad valley patchworked with forest and fields; before her lay the slope leading up to Uffington Castle, and the celebration she had no heart to join.

From below came a voice, casually breaking into the privacy she sought. "Poor wretch—he's become a sorry sight nowadays."

Blinking, Lune glanced down. A lithe sprite named Irrith climbed the side of Dragon Hill with the ease of one who has done it many times. The faerie nodded her head to the opposite slope, where lines were faintly visible in the long summer grass. The narrow trenches had been carved into the hillside, but their smooth curves were marred by greenery that stubbornly claimed a foothold in the chalk. The figure could not be made out well even from this, its best vantage point; it stretched itself out along the slope such that only the birds in the sky grasped its entirety. But Lune knew its shape. She had been there when the White Horse rose from the ground and descended to feed in the thick grass of the Manger below.

"Can you not clear the weeds yourself?" she asked, pushing her silver hair from her face with a futile gesture. The wind flung it back again the moment her hand left.

Irrith dropped casually onto the bare chalk at her feet. "Not our responsibility. There are families in this Vale whose task it is to scour the Horse—but with the Puritans watching over their shoulders, they fear to come up here."

Music came from around the bonfire, high above them, dancing on the summer wind. Puritans did not much approve of Midsummer fires, either, but that did not stop the fae—nor some mortals in the region. Not everyone agreed with the godly reformers. Fewer and fewer, as the years passed under their austere rule: first as the Commonwealth of England, and when that failed, the Protectorate, ruled over by the great General Oliver Cromwell. The Kingdom of England was no more.

The King is dead. There is no King.

Irrith said, "You are looking the wrong way."

"What?"

"London is that way." The sprite pointed left, toward the eastern horizon.

"I was not thinking of London."

A grin answered her. "Bollocks."

Irrith wasn't one of the ladies who followed Lune from the Onyx Hall nine years ago, when Ifarren Vidar drove her out. She wasn't a lady at all, as her insolent manner demonstrated. The sprite meant nothing by her discourtesy;

she was simply wild as the city fae were not. Tonight, for the Midsummer celebrations, she wore tunic and hose that had not been fashionable for centuries, and then only for men, and not woven from moss. Living moss, pricked here and there with tiny white flowers. In these parts, it counted as fine court clothing.

Lune still wore the bodice and skirts of the Onyx Court, impractical as they sometimes were. It was, she admitted, a matter of principle: if she dressed herself as the Berkshire fae did, she would lose one of the ties that bound her to her realm.

I still consider it my realm, despite these long years.

How could she not? She didn't need Irrith's reminder to tell her in which direction London lay; it called to her bones, a subtle, lodestone pull. She had crossed and re-crossed England in the early days of her exile, visiting the courts of other faerie monarchs, and at any moment could have pointed without hesitation or error toward the very heart of the City. So long as that sense remained, she was bound to her land. So long as she was bound to her land, she was its Queen. That was the very essence of faerie sovereignty.

But sovereignty was not politics, and she had not seen her realm in nine long years—nine years, four months, and twenty-three days, to be precise. *I count the time as if I were human.*

Vidar occupied her palace, and although every faerie monarch of England owed Lune for her aid to them ages ago, none would give her the army she needed to retake it. They sheltered her briefly, then encouraged her onward, until at last she came to rest here, in the Vale of the White Horse, where she did not and would never belong.

Lune became aware of Irrith looking up at her. Rising, the sprite said, "May I ask you a question?"

Lune wanted to say no. She had retreated from the festivities for a reason. But she knew all too well how dependent she was on the goodwill of those who had taken her in, and so she said, "Of course."

"Is it true you love a mortal?"

Love, not *loved.* Irrith understood that much, at least. "Yes."

"Why?"

Startled, Lune turned to look at her. Irrith's auburn hair, a careless tangle of loose strands and small braids, whipped back from her delicate features; she, unlike Lune, had the sense to face *into* the wind. In her eyes was honest confusion and perplexity. "He died ages ago, they tell me, and you'll grieve for him until the end of time. I don't understand why anyone would choose that."

Not so many ages ago. But an infinity of time would not dull the edge.

Lune sighed and turned her head, so that her profile was to the wind. "Imagine you lived all your life in a tower, and saw no more of sun and breeze, forest and grass, than what you could glimpse through your window. And then you had a chance to escape that tower—to walk in the grass, feel the leaves with your hands, and drink in the sun with your skin. Would you say no?"

"If I were to be locked in the tower again," Irrith said bluntly. "Imprisonment would be all the worse for having escaped it briefly."

A sad smile touched Lune's lips. "Ah—but the experience is worth having. The world seems more real to you thereafter, because the one you love lived in it. The colours are richer, the sounds more sweet, because you shared them with another."

Irrith had the courtesy to consider it for a moment before declaring, "I still don't understand."

I did not expect you to. Perhaps it was the touch of mortality shading Lune's vision, but she sometimes felt far older than the wild faerie at her side. "If you saw more of mortals, perhaps you would."

She hadn't meant to hint at the concerns that darkened her thoughts, but Irrith guessed them anyway; they were never far from her mind. "You will return, madam," she said, gazing across to the White Horse as if London lay before them, and not far to the east, as she had pointed out. The Onyx Hall, and Michael Deven's grave, which she had not seen these nine years. "And when you do, perhaps I will go with you."

ST PAUL'S CATHEDRAL, LONDON
14 July 1658

In the darkness, a horse whickered quietly and stamped one foot. The sound echoed off the thick stone pillars and into the vast heights above, far loftier than any stable.

Antony froze, breathing silently through his mouth. Only when he heard no one stirring did he ease forward again, feeling his way carefully across the littered floor, over the splinters of benches and choir stalls, around the pickets of sleeping Army horses, down the nave of the desecrated St Paul's.

The cathedral, relic of popery that it was, had seen ten hard years of abuse by the godly reformers who would eradicate every trace of Catholicism from their physical as well as spiritual world. Rain dripped through the broken roof in the south transept and elsewhere, and wind blew through the shattered windows, their painted glass smashed as idolatrous. Seamstresses slept in the portico outside, in flimsy chambers raised between the pillars of the classical face Inigo Jones built to beautify the western end of the aged and crumbling structure. Filth coated the floor from one end to the other.

But such neglect served Antony now. If caught, he would simply plead himself a beggar, seeking shelter from the rain that drummed on the lead-stripped roof. No one would question it. The soldiers quartered here might call him a vagrant and whip him back to whatever parish he named as his home, but no one would see in him the wealthy baronet of Lombard Street who had once served in Guildhall and Parliament.

That man was long gone. In his place stood a man who was, in truth, little more than a vagrant and beggar.

His hands shook as he knelt in the centre of the nave.

His hands, his knees, like he hadn't eaten in a fortnight. Desperation gnawed at his gut, as if he were a sot deprived of wine, and his mind held only one thought. *I cannot do this much longer. I cannot.*

The same refrain, for years now. And somehow, he kept going.

Soundlessly, his trembling lips shaped the words, praying extemporaneously in the manner of the Independents. *Almighty Lord, have pity on Your humbled son. Perhaps this is my punishment for my sins—but let me pass, I beg of You, lest I die.*

Filthy, stained, cracked as they were, the stones folded soundlessly away, opening a pit in the floor of the cathedral. No light came from below, but Antony's feet knew the path. He all but fell down the stair, letting the opening close behind him.

He collapsed on the bottom step, gasping, struggling to keep his harsh breathing quiet. The air was pleasantly cool, but it could have been life-saving warmth, penetrating his bones after too long in a winter storm. He pressed himself against the wall, weeping despite his will, and gave himself over to the embrace of the Onyx Hall.

How much longer can I endure?

Neither he nor Lune had realised, when she and her courtiers fled London, what the consequence would be. Queen and Prince, they were bound to the Hall. For both of them to leave it... whether that would have given Vidar a chance to claim the realm for his own, they never learned.

Lune could survive outside her palace, though she might lose her sovereignty in time. Antony could not.

The trembling grew worse, not better, as he huddled against the stone, and he wept silently, waiting for it to pass. Time spent in other faerie realms helped; he forced that as far as he could, driving himself to the limits of his endurance. The Onyx Hall was not safe for him. But in the end, it was *this* place he had bound himself to, when he became Prince of the Stone; this place, and no other. And humans so touched by Faerie died when they left it behind.

If he died, Vidar might win.

Therefore, he could not let himself die.

But God help him—he wanted to, sometimes. When the yearning grew too bad, and he thought about the dangers that waited below. This entrance was one of three Vidar did not seem to know about, and the safest for Antony; lying as it did beneath the cathedral, the place was uncomfortable to fae. St Paul's was also more accessible than the fortified Tower of London, and as for the third...

Vidar knew the London Stone was integral to the Onyx Hall, but not why. Very few fae understood the fundamental structure of the palace, and therefore the locations of its original entrances. Equally few knew the location of the Stone, the linchpin of the Hall. Its mortal half sat in Cannon Street above, but the faerie reflection was hidden, behind the very throne Vidar claimed for his own. And Antony would not do anything that might betray its concealment to the usurper.

So he crouched here, like a rat in its hole, fighting to

keep silent, and prayed that no passing fae would hear him.

He fell asleep at last, still on the lowest step, and woke painfully stiff. Touching the wall, he sensed that he had slept the day through, and night had come again. It was safe for him to move—as safe as it ever got.

Rising was the hardest thing he'd ever done, and it grew harder every time. But Antony forced himself to his feet, limped upward through the blackness, and left the Onyx Hall behind.

WAYLAND'S SMITHY, BERKSHIRE
6 August 1658

Sunset stained the grey trunks of the beeches with ruddy warmth, and elder and sweet cicely honeyed the air. Lune stood before the long, low mound that sheltered within the ring of trees, and watched as Teyrngar, the faerie hound Leslic had given her, sniffed along the margin of the woods in idle search of something to chase. *He* had proved faithful, if his giver had not, and Lune had in time learned not to see that traitor's face every time she looked upon him.

She appreciated how freely she could walk in the open, here in the Vale. She stood in front of the grey sentinel stones capping the mound's south end without any glamour masking her, and never any fear of being seen. It was a freedom unknown to her since an age so distant she could not recall it, and unimaginable in the city she called home.

But the quiet grated on her. Farmers lived in the Vale of the White Horse, and there was a village within easy reach, but she felt terribly isolated out here, with only the Berkshire fae and the remnants of her own small court for company. She had few dealings with mortals. Even a glamour only helped so much, when the laws against vagrancy meant any traveller was looked upon with suspicion. And so along with her freedom, she had ignorance: she was utterly dependent on others to keep her informed, as the world passed her by.

The still air was broken by hooves, beating a dull rhythm on the chalk-and-flint lane that passed near the mound and its concealing trees. If it was not who Lune expected, he would ride on by—or if he did not, she scarcely cared. The humans knew the tales of this place. But the figure who rode under the arms of the beeches was familiar, for all it had changed.

The sight of Antony Ware brought unexpected pain. Where once his association with faerie kind had slowed his aging, now it seemed to speed it. All but exiled from the Onyx Hall, he'd lost at least two stone, and most of the colour from his hair and beard. The shoulders under his buff coat were raw bone, and after two hard days of riding, his hands shook on the reins.

She would not insult him by pointing out the obvious, though. Lune took the reins and steadied his mare while he dismounted—a real mare, not a transformed faerie. "Leave a silver coin," she said, attempting humour, "and you'll find her shod ere we are done."

"Even I cannot be at two tasks at once." The voice came from behind her, a deep, friendly growl. For such an enormous man, Wayland moved far too silently.

The King of the Vale did not look obviously fae; at first glance, he seemed nothing more than a brawny blacksmith, with muscles cording his arms and straining his plain leather tunic across his chest. But Lune offered him a respectful greeting, never forgetting she owed this royal cousin her present sanctuary.

Wayland acknowledged her with a nod and gripped Antony's arm familiarly, then bent to scratch between Teyrngar's ears. "We have food for you within," he said to the exiled Prince, "safe for you to eat." Which meant some puck had stolen it from a nearby farm. But the fae here, never hardened by the old ways of the Onyx Court, were willing enough to do some good in return; Lune trusted the farmer had woken to find his house swept bare of dirt, his cows fed and milked.

It was the old way of things, simple and familiar, even though Lune herself had not dwelt in the countryside for an age. Wayland plied his hammer for any mortal brave enough to come and pay his fee, and though they were fewer with every passing century, his name was yet remembered. *Who remembers me?*

Fortunately, she had reason enough to put aside such self-pitying thoughts. "Your advisers have gathered," Wayland told them, unperturbed by any consideration that a king should not play messenger. Social distinctions were another thing that was simpler out here. "They wait on you."

"We will be there presently." She had one thing to ask Antony, though, before they went in. When Wayland had left them, Teyrngar frisking at his heels, she said, "What change?"

In all matters but this, she would not hesitate to speak in front of their advisers. But they had uncovered one planted spy and one suborned puck in the past, and would not risk this detail reaching Vidar. "He is still blind," Antony said, tethering his mare where she could graze, and pulling the saddle from her back with a grunt. "He tears the palace apart in search of the London Stone, but he has not found it, and he does not know what will make it answer to him if he does. He thinks this mortal partnership of yours nothing more than a foolish fancy."

Tiny points of tension unknotted in Lune's back. The Onyx Hall owed its existence to both mortal and faerie hands, and no one had ever claimed its sovereignty without mortal aid. She did not believe it could be done alone. And so long as Vidar remained ignorant of that, she would not have to worry he would overcome his arrogance and pride to take a human consort.

So long as she held that advantage and the London Sword, she held Vidar in check.

But she wanted more; she wanted her realm back. "Let another tend your horse," she said. "We have word from both Ireland and Scotland, that may at last be of use."

Four upright slabs guarded the front end of the barrow

mound, like turrets flanking the narrow, stone-lined passage that cut back into the soil. The cruciform chamber at its end was small; Lune had to crouch to enter it. Inside, the wall slid away with a quiet grinding she should have heard when Wayland came out—and how *he* ever fit through here, she could not guess. She straightened with relief into the space beyond.

Wayland's realm could not have contrasted more starkly with hers had he tried. Warm torchlight illuminated the high, round ceiling of the cavern they stood in, and dried leaves of scarlet and gold carpeted the dirt floor. Fae congregated here, but not in attendance on their King, who stood conversing with a tatterfoal off to one side. Hobs clustered around several pots that hung suspended over open fires, and a trio of pucks played an elaborate game that might have once been related to mumblety-peg, tossing a complex pattern of knives into the dirt.

The fae of the Onyx Hall stood out like London grandees tossed among farmers, even those who had given up the stiffness of court finery. Sir Peregrin Thorne, once lieutenant, now captain of the remaining Onyx Guard, demonstrated a complex sword pass to his companion Dame Segraine, who spun a dagger across her fingers as she watched. Tom Toggin, who commanded her household in exile, put the finishing touches on some elaborate marzipan subtlety, tongue protruding from between his buck teeth. Others were scattered elsewhere in the mound, no doubt pursuing their own accustomed habits as well as they could.

Lune knew all of them, far more intimately than she had when they were merely a few among many. Dame Segraine, for example: when in London, the lady knight had often disguised herself as a man to learn from the great fencing masters in their schools. Sir Peregrin, with enough wine in him, told harrowing tales of the hag Black Annis in Leicestershire, under whose rule he had formerly lived. Tom created enormous sweets for Lune's table, knowing she would not eat more than a fragment, so he could consume the remainder without feeling guilty.

They made their bows as she and Antony passed, still obedient to the manners of courtly life, and Peregrin fell in behind them. The Berkshire fae merely nodded, if they bothered to look up at all. Together, the exiled Queen and her Prince crossed the Great Hall and went out through one of the root-arched tunnels.

Their advisers waited in a smaller chamber, in chairs carved from beechwood, around an oaken table that might have seen William the Conqueror's day. The floor beneath them was carpeted with wild strawberries, blossoming out of season. The little group rose and knelt when Lune and Antony entered, removing their caps, and sat when she gestured. Peregrin took up a position behind them, standing guard as well as attending. "Thank you for coming," she said. "The journey was a long one for some of you. I hope you bring me good news."

Her council here was a motley thing, including in its number fae who weren't subjects of hers—one who was not even English. Lady Feidelm's clothing was more outlandish here than even Antony's buff coat, but she seemed at home in these caverns. Though technically still an ambassadress, her outrage at Eochu Airt's betrayal left her with no compunctions about giving her own aid to the court in exile.

The sidhe looked less than hopeful when Lune nodded to her, though. "I fear there's been little change. Few of the other kingdoms approve of Conchobar's alliance with Nicneven, but they do not disapprove so strongly as to take action against him."

The indecision was maddening. Lune said, "Vidar gained Conchobar's aid on the promise that he would control England to Ireland's benefit. Instead, Lord Protector Cromwell ground your people under the heel of his boot. How can they stand by him, after such a failure?"

Feidelm spread her white hands in a helpless gesture. "He has failed, yes—but if Conchobar abandons him, what good will that do? Vidar's success is his only hope, for certainly *you* will not view him favourably, should you regain your throne." *And Vidar has not your scruples against interference,* she left unsaid.

"We might have been able to do something on Ireland's behalf, had we not been driven out," Antony said. "It is more than Vidar's bungling; it is the loss of the good we might have done."

He rather overstated the case, in Lune's opinion; she was not at all certain they could have turned the tide of Cromwell's invasion, or even softened it. But such honesty had no place in politics. "And the Ard-Rí?"

Feidelm sighed. "Our High Kings, you understand, do not rule as a king does; they do not give commands, and the Dagda cannot bring Conchobar to heel. But he promises that no others will support Ulster against you."

In more peaceful times, Lune had viewed that High King with benign amusement. He was a crude fellow, extraordinarily powerful, but much concerned with earthy pleasures. His septennial ascendency at Temair, however, did not offer much hope for action; the Dagda was far more comfortable as he was. But the promise was not without value. Reinforcements from Ireland would turn this affair into a protracted war, and Lune had yet to figure out how to win even a single battle.

What if the fault of that lies not with me? The question haunted her, waking and sleeping. The monarchy of England had been abolished, by Parliamentary decree. Lune had not needed messengers to bring word of it to her; she knew the moment it happened. That sense of dislocation she felt when Charles was killed, the trembling in the foundations of the realm, was briefly an earthquake.

And then silence.

Wayland felt it, too, and every other monarch in faerie England. They did not lose their thrones as she had, but of course none of them were invaded, either. Or was it because none of their crowns were ever linked to the mortal one? Lune was not certain it was *possible* to regain her throne, with the King of England exiled from his, the crown jewels destroyed, and mortal sovereignty lying cold in its grave.

So she did what she could to aid Antony against the military rule of the Protectorate, and kept searching for hope in her own fight. And if she could not pry the Ulstermen away from Vidar, she would direct her blows at Scotland.

Amadea had spent a full year in embassy to the scattered Scottish courts, to little apparent result, but the true bounty of her efforts came in the form of fae willing to pass information south. Admittedly, the Lady Chamberlain made a poor spymaster, but Valentin Aspell had drifted away into careful neutrality, following neither Lune nor Vidar, and the Goodemeades had other concerns.

And she was not entirely ineffective. "The word from Fife," Amadea said when Lune turned to her, "is that Nicneven is daily more disaffected with Vidar."

That was enough to make even Antony sit up, despite his exhaustion. "How so?"

Amadea extended her hands, as if weighing the various sides. "He gained Ulster aid by promising he would control the mortal government and its Irish policy. But Nicneven—"

"—hates such interference," Lune finished for her. The Gyre-Carling had embraced it briefly in revenge for Mary Stuart, but with Charles's death, her purpose was done. "Why her people are still in London at all is something we do not know. Nor, for that matter, why she would work with Conchobar at all, when their aims are so far separated."

Light danced from the gems in Amadea's rings as she shrugged. "That, I've been unable to learn. I believe Vidar misled her as to the reason for Conchobar's involvement; the hints I gather are that Ulster promised to assist Nicneven in exchange for something else entirely."

Feidelm's chair scraped across the soil, and all eyes went to her. *"Claíomh Solais,"* the poetess whispered.

From farther down the table came a wry voice. "And what is that, when it's in English?" Irrith asked. She sat in for Wayland, who had little patience for these intrigues, though Lune doubted Irrith's patience was any greater.

"The Sword of Light," Feidelm said, her eyes shining with reverence. "The sword of Nuada, who was Ard-Rí before, and will be again. One of the Four Treasures of Ériu."

Lune swallowed an unexpected desire to laugh as the English around the table all exchanged baffled glances. Anything that merited renown as a treasure of Ireland could be real trouble. "What makes you name it?"

The poetess's eyes focused again, and she straightened, edging her chair back toward the table. "It has been lost for ages, but rumour has come of it again, and recently. This might be why. If it was in Nicneven's clutches…"

"With all the raids between Ireland and Scotland," Antony said, "mortal and fae alike, it's possible. Suppose Conchobar has the sword. What danger means that for us?"

Feidelm hesitated, fingers brushing the torc about her throat. "I cannot be certain. I may even be wrong about the sword. Properly, it is Nuada's, and Conchobar could curry great favour by returning it to the Ard-Rí. Perhaps he may do so, when Nuada reigns again."

"Nuada was on the throne two years ago," Lune said. "Conchobar had his chance then—for we must assume that if the sword was his payment, he has received it by now."

"Indeed." The sidhe nodded thoughtfully, and a line of worry creased her fine brow. "Which makes me think he has some use for it, before he gives it over. But in my honest opinion, that use will not concern you; more likely he will turn it against his enemies in Connacht. With no insult intended, madam, Lord Antony—to Conchobar, you are not that important."

If Ireland's internal strife distracted him from England, so much the better. "You said Nicneven was disaffected," Lune reminded Amadea. "Has she learned the truth of Vidar's promise to Conchobar?"

"He has not been subtle about it," Antony muttered blackly. Once they finished with the reports from abroad, he would tell her of Vidar's latest attempts to manipulate the Puritans and Lord Protector Cromwell's government. "I know Nicneven is in Fife, not London, but surely she has creatures who carry tales of his deeds."

"She does," Amadea confirmed. "But she had patience, because she believed Vidar when he told her he but delayed the Irish, while he worked to carry out her *other* purpose."

Other purpose? There had to be one; it was the only explanation for the Scottish fae still in London, long after Charles's death. But something in how Amadea said it made Lune's heartbeat slow in dread. "Which is?"

Into the silence of the council chamber, Amadea said,

"To destroy the Onyx Hall."

The blood drained from Antony's already pale face. Lune covered his hand with her own, and found his fingers cold as death. *It would kill him.* This long separation already came far too close. She feared what would happen if he died before they could retake the palace; he grew frailer with every passing month. And without him, Lune might find herself crippled.

"Why?" Peregrin whispered, horrified enough to speak out of turn. "That—but—it is as if we threatened to destroy Fife itself. She makes war, not just against her Majesty, but against—"

"The foundation of my sovereignty," Lune said, through numb lips. The bond with London hummed in her bones. Nicneven's venom against her and all her court suddenly became clear as fine glass. "Because she objects to the joining of mortal and fae, and my realm itself is the source of that problem. The roots of my sovereignty lie in the land—but she considers it twisted, does she not?" At the edge of her vision, she saw Amadea nod. "It is a mortal place, not a natural one. A place never meant for our kind. To be bound to such a land corrupts me, and through me, my subjects. If she wishes to end what we do, she must destroy its source."

Now she understood the reports of destruction within the palace, chambers torn apart. Vidar was not merely searching for the London Stone; he was trying to break the enchantments of the Hall itself. Or at least creating the appearance of it. Lune had no doubt he would prefer to be the Onyx Hall's master, rather than its destroyer—but if it ever became more beneficial to his own survival that he bring the palace down, he would do it.

And if he found the London Stone, that choice would be his.

Urgency flared beneath Lune's breast. Living forever, it was easy for faerie-kind to take a patient view, and see nothing in the delay of years. This robbed her of such complacency. Delay, and she might not have a realm to retake.

The Onyx Court would die as surely as the Kingdom of England had.

Antony had removed his hand from beneath hers; now he said in an unemotional voice, "Then we must encourage Nicneven's disaffection. It will risk her sending someone else to finish Vidar's task, but if she withdraws her support, he will be vulnerable."

Lune opened her mouth to ask Irrith a question, but swallowed it when she realised Wayland was there himself, standing just inside the doorway. He had entered with his usual, unnatural silence, and now he heard what she had been about to say. Wayland shook his head. "I understand your fears. And if the Scots withdraw from the Onyx Hall, you may have the war you desire. But until then, my answer is unchanged. My people are too few, and this is not their battle. I will not ask them to throw themselves into defeat."

"I understand," Lune said, and she did. But the

desperation clawing its way up her throat made her add silently, *Then help me find a way to prevent that defeat. Before it is too late.*

HAM HOUSE, RICHMOND
3 September 1658

Dressed in the rags he wore about the City, Antony might have encountered trouble as he rode along the south bank of the Thames, and so he had changed out his clothing for the sober respectability of a minor tradesman. With his hair and beard trimmed, and the fortification of a recent visit to the Onyx Hall burning in him, he looked and felt more like himself.

He was alert enough to ride warily, and to depart from the river path well in advance of his destination. Picking his way along smaller lanes, he came at the palatial manor of Ham House from the back, through the gardens that lay on the far side of the house from the water. After tying his horse in a thicket, he slipped down the broad avenues of the wilderness to the well-manicured lawn below the south terrace, and a gnarled old sweet chestnut that stood to one side.

Antony laid his hand on the bark and murmured, "I am here."

The trunk had a protruding burl like a drunkard's nose, and a gap below like a moustached mouth; when Antony took his hand away, the wood moved, and eyes blinked open in the bark. "Good evening," the chestnut tree said with grave dignity.

Though not one of Lune's subjects, the spirit of the tree had proven more than willing to help Antony. Ever since Kate struck up a friendship with the Lady of Ham House, in fact; he rather thought the spirit liked his wife. "Is all quiet?"

"Yes," the tree said. "The harsh one has not been here in a long time."

"Nor ever again." Antony felt a surge of relief. "The harsh one, my friend, is dead. As of this afternoon."

After pondering this, the tree said, "Good."

"Are they expecting me?" At the chestnut's affirmation, he touched a branch and said, "Thank you. I will see to it that my Queen rewards you for your aid."

The old tree retired into sleep, nodding, and Antony climbed the stairs onto the south terrace. Silent approach was impossible; the gravel crunched beneath his feet, and so he was not surprised when the doors swung open, revealing a small, familiar figure.

He crossed the last distance at a half-run and caught her up in his arms. The house on Lombard Street had been a house, nothing more, and the Onyx Hall was simply the place he must go to survive. *This* was home, as much as he had one anymore: within the circle of Kate's embrace.

She buried one hand in his cropped hair, the other holding him hard about the waist. Neither of them said anything; their kiss communicated all that was needed. She feared for him, hiding in London under a series of false identities, all the more so because she did not fully understand why he did it. Even now, he could not tell her the reason they had fled nine years ago, nor who it was that hunted him, nor why he continually went back. His political sympathies made him suspect, but no more than others who had kept their names and their homes.

Those were issues they had fought through before; she did not raise them again. Instead Kate smiled up at him and brushed a strand of hair from his eyes. She was about to say something when the door on the opposite wall creaked open, and a young man stepped through.

Antony's heart ached without warning. He might have been looking at his own elder brother, stepped straight from decades past, so closely did his son resemble the man for whom he had been named. *Has it been so long since I have seen him?*

It had. Any of his children, in truth; the last he had seen of his daughter Alice was at her wedding, and Robin had gone to sea with the East India Company, helping to maintain the trade that was the family's sole remaining source of support. And Henry...

Kate had tensed under Antony's fingers. He gave her a reassuring touch before crossing to take his eldest son's hand. "You are looking well," he said.

"As are you, Father," Henry said stiffly, and falsely. He was clean-shaven, and his hair neatly trimmed; his clothing was sober, as befit one of his ideals. Not Puritan, but a Commonwealthsman to the bone—never mind that the

Commonwealth of England, like the Kingdom before it, had fallen victim to these years of instability.

Kate broke the silence before it could stretch long enough to be uncomfortable. "We had word you were coming, and so dinner awaits. I'll have a servant bring water for you to wash up."

Clean and surprisingly hungry, Antony presented himself to Elizabeth Murray, Countess of Dysart and lady of the house, who reigned in solitary splendour with her husband gone. The first words out of her mouth were, "Is it true?"

He studied the woman with some curiosity. Though in her thirties, and with unattractive strawberry-blond hair, she was still remarkably pretty—a detail that had not gone unnoticed by those who marked her friendship with Oliver Cromwell. Despite his best efforts, Antony had never been able to puzzle out just how true that friendship was, at least on her part. How true *could* it be, when Elizabeth Murray worked in secret with her Royalist father to end the Lord Protector's rule and restore the Stuarts to the throne?

Now was hardly the time to ask. "Yes, my lady," he said, with as much kindness as he could muster. "Lord Protector Cromwell is dead."

Henry made a satisfied noise. "Perhaps now we will have the freedom we once enjoyed, and no single person to rule England as King in all but name."

His son was right about Cromwell, at least; in the streets of London, they called him King Noll, and celebrated his death. And the House of Lords might have been abolished, but earlier in the year the Lord Protector had created a new upper house to control his unruly Parliament. Only the bishops had not been replaced, after the dismantling of the episcopacy. Many of the Commonwealth's ideals lay in tatters, thanks to Cromwell's establishment of the Protectorate; naturally Henry would see his death as a chance to lift them up once more.

Antony knew better, but he also knew better than to broach the subject of politics with his son. And Kate and Lady Dysart helped, diverting the dinner conversation to less dangerous topics, so that for a little while they could pretend it was nothing more than a meal in convivial company. Despite her precarious position, the lady maintained a good home, and good food with it.

When they were finished, however, Kate lured Henry downstairs on a pretext, and Elizabeth guided Antony through the long gallery to the library, a cramped room that already held an occupant. John Ellin rose as they entered and greeted him with all the honesty Henry had eschewed. "You look like hell."

Gripping the young man's hand, Antony said, "No doubt I do. And no doubt you will prescribe a course of bleeding or some such, to improve my health."

"Bleeding? Not a chance. An excess of the sanguine humour is hardly your problem." Ellin's long, wry face turned thoughtful. "Black bile, I imagine. In which case—"

"In which case, Mr Ellin, you shall do nothing." Kate entered the library and closed the door behind her. The space was cramped with four in it, but at least they were private. "You have not finished your training as a physician *or* a surgeon."

He acknowledged her point with a bow. "A shortcoming I strive to mend as soon as possible."

It would not take him long; though four years younger than Henry, Ellin was already well advanced in his study of both the intellectual and practical aspects of medicine. Antony suspected his involvement in the Royalist cause was of a piece with that training: John Ellin saw the body politic as grievously diseased, weakened by the upheavals it had wrought upon itself from the civil war onwards.

Another such upheaval faced them now, but it might offer the chance for healing. "Cromwell is dead," Lady Dysart told Ellin, who merely nodded. The man's health had been bad for months, so it came as no surprise. Though there was a good deal of irony, it being the anniversary of his great victories at Dunbar and Worcester. "Sir Antony—what word of his successor?"

In reply, Antony drew a crumpled letter from inside his doublet. "It would have been Fleetwood," he said. "But this was the only proof of it, and on his deathbed Cromwell named his son Richard."

Kate took it from his fingers, with a look that said she was carefully not asking him how he got it. Ellin grimaced and said, "We might have done better with Fleetwood. He's a milksop."

"And let the Army's council of officers consolidate its hold over England?" Antony said sharply. "I will lie dead in a gutter before I let that happen."

"But Richard is the Protector's *son*. Their loyalty to Oliver—"

"Is not an inheritance to be passed on in a will," Elizabeth said. Ellin fell silent, conceding her greater knowledge of the family. "Oliver was an inspiring man, passionate in his convictions, with the capacity to carry others into his visions, and moreover he was a hero to the soldiery. Richard is all but a stranger to them."

Antony nodded and took the chair next to Ellin, hoping no one guessed that the weakness of his knees betrayed him into it. "At best he will have six of the Council of State on his side, perhaps seven—and very little of the Army. What's more, it won't be long before he has to call a Parliament."

Startled, Kate said, "Why?"

"Why does any ruler call a Parliament?" Ellin asked ironically. "Because he needs money."

Lady Dysart claimed the remaining chair; Kate moved to settle on a cushion, but Ellin rose and convinced her through an argument of gestures to have his seat. The young man leaned against the desk instead, slouching his length so as not to loom over them. By the time this dance was done, Antony had his strength back, and asked their hostess, "What do you think will be the reaction abroad?"

He did not have to specify what he meant, and in fact rarely did; even here, in this safe house, they spoke obliquely when they could. The responses from the European states would matter, but what she had knowledge of was a much smaller group: the Sealed Knot, the alliance of exiled English noblemen who worked to restore Charles Stuart, second of that name, to his throne.

Elizabeth's mouth quirked. "When they hear? The same as it is now, but stronger. Mordaunt will want a rising, and Hyde will argue against."

"Hyde is right," Antony said. "The worst thing we could do right now is give the Army something to fight. The people are tired of military control, taxation to support a standing force, and soldiers at free quarter. The longer we go without a war, the more disaffected they will become." He heard in his own words an echo of the debate over Nicneven, and tried not to shiver. *I must live as if I might not drop dead at any moment.*

Ellin raised one expressive eyebrow. "But Charles will not claim his throne by neglect alone. He needs soldiers to control London and other key points—which means he needs a port to land them in, and someone must acquire that for him. Not to mention ships to get the forces across."

The ships would have to come from France or Spain, but Antony agreed with Hyde that for the King to be restored by an outside power would poison opinion against him. Which was a philosophical concern backed by a practical one: until Europe stopped fighting itself, from Portugal to Sweden and everywhere in between, no one would spare any time for a King who only ever reigned in exile.

"No rising has succeeded yet," Kate said. "And before you tell me, Mr Ellin, that only the last one ever succeeds—

yes, your thoughts are that transparent—let me remind you that they have been miserable failures, every one. Even when Scotland gave young Charles its support, he ended up hiding from soldiers in a Staffordshire oak tree. I doubt he is in any hurry to try again."

Ellin spread his hands in florid submission. "Then what do we propose to do?"

"Wait," Antony said.

"I had hoped for rather more than that."

"Wait for Parliament," Antony clarified. "I do not know everyone who will be elected to it, but I expect Hesilrige, Vane, and others from my own days there. I have ways of setting them at each other's throats, and Parliament against the Army."

Ellin frowned. "To what end? Other than pure chaos, which I'm sure you will achieve magnificently."

"Chaos is what we need, at least for a time. The Protectorate is not popular, and will be less so without Oliver Cromwell to hold it together. The Army is despised. The Commonwealthsmen are passionate, but they've lost the people; men are tired of godly reformers prying into every corner of their lives and outlawing their pleasures. And they cannot present a united front, because they do not agree half so much as they think they do, and scarce one in a hundred can see past the glowing radiance of their proposed community of saints to the practical considerations of how to govern a country. What we *cannot* let happen is the officers of the Army claiming the little power that yet remains out of their hands, and turning all of England into their servants. To that end, I will sow what chaos I must, so that when they reach their hands forth they find nothing in their grasp but smoke."

Where the vitality for that impassioned speech came from, he didn't know; it surprised even him. Judging by the expressions that faced him, he was not the only one. Once he had recovered his jaw, Ellin began to clap quietly.

Antony flushed and looked away. Kate laid one hand on his, and kept it there until he met her eyes, whereupon she smiled. Elizabeth spoke, perhaps to cover his embarrassment. "If you are right about the Parliament, I can think of others we might see elected, to work from within."

"Not my husband," Kate said, before Antony could identify the knot of emotions that formed in him at the thought. "He cannot be known so openly."

"They would not have me regardless," he said, taking his hand from hers. "All who were purged before the trial will still be disabled from sitting."

Elizabeth waved their concerns away. "I was not thinking of Sir Antony. But I will do what I can to foster others."

"And to keep Mordaunt on a leash," Ellin added. "I don't fancy bending knee to the Army."

Antony watched soberly as they worked out the details. This was not something he ever had a gift for, this underhand work—not like Lune did. He had relied on Ben Hipley for precisely that reason. But it was the only tool left in his hand. If he was to restore either his King or his

Queen, he must work from the shadows.

And pray for the day when he could live once more in the light.

WAYLAND'S SMITHY, BERKSHIRE
26 April 1659

In all the long ages of her life, Lune had seen her designs thwarted, her achievements overthrown, her hopes trodden into the mud. Every time, she clawed her way back up again, rebuilding that which had broken, and she was determined to do so again.

She was determined, but she could not see how.

Those who kept by her in her exile were loyal, but they were not enough to overthrow Vidar. Lune had no great enchantments she could bring to bear against him, no army sufficient to crush him, and no means of dividing him from his allies, except to wait and hope that Nicneven's growing fury accomplished that for her. They had seeded information about Vidar's involvement with the execution of the Queen of Scots, and it seemed to be doing some good. But every day spent waiting put Antony's life, and the security of her realm, in greater danger.

Antony distracted himself from it by throwing himself all the more fervently into the Royalist cause, as if determined to accomplish the restoration of that monarchy before he died. Lune wished him all the good fortune in the world, but she could no more see how to put Charles Stuart on his throne than herself on her own. They had this much in common, she and the mortal King: despite all the divisions among their enemies, neither of them could muster the force necessary to take back what was theirs by right.

The thought brought a bitter smile to her face as she paced the rustic chamber Wayland had given over to her use. The Almighty could anoint Charles as King, and the Onyx Hall could acknowledge Lune as Queen, but those rightful claims did them not the slightest bit of good, without the strength to enforce them.

She crumpled the letter in her hand—word from Antony, of the dissolution of Richard Cromwell's disastrous Parliament—and flung it from her, pivoting with such violence that her heel sank into the soft dirt of the floor. She found Irrith standing a mere pace away and staggered, off balance with surprise and the uneven footing. *These wild fae move too damned quietly.*

Irrith at least had the decency to ignore her clumsiness. Clad in leather, a short bow in her hand, the sprite said hesitantly, "I—the moon is full tonight, and partially in eclipse. I thought you might like to hunt, and breathe fresh air."

Hunting was not a pastime Lune often engaged in, but tonight of all nights she felt like killing something, if only for the brief illusion of victory. And if she could not be in London, at least she could walk free under the moon, and try to find some solace in its beauty.

Though there would be pain in that, too. It was under an eclipse that the Onyx Hall was created, by a mortal and a faerie.

"Lu—ah, your Majesty?"

Irrith's hesitant query made Lune realise she was staring unblinkingly at the sprite. Lune startled, and gave voice to the thought that had seized her. "I have been as blind as Vidar."

"What?"

"Nicneven thinks me tainted by my bond to a mortal city," Lune said. For the first time in more months than she cared to remember, laughter bubbled up inside her, carrying with it the bright spark of hope. "Well, if I am, let me embrace it. Since faerie strength will not regain my throne for me, I shall see what mortals can do. Where is your King?"

Irrith's face was a study in bafflement as she tried to keep up with Lune's erratic speech. "In his forge—"

Lune was on her way out of the chamber even before the sprite answered. She could no more muster an army from the mortals than she could from Wayland's court, and however much she hated Vidar, she would not try to unleash Puritan faith against him. But there were other possibilities.

No one guarded the smithy door. Lune swept through and found Wayland stripped to the waist, swinging his hammer in steady rhythm, hammering out a semi-circular shape.

He cannot be entirely fae. The piece in his tongs was an iron horseshoe, and even standing so near turned Lune's stomach. The wound in her shoulder throbbed in sympathy. From a safe distance she raised her voice. "I beg a moment of your time."

The blacksmith King quenched the shoe in a wave of steam. "Yes?"

"You have told me you cannot supply warriors sufficient to even the balance," Lune said, drawing as close as she dared. "Will you supply us with weapons instead?"

Wayland laid the iron aside and gave her a considering look. "I could."

Lune quelled her surge of triumph by force of will, letting only a fierce smile through. *The battle is not won yet. But for the first time, I think it may happen.* "Then here is what I would ask of you."

THE ANGEL INN, ISLINGTON
7 May 1659

"To the Rump!"

Antony did not lift his jack of ale in response to Ellin's pledge.

The young man raised an eyebrow. "The Protectorate is staggering to a well-deserved death, the Commons kicked out six years ago is sitting again, and yet you do not drink. I know you think the quality of the ale here has declined, but you cannot even bring yourself to one sip?"

"Not for the Rump." One of Prynne's friends had come

up with the contemptuous name for the reduced Commons left behind after the Purge, and now half of London used it.

Ellin sighed. "It's better than the alternative. When the Army forced our not-so-beloved Lord Protector to dissolve Parliament, I thought it meant rule by the sword for sure."

The same Army that had, on Cromwell's orders, illegally dissolved the Rump six years before, ending the Commonwealth and beginning the Protectorate. It was just one more upheaval perpetrated by the same fanatical men who had held England at the point of a sword since before the King's execution.

Antony thought he kept his face impassive, but Ellin suddenly paled and reached across the table. The common room of the Angel Inn was hot with candlelight, and busy with trade; sweat pricked Antony's skin in the stifling air, but he felt cold. Ellin pushed back the cuff of his sleeve, feeling for his pulse. "Your heart is racing, and you're feverish. Sir Antony—"

Antony pulled his hand back. "I do not need your physicking."

"You need *someone's*. I'm not fully trained; so be it. I can give you the best names in London." Ellin's mouth twisted. "I would send you to France, if I thought you would go. What ails you, I have no idea, but man—it is *killing* you."

The anger in his gut had turned to sick desire. *Too long away.* Antony shoved back from the table. "I know my medicine, and will go to it now."

The ironical face stared up at him, stripped of any

humour. "Will you not let a friend help?"

Was John Ellin a friend? Lady Dysart had brought him into their conspiratorial circle two years ago. Long enough for Antony to know him as more than just another hot-headed young man enchanted by Royalist ideas; Ellin had passion, but also common sense. Antony trusted him more than any man since Ben Hipley had died—but that was not the same thing as a friend.

A wave of dizziness broke over him, and only experience kept him from staggering. "You do help. But this is something I must handle on my own."

"And you'll not let me help you to your horse—I know better than to offer." Ellin stood and gripped his arm. "But have a care for yourself. I don't fancy having your wife on me for letting you fall in a ditch somewhere."

Antony managed a smile. "No ditches, I promise."

The cool, dark air outside cleared his head enough for him to walk more or less steadily behind the inn. *No ditches—but a hole in the ground.*

Bare, skeletal stumps thrust up from the soil where once a thriving rosebush had stood, and the ground around them was torn. But the charms held, diverting attention from this spot, and so Antony knelt and laid his fingertips on one of the splintered branches. "The moon is in eclipse."

The phrase was not his idea. But with the gift some fae had for mimicry, it wasn't enough to give his name, and so some wit in Lune's following had come up with a series of coded signals instead.

The mutilated remainder of the rosebush shivered and split, revealing cracked steps. Antony made his way down them carefully. The waning crescent of the moon had not yet risen, but enough light came from the coaching inn to guide him into the room below.

He was just as glad not to see his surroundings. Leaves and dirt had drifted in, and cobwebs stretched between the broken fragments of tables and benches. Scorch marks blackened the walls. *We used him*, Rosamund had said, and it seemed Vidar knew it. The brownies' well-practised innocence had not been enough to save them when a force of redcaps and Scottish goblins broke in.

Kneeling again, he felt his fingers tremble. Soon he would have to risk the Onyx Hall again—but not yet. Not yet.

"Soon its light will return."

The second half of the phrase, and the key to the second door. The scarred boards flexed aside, and light bloomed up from below.

Antony shuddered in relief as he descended into the welcoming glow. It was not the Onyx Hall, but the Goodemeades' hidden sanctuary helped him stave off the tearing need for his faerie home.

Gertrude bustled up to take his cloak before he was even off the steps, and a chair waited for him near the fire. *This* heat warmed him, and took the tremors from his fingers. Nowhere else—not even in Berkshire—could he relax as he did here; everywhere else, he feared spies, be they mortal or fae. But though the branches of the rosebush had been shorn, its roots ran living and deep, arching over this concealed room. Tiny buds and blossoms gilded the ceiling. And under that ancient sign of secrecy, he knew himself to be safe. Even the redcaps had not found this chamber.

Nor had they found the Goodemeades, hidden here since Antony freed them from imprisonment beneath the Tower. Rosamund pressed a cup into his hand. Wine, not their mead; brewing was one thing they could not do down here. But Antony gulped it down thankfully.

It is killing you.

He put Ellin's words from his mind.

Hands twisting about each other, Gertrude said, "Antony—"

"I know," he snapped, forcing himself upright. "I push it too far, yes—but what else can I do? I cannot live my life in this hole, safe but useless; I cannot abandon my own world to live wholly in yours. What would you have me do?"

He opened his eyes and found the sisters staring at him open-mouthed. Never had he snapped at them like that, and guilt warred with his annoyance. Then Rosamund recovered. "I—we've a message from Lune."

His temper died, leaving foolish shame in its wake. Antony grimaced an apology for his outburst and said, "What word?"

Firelight danced in Gertrude's eyes. "She has an idea, that she thinks may better our chances against Vidar. If she's right—she hopes to retake the Onyx Hall soon."

"How soon?"

"Well..." Rosamund picked up the thread from her sister. She, too, fairly danced with excitement. "You told us that Mordaunt is in Brussels with the King, planning some rising?"

Antony grimaced. "A foolish plan. If the Royalists try to raise the country, they'll fail. Bloodily."

"Lune hoped they might not."

Hope meant nothing; political reality dictated the outcome. Yet the way Rosamund said it implied something more. The brownie had brought up Mordaunt in the context of Lune's own plans; why? "Did she think to time her effort with theirs?"

Judging by their expressions, yes. "It used to be," Gertrude said, perching on a stool at his side, "that what went on in the faerie court had a real effect on the mortal one, and likewise the other way. It isn't true anymore—but we've wondered, at times, whether some little connection does not persist."

Lune had hinted at it before, but never explained herself. True, she had lost her throne on the day of the King's execution, but ordinary causes sufficed to explain that, and the other points of similarity. Vidar had simply chosen to strike when he knew she would be distracted. Yet—

Yet ordinary causes and mystical ones did not exclude one another. It was possible, he supposed, that the unease of Lune's rule had affected Charles's, or his had weakened hers. Certainly Vidar had used the one to trouble the other. Antony could not judge whether some arcane force still bound the two; it was impossible to disentangle such an effect from the practical events surrounding it. But if that were so, then carrying out their own assault while young Charles's loyalists raised the country in his name might better the chances of both.

The brownies left him in peace, letting him think it through. What could be lost by trying? A great deal, unfortunately. Failed violence strengthened the Army's hand, and set back the Royalist cause. And whatever Lune had planned, it would involve risk to her own people; if fae died in the attempt, and bought nothing with their deaths, it would be all the harder for her to convince them to try again.

He could not judge the chances of Lune's plan, not without speaking to her about it. But he could judge the chances of Mordaunt's all too well.

Antony shook his head. "I understand what you hope for, but no. If there *is* a connection, it will only cripple the fae. The Council of State has too many ways to learn of Royalist plans; a rising will never catch them unprepared. Whatever plan Lune has, we must carry it out on our own."

The sisters looked disappointed. And they were very good at it; Antony felt immediate remorse for crushing their hopes. But he'd spoken only the pure truth. "Unless you believe your 'some little connection' can hamstring the Puritan whole of the New Model Army, it cannot be done. If Lune's idea is some great enchantment to that effect, though—then by all means, tell me."

He knew the answer before Rosamund murmured a reluctant no. "We can tell you the details," she said, "at least a few of them. But Lune's asked for you in Berkshire. She needs your advice, and your aid in preparing her folk."

Antony tried to marshal his strength at the thought of the ride, and failed. He would have to visit the Onyx Hall before he went.

Which meant he would have time for one other task. Antony had no direct way of stopping Mordaunt; Lady Dysart could write to the Sealed Knot, advising them against an armed revolt, but he had no illusions as to what that would accomplish. No, the only way to prevent a failed uprising would be to make certain Mordaunt knew it would fail.

Which meant ensuring that it *would*.

"Before I go," Antony said to the Goodemeades, "there is one thing I must ask of you."

Heavenly Father, forgive me for what I am about to do.

"There is a man named Sir Richard Willis," he said slowly, "a member of the Sealed Knot—and a traitor. He is in communication with Thurloe on the Council of State. I will tell you what I know of Mordaunt's plans; you, in turn, must make certain Willis knows it."

The little hobs paled.

He clenched his jaw before going on, fighting down the sickness in his heart. "If the Council knows far enough in advance, they will prepare a response strong enough to forestall the rising. It is a lesser evil than letting it happen and fail." Antony curled his fingers around the arms of the chair. Did he even believe his own next words? "We *will* restore the King to his throne. But not yet."

Rosamund swallowed, then nodded, not quite hiding her own hesitation. "That's yours to say. We will give the help you need."

He was Prince of the Stone, even if the court of which he was Prince had lost its realm; it was his right to direct faerie involvement in mortal affairs. Lune trusted his judgement, and so the Goodemeades did, as well.

Antony just prayed they were not wrong to do so.

VALE OF THE WHITE HORSE, BERKSHIRE
31 July 1659

The grassy embankments of Uffington Castle sheltered the massed ranks of the invasion force with room to spare. They were not many, even now, with exiled courtiers, Berkshire volunteers, and what mortals Antony and others had persuaded to the cause. But Vidar did not have so many either; at their largest, faerie armies did not number a tenth the size of those mortals fielded.

Lune hoped it would be enough. Raising her voice, so the wind would not carry it away before it reached Antony, she said, "You have trained them well." The Prince was climbing the slope to her position on the embankment, with Wayland a step behind. "And you, cousin—you have worked day and night to equip our people. Name your boon, and it will be yours."

His shoulders blotted out stars when he stood next to her. "You have influence with mortals," the King of the Vale said.

Her stomach tightened in apprehension of what he might ask. "Yes."

"When you are in your realm again, use it on our behalf. Revive the duties the folk of this area once owed to us, before the Puritans grew in strength."

Her gaze flicked downslope, to the barely visible figure in the grass. "We will," Lune said, with a glad heart. *He asks no more than I would do, regardless.*

Antony did not comment. He was still trying to catch his breath after the steep climb. She swallowed the desire to dissuade him from coming; she would only fail, and anger him by trying. He had as much right to fight for their home as she did, and more need. Besides, he was their general.

There was a distinct irony in that, given his hatred for the officers of the New Model Army. But he knew more of fighting than Lune did—which was to say, he knew anything at all—and while he lacked tactical experience, he was good at coordinating the advice from their two squad commanders. A barguest named Bonecruncher, one of the exiles, would lead one group with Antony, and Irrith would lead the other with Lune.

Those two were down with their soldiers. *I think of them as soldiers, now—not warriors.* It was an odd thought for Lune, and a sign of the changes she and Antony had wrought. She only hoped they would be enough to surprise

Vidar, and gain the upper hand.

Antony had his wind back now, and so she asked him, "What of the other uprisings?"

His voice was pitched to carry no farther than the three of them. "Called off, for now. The Council of State has fortified the relevant areas; there are seven regiments around London alone, not counting the militia. Most loyalists—I hope all—have gotten word not to rise." His jaw hardened, muscle ridging his skin. "The Council has put out warrants against a dozen Royalist leaders, though."

She would have put her hand on his arm, if he would not shrug it off. Antony had explained his reasoning, and it was sound. But the betrayal came no more easily to him for all that.

Their army would stand alone—and hope *they* did not meet with those regiments.

"The sun has set," Wayland said in his quiet rumble.

How he could tell its last sliver was gone, Lune had no idea; heavy clouds veiled the sky, and there were no bell towers out here to ring the hour. The grey light was a bit dimmer, perhaps, and the wind carried a cooler dampness. This foul weather masked their march, but it made for a grim setting.

She nodded to Antony. "You should speak to them."

He shook his head, a faint smile lightening his countenance, though only briefly. "I am no great orator. What they need to hear from me, they have heard."

"Your modesty neatly shifts the task onto me," she said

wryly. "You, at least, once had schooling in rhetoric. But very well."

It was easy enough to charm her voice to carry; finding appropriate words was harder. "Good people," she said, looking out over the motley assemblage of their army. "When first you came here, you were strangers to one another. Some have lived in this Vale since before the dawn of memory; others call London their home. Some are faerie, some mortal—and that is as it should be, for the Onyx Court embraces both in brotherhood.

"Ifarren Vidar would see mortals dance to a faerie tune. Failing that, he would destroy one of the greatest works of both our kinds: the Onyx Hall, shadow of England's mightiest jewel. He would prostitute himself to foreign powers, solely for his own gain."

She walked a dangerous line there; many of the Berkshire folk were so provincial as to barely recognise themselves as English, and to such minds, the London fae were nearly as foreign as the Irish. Lune swept on, before they could consider it too closely. "But more than that, we tell you this: *in nine years of trying, Vidar has not made himself King.* He may claim the title all he likes, but the Onyx Hall does not recognise him as its master. We name him now for what he is: a pretender, a usurper to a throne that is not and never will be his. I once struck to remove a Queen who claimed power that was not hers; now I go again, to right a second wrong. I am the rightful Queen of the Onyx Court, and Lord Antony is its Prince. All who fight at our side shall find a welcome reward, when the realm is ours again."

It was not a speech deserving of epic memory, but it did its job well enough. The gathered soldiers cheered, from the elf-knights in their gem-bright armour down to the twisted goblins and capricious pucks, and the sky answered with a rumble of thunder.

Turning to face Wayland, she found herself looking past him, and an idea sparked in her mind. Grand gestures had their place, on a night such as this. "One more favour, cousin, if I might beg it of you."

He nodded.

"I should like to borrow your Horse."

LONDON AND ENVIRONS
1 August 1659

The faerie steeds carried them faster than any mortal could go, the ground whipping below at a pace that threatened to leave Antony's stomach behind. Fortunately, he saw little of it; the thick clouds served as cover, hiding the faerie host that shot through the sky like a flight of arrows.

He rode pillion, his arms wrapped around Lune's waist, for the White Horse would not answer to any mortal's hand. Their mount unnerved him more than their speed, or their height in the sky. He had never been in Berkshire when the Horse left its hillside to feed, and while he knew the story, he had imagined—foolishly—

that it would be an ordinary white horse.

But at Wayland's call, the chalk lines had lifted free of the grass, and that was what they rode: an incomplete, elongated white figure, mottled with green, far larger than any natural horse, and far less substantial. How they even sat upon its back, his rational mind could not comprehend. His decades of association with the fae told him not to try. Antony gripped Lune, closed his eyes, and waited for their ride to end.

The cold dampness that chilled his skin like fog broke suddenly; the wind tried to tear his cloak from his neck. He opened his eyes to the sight of dark treetops rushing up far too fast, and choked back on a scream. They missed the branches by the barest hair and thudded to a halt in a field, sheltered from any eyes, with the rest of his company landing around him. Most of the horses they rode fell away, transforming back into ordinary straws. The remainder, and the black dogs that had run alongside them, took on their more or less human aspects.

A troop of horses, riding into London, would bring the Army and militia down on them like a hammer. From here, they would go their various ways by foot.

One of the mortals helped him down from the Horse's lofty back. Lune shifted, as if to touch him before he went, but then he was on the ground and out of reach. "Give us until sunrise," she said.

Antony nodded. He could not tithe bread to the fae and have it be of use, but the humans newly gathered to their cause could. For the first time in ages, they had enough to protect all their people.

He stood alone with the Queen, while their soldiers—such as they were—prepared to march. She spoke quietly, for his ears only, gazing down from the height of the Horse. "If there is one thing you have taught me," Lune told him, "it is patience. Should this not go as we hope—"

"Retreat, and try again." Sound advice—but Antony wanted to tear his skin off with impatience. The Onyx Hall called to him, awakening the craving he had fought these long years. Yet he dared not let himself believe they would succeed. If he did, and then they failed—

That will *kill me. I cannot survive such a fall.*

He was not sure Lune could, either. Physically, yes; but for all her talk of patience, she showed little of it herself. The Queen wore a man's riding habit, with armour to keep her safe, and looked very warlike upon her strange steed. Anger burned silver in her eyes. She was not the kind to endanger herself recklessly—but was she the kind to retreat?

Antony hoped so. "Sun and Moon keep you," he said, in lieu of the Christian benediction that had risen, unbidden, to his lips.

"And you," Lune said. A faint smile told him she wanted to bless him in his own manner—but even if it did not hurt her, the Horse would not take it kindly.

The great beast pawed at the turf, and she somehow patted a neck that was not entirely there. "Back to the sky, my friend."

It reared, which became a leap that carried it into the clouds. Lune's company was gone by then, continued on, but the Horse would catch up before long.

Bonecruncher approached him, eyes flaming in the bleak grey light. With his horns and claws, he could easily have been mistaken for a devil, and Antony's jaw tightened. "Why are you not masked? Do you want some passing farmer to see you and raise an alarm?"

Unconcerned, the barguest shrugged. "We was just checking where we are."

"About half a mile from Tyburn, that way." Antony pointed without looking.

Bonecruncher blinked. "How did you know?"

The goblin had lived in London longer than Antony had been alive, and yet was appallingly ignorant of everything outside the City walls. Antony shook his head. "Glamour yourself, and be on your way. We do not have much time."

THE TOWER OF LONDON
1 August 1659

Lune's company arced north of the City and approached from the east, where the pestered suburbs had not yet spread quite as thickly and as far. Landing in an open field between the Tower and the dockyards farther downriver, they quickly constructed their glamours and readied themselves to move on.

Riding the White Horse had been an impulsive decision, one designed purely to impress and therefore hearten their following. Now, within sight of London, Lune slid down and placed her hand on the figure's neck. "Irrith—will he return home on his own?"

The wild sprite considered it, then approached and pulled the enormous head down until she could whisper in his ear. The Horse whickered and stamped. Somehow, without any change the eye could catch, he shrank in upon himself, until he was no larger than an ordinary stallion. Irrith gave Lune an amused shrug. "I think he wants to stay. Perhaps he's as curious as I am, what this realm of yours is like."

"It is not a place for horses."

"I guessed as much, by the way you ride." Grinning, Irrith slapped the Horse's neck and beckoned her company onward.

Lune sighed, and found the white circle of the Horse's eye contemplating her inscrutably. *They say a wish made while standing in his eye comes true. Whatever fortune we have tonight, I am glad I did not try.*

They made for the nearby bank. An advance guard of river nymphs had gone ahead a few days before and secured enough skiffs for their group; once in, the boats floated steadily against the current, towed from below, in perfect silence up the Thames.

Ahead, London gleamed under a quarter moon. The pale light marked the upthrusting spires of the City's many churches, and the truncated tower of St Paul's Cathedral. The close-packed houses lay in shadow below. The beloved silhouette struck Lune like a blow to the gut, driving all the breath from her body. *I am home at last.*

She felt it in her bones, as well as her heart. Love and longing, for the place that was not just her realm but her home. Lune could not imagine retreating again.

And that meant they had to succeed. Tearing her gaze away from the City, Lune attended to the task at hand.

This was, for their group, the most dangerous passage. Once inside a fortified place, it was easy to seem as if one belonged there; gaining entrance was the trick. The fae huddled under their cloaks, scarcely breathing, as their boats drew up to the Tower's water gate. Men called it the Traitor's Gate, for the prisoners brought through it; Lune tried not to think of the name as an omen.

In the front skiff, a willowy asrai helped a boggart into the water, and supported him while he scowled at the chain holding the gate shut. He muttered a curse, and water splashed as the asrai covered his mouth; with such a force as theirs floating under the very toes of the guards, they dared not risk any noise that might break the tenuous charms keeping them hidden.

But the jingle of the chain was sweet music, and the quiet slosh of the gates swinging open.

Sir John Barkstead, lieutenant of the Tower, served the late Protectorate assiduously in his command, and maintained a watch alert enough to spot any intruders, however quiet. Therefore Antony had arranged for the Rump Parliament to dismiss the man, replacing him with one much less dedicated. For all that London was on tenterhooks, expecting a Royalist rising, the guard *inside* the Tower was lax, and the fae slipped easily through the courtyard precinct, heading for the White Tower.

Now Lune took the lead, for she was the only one who knew the way. Antony's men were coming into the City by circuitous routes, in twos and threes, and had less fear of attracting notice; her own force had to move quickly, lest their numbers break their concealment. And sunrise, Irrith breathed in her ear, was not far off.

They reached the old Norman keep at the heart of the fortress, and silent as ghosts slipped into the cellar. Its three rooms were crowded with stores—beer barrels here, gunpowder there—but no one had covered over the well that pocked the earthen floor. Water glimmered cold and clear in its depths.

Lune knelt at its edge, and set a dagger to her palm.

Three drops of blood fell into the water below. Each one sounded a deep note, like the tolling of an immense bronze bell, audible only to the ears that knew to listen for it. In Threadneedle Street, the well's rope could lower a knowledgeable traveller into a small antechamber; here, the stones shuddered and changed their configuration. The water drained away, leaving a black, dank pit, that had been here since before the Norman conqueror built his Tower. Dripping stones offered uneasy footholds, spiralling down its sides.

Irrith, waiting at her side, offered a malapert grin. "You've been in my home for years; I'm eager to see yours." And before Lune could say anything, the sprite was the first down the stairs.

THE ONYX HALL, LONDON
1 August 1659

"Stay in stealth as long as you can," Antony whispered to his men, scarcely more than breathing the words. "You will only get one chance at surprise. Make it count."

Bonecruncher's expression suggested he was only just restraining himself from snorting. They had been over this a dozen times and more. But they crouched now beneath the crumbling weight of St Paul's, and Antony found his nerves as hot as any green young man's, facing his first battle.

It is my first battle. Old man that I am.

Old he might be, but just standing here gave him strength. "And remember," he said, glaring down Bonecruncher's impatience. "Wound them only, if you can."

Cheerful words. Most of his supposed soldiers would be lucky to find their targets. He prayed surprise would be enough.

Now they moved with speed, slipping out of the chamber and through the Onyx Hall. Every Berkshire faerie or mortal was paired with a Londoner; Lune had drilled them on their paths, but it was easy for a stranger to become lost. Antony himself waited with Bonecruncher and a wispy, unarmed sprite named Dandelion.

A chill rippled down his bones, and he startled. "What?" Bonecruncher growled, glaring at him.

"Lune is here." The words came without need of his mind. Had he always been able to feel her presence? Perhaps—but only now, with his body starved of the Onyx Hall's touch, was he raw enough to notice it.

Bonecruncher took his revelation in stride. "Then let's get moving."

They were the last to leave, and went by the most secret route. Antony's target was the treasury. Vidar would have claimed its contents for himself, of course, but the chamber was the most protected location for keeping the enchanted objects that belonged to the Crown; they were hoping he had left things of use there.

But they could not move entirely by hidden passages, not from where they began. They had to traverse some of the same chambers used by the palace inhabitants. Antony had planned a course that took them through the Hall of Figures, a long, sunken gallery filled with statuary; it was not often frequented. But as they reached the top of the steps leading to its floor, Antony saw movement ahead.

Bonecruncher reacted before Antony could think. Down on one knee, and up came the weapon Wayland Smith had forged for this attack. One clawed hand on the barrel, one on the stock, flaming eyes squinted close—

A deafening crack broke against the walls, and an elfin voice screamed.

God be praised—he hit him.

Even that thought was a delay he could not afford. Antony drew one of the pistols from his belt, and for the second time in its long history, the Onyx Hall rang with the sound of a gun.

He missed; pistols were less accurate than the firelock musket Bonecruncher carried. But the guns Wayland had forged were as much instruments of terror as weapons; fae had seen them in mortal hands—occasionally even been shot by them—but to bring them into a faerie war was unthinkable innovation.

At least for Vidar, who scorned humanity and its works as beneath him.

Two fae had been conversing beneath a statue of a man beset by snakes. One fled. The other collapsed to the floor. Bonecruncher stopped long enough to tap him into unconsciousness, with enthusiasm that made Antony wince—but fae rarely died of wounds that did not kill them outright, and the guns fired elfshot instead of ordinary lead.

They had not even finished crossing the Hall of Figures when Antony heard more gunfire in the distance. He prayed the fae were conserving their shots; muskets and pistols were slow to load, and he had forgone lessons of speed in favour of teaching them to aim.

"Keep moving, m'lord," Bonecruncher growled. "Your war isn't over yet."

* * *

Some of Lune's courtiers had switched their allegiance to Vidar, when he invaded. Others joined her exiled court in Berkshire. Most of the remainder had gone elsewhere, giving up on this war entirely.

Half a dozen languished in cells beneath the White Tower, from which Antony had been unable to free them.

Lune's force—or rather Irrith's—subdued the guards without resorting to the firearms they carried. The six fae in the cells stumbled out, weak and blinking; Vidar had kept them in darkness and deprived of food and water, such as would kill any human kept thus.

But those long, black years had refined their hatred. Angrisla bared all her teeth, and gladly claimed the knife someone offered her. "I will bring him to you screaming," the mara promised.

"Stay with us," Lune ordered her. "The time for revenge will come."

The mara's obedience to that order would be dubious at best, but Lune had no one to spare for watching her, nor the others. The Tower squad split, each group to their particular task. The White Horse was long gone, cantering off on its own inscrutable exploration, but that might be all to the good; its presence would baffle Vidar's folk, spreading confusion they could use.

The sudden ring of blades announced the commencement of battle just outside the chamber Lune sought.

Trusting Irrith and her companions to hold the door, Lune laid a hand upon a floor stone that would lead them into a lower passage, bypassing the royal apartments, which Vidar had claimed for himself.

When her fingers touched marble, her vision blurred. Instead of the floor, she saw—

"Antony!" The name tore free of her. He was leaving the Hall of Figures, and behind him—she could not discern details, but three figures were approaching at speed, and they were not friendly.

She reacted without thinking. Antony passed through the double doors at the end of the hall, and she flung them shut behind him.

The wind of the doors ruffled his hair, it came so close, and the bronze panels almost swung shut on Dandelion, who leapt clear with a squeak. Bonecruncher whirled and raised his spent musket. "What—"

Shouts from behind them, on the other side of the doors. *"Move,"* Antony snapped, and they went on at a run, ducking sideways into a little-used passage.

His first thought was that Vidar had closed the doors. But why would the usurper act to protect Antony's group? By the pounding on the bronze, those on the other side were hostile, and trying to break through.

And who else would the Onyx Hall answer to but Lune? *Who else, indeed.*

Antony halted Bonecruncher with one hand on the barguest's shoulder. The other went to the carved corner post at his side.

He'd felt it before, almost as a man might hallucinate a missing limb, that the Onyx Hall was an extension of his body. Now he reached for the connection, and found it tenuous, almost gone: starved from lack of contact.

Like a man half-dead of thirst, he dove into the waiting pool, not letting himself wonder if he could swim. Antony immersed himself in the power of the faerie palace, and found himself—not *seeing,* for it was not a thing of the eyes. But he felt movement through the chambers and passages, and knew, if he concentrated, who stood in each chamber.

Or at least whether they fought for him, or against him.

Me. For or against me. *I am not this place…*

His sense of self threatened to dissolve into the vastness of the Hall. Bonecruncher's claws, digging into his neck, grounded him in his flesh; the barguest had gone for the most tender place not protected by armour. "My lord—"

Claws in his neck, and Lune. He felt *her* like a cool silver beacon, matching and balancing him. Antony's senses cleared. "Send to Pollikin," he said, opening his eyes. "There are fae—Red Branch knights, I think—waiting for him near the amphitheatre."

Bonecruncher stared.

"*Send it!*" Antony growled, and grabbed Dandelion. The sprite squeaked again, then fished in one of the cages at his belt. The moth he extracted fluttered on his fingertip as he whispered to it, then flew off with remarkable speed and purpose, to warn Pollikin of the ambush.

Irrith had assigned Sir Peregrin Thorne to be Lune's guide. Lost in her awareness of the Onyx Hall, Lune could barely see where she was going. But it didn't matter; she had found an unexpected weapon, and was using it to the fullest.

She could feel the fear from Vidar's people, especially the Irish and Scots, to whom this place had never been home. Now it rose up to fight them. Working in concert, she and Antony blocked the paths of the defending knights while opening the way for their own, and a veritable storm of moths snowed through the passages, carrying commands to the different groups. Someone on Vidar's side had set a salamander to hunt the moths, and half their messages were being crisped, but Lune and Antony both were almost to the great presence chamber, and they were winning.

Not without cost. The Red Branch knights were unsurpassed as warriors, and some of the invading force lay dead. The elfshot of the muskets and pistols had claimed few lives outright, but it tore flesh and cracked bone where it struck, and that was not always in the enemy. *We should have trained them longer.*

Her own group had grown to half a score, collecting other pairs that had split off and rejoined them. Now they were hurrying through the night garden, an incongruously bloody assembly among the quiet of the trees.

Up ahead, a narrow bridge arched gracefully over the dancing Walbrook—until a roar and a surging form shattered it into pieces.

Lune's heart sank at the sight of the creature waiting for them. *I hoped they would not have one...* The fuath were water spirits, and not fond of leaving their homes. But Vidar or Nicneven had compelled this one south, and now it blocked their path, tainting the brook with its foulness.

Irrith stared at the twisted alloy of goat and human shape. "What is *that*?"

Lune could not answer her. All her attention was lashed to the presence chamber, the heart of the Onyx Hall. Antony was almost at its doors, and if he got there without her...

"I must go," she murmured, barely hearing her own voice. "I cannot afford to delay—"

There were other paths across the Walbrook, but the fuath could move faster through the water than she could run. Irrith gripped the hilt of her sword more firmly and nodded to Angrisla. "We'll cut a path through, as quickly as we can."

Desperation clawed in Lune's gut. *That will take too long—*

She felt more than heard the approaching hoofbeats. Tearing herself free of Sir Peregrin's supporting arm, Lune threw her hand out and caught an insubstantial mane. With a wild twist of her body, she swung herself upward and over, and settled onto the back of the White Horse just as it gathered its hooves beneath and *leaped*.

The fuath roared and clawed upward, but the sudden rush of the Horse took it by surprise, and its claws caught nothing of the half-material body. Lune's teeth jarred together hard enough to break when they landed; then they were out of reach, past the Walbrook and running for the far entrance with terrifying speed.

Fortunately, the passage on the far side was a lofty one, suitable for the giants of the Onyx Court, and the White Horse crossed from soil to marble without missing a stride. With a wrench almost as physical as the one that put her on the Horse's back, Lune dragged her concentration inward, clearing her mind of all the rest of the palace. The presence chamber was just around the corner.

As was Antony. Lune slipped from the Horse's back at the corner, and the beast charged on without her. Whether it had any sense of what was going on, she couldn't say, but it took the doors of the presence chamber at a dead run and slammed them open with all the weight of a charging stallion backed by the hillside that was his bed. The panels came half off their hinges, leaving Lune and Antony a clear view into the chamber—and robbing them of any chance to prepare.

The invasion had taken Vidar by surprise. They knew that by how scattered his forces had been, dispersed around the Onyx Hall, and relatively easy targets for the fast-moving scouts of their two companies. But he was not stupid; he guessed who had come, and knew they would seek him out.

Fully half a dozen Red Branch knights waited in

gleaming array across the presence chamber floor. That much Lune saw, before they scattered like leaves in the face of the White Horse's charge. They were great charioteers, the stories said, but the Onyx Hall was no place for chariots, and they were *not* expecting cavalry.

Behind the knights, though, another figure stood his ground.

A fist like granite slammed into the side of the Horse's head, and *this* attack struck home. The Horse's scream sounded almost human. All its speed went abruptly sideways, the white lines of its body flying into one of the fluted black pillars that arcaded the chamber's sides.

Kentigern Nellt's answering growl shook the ceiling.

Lune had arrived at the doors with no allies save the White Horse. Antony had a bloodstained Bonecruncher and a Berkshire goblin. She bore the London Sword at her side, and had learned something of its use during her exile, but the four of them did not stand much chance against the giant.

She drew the blade anyway—and Antony stepped in front of her.

Antony moved to protect Lune without thinking, drawing his last remaining pistol and firing. The giant was coming for them, advancing like an earthquake across the floor; he thought his shot struck home, but Kentigern did not so much as stumble. The Red Branch knights were recovering. Four against seven, and those four outmatched; their allies would not reach them in time. They had overreached themselves, and now would pay the price. Even if they retreated, the battered doors would not hold Kentigern for more than a heartbeat.

The Onyx Hall had moved in their defence when they bade it.

How far does that go?

Antony spun, reaching for the hilt of the London Sword. He got Lune's hand and the pommel, and forced the tip down. Throwing the full weight of his body behind the strike, he stabbed the blade downward, into the floor.

Whether it was intuition or the rapport they shared through the Onyx Hall did not matter. Lune joined his motion as smoothly as water, and when the Sword pierced the marble, they gave the command together.

With no more warning than that, the ceiling of the presence chamber gave way.

The collapse felt like it snapped Lune's own spine. Her scream and Antony's were lost in the deafening thunder, until the dust cut them off. Choking and blind with agony, she fought to control what they had unleashed. The rain of stone stopped just short of where the two of them knelt, still gripping the Sword, but it was long moments before she felt safe to pry her hand loose from the hilt and ease the shoulder wrenched by that downward strike.

The Sword stayed upright, wedged between cracked blocks of marble. Antony had released it, too, but he remained on his knees, gasping for breath.

In front of Lune, the dust was slowly settling. The main weight of rock had fallen, as they intended, on Kentigern Nellt; of the giant she could see nothing, just an unmoving mass of stone. But some of the fragments had caught the Red Branch knights, who lay broken and stunned along the edges of what had been the presence chamber.

Beyond them, she could just make out, through the dust, the silver shape of her throne.

It was empty.

She flung her senses outward, through the reaches of the Onyx Hall. Irrith and the others had defeated the fuath; Amadea's group had secured the royal apartments; one by one, she identified the pieces of her army and her enemy's, but nowhere in all those chambers and halls did she find the presence she sought.

The invasion had taken Vidar by surprise. Knowing they would seek him out, he had gathered what forces he could to this chamber...

...and then fled.

Bonecruncher was making sure the downed knights would stay down. Irrith entered just in time to catch Lune as she sagged. "Your Majesty!"

Extricating herself from the Onyx Hall hurt, and left in its wake a roaring abyss of exhaustion. Speaking took all Lune had. "Vidar—fled. Chase him. Secure others. Take c—" Her knees gave out completely, and Irrith shouted for help. "Take care of Antony."

For while she had searched in vain for Vidar, the Prince of the Stone had slumped to the floor, where he lay as pale and drained as a corpse.

THE ONYX HALL, LONDON
1 August 1659

"Her Majesty is not to be disturbed."

Amadea's calm declaration angered Irrith far more than the lady deserved. "What *happened* to her?"

The chamberlain adopted the discreet, infuriatingly polite expression that so many of the London court hid behind, instead of wearing their feelings plainly. "She is tired, nothing more."

"I've *seen* tired. That? Was something more." The Queen was pale by nature, but she had been white as snow when she collapsed. And that mortal of hers... Irrith was surprised he wasn't dead already.

She clearly wasn't getting past Amadea, who had placed herself at the door to the royal bedchamber like a silk-clad guard dog. Irrith took careful hold of her temper and said, "When she wakes, please let me know. Bonecruncher and I have things we must ask her about."

All she got was a nod—not even a promise. *These damned London fae,* Irrith thought. *Now that they're home again, they would be glad for Wayland's people to vanish.*

Scowling, she went out into the corridor—and promptly

got lost. The moment the battles were over, her mind had discarded its map of the Onyx Hall, as if it wouldn't be needed anymore. The place was stifling to Irrith, capped with stone everywhere she turned, and she kept thinking about the mortals who walked not far above her head. She wanted to go up and see the City, but she had nothing to protect herself, and Lune had made it abundantly clear how dangerous it was to go around showing her true face.

Besides, she wasn't sure how to get out.

Her wanderings took her at last into an area she recognised. Irrith had been here twice, first when they launched the invasion, then again when she and others helped Bonecruncher herd their prisoners into the cells beneath the Tower of London. A black-haired elfknight glared wordlessly at her through the grate in his cell door, and she shivered. What Lune was going to do with these captives, she had no idea. Murdering them all seemed a bit excessive—but then, so was keeping them locked away for eternity.

That one giant might just grieve himself to death, in the cell he practically filled on his own. *Which would save the Queen some trouble.*

The dungeon was too gloomy. Irrith wandered with determination, forging on despite her complete loss of direction, passing goblins and pucks and courtiers, none of them her own people, none of them with particularly friendly faces. When Lune awoke, Irrith decided, she would hand over what she knew about the prisoners, then ask for a bite of bread to get her home. Once clear of the City, she wouldn't need to worry about mortal charms against fae—and she belonged back in the Vale.

She turned a corner and found herself confronted with a pair of nearly identical brownies hauling a basket almost as big as they were. "Good day," one of them gasped out, smiling through her breathlessness. "Would you be a dear and help us carry this? To the garden, I should think—"

"To start with," the other one agreed. "We can unpack it there and have people take things where they're needed. Come along; it isn't that heavy, just too large for us—there's a darling. You're stronger than you look! Oh, you have it all, how *wonderful*. Follow us now; you look a bit lost. From Berkshire, are you?"

Bemused, and not entirely sure how she ended up bent beneath their basket like a snail, Irrith followed the two curly heads toward the garden, wondering who they were.

THE ONYX HALL, LONDON
3 August 1659

Bolsters and pillows propped Lune up like an oversized doll, allowing her what semblance of dignity was possible when Gertrude was spoon-feeding her beef broth. She tried to ignore the childlike helplessness of her condition while she listened to Irrith's report.

The Berkshire sprite had trailed in behind the Goodemeades like a duckling picked up by two mother hens, scant minutes after Lune awoke. Some intuition of the brownies' must have sent them her way at the right moment, for she was ravenous, despite crippling weakness that made eating a herculean task.

Amadea wanted her duties to wait, and the sisters agreed with her. But Lune could not delay; already she had lain unconscious for two days, and only thanked fate that her enemies had not staged some counterattack while she was incapacitated.

She owed thanks to Irrith and Bonecruncher, who had brought things admirably under control. Some of the Irish and Scots had escaped, but the traitor courtiers were imprisoned, and they were the ones who worried Lune the most—aside from Vidar, who had slipped their grasp.

"There are two asking to see you," Irrith finished. "An elf-knight and a giant, uh—"

"Sir Cerenel and Sir Prigurd," Rosamund supplied, when Irrith floundered for names. "Sir Prigurd is begging your mercy."

The beef broth churned uneasily in Lune's stomach at the memory of his betrayal. Or perhaps not; the cause might be her own handling of Cerenel.

Prigurd would have to wait. She had to appear strong when she faced him. Cerenel, perhaps, should also wait—but that was expediency talking, not honour. She had already kept him too long.

Even Irrith argued against that one, but Lune insisted; in the end, they gave in because it was the quickest way to get her to rest. Then there was the question of who would be present for that audience. Lune wished it to be private, but she had to admit she did not trust what Cerenel's response would be. And if he turned against her, she would be helpless.

Not the Goodemeades. Neither of them was a warrior, and she had endured too much of their silent disapproval over the oath she forced on the knight. She chose Irrith instead, who cared little about Onyx Court politics, and would be going back to Berkshire soon. "Keep behind the arras," Lune said, "and as silent as you can. You are for security only, in case all should come to the worst."

Irrith, to her credit, asked no questions. And when she was concealed, even Lune could not tell she was there. Soon Sir Peregrin Thorne escorted the prisoner knight into the chamber, bowed, and exited.

Leaving Lune in private with the one fae she had wronged most in all this war.

He was thinner than he had been—or perhaps it was just his manner that made him seem raw and hard. He stood like a hooded falcon, blindly obedient, but capable of murder if unleashed.

"Sir Cerenel," Lune said, putting what strength she could into her voice. "In ancient Mab's name, I release you from your oath."

He jerked in surprise. She had framed a number of speeches to preface the declaration, during the long minutes while she waited for him to be brought, but in the end it was nothing more than fear. If he felt any charity toward her still, then he would wait and hear what she had to say, even once unbound. If he did not, then all the prologues in the world would not change that.

His eyes burned violet as his chin came up, as if her words had loosed the chains that held his fury in check. She saw his lips part, his balance shift, as if he almost spoke, almost moved. But it seemed he had no words, and did not know what he wanted to do. She took advantage of his hesitation to speak on.

"You served your penance to me when first I sent you to Fife. Returning you there was a decision of politics, not honour. You were the tool I had to hand, and therefore I used you. Speaking as Queen, I do not apologise; had you not gone, I might not have learned the Lord of Shadows' identity, and suffered all the worse for my ignorance. But speaking as a private individual—I have wronged you, and forced your loyalty too far."

Cerenel found a voice at last, strained and unmelodic. "Yes. You have."

Lune concealed the pity she felt; he would only perceive it as an insult. "Your position in the Onyx Guard is restored to you, do you wish it. Moreover, I will grant you a boon of your choosing—reparation for the service you have done. You have but to name it."

The knight stood motionless, head bowed, black locks falling forward in disarray. Finally, meeting her eye once more, he said, "I wish only to leave this place, and make my home elsewhere."

Sorrow gripped her heart. *Be honest—you hoped the*

handsomeness of your apology would reconcile him to you, and make all well again.

But some hurts cannot be undone so easily.

"You are free to go," Lune said. Despite herself, a waver marred the words. "Wait but a moment without: I will have someone bring your possessions, and enough bread to see you safely on your road."

His body stiffened, as if he almost bowed and stopped himself. Silently, he turned and left the chamber.

Lune closed her eyes and let her head sag back against a pillow. Exhaustion had drained her to the bone once more, but she could not rest *quite* yet. "Irrith?"

The faintest of rustles told her the watching sprite had stepped out. "Yes?"

"Please give Sir Peregrin my command. And when you have done that…"

She was not a private individual. She was the Queen, and must do what was necessary.

"Tell the Goodemeades to have one of their birds follow Sir Cerenel. I must know where he goes."

THE ONYX HALL, LONDON
7 August 1659

Irrith did not have to ask where to find Lune, when the Irish ambassador sent her in search. The Queen still rested for long hours each day, and spent most of her waking time handling the myriad of tasks involved in rebuilding her court, but when she couldn't be found in her chambers or public rooms, she was invariably in one other place.

The guards let the sprite through into Lord Antony's chamber. The furnishings had been ravaged during the occupation; the hobs of the court had swept out the detritus and brought in a new bed, but it was still one of the only furnishings in the room.

The bed, and the chair beside it, where Lune sat like an alabaster statue. "I beg your pardon," Irrith said softly, regretting the interruption, "but Lady Feidelm sent me with word."

One slender finger lifted, indicating she should continue.

"She has word from Temair. They found the sword—the *Claíomh Solais*—and King Conchobar is in a great deal of trouble for it." Feidelm had used an earthier phrase, but the fine manners of this court were beginning to curb Irrith's tongue.

Besides, vulgarity seemed out of place in this room. The Prince of the Stone lay unmoving beneath the coverlet, as he had for the last week. Breathing was the only motion Irrith had seen from him in all that time, and even that was barely discernible. He might as well have been dead.

Nearly everyone behaved as if he already was. The courtiers arrayed themselves into complicated factions, and several groups were grooming candidates for Lord Antony's successor, mostly from the mortals who participated in the battle.

Lune spoke, and it took Irrith a moment to realise she

was not responding to Feidelm's news. "I do not know what to do for him."

Irrith blinked. Conchobar—no, Antony. What response could she make to that? "Age happens. Mortals tire of life. Their flesh breaks down."

"It is more than age." Lune moved at last, leaning forward to straighten the pristine counterpane over the Prince's body. "Neither of us had ever called on the Onyx Hall so intensely. It has drained him, as it drained me."

But the Queen was an immortal faerie, and could survive what killed a human—especially an old one. *She doesn't want to admit that she must let him go.* "Perhaps..." Irrith began hesitantly. *How to make it clear—without being unforgivably rude?* "Perhaps what he needs is to be among his own kind. Away from all of this."

It would no doubt kill him, but that would be kinder than this living death. And Lune's eyes widened, as if Irrith had lit a candle in the dark room of her thoughts.

"He is lost," she whispered, hands hovering in the air. Then she stood in one swift motion, showing more vitality than Irrith had seen in her since the invasion. "Go find the Goodemeades. They will know where Antony's wife is. Have someone bring her to London—we'll move Antony to his house." Lune dismissed those words with a sharp cut of her hand. "No, his house is gone. We will arrange for another. *But find Lady Ware.*"

* * *

369

ST MARTIN'S LANE, LONDON
10 August 1659

Jack Ellin reached for Sir Antony's wrist, less out of need than a desire to be *doing* something. The unsmiling woman who lived in this house had forbidden him to feed the unconscious baronet any medications; she was sterner than Lady Ware.

He did not actually believe she lived here. Anne Montrose, as she called herself, didn't show any of the comfortable familiarity that characterised a woman in her home. But Jack was familiar enough with conspiracy not to question it. The woman wanted Sir Antony to recover—despite her orders regarding his treatment—and that was enough to make her Jack's friend for now.

Mistress Montrose stood sentinel in the corner, hands clasped across the hard front of her bodice. Her steady, grey-eyed gaze made Jack uncomfortable: another reason to attend to Sir Antony. He picked up a basin, wet a cloth, and used it to dribble more water into the man's mouth. How long he had been in this coma was another thing no one would tell him, along with how the baronet came to be in this condition to begin with.

Footfalls on the staircase, the frantic steps of a woman who couldn't clear her skirts enough to take them two at a time, as a man would. Jack rose from his chair just in time to get out of Lady Ware's way.

She drank in the sight for long moments, while Jack held

his peace. He'd endured enough letters from her over the last few weeks, demanding to know where her husband was, that he understood how much it meant for her merely to see him. Only when that need was filled did she begin to *see,* to take in the slack limbs, the grey-tinged skin, the dry, cracked lips.

Then, right on cue, came the anger.

She whirled on Jack first. "What has happened to him?"

He nodded at Mistress Montrose. *I would lay odds Lady Ware did not even notice her.* "This good woman brought him to me, as you see him now."

After dealing with that uncommunicative presence for the last day, Jack took a certain pleasure in unleashing Antony's wife on her. "What have you done to him?"

Katherine Ware needed no watching, except insofar as she might employ her claws; Jack kept his attention on the stranger. He therefore caught the brief tightening about her eyes. *Guilt? I do believe so.*

It went no further than that fleeting sign, though. Mistress Montrose answered, in a quiet, unremarkable tone that nonetheless checked the lady's incipient harangue. "If you act quickly, you may yet be able to gain the answers you seek from your husband. I sent for you, Lady Ware, because Antony needs you. Indeed, you may be the only one who can help him."

Which piqued Jack's curiosity enough that he almost overlooked her unadorned use of Sir Antony's Christian name. *Physicking now; questions later.* "I don't know what ails him," he admitted, coming forward a step. "He's been weakening for as long as I have known him; now, his body seems stronger, and yet…"

"His mind is lost, I fear." Mistress Montrose also left her post, holding up one delicate hand to forestall Katherine Ware's frightened response. "I do not mean madness. I mean that he has gone far away, and what it needs is for someone to call him back. This is something no physician can do for him. You have been the foundation of his life, the means by which he keeps himself grounded in this world; you, I believe, have the capacity to bring him back to himself."

Katherine looked unwillingly down at the motionless body on the bed, as if she could scarcely believe it belonged to a living man. "How?"

The other woman shook her head. "I do not know. Your instincts, not mine, must guide us now."

Lady Ware's hand descended slowly, then took Sir Antony's limp fingers into her own. Her other hand clutched the air behind her until Jack realised she was reaching for the chair; he pushed it forward, and she sank down beside the bed. "Antony," she whispered, hesitant but determined, "I am here."

They withdrew from the room, granting the two some privacy. Jack looked in from time to time, bringing wine to wet Katherine's throat when her voice began to flag. But he was not above discreet eavesdropping, and through the door he heard her speaking of anything that came to hand, from their children to politics. *This world*, Mistress Montrose had said. Another wife might have read to Sir

Antony from the Bible, but they did not want him thinking of God and Heaven—not if the goal was to keep him here. It was not, perhaps, the best course of action for his soul, but Jack didn't fault her tactics.

Except they produced no change. Sir Antony's body lived, but his spirit might as well have departed it for another realm. Jack was there when Katherine looked up at their hostess and said, ragged and despairing, "I do not think he hears me."

The grey eyes regarded her, and Jack was more sure than ever that they hid a wealth of thought and feeling. Who was this woman, to whom Antony was important enough to save—and yet Jack had never heard her name? He understood that the baronet had other allies, but he couldn't fit this one into any position he knew, and that bothered him.

As did the words she spoke at last. "He must be called by a human voice. What distinguishes humanity from the soulless beasts of the field?"

"Love," Kate whispered. "But I have said it a dozen times, and he does not hear."

"Then don't *say* it," Jack said. A strange, unspoken communion of urgency breathed among the three of them, in this candlelit room, with the noise of the St Martin's Lane tenements distant and faint. *We all want him back. We refuse to lose him in such fashion.*

He knelt at the side of the bed, taking Antony's other hand. Discarding the delicate touch of before, he gripped the unresisting fingers, hard enough to feel the bones beneath. *A friend may love, as well.* Capturing Kate's gaze, he said, "Speak to him by means other than words."

Understanding sparked. Bending over her husband, Kate took his face in her hands, cupping the line of his jaw, brushing his thinning hair back with one gentle thumb. The devotion in her eyes was uncomfortable to see; such things were meant for private display alone. Jack felt like an unwelcome spy. But he held fast to Antony's hand, and stayed as Kate lowered her head and kissed her sleeping husband.

Time might have stopped. Or perhaps it was only Jack's breathing, held tight in his chest, for fear of shattering something fragile. Kate pulled back at last, and whispered her husband's name.

Antony's eyes fluttered open.

His pupils were wide and drowning, his gaze unfocused. Then it sharpened, and Antony seemed to be looking past the two of them, to the figure that stood at the foot of his bed.

But when Jack turned to see, Mistress Montrose had vanished.

ST MARTIN'S LANE. LONDON
11 August 1659

Kate held her peace while Jack Ellin fed Antony beef broth, while he rose and walked a shaking circuit of the room, while he drifted into the embrace of true sleep, restorative as his previous stupor had not been.

But when he woke in the small hours before dawn, she still sat in the chair, and in the light of the one candle he saw the questions she had suppressed for so many years.

His wife, noticing he was awake, poured him a cup of wine and helped him drink. Red wine and beef broth—meat as soon as he could manage it—for Jack had told him in no uncertain terms that he needed to strengthen his blood. At least he was spared any foul-tasting potions.

When he was done, Kate set the cup aside and asked, very controlled, "Who is she?"

"A friend," Antony said. *What else can I call her, that will not open a Pandora's box of trouble?* Once he had been certain that God had placed the fae in the world to show humanity what they might be, without their immortal souls and the salvation of Christ. Capable of both great good and great evil, but lacking a guiding star by which to steer their choices. That certainty, like so many others, was long gone. And in its absence, he did not honestly know if he could explain his association, to Kate or anyone else, in a fashion that would render it into sense.

Kate's expression hid in the shadows of her face, fragmented and unreadable. "How long have you... known her?"

The brief but telling hesitation wounded him. "She and I have served the same cause for years. Since before the wars." A dangerous admission; the face Lune had showed here was young. But Antony was loathe to tangle himself in more lies.

"And what cause is that?"

Antony flinched. What could he tell her, to ease the pain she held behind those walls? "Kate..." He reached out and took her hands. "The Sealed Knot serves Charles abroad. They operate in secrecy, working underhand to achieve a restoration of stability for this land, and it is not for those who aid it to speak openly to others. The woman who was here... she is part of another group, one that has existed longer, and for a simpler purpose: the well-being of England. When Charles declared his personal rule, they worked for the calling of a new Parliament. When Parliament arrogated royal authority for itself, they struggled to restore the ancient balance. And now that the Army stands over England with a naked blade, they do as we do: they seek the sanity this land has lost."

His fingers tightened on hers. "And I swear to you, in the name of the Lord God and His most holy Son, that she does not hold my heart—nor I hers. You are the only one for me, Kate, and I have ever been your faithful husband."

Her chin hardened, a sure sign that she strove to keep her lips from trembling. "Faithful to me in body—perhaps even in heart. But this woman, this Mistress Montrose... you have given her a piece of yourself withheld from me. I have not even been permitted to know it was gone."

He had known it for years: Kate hated secrets above all. By keeping this one, he had betrayed her trust.

All he could offer her now was his own truth, simple and insufficient as it was. "I am sorry."

She stared at him, and then the hardened jaw gave way; Kate buried her face in his shoulder, tears soaking through his linen shirt to chill the skin below. Antony held her close, laid his lips on the kiss-curls at the back of her neck. *Forgive me, Kate.*

He would not say it. Forgiveness was not his to ask.

"I almost lost you," she whispered.

His arms tightened around her shaking body. "I know. I—I fought so hard for my cause that I almost lost hold of my purpose, my reasons for fighting. I was so tired... it would have been easier to let go."

She came up, then, and gripped him hard. "Do not say that. If it is rest you need, then you shall have it—if I must carry you out of England to find it."

How long had it been since he laughed? Kate knew as well as he that such exile would be the end of him, not because of the Onyx Hall, but because he could not abandon London. But he believed with all his heart that she would throw him over one shoulder and drag him bodily onto a ship if she thought it necessary. His Kate was a fierce one.

"I love you," he said, tucking an errant strand of her hair behind her ear.

"And I you," she replied.

She did not need to say she forgave him. The message was there, unspoken. And with that, Antony could truly rest.

* * *

THE ONYX HALL, LONDON
13 August 1659

From Lune's elevation on the dais, the greater presence chamber was a sorry sight. The rubble of the ceiling lay in piles beneath the arcaded galleries along the sides, and raw earth showed above. The intricately laid patterns of the floor were cracked almost into gravel, and stained with Sir Kentigern's blood.

Nor was the damage confined here. Bedchambers had been ransacked, and gardens despoiled. The obelisk in the night garden was shattered, the apple trees burnt—but some force in the Onyx Hall, still loyal to its former master, held firm; the soil had refused to yield up Michael Deven's bones to desecrating hands. That one salvation, amidst all the destruction, reduced Lune to tears.

They came so close to destroying it.

Not just his grave, and not just the palace. With the help of her allies, she had saved the Onyx Hall—but what of the Onyx Court?

The battered, broken remnants of that stood before her as well. Looking out over them, Lune could not delude herself into thinking she had won some great victory. At best, she had regained the ground she held ten years ago: mistress of her realm, still threatened by enemies without. But along the way she had lost friends, power, and the Kingdom of England itself.

Vidar had escaped. Nicneven sat untouched in Fife.

Conchobar was in check, facing the wrath of Temair, but that was small consolation for the wounds inflicted on this court. Her people were fragmented now, divided from one another, no longer the unbroken fabric she had once believed them to be.

But that had always been an illusion. Traitors lived all this time amongst them, and their betrayal had torn rents that would be years in the mending.

Their common purpose had united them long enough to retake the palace. But it did not make them whole.

What can?

"Stand," Lune said, and her voice carried like a bell.

Her subjects rose. There, the surviving remnant of the loyal Onyx Guard, under Sir Peregrin Thorne's command. Clustered around one of the fractured pillars, the Berkshire fae. A glowering clump of goblins, Bonecruncher's followers—she would have to watch them carefully. They had tasted blood, and wanted more.

Lune curled her fingers around the arms of her throne and spoke. "We shall address three matters today.

"First: the succession of the Prince of the Stone." Several fae shifted at her words; a few had the temerity to look eager. Lune wielded her contempt like a whip. "Those who have eagerly anticipated Lord Antony's death shall be disappointed to hear that he yet lives. Let me make myself clear: those carrion crows who think to profit when he passes shall find *no favour* in this court. The Prince is no pawn to be manipulated by those seeking advantage. When the time comes for a successor, he and I will choose that man ourselves—or I alone, should he be gone. *None other.*"

Some looked abashed. Not all. They would continue to place humans in her path, hoping one would catch her eye. The prospect curdled her stomach. She was determined to take none of their candidates, when the time came.

How soon that would be depended on Antony.

"Second," Lune said, when the last whispering echo had faded from the chamber. "We shall hear a plea from the traitor Prigurd Nellt."

The doors were still warped and unusable. Prigurd simply appeared in the opening, flanked by Bonecruncher and an escort of tough goblins. She had to send them; the Onyx Guard, betrayed almost as badly as Lune herself, might have chosen to expiate their failure by murdering its architect.

The giant advanced slowly, hobbled by rowan-wood chains that gave him barely enough freedom to shuffle his feet. No strength could break those chains, not even his. They were one of the less pleasant objects Vidar had brought out from the treasury for his own use—things Lune had ignored for years, to her detriment.

When he fell to his knees, the graceless impact shook the floor.

Lune gazed pitilessly down upon his head. "You are a condemned traitor to your Queen. For years, you worked to undermine the Onyx Guard by bringing in disloyal knights at the behest of your exiled brother Kentigern. Your betrayal led to the deaths of our loyal subjects, both mortal and fae." Of this, everyone was aware; but the litany of his sins stoked their anger, against the pitiful sight of his bowed shoulders. "Why should we grant you mercy?"

His voice was a broken rumble, audibly wracked with guilt. "Your Majesty—I helped you escape."

Her eyebrows rose in surprise. "You claim so? Had we not slipped your grasp in King Street, we would have been prisoners from the execution onward. Later, by order of the traitor Ifarren Vidar, you were marching our person and that of Lord Antony to the cells beneath the Tower. Were it not for Benjamin Hipley's intervention, you would have carried out that order. *Wouldn't you?*"

Prigurd's shoulders jerked, and the chain binding his wrists rattled. He shrank even further into himself. "Y—Your Grace remembers the execution. I was there. I was protected. When Hipley started singing… it didn't hurt me at all."

It was so unexpected, Lune's anger faltered. Was he telling the truth? She remembered the psalm washing over her, deflected by the tithe.

Which *all* of them had eaten, before going to Westminster. Not Essain and Mellehan, who did not accompany them—but Prigurd had.

She should have noticed the incongruity. Had she been thinking at all clearly that day, she would have. But with the death of the King ringing in her bones and Vidar upon her throne, such lesser considerations had fled her mind. And later, when she had more leisure, she had not given it a second thought.

Yet why should he have carried out such a ruse?

Irritation sparked, irrationally. She had granted him this audience believing she knew what path she would follow. Now, thanks to his revelation, she could not condemn him out of hand—however much she wanted to. Having chosen to hear him publicly, she had to ask him the question all her subjects, like her, wanted answered. "Why?"

Prigurd's head rose just a hair, then dragged itself farther down. Had he tried to look her in the face, she would have ordered him to drop his gaze, and he knew it. He had lost the right to behave so familiarly. "I wanted to be loyal, your Majesty."

If that was supposed to excite mercy, it failed; her rage recovered from its stumble. Rising from her throne, Lune spat, *"Then why did you betray me to Vidar?"*

"Because of Kentigern." The anguished whisper, tearing from the giant's great chest, still carried through the hall. "Majesty—he was my *brother*. He asked it of me, he—he told me we owed it to Halgresta—he was all the family I had left!"

She did not want to pity him. Prigurd was an *idiot,* a blind fool, too easily led by others; she should never have given him command of the Onyx Guard. But the mistake was of her own creation: she had always known him to be the only one of the three Nellt siblings moved by true duty and loyalty.

Which bound him from two directions. His sister dead, his brother exiled, Prigurd must have felt his failure keenly. And Kentigern—less cunning than Halgresta, but just as vicious, and utterly without principles—had used that to manipulate Prigurd into betraying his Queen on behalf of his kin.

An error Prigurd had tried, in his pathetic way, to remedy.

Lune gestured sharply at Bonecruncher. "During the retaking of the Hall—what did the traitor do?"

The barguest pointed one hooked claw at a fetch in his group. "He brought the giant in. Said he found him hiding in his chambers."

"I didn't fight," Prigurd insisted.

"Silence!" Lune's shoulders ached with tension. Kneeling humbly, awaiting judgement, Prigurd infuriated her, because now she had to decide what to do with him. A mortal could be imprisoned, to be let out when old, or left there until dead; Lune had no such luxury with her immortal subjects. Locking him back in the dungeon would only postpone the problem.

Unless, of course, the Onyx Guard murdered him in his cell. Which was entirely possible.

I must execute him myself, or send him away; he cannot stay here. And if she killed him, it would annihilate any chance of healing the breach in her court. No one could expect mercy from her then. If exiled, though, he would be a ready pawn for her enemies.

Once, this court had possessed a gem that could bind anyone, faerie or mortal, to a specified ban, bringing death to those who broke it. And for one sick, horrifying instant, Lune wished she still had it to hand.

She turned to hide her face from the watching fae, and seated herself once more upon the throne when she had mastered her wrenching repugnance. *Must this be my fate? By ruling London, am I doomed to become like Invidiana?*

It must not be. "Prigurd Nellt," she said, coldly calm once more. "Do you abjure Ifarren Vidar, Nicneven of Fife, Conchobar of Ulster, and all their allies?"

The giant raised his gaze as far as the hem of her skirts and placed one massive fist over his heart. "Your Majesty—I will never again oppose you, the Prince, or the Onyx Court. I will take no action against you, and I will keep no secret that might threaten you. I will never again raise my hand against you or any of your subjects. This I swear, in ancient Mab's name."

Her heart beat painfully in her breast. An oath had not been her intent—not after Cerenel. She had some idea of how to frighten Prigurd sufficiently to keep him away from her opponents. And a vow so broad... his choice of terms was nothing short of asinine. It rendered him as useless *to* her as he was *against* her.

But bound in such manner, she could release him without fear.

Sun and Moon. Were my courtiers bound half so stringently, I need never again fear rebellion from within.

Another sickening thought. Parliament and the Army had tried that course, demanding varied and repeated oaths from members of the puppet Commons and other officials. The result had been to cheapen them into mere words. She would not risk the same here.

She had to reply. Lune gathered her wits and said, "We accept and recognise your vow. Despite it, however, your face is an unwelcome reminder of your treachery, and the price this court has paid for it. We therefore exile you from London and its environs, not to come within one day's journey, on pain of imprisonment and further punishment. Go now, and let us not look upon you again."

Prigurd's breath caught. Slowly, awkwardly, he bowed until his face almost touched the floor. Then he stumbled to his feet and stood, broken-shouldered, while Bonecruncher unlocked his chains. No one spoke a word as he turned and made his way from the chamber, steps dragging, and out the shattered doors.

When he was gone, Lune said, "And now to our third matter."

Every eye was upon her as she formed the words, enunciating them with razor-edged precision. *"Bring me Ifarren Vidar."*

ST MARTIN'S LANE, LONDON
14 August 1659

"You should have waited for me," Antony said.

"I could not." Lune wore a different guise today, a younger version of the stern woman he had accompanied to the King's execution. Whether she wished not to show the

Montrose face again, or was thinking back to that terrible day, he could not guess. "I must return the court to order as quickly as I can, and that means addressing such matters."

Impatience flared at the edges of his temper. That was good, in its way; he had the vigour to feel impatient. Owing, at least in part, to the vast meal he was currently gulping down. He had gone to church that morning, for the first time in far too long, and thanked God for the gift of his life—and the wife who had preserved it. "I am not so far away. You could have sent a messenger for me."

The faerie woman shook her head. "No. You must stay above, and re-establish your roots in this world."

There was a grotesque irony in her words: that, having wasted halfway to death because he was too long outside the Onyx Hall, he should nearly have killed himself by flinging his spirit so deeply into its embrace. In his waking moments, Antony could remember little of what he felt after pulling the ceiling down, but it returned to haunt him in dreams.

Compared to that, the world of this small house was gloriously solid and bright. "But I cannot stay here forever; I *must* come below again, and soon."

Lune hesitated. He wished she would show her true face; masked by humanity, she was harder for him to read. "Antony... do you wish to?"

"What?" He put down the pheasant bone he had just torn half clean. "Wish to stay here, or to come below?"

"To be free of us."

She spoke the words with an abruptness that could only

be born of inner turmoil forcibly chained. Staring, Antony fumbled for a napkin and wiped his fingers clean, then rose from his chair. "Lune…"

He got no further than her name; he was not sure what to say. She lifted her chin and went on. "I do not know if it's possible. But we could try. Your bond to my world has almost killed you, more than once, and I know it has almost cost you your marriage. I never meant for this to bring you pain, but it *has*. I would spare you more, if I can."

To be free of Faerie… he could not think what to feel about that. *I have been with them two-thirds of my life.* The realm beneath his feet was as much a part of his world as the one he stood in now.

But perhaps he was not so much of *her* world. "You have no more use for me, then."

"No!" Lune reined herself in, but that unguarded cry rang in his ears. "If anything, *we* are of no use to *you*."

The conversation was stumbling further and further from reason. "No use? How can you say that?"

She laughed bitterly. "What have we done for you, for your world, that you can say has bettered it? I do not mean the distant past. Since the start of these struggles, we have been leaves in a flood, deluding ourselves that we control where the torrent will carry us.

"When England was a Queen and her court, we—the fae—had some chance of steering a course. But England is grown too big for us; its concerns are grown too many. It is a hydra with a thousand heads. Parliament is the heart of this land now, speaking in contradictory voices, and I cannot control it by any honourable means."

The words stung like wasps. Antony had never heard Lune like this, scourging herself with her failures. He could not say she was wrong in the substance of it—but what provoked her to such self-recrimination?

Me. I have done it. He saw it in the way her gaze fixed on him. Her world had nearly destroyed him, and the guilt of that tore deeply into her.

No other fae he knew would care so much, with the possible exception of the Goodemeades. It was the love of a friend, such as her kind were scarcely capable of, at least for *his* kind.

And it blinded her. "You may be right," he said quietly, and did something he had not done for years; he took her by the arms, fingers curling into the cambric that draped her shoulders. "The whole of England is too much for us alone. We cannot control it, any more than Charles could, or John Pym, or even Oliver Cromwell. But we can help, as any of her loyal people do, for love of their home. There are smaller moments, and there is London; you should not give up on those. Certainly I will not."

Was it accident or conscious choice that altered her eyes? When she looked up at him, they shone silver—Lune's eyes in a mortal's face. And her voice, saying, "You wish to stay?"

"I do," Antony confirmed. Even if the enchantment of his bond released him, he would not abandon her. "And together we will do what we can, however small or great."

THE ONYX HALL, LONDON
25 October 1659

Hasty work had converted Sir Mellehan's former chamber over to an armoury, while its previous occupant enjoyed the hospitality of the dungeon. Racks held the shining brass of the muskets and pistols Wayland Smith forged for Lune and Antony's army—locked away for the time being, except for those few Sir Peregrin permitted to trusted hands.

"We can provide you with means to carry these back to Berkshire," Lune said to the sprite who stood near the door.

She heard Irrith's weight shift. "That won't be necessary, madam. He's *Wayland Smith*. He makes things; he doesn't keep them."

Lune suppressed a smile at the awkward manner of Irrith's address. The wild faerie was learning courtesy, but did not yet use it well.

Keeping the firearms made her uneasy, but she recognised that sending them back to Wayland would not solve anything. Over time, the fae adopted any mortal thing that interested them; sooner or later, *someone* would have picked up a gun. And she might need them again.

She took her hand from a musket stock and faced Irrith. "You may tell your King that I am looking into the fulfilment of my promise. The Army has dissolved Parliament—"

"*Again?*" said Irrith in disgust. She was learning mortal history, too, and found it inexplicable.

"Again. But I think it shall not last for long. Without

the Rump, the Army has nothing to legitimate itself save the sword; we shall have new war or a new Parliament before long. Either way, they have greater concerns than the maintenance of your Horse, but there are other means of achieving it. The people are tired of having Puritan morality imposed on them from without."

The Horse had gone back to its hillside; Lune wondered if Irrith would follow suit. The sprite asked endless questions about the mortals of London, but passing fancies were common among fae. She might not return.

Concealing her disappointment at that thought, Lune said, "And please also convey to your King what I have said regarding Vidar. I will reward handsomely anyone who brings word of him to me."

The delicate face broke into a fierce smile. "I should not like to be your enemy, madam. I'll carry your message, and search for Vidar myself."

THE ROYAL EXCHANGE, LONDON
5 December 1659

Throwing roof tiles and chunks of filthy ice had seemed like a good idea at the time. London's apprentices had presented a petition to the City's Common Council; they wanted a new Parliamentary election, or at least the return of the Rump ejected in October. When Dendy showed up to post a proclamation from the Army's so-called

Committee of Safety, outlawing petitions, it didn't take much encouragement from the handful of disguised pucks and goblins among them to provoke the apprentices into standing up for their demands. And the sergeant-at-arms, ducking the missiles, had withdrawn with his men.

But now a regiment had come, with horsemen to back them up. It didn't stop the apprentices; a knot of them descended upon one unfortunate soldier not wise enough to keep up with his fellows, and disarmed him by force. Antony could not get through the crowd to them as they kicked the man to the ground outside the Royal Exchange.

And what could he do, if he did? Tell them he was an alderman of London? The Court of Aldermen was not in high esteem at the moment, though Antony had been working since his restoration to better that. He might join the soldier on the ground.

The regiment's commander was going to carry out the duty Dendy had failed at, come the forces of Hell itself. Ignoring insults from the crowd and the football some of the apprentices were kicking about, disregarding—or perhaps oblivious to—the fate of his soldier, Hewson was reading out the proclamation in a determined bellow.

And then someone threw a stone.

Antony didn't see where the first one came from. He saw some of those following, though, as other apprentices took up the idea and began to pelt the soldiers with anything that came to hand. The shopkeepers of the Exchange had long since cleared away, but there was rubbish aplenty, and some of the apprentices had strong arms.

This goes too far. He craned his neck and caught the eye of a starveling beggar child on the roof, crouching on the shadowed balcony of the clock tower; the puck gestured helplessly in response. Fae were much better at sowing chaos than stopping it. *Christ. I've started a riot—just as Vidar used to.*

Then the child shrieked a warning, his thin voice unintelligible over the clamour.

Antony cupped one hand to his ear, uselessly. The child was waving his arms wildly. *What does he—*

A shot shattered the air, deafening in the confines of the courtyard. Someone screamed. Antony ducked, instinctively sheltering behind the brawny apprentice in front of him.

God help us all. The soldiers were firing on the crowd.

The mass of bodies became a flood of rats, battling their way toward the arch that led to the street. Antony was buffeted from all sides, stumbling, keeping his feet only because to fall was to die, in this madness. Out onto Cornhill; he went with the current, which took him left, toward Gracechurch Street. All around him, apprentices split off into alleys and byways; he kept on straight, thinking vaguely to lose himself in the Leadenhall Market up ahead, and to hide among the patrons there—should the soldiers follow so far.

But it seemed no one was pursuing them. Antony staggered to a halt at the entrance to Leadenhall, air rasping in his lungs, and bent nearly double with coughing. One of the young men had followed his same path, and put a hand on his shoulder. "Careful, old man."

Spasm ended, Antony forced himself upright. "I am perfectly—"

He choked on the last word and nearly started coughing again.

If a soldier had ridden by and poleaxed Henry in passing, Antony's son could not have looked more stunned. "Father?"

The boy sounded disbelieving, as well he might. Antony was dressed to blend in with the apprentices; the Court of Aldermen would need to believe they were telling the truth when they promised the Army they had nothing to do with the riot. Henry's face settled into sardonic lines. "I didn't know you fought for the good old cause."

Antony almost laughed. Good old cause? Henry was scarcely old enough to remember the days when that phrase had been coined, and he was hardly an Army man, to talk of fighting for it. "The Commonwealth? Not hardly—nor the Rump, neither. I'd fight for my seat in Parliament back, if I thought it might do any good. But since it will not, I side with your apprentice friends: our soldier-masters should at least arrange a new and free election."

What possessed him to say it, he did not know. Even supposing he wanted to break their tradition of never discussing politics, the entrance to Leadenhall was hardly the place to do it. But Henry had caught him off guard.

Predictably, his son's expression turned mutinous. "Of course you wish your old place. You and your friends would vote for the restoration of the monarchy before the opening prayers were done."

Henry had no sense of discretion—but then neither did he, it seemed. They were far too public. Antony took his son by the arm and dragged him, protesting, around the corner of the market, into a narrow alley reeking of piss. After years of skulking about London, hiding from Vidar and Cromwell alike, he knew all the hidden byways.

"Do not speak so openly," he growled at his eldest, voice echoing off the overhanging jetties of the houses. "Unless you wish me disbarred from the aldermen again, and perhaps imprisoned."

"You've created that danger yourself," Henry said, jerking free. "Why, Father? I once thought you too wise to have a romantic view of the past, yet you cling to it more with every passing year."

"Romance?" This time, Antony *did* laugh. "Say rather 'cold-eyed practicality'. A body cannot live without its head."

Henry scowled, at the words or the laughter, perhaps both. "It has lived so far. And what if that head be diseased? For the love of God—*you* remember that man of blood."

More Army phrases from his son's lips. Did Henry realise how much he parroted them? Antony doubted it. Henry was a Commonwealth man, to the bone. He hated the Army, but did not see how it was the only force propping up the Rump—and then only when it chose. "I remember a great deal more than King Charles. At least in those days, we knew the tools in our hands; we knew the ways in which King, Lords, and Commons could be made to balance one another. If at times we failed, at least the ground we fought on was familiar."

How old had Henry been, when Charles fled London? Not even breeched. He did not remember a world in which that pattern held true. He had never known a King on the throne.

Nor did he wish to, by the contempt on his face. "So you would hold fast to what you know, for fear of anything different."

"If the men peddling difference had any plan," Antony said, answering contempt with contempt, "I might see it differently. But ask yourself: when was the last time you heard someone argue for a republic, *and* provide a notion of how to create it? I do not mean some Utopian dream of government; I mean a practical, practicable scheme for getting from here to there."

Hot-headed Henry might be, but he had a brain. He opened his mouth, but when he found no answer inside, shut it again. The Commonwealthsmen kept believing that success lay simply in finding the right design for England's government; they did not see the obstacles along the way. So long as that was true, they would only tear the realm down again and again, and never build anything stable in its place.

"Give us time," Henry said at last.

Antony shook his head. "There *is* no more time. The hunt for that dream has let in a wolf worse than the one killed ten years ago. Do you know the Protectorate sold Englishmen into slavery in Barbados? Do you know how many men have been imprisoned without proper trials? *I* do not; God Himself might not be able to count them."

"But the monarchy—"

"Is what the people want."

"Then the people are *fools*," Henry cried, full of young fury. "Blind, damnable fools, who do not see what they are asking for!"

The wall behind Antony was filthy with coal smoke, but his doublet was of no consequence; he leaned against the surface and crossed his arms. "Then you must make a choice," he said flatly. "A republic is guided by the will of its people, is it not? And the people want the world they had before. They may be fools, but if you stand by your principles, then you must support a new election and accept its consequences. Your only alternative is oligarchy, under the false name of republic."

His declaration carried a certain necessary cruelty. Henry called the people of England blind, but so was he, in his own way. And Antony could not let his son blunder onward, ignorant of the tangled, bloody truth. Change was coming. Henry must be prepared.

The question was whether, having laid his own sympathies out so plainly, he had lost his eldest son.

Henry was floundering for words. Antony decided to play one final card. "General Monck is moving in support of Parliament. If the Army does not comply, there's a good chance he will bring his troops down from Scotland and ensure a Parliament free from their control. Paradoxical, yes, that military force should free us from military force—but he is possibly the only honest leader the Army has. This much, I think, we can agree on: that a free Parliament must be England's next step."

The step after it might be indeed restoration of the monarchy. Antony hoped so. It was to that end that he and Lune worked now, not controlling, simply helping the people where they could. The same people Henry railed against just a moment ago. But principles won out over ideals; Henry nodded, reluctantly. The right of the people to elect their representatives was his paramount concern.

"Then come," Antony said, reaching for his son. "This alley stinks, and I am hungry. We shall have supper together."

THE ONYX HALL, LONDON
9 February 1660

A shiver ran down Lune's body. She broke off what she was saying mid-word and closed her eyes, reaching for the source of that reaction. Something in the Onyx Hall...

No. Not in; above.

"Lord Valentin," she said, and heard him murmur in reply. "Send someone into London. Find out what is happening at the gates."

"Which gates, madam?"

Another shiver, like bones grinding in their sockets. "All of them."

She opened her eyes to find Sir Peregrin regarding her with a strange mixture of reverence and disturbance. A faerie monarch was tied to her realm, but not until the retaking of the Onyx Hall had her subjects realised how far that went here. They seemed to fear she would drop the ceiling on them, next.

She could not do it without the Prince of the Stone; though she could sense things when she tried, the Hall only answered to its master and mistress in concert. But there was no profit in explaining that.

"Carry on," she told the captain, as if the interruption had never happened.

He blinked, re-gathering the scattered threads of his thoughts. "We have found no sign of Vidar in England, madam. Your cousin Kings and Queens would not give him refuge after Invidiana's downfall; they are no more likely to do so now."

"And Ireland?"

Peregrin shrugged helplessly. "He is not in Temair, nor in Connacht, Lady Feidelm tells us. Leinster and Munster claim they do not harbour him, and I see no reason to doubt them."

"And Ulster," Lune sighed, "is not likely to answer if we ask."

"No, madam."

She brooded over the fan she held, trying to weigh her enemy's mind. Would he flee to Ireland? Conchobar was disappointed with Vidar's failure to control the English government, but the traitor lord was still a closer ally to Ulster than Lune would ever be. Then again, Conchobar was busy with his own troubles over the *Claíomh Solais*.

Her heart told her Vidar was not in Ireland. No, he would crawl back to the same hole from which he had emerged to devil them before.

Fife.

To which Cerenel had returned, after Lune released him from his vow. His brother Cunobel was there, living in relative peace, separate from all the squabbles between Nicneven and herself. Lune wished them well, with sorrow. *Cerenel is no resource I can call upon. Not anymore.*

Which left her with no intelligence on Nicneven's movements, and what Vidar might be planning.

Blind again. Have I won nothing for all my struggles?

Valentin Aspell returned, giving her some small relief from that question. "What of the treasury?" she asked him; as Lord Keeper, it was his province.

"There has never been a thorough inventory, madam," he admitted. "What Vidar may have taken, we cannot tell; but we are finding a great deal we did not know we had."

Vidar had once been Lord Keeper himself. He would know precisely what to take. "Anything that may hunt him?"

She watched Valentin's face sharply as he formed an expression of regret. Aspell had been in the company of the late Sir Leslic, but more, she believed, out of a desire to protect his own political influence than because he had any alliance with Nicneven and Vidar. He had drifted away during the exile, rather than stay under Vidar's rule. But he was greedy, and ambitious; Lune wondered, as he denied having found any such enchantment, whether he would tell her the truth.

I should have councillors I can trust.

But she could not afford to replace him. Lune listened to his account of the things he had found, then made arrangements with Sir Peregrin to hear pleas from other traitors who were tired of their cells. "But not until I may arrange a joint audience with Lord Antony," she said, remembering at the last moment that the Prince wished to be a part of it.

The captain of the Onyx Guard nodded, and then her usher opened the door to the privy chamber where they sat. "Your Majesty, the mara Angrisla."

"I sent her above," Valentin said, and Lune gestured for the usher to show her in.

The nightmare's narrow, slitted eyes were uncommonly wide as she knelt. "What have you discovered?" Lune asked.

"Your Grace—those soldiers are in the streets. The new ones, from Scotland."

"General Monck's regiments." Largely English, as their general was, but everyone thought of them as the Scottish troops, as that was where they had marched from. The news of his advance south had been threat enough to put the Rump back into session just after Christmas, but after a mere six days in London, it seemed Monck's men were already interfering. *They are, after all, part of the Army. Did I expect otherwise?*

Angrisla nodded at the name. "They say Parliament has

ordered them to unhinge and destroy the gates."

"What?" Lune startled in her chair. London had long since grown past its defences; during the war, Parliamentary forces had dug a great ditch some distance out, in recognition of the wall's uselessness. To destroy the gates, though, meant rendering the City incapable of even the slightest resistance.

Which must be why they had ordered it. People wanted a Parliament, but they were tired of the Rump. In the City especially, they were not well disposed toward England's illegitimate masters, and had thrown up chains at the gates to announce their discord.

She was surprised that Monck would agree to cripple them thus; as a rule, he seemed honestly concerned with defending the liberties of the people, and not merely mouthing the words. But she was more concerned with its effect on the Onyx Hall—

Lune's breath stopped. Could it be Vidar? It did not take a clever mind to know the City wall was part of the faerie palace, since the Hall did not extend beyond that boundary. And Monck had marched down from Scotland. Lune pressed her fingertips into her eyes, striving to sense any weakening in the enchantments.

"Madam?" Sir Peregrin asked quietly.

Lune sighed. *Or perhaps Monck simply is obedient to the Parliament he restored. Not everything has a faerie cause. And I could easily drive myself mad, looking for one.*

She lowered her hands and found everyone watching

her. Whatever Angrisla had said in response to her startled cry, she had not heard a word of it. The Onyx Hall was not crumbling around her ears, though, and showed no sign of doing so anytime soon. They were opening the gates, nothing more. That would not destroy the palace.

Still, she would ask Antony about Monck's decision. If there *was* some hidden influence there, she would like to know about it.

"Thank you," she said to Angrisla, and made herself smile. "The news startled me, nothing more. Carry on, my lords; we have business to conclude."

GUILDHALL, LONDON
11 February 1660

So this is the man in whose hands England now rests.

George Monck did not look remarkable enough for the burden of fate that lay upon him. The general of the Army's regiments in Scotland dressed as a soldier, and his fleshy face was stolid as he listened to Thomas Alleyn, the Lord Mayor of London, belabour the obvious. "Given the recent unsettlements of the City, you understand, the people are most uncertain as to your intent—the soldiers gathering in Finsbury Fields—"

Monck bore it with patience, but eventually held up one hand. "Lord Mayor, I assure you, my intentions are as they have always been: to protect the liberties of the people. I've sent a letter this morning to Parliament, requesting them to issue with all possible speed writs to fill the vacancies in the House. By this, I hope to dispel the impression that they intend their sitting to be perpetual."

Had Antony's heart been pounding less heavily, he might have snorted. Impression? No, it was a certainty: the Rump had no desire to give way, and let go of the power currently in their hands. It was the same disease that had gutted the Army, seducing the officers to aggrandise themselves, until their own soldiers abandoned them.

The general *had* to know that, or he would not be here. Monck had never been a political man, unlike his Army brethren Ireton and Cromwell; only the greatest distress at England's situation had persuaded him to take action. Yet everyone seemed reluctant to condemn the Rump outright, as if speaking would make its faults real.

Hence the pounding of Antony's heart. He felt as if he held a butterfly in the cage of his hands. If he could but persuade Monck...

He cleared his throat, and all eyes snapped to him. Betraying nothing of his inner tension, Antony said, "Promises to fill the vacant seats go only so far—especially when the Rump may pass whatever restrictions they like on who may elect, and who be elected. They have done it before, sir."

Monck said mildly, "If those are the laws Parliament passes, then so be it."

Frustration welled in Antony's throat. Monck had gotten this far by moving one careful step at a time; were he less attentive to practicalities, he might have been checked in Scotland by his own disloyal officers. But the general put his own house in order before moving south, and had held to that pattern ever since, addressing concerns as they arose.

It was a strength, but also a weakness. When looking to the future, his vision stopped at next week. "Please allow me to remind you that they have set no date for their own dissolution, nor do they seem likely to do so. What else is that but a perpetual Parliament? We must have a *succession* of Parliaments, as is meant to be."

"And so I have advised them," Monck agreed.

"But what if they ignore it? They are not representative, sir; they are the remnant left after the greatest affront to privilege and liberty this realm has ever seen." Antony looked not just to Monck now, but to the Lord Mayor and his fellow aldermen—some of them victims of similar interference in the government of London. "The *only* legitimate authority in this land is that elected twenty years ago: the full Parliament, such as has not perished in the interim."

By the finer points of law, it had never gone away. Back in Pym's day, they had manoeuvred Charles into signing an Act that Parliament could not be dissolved save by its own will. From the original purge to Cromwell's ejection of the Rump at the start of the Protectorate, through the myriad of upheavals since then, that longest of Parliaments had, in legal terms, never ended.

Monck folded his hands on the table before him. "You mean the readmission of the secluded members."

"Forgive me, Sir Antony," Alleyn broke in, "but it seems to me that you speak in your own self-interest—as you were one of those purged."

"I speak in the interests of England," Antony said, glaring at the Lord Mayor. "Unless you wish to argue that the Army had the rightful authority to force us out, then you must admit that seat is mine by law—for the laws barring me from it were passed *after* my seclusion. And if you wish to argue in the Army's favour, then by all means, say so."

Alleyn flushed and mumbled something unintelligible, but clearly negative. Enough men in the room had bristled at the mention of the Army that only a madman would have tried to argue Antony's point.

Addressing Monck once more, Antony said, "Sir, I beg you. You are Parliament's support—not the Rump, but the freely elected Commons of England. You have said so many times. Use your influence to return us to our places, and you shall have the succession of Parliaments you seek. But I tell you with certainty: the Rump will never vote for the end of their own power."

He held the man's gaze with every word he spoke, and prayed as he did so. Antony had come so very close to asking Lune for aid; a few well-crafted dreams would be enough to sway the man's sympathies to their side. But Monck had resisted tearing down the gates and trespassing on the rights of the City; though he had finally given in on those matters, his patience with the Rump was already near its end. He must make his decision freely, not constrained by faerie magic. Nothing else would be honest.

And honesty, as much as monarchy, must be restored in England.

"I will consider what you have said, Sir Antony," the general told him. With that, Antony had to be content. But he saw doubt in the man's eyes.

It may take him some days yet—but we have him.

ST STEPHEN'S CHAPEL, WESTMINSTER
21 February 1660

Applause and cheers greeted the line of men as one of Monck's captains led the way through the lobby of the Commons. Whether those watching were petitioners with business for the House, or whether news had gotten out of Monck's plan, Antony could not guess; he, with the others, had been gathered since well before dawn at the general's chambers in Whitehall. But either way, the onlookers roared their approval as the secluded members marched through.

It had the feel of a triumphal procession. Prynne wore a basket-hilted sword that looked as old as he, and waved vigorously at men he knew, until the sheathed blade tangled the legs of Sir William Waller behind him, and he had to attend to its management.

Dodging Waller's stumble, Thomas Soame grinned at Antony and said, "The place seems smaller than I remember."

"That's because we scarce have room to breathe." Up

ahead, the soldiers had stopped at the bar to the House: a nice observation of propriety. The secluded members filed past them and found the chamber empty. "Do you think they know we are coming?"

"The Rumpers? I hope not. Bit of a surprise for them when they find out, and I confess feeling some glee at the thought."

Hesilrige at least knew; he and his minions had an unpleasant surprise when they came to call on Monck that morning. But as current members began to trickle in and found their old companions in their seats, their reactions were more than sufficient to entertain Soame.

Antony left his friend to enjoy their discomfiture, and settled more agreeably into his seat. Monck might delude himself that they had come to establish England once more as a commonwealth; at the very least he struggled to avoid war. In that latter, Antony would be more than happy to oblige him. But the time had come for a return to the old constitution.

The House of Commons. The House of Lords. And the King upon his throne.

England would be a kingdom once more.

THE ONYX HALL, LONDON
19 April 1660

Convincing all her ladies to leave her in peace took some effort. Some had been with Lune in exile, and some had not, but to a lady, they were all determined to behave as if no disruption had ever occurred—which meant they stuck to her like burrs, as if sheer intensity of service could make up for long deprivation. She had to speak quite sharply before the last of them understood that when she said she wished to be alone, she meant true solitude.

With that achieved at last, she sat in one of her antechambers, hands playing over the keyboard of her virginals. She had no skill at the instrument: no expression such as mortals could evoke, no faerie entrancement, not even physical expertise. But it was new to her, and the challenge was diverting.

Enough so that when the door opened, unheralded, letting Antony into the chamber, she offered him an easy smile. He held a folded sheet in one hand—no small scrap of paper, but fine vellum, sealed with wax. Lune could not see the impression from where she sat, but a ribbon dangled from the seal; it was something formal. "What is that?"

"A letter I fear will damage your good spirits," he said, extending it to her. "From Nicneven."

The vellum perched loosely on her slack hand as Lune stared at him, taken utterly by surprise. Not *once* since her accession had the Queen of Fife deigned to communicate directly. Why now? And why did Antony have it?

"As to the second," he said when she asked him, "it is because I found Valentin Aspell pacing outside your door, trying to devise a means of presenting it to you that would not result in him running for his life. I offered to hazard myself instead. But for why she has written to you—we must read it to know."

She did not *want* to know; she wanted to throw the letter in the fire unread. Instead Lune settled into a chair by the hearth and cracked the seal with her thumb.

The missive was addressed to Lune alone, but that was no surprise; Nicneven would hardly wish to acknowledge a mortal as her co-ruler. She turned so Antony could read it with her, from the chair he pulled to her side. The script inside was sharp and unadorned, and its message unmistakably clear.

"Heaven and earth," Antony said. "He is not in Fife?"

For his betrayal of our trust and goodwill, we lay claim to the life of Ifarren Vidar. Should you or any of your court apprehend him, surrender him to us at once, or we shall once more make war upon your realm, and destroy it utterly.

A breathless laugh escaped Lune, born more of disbelief than amusement. "It would appear not. And for good reason."

During the long years in Berkshire, they had tried to encourage Nicneven's disaffection with Vidar. It seemed she no longer needed prompting. Vidar was not in Fife; he had squandered any goodwill there by his failure in London.

Then where *was* he?

Antony sat back in his chair and raised his eyebrows. "Well, that is a weight off your shoulders, I should imagine. Let the Gyre-Carling dispose of him."

"She must find him first," Lune murmured.

The Prince knew her too well; he gave her a curious look, leaning forward once more. "You do not seem pleased."

409

Lune folded the letter carefully, along the original lines. The seal was too battered now to make out—presuming it was Nicneven's at all. Did the Gyre-Carling often send letters? Or had she borrowed someone's seal, in an attempt to follow civilised standards? "It is blackmail, Antony."

"But it would buy the security you have sought all this time."

"Would it?" The words came out sharp. "Nicneven despises this place. She will not cease just because I help her kill Vidar. But that is not the point, Antony: the point is the threat itself."

He paused, then said, "You do not wish to be seen bowing to it. I understand. But no one knows of it save us two. Aspell did not read the letter. If Vidar were found quietly, and sent north—"

"You do *not* understand." Lune rose from her chair in an angry burst, the letter crumpling in her hand. "She threatens *my realm*. Not myself, not my subjects; the Onyx Hall itself. The very foundation of my sovereignty. If I bow to that—" Even speaking the words made her bones shiver. It was the same instability she had felt when they cut the head from Charles in King Street, the tremor that preceded the earthquake.

"If I bow to that," Lune repeated, almost too faintly for herself to hear, "then I will be Queen no more."

Antony shifted behind her, uneasy. "How so?"

She shook her head. "I—Sun and Moon. I cannot explain it, but I *feel* it. Beyond question. I know I ceded the palace to Vidar when I fled, but that was not the same..."

Her breath caught. Lune swallowed painfully. "It would be as if, in his trial, Charles had renounced the divine, in order to spare his life. Or no—that is not it at all—" Frustration closed off her throat. She had never been a philosopher, to seek out the reasons for faerie customs, much less to explain them to others. "I do not have the words. But if I allow Nicneven to use my realm to force me to my knees, I will *lose* that realm. Likely to her."

Lune turned and found Antony now standing as well, confused and worried in equal measure. "We must find him first," she said, her determination hardening with every word. "Find him first, and dispose of him quietly, so that he cannot threaten us again. And if Nicneven does not like it—then we shall answer her as befits a Queen." And she flung the letter into the fire.

LONDON
29 May 1660

The City had burst into bloom, the warm spring sun calling out all the colours and gaiety the long, cold winter had suppressed—a winter that had, in some senses, lasted for more than ten years. Everyone wore their brightest, and banners hung from every jetty and balcony along the processional route. The fountains in the streets ran with wine. The roar was deafening, but above it all, trumpets rang out in brazen triumph as the procession made its way up London Bridge.

At the heart of all the pageantry was a tall, smiling man, his black hair hanging in thick curls past his shoulders, receiving with benevolent goodwill all the accolades of the City his father had fled nearly twenty years before. Antony knew well that Charles Stuart, second of that name, had no particular illusions about the circumstances of his restoration, but he was willing to accept the fiction thus offered. Indeed, the King laughed that it must be his own fault that had kept him away, for everyone so clearly desired his return. These smiles and jests were the bandages that would hold England's wounds closed—to heal in time, they hoped.

"God save the King!" echoed from every window, when not long before those same voices had sworn never to accept a single person at the head of their state, be he King or Lord Protector. But here came this merry man, thirty years old today, with splendid display the likes of which had not been seen since Puritan rule began, and it was excuse enough for rejoicing. The trouble could come later.

Tears prickled in Antony's eyes. So little of it made sense! The struggle now ended was not the one they had begun so long ago. The issues that troubled men back then were all but forgotten now. Few concerned themselves anymore about the Anglican episcopacy, or ship money, or control of the militia; though the New Model Army was far more dangerous a weapon, Parliament had ceded it to the King without a quibble. Half the names that led the fight twenty years ago were dead now, or retired from the field of political battle. After so many wars and risings, the restoration of the monarchy was achieved not by arms, but by a few simple votes in the Commons.

It was the greatest of all ironies. Old Charles had rightly disputed Bradshaw at his trial, when the lawyer tried to call him "elected King"; a sovereign was not chosen by the people, as if he were a member of Parliament. Yet this celebration today was a triumph for those who held that sovereign power arose from below, rather than being bestowed from above; though the people of England had not chosen their King, they had chosen to *have* a King. All the divine right in the world had not brought young Charles home, until his people willed it.

Henry might be right. Charles the Second was a dissolute man, given to wenching and drinking, and he might be a bad king. Riding with his fellow aldermen in the bright May sun, Antony could not guess what the future would bring.

But for today at least, he refused to worry about the future. Today, the King enjoyed his own again, and England was at peace.

Tuesday 4 September 1666

THE BATTLE FOR ST PAUL'S

"The stones of Paul's flew like granados, the melting lead running down the streets in a stream, and the very pavements glowing with fiery redness, so as no horse nor man was able to tread on them; and the demolition had stopped all the passages, so that no help could be applied, the eastern wind still more impetuously driving the flames forward. Nothing but the almighty power of God was able to stop them, for vain was the help of man."

JOHN EVELYN
DIARY, 4 SEPTEMBER

All through the night the Dragon has prepared, nurturing the power stolen from below, and as dawn breaks it begins its attack.

The fall of the Bow Bells heralds the onslaught. The inferno roars up the southern streets from Soper Lane to Old Change, crushing the church of St Mary-le-Bow in its maw. The great bells, emblem of London's soul, toll their last against the hard ground. East and west, all down the broad lane, Cheapside burns.

The precious works of the goldsmiths have been stolen away to safety, but other treasures cannot be moved. The Dragon strikes fast at the Standard, disabling the water conduit, further crippling the City's defence. The Mermaid Tavern of story and song crumbles into cinders and ash.

In the narrow lanes to the north, where the houses stand so close together their jettied upper floors almost touch, the people flee like rats. Some drag beds, makeshift litters for those who cannot move themselves. Upon one, a mother clutches her infant daughter to her breast, baptised not two days ago at the church that now burns so fierce.

Had the defences been ready, Cheapside might have stayed the beast; the broadest street in the City offers a natural place to stand. But those who have fought for two days straight now falter in their weariness, and what might have been a bulwark instead becomes a highway.

Riding the wind, the Dragon flies westward, into the Newgate Shambles, and beyond.

THE ONYX HALL, LONDON
eight o'clock in the morning

Jack winced as Lune pulled a deerskin glove over the ruin of her left hand. He knew a bad burn could render flesh insensate, but all his medical instincts screamed at him to prevent the damage she would do by continuing to use the injured limb. *It will putrefy and fall off...*

But fae were proof against such infections, and Lune had work to do. As did he.

"The wall," she said, flexing her fingers to settle the glove. "Soon the Dragon will reach it—at Aldersgate first, I expect. We can make a defence there."

They spoke in her council chamber, surrounded by half a dozen others with knowledge of warfare, from the barguest Bonecruncher to the noble Captain of the Onyx Guard. To a man—*to a faerie, rather*—they stood straight and proud, unbowed for the first time since the Cailleach's cold wind began to blow. The Dragon had drawn power from the

Onyx Hall, but the fire Jack and Lune had transmuted gave new strength to the fae. And, it seemed to Jack, united them in a common purpose: they were more than ready to fight.

Yet dispatching them to the City wall could hardly accomplish much. "We haven't enough people to cover the entire wall," Jack said, "and even if you defend the gates—what can you do that the human defenders cannot? They're bringing in sailors and dockhands, with gunpowder to blow up houses and make firebreaks." Samuel Pepys might have suggested it with the protection of the Naval Office in mind, eastward in Seething Lane, but it would be useful elsewhere, too.

Lune smiled faintly. That strange fire still burned in her, too, though she was no longer the eldritch creature he had kissed. *And I still cannot believe I did that.*

"We will not be at the wall," she said, either oblivious to or ignoring his flush. "Not outside. As above, so below: we can strengthen it from here."

Several of their lieutenants looked puzzled, but Jack followed her meaning. The wall was one of the physical anchors of the Onyx Hall—though not, thank God and whatever powers the faeries honoured, one that afforded access into the palace. Because this place reflected the land above in twisted fashion, its edges were not those of the City; Jack's head hurt, trying to trace the path the wall followed through the chambers and galleries.

Judging by the orders Lune gave, she traced it without having to think. It would be a strange defence indeed, fae stringing themselves in a tortuous line through the palace, but she seemed to believe it would hold. Or was that merely the confidence one played when one's subjects needed to hear it?

He didn't think so. There was a serenity in her now, despite the paired dangers that threatened them; it had been there ever since the kiss. She seemed to float an inch above the ground, though he had looked and found her shoes firmly planted.

Jack himself did not feel so serene. Not with the words currently burning a hole in his throat, waiting for the right moment to be spoken.

There is *no right moment*. There were wrong moments, though, and included in their number any moment in which they were not private. The court's advisers knew Nicneven wanted Vidar, but no more. Lune would not thank him for revealing the rest publicly. And while he didn't need Lune's thanks, he *did* need her to listen.

So he waited while Lune gave her orders, and when she turned to instruct the nightmare Angrisla about a final group on the surface, he spoke in an undertone to Amadea. "Please see to it that we are not disturbed. I have a matter I must address with the Queen."

The Lady Chamberlain raised her eyebrows, but curtsied in acceptance. She left on Angrisla's heels, and the instant the door swung closed, Jack began. "I'm still new to my title, so forgive me if I misunderstand. But I'm here to speak for the good of London's mortals, am I not?"

"You are," Lune agreed.

"As I thought. Then on their behalf, I say this: *you must negotiate.*"

Lune's gloved hand curled into a claw, and she held it against her breast as if the shattered nerves pained her. Were she a mortal woman, he would be a monster for demanding anything of her; she deserved quiet rest, and relief from the burdens she bore. But she was a faerie woman, and moreover a Queen. She would find no rest while her realm was in danger.

Jack spoke with deliberate bluntness. "Half the City is burnt already. With the strength the Dragon stole from this place, it bids fair to burn the other half by day's end. The men above slow it in any way they can, but the wind is driving the flames onward like a fleet of fire-ships, and carrying them over every break we create. If there's to be anything left standing next week, then the Cailleach *must* be stopped. And that means you must reach some terms with Nicneven."

Her lips thinned into a pale line. Lune had been here, trapped in the freezing chambers of the Onyx Hall, while he fought the Fire above; he suspected she didn't understand the extent of the destruction there. Oh, she could trace it, through her bond with the palace—but she had not *seen* it. It was easy to forget what one had not seen.

Lune clenched her jaw, then said, "You would have me give in to her?"

"Did I say that? Negotiation is not agreement. Send for

the ambassador," Jack said. "Tell him—oh, whatever you have to, even if it's a lie. Pretend you're willing to consider the Gyre-Carling's demands. Even if it buys us nothing more than a temporary reprieve, that may be enough to save the City."

"I have *asked* for a reprieve, and been spurned."

"That was a reprieve for London," Jack reminded her. "I'm talking about a truce. Promise them something, but on the condition that the Cailleach ceases her assault while they send word to Nicneven in Fife. That will give us— how fast can fae travel? Surely at least a week. Enough time to—"

He broke off, because Lune's eyes had gone very wide. "What?"

She stood silent for a moment, then said, "Not a week."

"What?"

"To send to Nicneven. Because she is not in Fife."

Jack blinked. "Why not?"

"The Cailleach." Lune spoke with more vitality now, no longer sheltering her hand. "She would not answer to anyone less than a Queen. If the Hag is not attacking us from Scotland—and I do not believe she is—then Nicneven must be near, to bid her begin and end her assault."

"Then she would be with the Scots outside the City, I presume," Jack said. "What do you intend—a knife between her ribs?"

Lune shuddered, recoiling from him. "No! Sun and Moon—that would prove Vidar right indeed, that I have

422

become Invidiana's echo. No, but if I sent word, demanded to speak to her face to face…"

Invidiana. He'd heard that name before, regarding the days before Lune's rule. If Jack was to be of any use in the negotiations—if he was to have any chance of persuading Lune to end this conflict for good—he would have to learn more about that, and fast. "Will Nicneven come?"

"I believe she will," Lune said. "And if I am right, it will gain us some time."

"To fight the Dragon."

Her answering smile was fierce. "To kill it."

FLEET STREET, LONDON
ten o'clock in the morning

"I don't think it's working!" Irrith screamed at Angrisla, and the mara snarled in reply.

The tower of St Paul's stood veiled in smoke, a rare island of sanity in the midst of chaos. The squat, rectangular shape betrayed no bright flicker, and surely it would do so if the cathedral had caught. Which meant the troop the Queen had dispatched to protect its grounds was succeeding.

The ones who *weren't* succeeding were underground, in the Onyx Hall. The Fire had climbed Ludgate Hill, moving up from Blackfriars and Carter Lane to claim the high ground, until the whole rise seemed like a volcano, belching thick black clouds. From that height it flung out sparks, riding the wind toward the wall.

Which was not stopping them.

For a time it had worked. Irrith had watched, holding her breath, as the incandescent flakes snuffed themselves against an invisible barrier. Angrisla, barely bothering to disguise her hideous face, kept up a continuous stream of curses and speculation, identifying for Irrith all the buildings and streets she could not name on her own. And it seemed that the stout brick courses of the City wall, bolstered by the fae, would hold the beast back.

But Ludgate itself, which had long formed a stark profile against the glare behind, abruptly vanished into the flames. The debtors usually imprisoned within its walls were scattered—released by their jailers or broken free on their own, Irrith didn't know—and the proud statues of old Lud and the Tudor Queen Elizabeth were lost somewhere inside the blaze. The Dragon had passed the gate, and was coming toward them fast.

Angrisla spat a foul oath and ran for the Fleet Bridge—not away from the Fire, but toward it. *These London folk are mad,* Irrith thought in disbelief. *She* would never run to save the village near Wayland's Smithy; the mortals could just rebuild, and breed more of themselves to replace the ones they'd lost.

Fae, however, were harder to come by. *I must be mad, too,* Irrith admitted, and ran after Angrisla.

The mara at least had not charged straight into the flames. She halted on the Fleet Bridge, leaning out between the iron pikes that lined its stone edge. Irrith cringed back from joining her, though whether because of the iron or the sheer filth of the river, the sprite could not say. If the searing air hadn't roasted all sense of smell from her, she would have gagged on the water's stench.

Angrisla was shouting down into that fouled water. Irrith couldn't hear her clearly over the whirlwind roar of the advancing Fire, and she was not even certain the goblin woman was speaking English.

Except for the last bit, where Angrisla screamed, "Do it, bitch, and I'll feed you a corpse a day for a year!"

Which was almost enough to make Irrith shy off the bridge entirely. She made the mistake of looking down, though, and what she saw there transfixed her to the stone.

Something moved in the choking sludge of the Fleet. Flowing sluggishly between the wharves and crumbling embankments, its surface clogged with debris and snowed under with ash, the thing was hardly a river at all—and Irrith had never seen a river spirit like the one that rose from it now.

Angrisla ran off the bridge as if for her life, hauling Irrith with her as she went. "Blacktooth Meg," she said when they scudded to a halt on solid ground once more, and gave a feral grin. "The hag of the Fleet. Not so powerful as the Cailleach Bheur, but more than you or me."

"Were you asking her for help or threatening her?" Irrith asked, unable to look away from the monstrosity before her.

The mara shrugged. "Both?"

The oil-slick skin might not have been skin at all, but an accumulation of the river's filth. The shoulders were huge, but uneven, studded and twisted with lumps of either muscle or trash. Patches of stringy hair sprang from the scalp, debris caught in their strands, and the clawed hands that rose from the water's surface could have crushed Irrith's face, in concert or alone.

Irrith was *very* glad she could not see the hag's face.

A voice like a thousand mutilated ravens screamed some unintelligible challenge at the Fire. *I don't think she needs the bribery of corpses,* Irrith thought, backing another few steps away. *This is her territory, and she does not like invaders.*

What coiled up to meet the hag was not the entire Dragon. Irrith was not certain there *was* such a thing anymore; the beast had grown so huge under the wind's encouraging hand that it could probably manifest itself in half a dozen places at once.

It was not the entire Dragon. But it was big enough.

Blacktooth Meg didn't flinch back. She yowled in fury and threw her clawed hands skyward, burying them in the creature's molten flesh. A stench bad enough to punch through to Irrith's dulled senses struck her like a giant's club, knocking her to the ground. The sprite writhed on the hard-baked dirt, until she felt Angrisla's bony fingers wrap around her arm and haul her upright.

The river hag was lost from sight, buried in a twisting,

tearing mass of flame. The stones of the bridge next to that battle were beginning to glow with the heat. The Dragon—that part of it—was pinned down.

But for how long?

The hag was no great spirit, not like Old Father Thames. Sparks glided by overhead, seeking the dry, close-packed houses of Fleet Street.

And from inside the raging battle, the sprite and the mara heard Blacktooth Meg scream.

"I don't think it's working," Angrisla said, and Irrith swore in agreement.

ALDERSGATE, LONDON
four o'clock in the afternoon

The sudden crack of an explosion made the man next to Jack startle and look around in fear. The physician had him by the shoulder before he could run. "It isn't foreigners," he said, weary with having repeated it a thousand times. "The duke's men are blowing up houses around Cripplegate, to stop the Fire's spread." Also by the Tower, though most if not all of the powder had been removed from the fortress. Jack hoped someone had the sense to clear breaks in the liberties west of the City, too—but he had no sense of that land, which lay outside the borders of the Onyx Hall.

That strange, extra sense was ravaged almost beyond capacity for life, though. Jack had been forced to ride halfway around the City to reach this spot; of all the entrances to the faerie palace, only the Crutched Friars and Tower doors stood unscathed. St Paul's was yet intact, but besieged on all sides by flames.

Everything else had fallen to the Dragon.

The western wall collapsed early—not physically, but in its magical fortification. Here, where the northward run of that defence bent eastward for a time, the line was breached, but not by much. The narrow gap of Aldersgate strangled the flames, letting only a slender arm through, and the wind lacked enough northward bent to carry the sparks over the height of the bricks. They battled the Fire for every inch it claimed.

Too many inches, though. The message was sent; now they waited for Nicneven to answer, losing more of London with each minute that passed. And Jack, well aware of the irony, prayed to God that Lune was right—about the Gyre-Carling being here, about her willingness to meet, about the killing of the Dragon, about everything. Otherwise they would lose all they hoped to save.

He could not sit below and wait; it would drive him mad. So he came out here again, joining the men who still fought, slowing the Fire with every means at their disposal.

Shouts rose at the corner across from Jack. An ember had wormed its way into the wood, unnoticed by the men busy fighting to extinguish another blaze, and now a whole wall was in flames. Staggering, weary past the telling of it, Jack grabbed the nearest fellow by the sleeve—some fine gentleman, whose rich clothes would not be fit for rags when this was done—and dragged him toward an unused fire-hook. Somehow the two of them got its heavy iron point up; then others joined them, helping manoeuvre the hook into a ring under the eaves of the burning house. "We have it!" Jack cried in a voice gone hoarse with smoke and overuse, and a dozen hands seized hold of the ropes set along the thirty feet of the pole. Together they all heaved, bellowing, until the timbers gave way, and the house front came crashing down.

Sparks erupted skyward, but others were there with buckets. Jack and the fine gentleman positioned themselves as close to the heat as they could, flinging water over the crackling wreckage, until the last of it sputtered out. A small victory: one more house destroyed, true, but it would not spread to others.

Chest heaving, Jack dropped the last bucket from his blistered hands. His companion gave him a soot-blackened smile, shoving the lank, sweaty mass of his dark hair back toward the ribbon it had escaped from.

There were other places to fight. Jack opened his mouth to suggest they join a group farther down the road, but left it hanging as a horseman trotted to a halt at their side.

He knew the man on that horse, who had been everywhere around the City since yesterday morning. The prominent nose of James Stuart, Duke of York, would have been recognisable through any amount of grime.

Jack could only blame desperate exhaustion for his

failure to recognise that same nose on the fine gentleman at his side.

"We have the Fire under control here," the duke said to his brother, ignoring Jack. "The men fighting in the liberties, though, could use encouragement."

Charles Stuart nodded. "But reward those working here. By their efforts are these northern parishes saved." Reaching into a bag slung across his body, the King of England pulled out a shining guinea and offered it to Jack.

Who merely gaped at it. The coin was so clean, winking brilliant gold in the afternoon light, that he could not comprehend it. Nor the hand that held it. The King and the duke had been in and around the City all day—that much Jack had heard—and yes, that they worked with their own hands alongside the citizens of London, but...

But the tall, long-nosed man before him, however fine his clothes had been, was so far a cry from the drinking, wenching, merrymaking ruler of England that Jack's tired mind simply could not put the two in the same body. And so he stared, until Charles said, "Take it. You have earned it, in defence of my City."

Jack found the wit to shake his head. "Keep it, your Majesty, for some other man—one who needs it more." The part of his mind that still possessed an ounce of sense reminded him that his house in Monkwell Street was gone, and so was the Royal College of Physicians, and the Barber-Surgeons' Hall.

Yet I have the fae. Others are not so fortunate.

Charles smiled again. It was friendly and open; no wonder so many liked this man, for all his failings as a king. Replacing the coin, he offered Jack his hand instead. His strong grip infused Jack with strength—not by magic, but the simple charm of his confidence and goodwill. "Your name?"

"Jack Ellin. Doctor."

"God send me more subjects so charitable as you, Dr Ellin. Keep fighting; we will kill this beast yet." A gentleman brought up another horse. Charles mounted, and was gone.

We will kill this beast yet. Jack prayed it might be so.

But the wind was growing stronger.

THE ONYX HALL, LONDON
eight o'clock in the evening

They had abandoned the defence of the wall. At the end of Basinghall Street, just east of Cripplegate, the Fire had battered itself into exhaustion against the high bricks; westward, from the gate itself, the reinforcement held enough for the mortal defenders to wrestle the flames into a standstill, scant paces beyond the line.

Those along the wall's farthest reach, though, from Newgate down to the river, now lay in exhausted stupor, tended by sad-faced hobs.

Any faerie with an ounce of vitality left in him, Lune had sent above, to form a ring around St Paul's. The Dragon was driving hard at the cathedral, and they must not let it break through. Like the Stone, it was a foundational piece of the Onyx Hall; if the Dragon conquered it, the palace would soon follow.

Lune kept back only her knights, who now stood in thin ranks on the white sand of the amphitheatre. Their numbers had never fully recovered from the war and Prigurd's betrayal; she could only hope they would be enough.

Jack stood at her side, kept upright only through grim force of will. There would be no speeches from him, and none from her, either; the Onyx Guard needed no convincing for this battle. "The Dragon wants the cathedral," she said simply. "This means it has focused itself in one place, and this means we can fight it. Not fragments of its power, not the salamanders it has birthed: the Dragon itself. And we must kill it."

She did not add, *for the sake of London.* The appalling truth was that London was lost. A remnant of it survived in the northeast, forming a crescent down to the Tower; the suburbs that lay outside its walls were mostly untouched, save for the liberties immediately to the west. But the City itself was gone. They had suffered terrible losses on Sunday and Monday, but today the Dragon, fuelled by its stolen power, had devoured as much again. If there was anything yet to be saved, it was the Strand, Covent Garden, Westminster.

But London was more than just the City within the walls. They would not abandon their defence so long as one outlying village remained under threat.

Sir Peregrin cleared his throat. "Madam—you wish us

to let it through into the Onyx Hall?"

"No," Lune said. "You will battle it outside the cathedral."

In the mortal City. Not hiding under glamours, pretending that what they did was something mundane; a fight such as this could not be concealed. But who was there to see? The cathedral mount was an island in a sea of fire. The humans were fled. Their church bells had fallen silent, brazen tongues now melted slag in a desolation of cinders. If London was not quite safe for her people, it was the closest it had come since mankind settled on the banks of the Thames.

The Captain of the Onyx Guard touched his hand to his heart. Lune knew his doubts, as clearly as if he had spoken them: his knights were brave, but few, and the Dragon a foe more terrible than any had faced.

She would be sending some of them—perhaps all—to their deaths.

But any who lacked the courage for this battle had already fled.

"Let me fight it."

The voice came from the amphitheatre's entrance, rumbling in the hollow pit of Lune's stomach. Broken and hoarse, but still familiar, and her throat closed up tight.

Prigurd Nellt was coarsely dressed, his hair grown long and shaggy beneath the helm he now removed. Deep lines seamed the hard skin of his face, marking the lonely years of his exile. But his shoulders were straight, and the hilt of his great two-handed sword rose above one of them, wrapped in well-worn leather.

Peregrin's own sword hissed out of its sheath, and the tip flashed fire as he levelled it at the giant. "You have been banished. Why are you here?"

"To defend London." Prigurd said it without flourish. He advanced carefully, Peregrin's blade tracking his every step, and stopped well shy of Lune, kneeling on the sand. "Your Majesty. Lord—" He caught Antony's name before it came out, blinking at Jack in confusion. "Er—Prince. Let me fight for you."

Jack was staring in manifest curiosity, but Lune did not have time to explain. She frowned down at the exile. "You are no longer of our guard."

The giant's doubt spoke frankly as he eyed the knights. "I know. I—I haven't forgotten. But I've had time to think, and to—regret. I don't expect you will let me back, your Grace. That isn't why I'm here. I just want to do *something*. So that when I think about this place, I can remember something other than how I betrayed you."

The constriction in her throat grew tighter. Against shame, against the threat of punishment, he returned to them in this desperate hour. Not for reward: she believed him when he said that. But for honour, and duty, and loyalty. Because this was his home, even if she had driven him from it.

Peregrin's body was practically humming with distrust. Lifting her fingers, Lune gestured for him to back away. "Madam—" he began.

"We need him," Lune said. "His size, his strength.

Would you face an enemy whose head you cannot reach? We will not turn away a sword arm, Peregrin—not when our realm is at stake."

An intake of breath from Prigurd, that from a smaller creature might have passed unnoticed. His thick fingers dug into the sand.

From Lune's side, unexpected support. "I wasn't here when this…fellow's crimes were committed," Jack said. "In fact, I have no idea who he is. Which makes me, I think, as close to a neutral party as we'll find in this room. I make no judgement regarding his past actions, but if he will fight for us, then he has my favour."

Prigurd's head came up in startlement. Purest joy flickered there, just for a moment, and it struck Lune like a blow.

He deserves this much of me.

"For this battle," she said, "he shall have mine as well." Fumbling, she unpinned the diamond brooch holding her cloak shut, and extended it toward the giant. The star buried in its depths winked in the light. "And when this is done, he shall have three days and nights' safety here in the Onyx Hall, with no hand raised against him." Could she grant more than that? It depended on his former brothers-in-arms—who, if they did not precisely forgive him, looked more than a little relieved to have the giant's strength on their side. After the battle, they might view him with renewed charity.

Disbelieving, Prigurd rose, ate the ground between them with two strides, and took the brooch from her hand.

His calloused skin rasped against hers—and then Jack and Lune gasped as one.

Sir Peregrin leapt forward, ready to defend them, but he had barely moved before a tiny sprite shrieked into the air above their heads, screaming what the Queen and Prince already knew. "The cathedral burns!"

ST PAUL'S CATHEDRAL, LONDON
eight o'clock in the evening

The Dragon found its foothold on the very scaffolding erected for the cathedral's repair. Eight days before, the architect Dr Christopher Wren had met with others to discuss its restoration: the mending of its broken roofs, the straightening of the leaning walls, the support of a pillar that had settled askew under the weight of the central tower.

Now a spark alit on the edge of a board laid to patch a hole in the leads, and burrowed its way inward.

The exhausted defenders in the hellish oven of the churchyard fell back, defeated. The Dragon dug its claws into the board, flames licking across the parched timber. Stone could not burn, but its fittings could, and with ravening hunger the Fire tore inward, seeking the power below.

In the cracked, chipped floor of the nave, the entrance opened up. Marching in grim, battle-ready file, the knights of the Onyx Guard and their erstwhile commander emerged, weapons in hand.

They arrayed themselves across the south transept, Sir Peregrin Thorne anchoring one end of their line, Dame Segraine the other. The tombs of London's worthy forefathers and foremothers stood between them like shield brothers. The vaulting stone heights of the ceiling concealed the flames for now, but the blocks ground ominously against one another, shifted by the thundering heat. The wooden roof above was too high for anyone to douse the flames, even if water could be brought. All they could do was wait.

Wait, and prepare. Gripping the hilt of his sword in both hands, Prigurd Nellt drew in a slow breath, letting his great chest expand—and *grew.*

The days when a giant could walk the land in his true form had passed. To live in the Onyx Hall, or the home of any other faerie monarch, he drew himself inward, diminishing his bulk until he could live—if not comfortably. But here, hidden by walls of stone and flame, with the ceiling so high above, Prigurd could be as he once was.

The giant's shoulders swelled upward and out. Head bowed, Prigurd grew, flexing arms as thick as an ox's body, shifting legs the size of mighty trees. In his hands, the sword kept pace, until three men together could not have wielded it. Hewn from the stone of his rocky northern home, the blade held a touch of that cold chill, and the giant smiled to think of what it could do.

No Dragon would eat his home. Not this day, nor any other.

The wooden roof was well in flames, but the Fire had

not the patience to wait. With a roar, its power struck downward, and the stone of the ceiling shattered as if blasted by gunpowder.

A blazing column punched through to the floor, smashing into ruin the recumbent monument of some long-dead knight. Upward curved the flames, a thick band coiling about itself, until the gathered fae could barely look at it, or breathe the searing air. The stone beneath calcined white, crumbling into powder that spun into a stinging whirlwind, the herald of the Dragon.

Eyes squeezed shut against the dust, Prigurd did not need to see. He knew which direction was forward, and the enemy, like him, was too large to miss.

Bellowing a war cry, Lune's brooch a tiny star upon his shoulder, the giant hurled himself into battle.

The tip of his ancient sword carved a broad slash through the twisting mass of flames. It was not like striking flesh, nor like insubstantial fire; the Dragon's body was semisolid, offering a modicum of resistance to his blade. Expecting more, Prigurd had thrown himself with too much force. He fell forward, one shoulder slamming into the body of the beast.

Skin crisped, and Prigurd roared, but the Dragon felt it as well; the vortex shuddered backward, colliding with the transept wall. The cathedral shook, and more stones fell from above. Several of the knights staggered, but they recovered their feet quickly enough when they saw they had an enemy to fight.

For Prigurd's sword had carved free a writhing mass that fell to the floor below, where it quickly reshaped itself into a monstrous salamander, as tall as a cart-horse. Two of the knights charged it, driving it back from the main battle, and Dame Segraine cupped one hand to her mouth, shouting into the howling chaos of battle above. "Prigurd! Cut it small—we shall do the rest!"

Trapped beneath a suffocating wall of flame, Prigurd had no breath to reply. But he was a child of the earth, born of solid stone, and did not burn as softer flesh might. Setting his hands against the blaze, he *shoved,* and sent the Dragon spiralling backward, out of the transept and down the long reach of the nave. Its substance split around the thick pillars, regrouping on the other side, but by then Prigurd was there, swinging his sword in a two-handed grip that hacked away one lump after another.

He drove it down the nave, shouting in wordless joy. For the first time in forgotten ages, Prigurd was a giant again, and battling an enemy worthy of his strength. If tombs split under his blows or the Dragon's, if columns cracked and stones exploded outward from the raging heat of this contest, he did not care. The house of Heaven's divine Master was no concern of his, nor the decaying bodies of the mortal dead. This creature threatened his home. He would throw the beast out the western doors and drop the portico on its head. He would kick it down Ludgate Hill and drown it in the stinking waters of the Fleet. He would tear at it until nothing remained to be torn, and when that was done—

The arching ribs of the ceiling collapsed in the western end of the nave, raining burning shards of timber behind the stone. The sudden inrush of air breathed new life into the Dragon, which recoiled upon Prigurd with a dizzying blow. It knew where the entrance lay, though the floor had closed behind the Onyx Guard, and knew the giant drove it from its prize.

Whips of flame lashed Prigurd, pinioning his arms, stilling the cold blade that kept biting into the Dragon's flesh. The Fire lifted its prey bodily and flung him the length of the nave, two hundred feet, until Prigurd's slide was halted by the mighty pillars of the crossing. In a flash it reclaimed all the distance it had lost, and bent to strike at the vulnerable stone beneath.

But the rest of the Onyx Guard were there, harrying its sides like rats, ramming long pikes into the boiling heart of the flames. It flicked them aside like ninepins, then found Prigurd had recovered. The giant set his feet wide and seized the Dragon in a wrestler's grip, dragging it backward into the quire, where the benches fell instantly to ash. With a wrenching twist the Fire smashed Prigurd into the south wall. The towering monument to old Elizabeth's Lord Chancellor Sir Christopher Hatton cracked and fell, and crushed beneath it the simple tablets of Sir Philip Sidney and Sir Francis Walsingham.

Peregrin shouted. By supreme effort, he and another knight had moved Prigurd's sword close enough to grab. The giant took it in hand once more and stabbed it into the Dragon's flank; with that as a lever, he forced the beast off him, and gained his footing once more. Working like a peasant hewing wood, he chopped again and again, raining blows down upon the beast, sending its salamanders in all directions, where the other knights chased them down.

Yet now he was in the wrong place: the Dragon stood between him and the entrance, not the other way around. Prigurd realised this too late, as the Fire eddied suddenly backward, into the crossing once more.

He leapt after it with a desperate bellow. If it had but an instant to draw in its power, it would break through. Not into the chapel below, the little chamber in which the parishioners of St Faith met, but into the space that could be reached by no mundane path.

He could not let it happen. And so Prigurd, knowing little of what he did, knowing only that he must stop his enemy by whatever means he could, and trusting to blind hope that this would crush the beast for good, reached for a strength greater even than his own.

His sword struck, not at the Dragon, but at the four massive columns surrounding them.

Weakened by long neglect, off balance from the tremendous weight of the tower above them, they gave way like twigs. The pillars snapped, and all the height of St Paul's crashed down into the crossing.

The Dragon vanished beneath the onslaught. So, too, did Prigurd. And the stones of the floor, supported from beneath by the arches of the Jesus Chapel, pulverised into dust.

The burning wreckage fell through into the little church of St Faith, and blazed into terrible light. For in that space—bounded by stone, sealed with care, and thought by its bookseller parishioners to be the safest place in all of London—rested the close-packed volumes of their printed wealth. From cheap broadside ballads to leather-bound editions of Virgil and the Church Fathers, it was the greatest library in all of England.

Gone, in an instant of annihilating flame.

Above, the knights of the Onyx Guard staggered to their feet, coughing and blind. Segraine wiped her streaming eyes and saw the infernal pit where Dragon, giant, and entrance had stood. Flames danced everywhere around them, more and more of the ceiling collapsing in, but those were small creatures, scarcely more than flickers of spirit, not the great beast that had been.

Peregrin stumbled to the edge of the pit and seized hold of something. "Help me!" he choked out. Going to his side, Segraine found he had an arm—shrunken and black, but still gripping the hilt of a sword. It gave her brief hope, and together they pulled... but what came out of the blaze was nothing living.

She would never have recognised it as Prigurd, were it not for the helm and sword. All the giant's size had shrivelled, leaving behind a decrepit, withered body that might have belonged to an ancient and long-dead human. She and Peregrin dragged it eastward into the relative safety of the quire, where a portion of the ceiling yet held, and there they collapsed, joined piecemeal by the knights of the Onyx Guard.

"We must take him to Lune," Segraine said, coughing. If they stayed much longer, it would be all of them dead, and not just the giant.

Peregrin stared down at the corpse, his expression broken and lost. Before him lay his terrible enemy, the traitor of his brotherhood: gone, with a hero's death. The fire that burned in the underground chapel was fire only, not the Dragon. And *nothing* was passing through that entrance—perhaps not ever again. Prigurd had destroyed St Paul's, but saved the Onyx Hall.

Finally the knight shook his head. If tears made tracks through the filth on his cheeks, no one could tell them from the sweat. "We must flee," he said, "and we cannot carry him."

As one, they all turned and looked past the roaring pit of St Faith to the cathedral's western end. The new portico there yet stood, but outside was all the burning City, with no clear path to safety.

Peregrin was right. They would be lucky to bring themselves out.

Segraine folded the hands of Sir Prigurd Nellt over his chest, tucking the now-reduced sword beneath them. "We will remember you," she whispered, and gave her former captain one final salute.

Then the knights of the Onyx Guard left the wreckage of St Paul's.

THE ONYX HALL, LONDON
eleven o'clock in the evening

Jack fought his way into awareness one inch at a time, his head throbbing as if it had been split by an axe. Lune's hands were supporting him, though when his vision cleared, he saw that the faerie Queen looked no better than he did.

St Paul's. Now he remembered.

He would call it a miracle that the Onyx Hall survived, but he was not certain what, if anything, God had to do with faerie palaces and the preservation thereof. *Perhaps the Almighty answered my prayers.* He somehow doubted it.

Lune's words drove all thoughts of God from his head. "The wind has dropped," she said, her voice cracking on the last word. "Nicneven has come."

The silence rang in his ears. No voice whispering of sickness and death, no wintry blast chilling the Onyx Hall to black ice. Blessed, blessed quiet, and a breath of warmth to carry it.

And the Gyre-Carling had come.

Jack reeled to his feet, went to wipe his face on his sleeve, and realised there was nothing to choose between the two. Lune managed a faint smile. "She is not inside yet," the elfin woman said. "We have time to bathe and dress." For once Jack didn't dread the finery that was no doubt in store; he had no desire to meet Nicneven looking like the inside of an oven.

As for what happened when he did...

One thing he had decided, after the knights went above to do battle, before the cathedral's collapse felled him like a tree.

We will give her Vidar if I have to dig the whoreson up myself.

Molten lead runs like blood down Ludgate Hill, streaming from the dying body of London's great cathedral. In the north, the roof timbers of the venerable old Guildhall shine gold in the night, a second beacon for those watching from the fields to the north, or those across the river. The papier-mâché statues of the giants Gog and Magog have fallen at its feet. In the heart of the city, embers smoulder, and here and there small blazes still dance, but three days of destruction have reduced it to a desolate plain, smoking like Hell itself, and spiked by the broken fingers of brick chimneys and stone walls, survivors of the holocaust.

Those who fled before it huddle under blankets if they are lucky, nothing but their shirts if they are not. Guards watch over them, keeping the King's peace, trying—where they can—to capture those who would plunder others in their misfortune. Elsewhere the battles continue, for with the dropping of the wind hope comes for the first time that they may, at last, be able to extinguish the Fire.

Any man who has fought these three days breathes the same prayer, hoping it will rise with the smoke into the heavens, and to the ears of the Almighty Lord.

Let the wind keep down, and what is left be saved.

PART FOUR

THE LIVING FEW
1665–1666

"It had been a year of prodigies in this nation: plague, fire, rain, tempest and comet."

JOHN EVELYN
DIARY, 6 MARCH 1667

LOMBARD STREET, LONDON
9 May 1665

Jack Ellin barely waited for the hackney coach to rattle to a halt before he leapt free like a schoolboy released on holiday. Flicking a coin up to the driver, who caught it adroitly, he dodged through the press of bodies, horses, and carts that filled Lombard Street, and across to a familiar door.

Two clerks sat in the front room, tallying up accounts for the goods that filled the rest of the ground floor. Once there had been more, but Antony's wealth had suffered almost as badly as his health during the King's long exile. He had regained the house, but not all his former stature. The clerks nodded greetings at Jack when he passed them, heading for the staircase that led to the family's living quarters.

The manservant Burnett met him at the top. "Is Sir Antony in?" Jack asked.

"He is, Dr Ellin, but not in good spirits. Ill news came today, I believe, and Lady Ware is away—visiting family in Norfolk."

Jack had forgotten. Kate's absence was a great pity; she, more than anyone, could lift Antony from his black moods. *Well, I shall have to do my best.* Jack slung off his cloak. "He needs distraction, then. He's in his study?"

He found Antony bent over a stack of papers. Guildhall work, most likely; the baronet had withdrawn from Parliamentary life just before the restoration of the monarchy, but he stayed firmly engaged with the politics of London. Last year he served as one of the City's sheriffs. Jack would lay money on his election as Lord Mayor some day.

If he didn't fret himself into his grave first. "Jack. I apologise for my distracted state—some business has me concerned."

The ill news Burnett had mentioned, no doubt. "Oh?"

"A plague death in my ward. On Bearbinder Lane."

It dampened Jack's good cheer, and more than explained Antony's own mood. Plague raised its ugly head year after year, but to find it in Langbourn Ward was worrisome indeed. Professional curiosity sparked. "I knew there was plague in the pestered suburbs, St Giles-in-the-Field and the like—but here? Are you certain?"

"The searchers verified it. But there's some suggestion the man was a foreigner, a Frenchman, who had only just removed from St Giles; we may hope the distemper will not spread here." Antony rubbed his eyes tiredly. "But you did not come here for that. I judge by the spring in your step that you have some good news to share."

It seemed less bright, after speaking of the plague, but Jack put on his best grin and offered Antony a florid, courtly bow. "And so I do. You see before you, my good sir, the newest Fellow of the Royal Society of London."

"Wonderful!" Now the smile was genuine. "I should mock you for this; is it not enough to be both physician and surgeon? Now you must be a natural philosopher as well."

At Antony's gestured invitation, Jack claimed the room's other chair. "My love will always be the physicking of people, I promise you. But theories have their uses. Take Harvey's work on the blood—"

"My dear Dr Ellin, if you are about to subject me to some abstruse lecture on anatomy, you may save your breath; I will not understand it."

Jack waved the objection away. "Nothing abstruse, I promise you. Merely this: that Harvey showed the heart is a sort of pump, propelling blood around the body with its action. Now, knowing this does not change the fact that if you put a hole in a man, his blood will all come out, and he will die. But! Harvey's observations suggest that the veins carry blood only *to* the heart, and the arteries *away* from it."

The old man's expression said clearly that he did not see the point.

Jack sighed. "It all depends on where a man is wounded. What has been damaged: an artery or a vein? We might find ways to improve the efficacy of bloodletting, were Harvey's notions more widely understood. And you see, that is what the Society is about! Sharing knowledge, and *testing* it— deriving knowledge from observation of the world, rather than relying solely on ancient authority."

Chuckling, Antony turned back to his papers and

straightened them, sweeping aside fragments from a newly cut quill. "I have no doubt you will fit with them like a hand in a glove. You certainly have the curiosity."

"And the disrespect for authority—only you're too kind to say it." Jack leapt to his feet, still bursting with excitement. Once he was sworn in, he would have the Society's patronage behind his work, and the Society had the King's. What could he not do with that? "Come! Let us have a supper to celebrate. We could see one of those Punch shows in Covent Garden, or go to the gardens at Vauxhall. I only wish Kate were here to join us."

A shadow crossed Antony's features, most unexpectedly. What ailed the man? Something more than a single plague death, or even the larger threat in St Giles.

Simple loneliness? His children were all gone: Alice married, Robin at sea, and Henry maintaining polite distance, with letters and the occasional visit, but nothing more. The thriving trade Antony had once ruled over now faltered; though still enough to keep body and soul together in decent comfort, it no longer seemed to give the baronet much joy in life. Kate's journey to Norfolk could turn a man's thoughts to his empty house.

Or more than that. "Did you and Kate quarrel?"

Antony rose and crossed to the window, gazing out into the cloudy day—and, as it happened, hiding his expression from Jack. He stood there a long moment, hands braced on the sill, until Jack almost gave up and changed the subject. But then Antony spoke. "I dislike keeping secrets."

Jack blinked. "Then don't."

His old friend shook his head. "I do not—in every respect I can. But there are some few things in my life I can never tell her about."

Which meant he should not be saying anything to Jack, either; it only roused the physician's curiosity. Asking would gain him nothing, though. Jack said, "For fear of what? That she'll turn against you? Antony, your wife loves you. You could burn down a church with a hundred parish orphans inside, and she would try to find out what good reason you had for doing it."

"Not that." Antony bowed his head, and the grey light gleamed through the grey hairs on his scalp. "I simply cannot explain my actions to myself. I surely cannot explain them to anyone else."

Though rarely at a loss for words, Jack had little notion what to say to that. Antony was not the sort of friend who shared the confidences of his heart—and while Jack might know about the circulation of the blood, he had no skill for dealing with that organ's less physical functions. He bit his lip, thought it through, then asked, "Do you regret what you've done?"

Antony went still. "No."

"Then why do you need to explain it, to yourself or any other?"

After a moment, the old baronet laughed ruefully. "I suppose I do not."

"Just so. Now come." Jack came forward and took his

friend by the arm. Antony, surprisingly, permitted him the touch. "Supper, and some good cheer, and I will tell you about this ridiculous chymical physician who's trying to gain entrance to the Royal Society."

THE RED BULL THEATRE, CLERKENWELL
15 June 1665

The audience roared with laughter as a gaily painted actor tumbled to the boards of the stage. The air in the Red Bull was stiflingly close and none too sweet, its foulness hardly veiled by thick clouds of tobacco smoke, but Lune laughed with all the rest, as coarsely as the red-faced mortal she pretended to be. Carline had persuaded her to come and see the new innovation of women actors, and while Lune thought the Bull's lady shrill and overwrought, she was glad of the chance to distract herself.

The decision to come was not easy. There were six fae in the theatre that night, which meant six pieces of bread consumed—or rather, four pieces of bread and two swallows of milk, though the latter was rarely seen in the Onyx Hall. Scarce resources nowadays; of the mortals who followed them from Berkshire, some had drifted away slowly, others with more speed, once the plague broke out in London's parishes.

But Lune needed the diversion. Her messengers—she might call them spies—had returned again, footsore and annoyed, without word of Vidar. It worried her, not to know where he hid; she did not believe he would flee so far she could not find him. Not that her reach was so long, but she knew Vidar, and knew his arrogance. To take refuge in Italy would be to admit that he had failed, and that he would not do.

Nicneven had not found him either. Which was less of a surprise, the Gyre-Carling having a shorter reach than Lune's own—but it did not put her heart any more at ease.

The Red Bull Theatre was glad to provide the diversion she needed. Why exactly the man now onstage was wearing a wooden tub around his naked body, Lune did not know— she had missed the explanation, if indeed there had been one—but the sheer absurdity of it was infectious.

All her amusement fled, though, when she spotted a figure forcing his way through the patrons of the Red Bull. Antony did not belong here; his back was stiff with disapproval, and more than a few of the men he shouldered aside glared at him. The baronet paid them no heed.

It did not take a great sage to realise some pressing errand brought him. Lune touched Carline's arm and murmured in her ear, then rose to greet Antony.

"A moment of your time?" he muttered.

"Of course." A man behind her was already complaining that she blocked his view; she eased her way clear, stumbling as someone's foot snagged her hem. *I am no Queen here,* she thought wryly. *Were I mortal and Christian, I would call it a lesson in humility.*

Being neither of those things, she had no particular appreciation for humility, and was glad to gain the freer air of St John's Street outside. Straightening the disarray of her skirts, Lune opened her mouth to ask Antony what was so pressing it could not wait a few hours for her return.

He spoke before she could get one word out. "What in God's name do you think you are doing?"

The harshness of it put her back up, for it evoked the guilt she felt in spending their scarcity on an evening's entertainment. "I've hardly spent a moment outside since returning from Berkshire," she began, prepared to defend her choice.

Antony cut her off with a violent motion. "That theatre is supposed to be *closed*. All of them are, by command of the King and Lord Mayor. And I find you in their midst, with no regard for the law!"

Lune winced. She could not pretend she hadn't known. Kings came and went, but the plague orders remained the same: in times of sickness, all such public gatherings were banned, to prevent the spread of the distemper. After the strangulation of the Puritan era, though, London's inhabitants, mortal and fae alike, were wild to partake of the licentious mood fostered by King Charles the Second— even in the face of danger.

"Fae are not vulnerable to disease," she said, in vain defence. "We can neither contract it nor spread it; our presence here makes nothing worse."

"It makes nothing better, either." Antony snatched off

his hat, crumpling the brim in his fingers. The hair beneath was thinner than she remembered it, and brittle. Their exile had broken his health; Antony had never fully recovered. But there was life in him still, and most of it currently burning with anger. "Lune, the plague is *spreading,* and at such a rate as to frighten me. They say it is God's judgement for our licence. I do not know about that, but certainly such behaviour does not help."

Lune spread her hands in bafflement. She was not to blame for the folk inside, and she could not see why Antony behaved as if she were. "What would you have me do? Send Bonecruncher and his friends in without glamours, to frighten everyone out?"

"It would be a start. But I had in mind a great deal more than that."

She blinked. "Such as?"

He stepped closer, until only the crown of his hat separated them, so his voice would not carry. The passion in him had faded, leaving behind something less easily read. "You have more at your disposal than simple plague orders and medicines."

"Magic?" Lune, too, kept her voice low. "Antony... our enchantments have no power over this sickness."

"None ? "

She let him see the honest regret in her eyes. "Disease is not something we know. We may speed the closing of wounds, a little; there are tales of greater things, that have more power to heal. But none in our possession. And none, so far as I know, that can banish the plague."

Frustration hardened his features anew. Deven had asked this once, too; the plague was a frequent visitor to London. Lune had expected it from Antony during the last great visitation, some years before the war. It might have been easier for him to accept back then, before his own age made him so aware of his inevitable death.

Or not.

The Prince half turned away, jammed his hat back onto his head. Then he said, "There are other possibilities. Some of your stealthier folk could watch shut-up houses. The watchmen assigned to keep them closed are sent away on errands, and then the people escape; or else they threaten their watchers outright, hold them off with pistols or swords while their families flee, carrying the plague with them."

"Antony—"

"Or the gentler ones, they could bring comfort to those in confinement, and perhaps keep healthy those who have not yet fallen sick."

"Antony!"

Her call silenced him for just an instant, and into that gap came the sound of a bell. It did not ring the hour, which had passed just a short while ago, but tolled six times: the death of a woman.

It might not be plague, but she knew they both thought it.

As the holy sound washed harmlessly over her, Lune

said, "How often are the bells heard? Too much for safety. You will tell me I should not have spent bread on this visit to the theatre, and you will be right. But even without that— Antony, we cannot afford to be in the streets, not such as you ask. Not with people praying constantly for deliverance; not with crosses painted on the doors of the sick."

"We said we would protect London," he said, with ragged determination. "If not all of England, then at least the City. Lune, you have to try!"

Something black and desperate curled in her stomach, shortening her breath, making all her nerves hum. The bell was still sounding, ringing out the age of the unknown dead woman. Somewhere nearby, a parish servant pulled on the rope, fearing that soon someone else would ring the bell for *him*.

"I cannot," she said, through the thickness that made her tongue stumble. "This is not something I can affect, Antony. I am sorry." And without waiting for his reply, she fled back into the desperate frivolity of the theatre.

ROSE HOUSE, ISLINGTON
20 June 1665

"Oh *dear*," Rosamund said, somehow communicating a world of concern and frustration in that short exhalation.

The new rose bush planted behind the Angel was yet a slender thing, but the house below had been more than restored; one of Lune's first actions after retaking the Onyx Hall had been to lend the sisters aid in improving their home. The bedchambers were enlarged, and each had its own hearth, until the place had the feel of a sumptuous little inn that just happened to be underground. The courtiers were calling it "Rose House" now—a name that caused Gertrude endless vexation.

As a concession to her, the upholstered chair Antony rested in was embroidered with daisies, instead of her sister's endless roses. The two sat in their own small chairs, having listened to his frustrated account of the argument with Lune, while food sat untouched before him. He had no stomach for it, not with the problems he faced.

Gertrude nobly did not comment on his refusal, though her eyes followed the dish as he pushed it aside. "She's right, I'm afraid. We have no charm to simply banish disease. Not once it's taken hold in the body, and we are none of us great powers of Faerie, to bless the whole City of London."

"But that is not what I asked for!" Antony sighed and clenched his fists. "Very well, it *is*—but I understand why you cannot. What of my other suggestions, though? Why will she not even consider those? She all but *ran* from me when I asked!"

The sisters exchanged a glance—an ingrained habit that today only made Antony's useless anger worse. His ill temper was not for them, and not even, he thought, for Lune; but it was hard to be anything like calm, when every day brought news of more parishes infected. The further it spread, the dimmer his hope of doing anything to combat it.

Their silent conference seemed to pass the responsibility for answering to Gertrude. "She's afraid," the little brownie said.

"Of church bells, yes, and crosses on the doors, but there are ways to shelter oneself—"

"Not of those," Gertrude said. "Of death."

Antony's brow knitted in confusion. "Death? By the plague? She told me herself, fae are not vulnerable to it."

"That isn't the point," Rosamund said softly. "The point is death itself. To see humans in such a state—not just one or two, but dozens, hundreds, and all the rest living in fear. *Mortality*. Some of the crueller goblins find sport in it, but not Lune."

Gertrude nodded. "She's touched mortality too closely, with all the bread she's eaten, and loving one of your kind. She understands it just enough to fear it even more than most. But you'll find few fae who would like the thought of being surrounded by the dead and dying."

"*No one* likes it," Antony said, staring. "No one with any spark of compassion in them. That does not prevent us from caring for those in need!" Except that it did. Already, those who could afford to were retreating from London, the wealthy going to their country estates, or imposing themselves upon cousins. He could understand the King leaving; they could not afford the risk of *him* dying. But others fled, too— even doctors, who of all people should stay to help.

People fled, though, because they feared the danger to themselves. What the brownies were trying to say was that fae feared the thing itself: death, stark and omnipresent, as incomprehensible to them as love.

They could love. And they could die. But it came rarely, and few of them understood either one.

He tried to have sympathy, without much success. He had greater concerns than to coddle the fragile feelings of immortal creatures who were in no immediate peril. But sympathy or no, at least now he understood the source of the Queen's reluctance. And knew, too, that it would go beyond Lune alone, if he tried to seek help elsewhere in the court.

He would just have to find a way to move them past that reluctance.

It could start here, in Rose House. "Will *you*, at least, do what you can to help?"

"We always do," Gertrude answered him stoutly. "Though it's little enough, I fear."

Antony sighed. "It will be no worse than mere mortals can do."

THE ONYX HALL, LONDON
16 July 1665

Someone was stealing Irrith's bread.

The realisation annoyed her; then, a few moments later, her annoyance surprised her. The mortal food was a gift from the Queen—more like wages, really, given over the years both for reward and practical use, as Irrith played messenger to the Vale and other faerie courts. Despite seven years in Berkshire, where such protection was rarely necessary, Lune had soon reverted to the assumption that one could not set foot in the mortal world without being armoured by their food.

Now that she had experience of London, Irrith understood it. The fae of the Onyx Court lived with *one hundred and nine churches* above their heads, and more iron than any sensible faerie should get within smelling distance of. But once clear of the city, Irrith had no need of bread on her journeys, and so she hoarded much of her allotment. Sometimes she traded it for favours, using the little morsels like currency, but more often she ate it so she could venture outside in safety.

Proof of her own madness, really. She hadn't done it as much of late, because of the plague; London was not a friendly place nowadays. She even thought about returning to Berkshire, where she wouldn't have to worry about such horrors. If she did leave, though, Irrith knew she would return. The mortals here kept *changing!* New plays, and new broadside ballads, and men's clothing had recently sprouted masses of ribbons like brightly coloured fungus. She couldn't give up the chance to stare at them.

But she could only do that if she had bread to protect her, and someone had begun pilfering it.

When she realised it, she thought of informing the

guards—not the Onyx Guard, who protected the Queen, but the lesser warriors. She preferred not to bother them, though, and so one day, after receiving her allotment from Lune, Irrith left her bedchamber and passed very obviously through a public area where other fae gathered, then circled back by a more secret route.

For all that dwelling encased in stone bothered her, she liked the bedchamber Amadea had found for her. The Lady Chamberlain, searching for something that would evoke Irrith's home, put her in a room where pillars of silvery marble had been carved to look like birch trees, sprouting leaves of green agate along the arching branches that supported the ceiling. It was in the shadow of one such pillar that Irrith concealed herself, to catch the thief.

She was a patient creature, when she had to be. Fae ate when they felt like it, and so Irrith could sit there for days, if necessary. And she was prepared to.

Patience, unfortunately, was a tedious thing. Irrith didn't even realise she had dozed off until she heard a click—the lid of the box in which she kept her bread. By the time she had her wits about her, the door to her chamber was swinging closed.

Irrith was on her feet instantly, but not fast enough. The corridor outside was empty, with no footsteps to be heard. Charms for silence were easy things, though; she called one of her own, and stole with rapid, noiseless strides to the corner.

A shadowed figure vanished down another passage just as she peeked around the edge.

Despite herself, the sprite grinned. *Very well, then.* This was not the woods of Berkshire, and she lacked her bow, but it was a hunt all the same. She would track her quarry, and see where the creature went.

He—she thought the indistinct figure was male—knew the Onyx Hall well, whoever he was. The doorways and turnings he chose were familiar to Irrith only because Lune made her memorise them six years ago. They led her through parts of the Hall rarely used, leaving behind the bedchambers of the courtiers and common subjects. The warren she entered lay near the cathedral entrance Lord Antony had used, though its own passage to the surface came out in Billingsgate, near the Tower.

She suspected her quarry did not aim to go above, though. Her suspicions were confirmed when she stole a glance around another corner and found no one in sight.

There was a door in one wall, though, leading to Mab knew what. And the stone nearby was suspiciously clear of dust—the work of either some hob of single-minded cleanliness, or someone who didn't want to leave his footprints on the floor.

Irrith had assumed the thief was just some courtier, hoarding the food so he could visit a lady-love in the City, or trade it to get political advantage over an enemy. It was the sort of thing courtiers did.

Now, she was not so sure.

Against her better judgement, Irrith crept forward, ready to bolt if her quarry should emerge, and laid one ear on the door. Faint scuffs came from inside—he had released his charm—and a clunk, as of a heavy object set on a table. Irrith wondered, biting her lip, whether she remembered her path to this room well enough to lead someone else back here.

Someone like a guard, or three.

She got no chance to answer the question. A crippling wave of nausea struck her without warning, dropping her to the stone. It vanished a moment later, and she fled like a wild thing, back around the corner to relative safety before she could even think about it.

Iron.

Her own charm of silence was gone, shattered by the cold aura. Iron, and a lot of it. Irrith gulped, swallowing down her nausea. Then held her breath, shaking, as she heard the door open once more.

She pressed herself into another doorway, trying desperately to keep the movement quiet. The faerie lights that floated through the palace were thinly scattered here, and the shadows were deep. They were enough to conceal her as the figure went by, carrying something before him.

Irrith felt no taint from the box he held, and the faerie she saw was not the one she had pursued. But if he had eaten the bread to protect himself from the iron in that room, he could also be wearing a glamour no faerie could easily break.

There was no time to summon anyone else. She had to follow, and hope she knew what she was doing.

* * *

Antony rarely used his bedchamber in the Onyx Hall. It meant a great deal to him, when he first came to this place, that he not treat the faerie palace as his home; his place was in the world above. And Lune had warned him that too much time below could warp his mind. But he made greater use of the other chambers allotted to him, particularly the study, for he also understood that as Prince, he must have a visible presence in the court.

He was less and less in those chambers of late, though, as his work above consumed more and more of his time. The papers spread on the table before him told the tale: the Bills of Mortality, numbers gathered from each parish, organised by cause of death. Plague dominated the list. Every week, more hundreds fell. In the parishes outside the walls, they had begun to dig great pits, into which the bodies were thrown without even the dignity of a coffin.

And in his hand, another list, which told him how little he could do to stop it. At his request, Amadea had compiled an estimate of the bread available within the Onyx Hall. It was shockingly small. Few mortals remained at court, and as for the city... people would not give bread to the faeries, when their own starving children needed it more.

That was the work that devoured almost his every waking minute: keeping London on its feet. Half of the Guildhall was gone, its wealthy men fled to safer homes, but Antony toiled on, with his deputy and councilmen and parish officers of his ward—those of them who stayed. Faerie London was at peace, at least for now; mortal London was coming apart at the seams. Orphans and widows, without anyone to feed them; merchants with no one to sell their goods to, for trade was at a standstill. There were no grand gestures that could sweep those problems away, only one small thing after another, alleviating what misery he could.

Which wasn't much.

The knock on his door startled him. Few fae had anything to ask of their mortal Prince, when they were so reluctant to go above. Antony did not even have a servant attending him. He sat in a circle of warm candlelight, preferring that to the cold illumination of the faerie lights, and had little sense of the hour; it was easy to lose track of time here. The candles, and the darkness beyond them, always made him think it very late.

Shaking his head to clear it of bleak thoughts, Antony rose to answer the door.

The faerie outside was one of Valentin Aspell's minions, though Antony could not remember his name. He bowed as best he could, despite the burden he carried, and said, "M'lord Prince, if I might beg a moment of your time."

Antony gestured him in, curious. The box in the fellow's hands was a simple thing, built from unfinished hawthorn wood, but it seemed very heavy for its size. "I presume your request has to do with this?"

The faerie nodded. He was a broad-shouldered hob, taller than most, but ugly as male hobs usually were. He carried himself stiffly—though perhaps that was merely his scrupulous care as he laid the box on Antony's table, covering two Bills of Mortality. "Begging your pardon, but—I'm told you look for a way to help those above."

He had all of Antony's attention. "Have you found something?"

"In the treasury. Many things in there, and half of them we don't know what they do, so m'lord Valentin, he laid this aside at first. But I have a notion." The hob removed the lid, and beckoned Antony closer. He reached inside as the Prince approached, shifting something, and it seemed to Antony that chill air breathed outward, raising the hairs on the back of his neck. Shivering, he reached the table and looked inside—

A squat iron box sat within, its interior black and deep beyond all nature, as if leading to oblivion itself.

The sight shocked him so badly that he didn't see the hob move. And he was an old man now, slow, while fae were unageing; before he knew what was happening, the hob had his wrist in a crushing grip, and was slashing at his hand with a knife.

Pain tore across his fingers, and blood sprang free. Not much—the cut was not deep—but a drop fell into the blackness, and something seized Antony at the core of his soul, dragging him toward that abyss.

It paralysed his tongue, locking all his muscles tight. Antony fought to speak, but his throat would give forth no sound, not even Christ's name. And could that save him from whatever enchantment might reside in *iron?*

A second drop slid down his fingers. As he tried to pull

loose, it too fell, and the terrible pressure increased.

A third drop gathered, hovering at the edge of his palm—

Through the roaring in his ears, he heard a higher-pitched scream, and then the hob was slammed off balance. The third drop of Antony's blood spattered against the hawthorn. The hob's grip broke, and half blind, Antony found the discarded lid and clapped it down atop the wooden casing. All at once he could breathe again, and see the chaos before him.

Irrith straightened with renewed vigour and ploughed into the hob a second time, clawing and biting, tangling his feet with her own so he fell to the ground, where she kicked him until his own flailing defence upset her balance. But she collapsed with intent, her knee colliding with his head, and he went suddenly limp.

She stumbled to her feet almost immediately, recoiling from the table, although the hawthorn shielded her from the iron within. Antony's candleholder had been upset by the struggle; he righted it, and beat out the flaming papers with his hat.

Then, and only then, did he look at the figure on the floor.

Ifarren Vidar.

We should have known.

The accusation would not leave Lune's mind. Yet how could they? Who would have dreamt that Ifarren Vidar would find his refuge beneath their very eyes?

They found evidence enough of it in the Billingsgate warren. Vidar lived there like a rat—the sight afforded her some vindictive satisfaction—but he had been there for a long time. Perhaps years. There was no safety for him in Scotland, or elsewhere in England, and so he had concealed himself in the one place no one would think to look for him. Lune had not sought him there since the battle ended, and to know who was in the Onyx Hall required effort she no longer had reason to exert. He could have returned to the palace the very next day.

And somewhere in that chaos, he had stolen the iron box and its protective shell from the treasury. Lune should have paid heed to the things there far sooner, but too many of them had been gifts to Invidiana; she was loath to see what the old Queen had kept. From Antony's description, the thing was obviously a prison—one that would hold even a faerie.

"I expect I was to be a peace offering to Nicneven," the Prince said, with more equanimity than Lune thought the situation deserved. "She has threatened to kill me before."

"Perhaps." Lune tried to think past her instinctive revulsion, and the throbbing of the old wound in her shoulder. Irrith had been green, and understandably so, when a few brave souls came running to see why there was iron in the Prince's chambers. The sprite was abed now, with a draught from the Goodemeades to restore her, and Lune had every intention of rewarding her with a knighthood. Irrith would likely not see the point of such a title, but Lune meant to acknowledge her valour. "Or perhaps Vidar meant something worse."

Antony paled, showing he was not so sanguine about his close escape as he had seemed. "Worse?"

She paced across the chamber, stabbing the heels of her shoes into the Turkish carpet. She wanted stone beneath her feet, the hard impact and ringing noise. "It is no secret any longer that you are an integral part of my connection to my realm. What if you were severed from me by iron?" Despite her control, her voice wavered on the last word.

He did not answer. Like her, he could only imagine—but the possibilities ranged from bad to horrific. Lune doubted it would destroy the palace on the spot, but it might vitally weaken the enchantments, and at the very least it would leave her vulnerable, lacking half her power.

She had been one drop of blood away from finding out.

Vidar was locked beneath the Tower now, and the hawthorn box with its dreadful contents secured. But too many fae knew what had happened; they knew Vidar had been found.

Sooner or later, Nicneven would hear.

Antony knew that as well as she did. Leaving aside the question of the traitor's purpose, he asked, "What do you intend to do?"

It was not a safer or more cheerful direction of thought. Lune was no faerie philosopher, but she had spoken to a few, in roundabout fashion, of Nicneven's threat. She began with the death of mortal sovereignty in England, reborn when Charles the Second reclaimed his throne, and the philosophers found much of interest in that. But when she asked them to consider faerie sovereignty, their speculation had turned much grimmer.

Her instinct was correct. If she permitted Nicneven to hold the Onyx Hall to ransom—if Lune, a sovereign Queen, bent to the will of another—then she surrendered her realm. To give in to the threat would be to recognise the Gyre-Carling as a greater authority than Lune herself, one with power over the Onyx Hall she could not contest.

And if she did that, she would be Queen no more.

What came after that, even the philosophers could not say. Either Nicneven would be Queen in London, or no one would—but neither fate was acceptable.

She had shared this with Antony, reluctantly, and even begun to hope in the privacy of her heart that the Gyre-Carling would find Vidar before she did. It didn't matter whether the Queen of Fife got what she desired; it only mattered that Lune not let her realm be used to force her into surrendering him.

But Vidar's attempt on Antony, and Irrith's valour in stopping him, had left her with only one option. "I must execute him," Lune said.

Antony nodded. "So I presumed. I meant something more, though. What will you do *before* that?"

Lune's brow furrowed. "Summon all my court... do you think I should send word to Berkshire, and wait for any who wish to attend?"

473

"If you like. Let me put it more bluntly: will you place him on trial?"

He might as well have spoken French, so little did Lune expect his words. "Trial? Antony, you cannot doubt his guilt. Even were his earlier crimes in question, you saw what he tried to do to you!"

"I do not doubt it," Antony said. "But if it is certain, then it is easily proved—and why not do so? Conduct a proper trial."

"Proper?" It came out a disbelieving laugh. "We are not mortals, Antony."

What made him propose this so sombrely? "No, you are not," he agreed. "But that does not mean you have no concern for justice."

"*Justice* will be his death."

"Because you will it?" The question startled Lune into silence. "That is your royal prerogative, Lune. But you know my opinion on such things; it has not changed these many years. I disagreed with Pym on too many points to count, his endless attempts to strip power from the King and place it in Parliament's hands, but in one matter he and I were in accord: we detested Charles's prerogative courts. Justice must be an orderly thing, not the whim of a single person."

"You think it a *whim?* " Pain tightened Lune's heart. "Antony, the fate of a traitor is death, among fae as well as mortals."

He nodded again, but this time there was irony in it.

"I see. And that, of course, is why you executed all the other traitors—like Sir Prigurd."

A dozen answers, all trying to emerge at once, choked Lune's attempt to reply. Prigurd had tried to help, in his belated fashion; as for the others, to kill them all would have been an act of unthinkable murder. She had her reasons—

But that was Antony's point. She had made her decisions alone, on her own judgement, without recourse to any standard save that she set for herself.

Quietly, without accusation, Antony said, "Arbitrary behaviour is made no more attractive because it comes from a faerie."

Lune winced. "You were upset that I dealt with Prigurd in your absence; I understand that. I will not exclude you a second time. The exile almost killed you, Antony, and it was Vidar's doing; you have every right to take part in his judgement."

He smiled, as if she had said exactly what he hoped she would. "Good. Then for my part, I demand you put Ifarren Vidar on trial, and prove his guilt before all."

Lune closed her eyes, despairing. "You will not give this up, will you?"

"Indeed I will not."

She gritted her teeth. "He will be shown guilty."

"I have no doubt of it."

Then what was the point? To establish a procedure; to make the judgement of a traitor an orderly thing. And, Lune suspected, to give the people of her court some voice in punishing the author of their suffering.

Antony had absorbed more of the Commonwealth's ideals than he realised.

"Very well," Lune said through her teeth. "You shall have your trial."

THE ONYX COURT, LONDON
28 July 1665

She had cause to regret that concession as the next fortnight passed. Promising a trial was one matter; deciding how to conduct it was another. While Vidar languished in a cell, bricked up so thoroughly that only a tiny sprite no bigger than a dragonfly could get through to verify his presence, she tried to sort out a basis for the event.

The problem, which Antony no doubt had foreseen, was that trials were a thing of law, and the fae had none. They ran their world on common sense and royal prerogative: if the Queen deemed something a crime, it was, and she had the right to pass sentence. She suspected Antony's true hope was that they would write themselves a proper code of law—but she was certainly not delaying Vidar's execution for *that*.

We are not humans, she thought, but wondered how much strength lay in that defence. True, her realm was smaller, her subjects fewer, their society much simpler than the one above. Did they truly need laws and trials? But though she could reassure herself that she was a better Queen than old Charles had been King, she had enough perspective to understand how little that meant. Royal prerogative was royal prerogative, whether exercised with good judgement or bad. The rightness of the thing itself was separate from her person.

She damned Antony for putting such thoughts into her head, where they buzzed about like bees, and did not give her a moment's peace.

In the end, she prepared for the trial by dividing her court into groups: the Onyx Guard, the Berkshire fae in residence, her privy council, and so on, allowing each one to select a single individual to serve on the jury. She ended up with nine, not the twelve the mortals liked, but no matter. Nine or twelve, she had no fear any of them would find Vidar innocent of his crimes.

The final problem came when she turned to the mortals, and discovered just how few of them remained. She knew the plague had thinned their ranks, either by killing them or sending them into flight, but she was disturbed to find only two left, not counting Antony.

While she was distracted, a vital part of her court had all but melted away.

I will fix it, Lune promised herself. But, as with so many things, it would have to wait. The mortals met to choose their juror, and by a vote of two to one chose Antony. "This is a faerie matter," he said when she expressed her doubts. "You will be the judge of this case, not I. It would have been better for one of them to serve, but I will do it."

He was playing a lawyer's game, asserting his authority when it suited him, discarding it when it did not, but by then Lune's patience had worn so thin she did not quibble. She just wanted the trial to be done.

They met beneath the mended ceiling of the great presence chamber. The jury sat in a line to either side of Lune's throne, four to her left, five to her right; Antony's own seat had been removed, and he sat at the far end of the line, so as to avoid the impression that he sat in judgement as the Prince. A chair faced them, awaiting the accused, and from behind it her subjects watched in silence.

"We hereby open the trial of Ifarren Vidar," she said into the still air, "formerly a subject of this realm, having the title of Lord Keeper, which was stripped from him when he fled into foreign parts after our accession. His guilt will be judged by this assembly of nine, chosen out of the groups most affected by the late rebellions and invasions that have afflicted this realm. Let the—" *Do not call him traitor; not yet.* "Let the accused be brought in."

A path had been left for him, down which a pair of goblins marched him under guard. The rowan-wood shackles once binding Prigurd were on his ankles and feet, though simple chains would have been enough to hold his bony limbs. Vidar wore them with disdain, and did not acknowledge the presence of any others in the chamber. His black eyes fixed unblinkingly upon Lune.

Now their positions were reversed; she sat upon the

throne from which he had revealed his invasion of her realm. The throne that had been Invidiana's.

She had not dared destroy it; the great silver arc of its back concealed the London Stone, and she could not risk that secret being revealed. But Vidar's regard made her unpleasantly aware of the throne's history, and of the crown upon her head. He gave her a brief nod, a faint smile—as if approving her achievements. As if to say, *You have won the game I once played.*

But it had never been a game to her. She was not like Vidar.

The contact between them broke when he sat, sprawling elegantly in the chair provided. Lune spoke again, words prepared with care. "Ifarren Vidar. You stand accused of conspiring with two foreign powers for the overthrow of our authority; of abetting the efforts of the late Kentigern Nellt to subvert our royal guard; of giving information to our enemies so that they might send murderers and other attackers against our safety; of attempting violence against the Prince of the Stone, and the final destruction of this palace that shelters us now. You also stand accused of fomenting riots and conflict among the mortals above, to disrupt our realm below. How do you answer these charges?"

Vidar's bone-white skin was unmarked, and his black clothes were immaculate. Someone had given him water to wash in; perhaps Antony. It would be like the Prince, to insist on giving the accused his dignity, despite everything. If there was to be a trial, it must appear—must *be*—legitimate.

Yet trials were not a thing fae did. Lune expected the mocking smile that spread across Vidar's face. He might sneer at mortals, calling them pawns, but he would have paid at least enough attention to know the farce Charles had made of his own trial, denying the authority of the court that faced him. But unlike the Lord President then, Lune was prepared for it. Her prerogative was to dispose of traitors as she pleased; if it pleased her to delegate that authority to others, she had the right.

"I am guilty," Vidar said.

What?

He laughed outright at her dumbfounded expression. "What, should I dance for your pleasure? Plead my innocence, when not a faerie soul here would call me anything other than guilty?" His voice dripped venomous emphasis on *faerie,* dismissing the mortals as without consequence. "I could deride this *trial* of yours, but it hardly seems worth the effort. I am surprised you do not let the humans drip holy water on your head and wash your immortality from you, you love their world so much."

Lune fought her breath back under control before she answered him. Murmurs ran through the hall, and the jurors were shifting in their seats. Antony was as startled as she—but she could not look to him for help. It would only lend credence to Vidar's words.

"You are guilty, by your own admission," Lune said, striving to sound neither surprised nor displeased. "Therefore there is no need for trial."

Vidar bared his teeth at her in a terrible smile. "Indeed. This is my favour to you, Lune. After all, you have thirsted for my blood since before you stole the throne you sit upon now. I am your enemy, and I threaten the security of your power. Does this sound familiar? Speak the words! Order my death. *It is what Invidiana would have done.*"

Bile scalded her throat. *Sun and Moon...*

How many had Invidiana sent to their deaths, from this very seat? For a whim, for an evening's entertainment—Lune was not like that. But amusement was only the secondary force driving the former Queen's actions. Foremost, always, was the security of her own power.

Invidiana did not always kill those who posed a threat. If they could be punished in other fashions—disgraced, exiled, forced into penance, and thereby used to serve some larger scheme—then they lived.

Lune tried, and failed, to banish Cerenel's voice from her memory, swearing the oath she forced upon him.

But if a courtier had no further value to Invidiana, if the danger they presented outweighed their use... then she ground them beneath her heel, to keep all the rest in line.

I am not like her.

Or was she? How often had she dreamed of Vidar's death, sought it with every power at her disposal? She hesitated to kill—except for him. Not because he threatened her immediate safety, as Kentigern had when they called down the stones to crush him, but simply because he could serve no purpose but to threaten her power.

Silence reigned in the chamber. Few even seemed to be breathing. Vidar waited, smirking. *Why would he do this? He gains nothing by admitting his guilt, save his own death!*

But his death was a foregone conclusion. By advancing to meet it, he achieved the one victory left to him: he hurt Lune, struck at the very heart of her confidence upon the throne.

And if she executed him, every faerie who remembered Invidiana would recall his words forever.

Yet he could not live. Casting desperately about for any escape from this trap, Lune felt a smile spread across her own face, rising out of the vindictive triumph growing in her soul. He thought to claim one final victory, but she would deny him.

"Lord Valentin," she called out, not looking away from Vidar, and heard a startled reply from the audience. "We have need of the item we recently entrusted to your safekeeping."

"The b—" The Lord Keeper's answer cut off abruptly. "Your Majesty—"

"We are waiting, Lord Valentin."

At the edge of her vision, she saw him bow and exit the chamber, dragging one of the remaining mortals with him. Murmurs ran through the hall, fae asking one another what the Queen referred to.

"Silence," Lune commanded, and received it. "We have delegated our authority to judge these crimes; we therefore ask the jury to render their verdicts." How long would it take Valentin to return? Once out of her sight, he would run very fast. "Ifarren Vidar has confessed his guilt to all the crimes named. Do you acknowledge and confirm that guilt?"

Mere pageantry, making a grander occasion out of the truncated trial, and giving Valentin time to return. Vidar waited with the patient smugness of an incipient martyr. One by one, the nine jurors stood and stated their recognition of his guilt. *We shall leave it beyond all question.*

And when they were done, she said, "What sentence do you advise for such a traitor?"

Fae were often reluctant to kill, but not now. Every group had chosen the individual most eager to have a part in punishing Nicneven's chief lieutenant in the long struggles between London and Fife. One by one, the jurors stood and called for death, Antony last of all.

The Prince would not like what she was about to do. But in the end, she was the Queen; she might listen to advice, but in the end the decision was hers, for the good of her realm. Antony was not here as Prince, and this faerie matter was not his to judge.

Vidar thought it nothing more than a means of shedding the guilt for his death. His smirk grew ever wider. But when Aspell and his companion re-entered at the back of the hall, and Lune dismissed the jurors from the dais, a hint of confusion began to creep into the traitor's expression.

The watching fae turned, and saw the box of hawthorn in the mortal's hands.

The chamber rang with a gasp of horror so loud it was nearly a shout, and everyone shied back, forgetting the solemnity of the occasion. It left a wide aisle down which Valentin passed, followed by the mortal bearer.

While all eyes in the hall were upon them, Lune slipped a piece of bread free of her pocket and swallowed it. She carried some with her always now, for safety, and was glad of it.

The two reached the dais. All others had shifted well back, save Lune, Vidar, and Angrisla, who held the traitor forcibly in his chair. At Lune's gesture, the mortal placed the box at her feet, and then gladly joined Valentin in retreating.

"Ifarren Vidar. For your crimes," Lune said, "you merit death. But the murder of fae is abhorrent to us, and so we grant you this measure of mercy. We sentence you to imprisonment eternal—guarded not by lock and key, which may be broken, nor by watchmen, who may be bribed, but by the elemental forces that bind all fae."

She lifted the lid of the hawthorn box.

The thing inside was small, no wider than the span of Lune's hand. But it exuded a cold aura far beyond its size, that chilled her even through the protection of the bread. Iron had tasted of her flesh; its taint lingered in her blood, inside the defence of the mortal tithe. Lune had not expected that. Her intention had been to lift the box free herself, but she could not bring herself to hold it so closely. She had to gesture the mortal forward again, and have him set it atop the replaced hawthorn lid.

Now everyone could see it. The black sides were unadorned; its lid bore only a blank shield. But it was the one prison nothing could break free of, not even a faerie spirit—and she had in mind a way to ensure no one would ever let him out.

Vidar knew it, too. All the smugness was gone, and sick horror had descended in its place. But this was the fate he would have condemned Antony to; Lune remembered that, and used her fury as armour and goad alike. *It is no mercy, but then again, he deserves none.* She forced herself to reach out.

The touch of the iron was like the hottest fire and the coldest ice, and it called forth an excruciating answer from the half-healed wound in her shoulder. Lune was dimly aware of a scuffle, but had no attention to spare; clenching her teeth until she thought her jaw would break, she lifted the lid, and snatched her hand back the instant it was done.

The scuffle, it seemed, had been Vidar's attempted escape. He now lay face-down on the floor three paces from his chair, with Angrisla on his back, twisting his hands in a tight grip. He might be sanguine about his death, but not this.

Lune was more than ready for the box to be gone. "Bring me the prisoner's blood," she said, and the mara grinned toothily. A demented light shone in her eyes as she faced down the iron aura, holding her position by will alone. Bonecruncher would not come near, but slid a knife along the polished floor to her. Angrisla carved a long slash down Vidar's arm, then glared at the mortal until he fetched it and bore it to Lune.

She took the dagger and held it over the black interior of the box. "Thus do we carry out the traitor's sentence," she said, through her nausea and pain. Three taps of her finger sent three droplets flying from the tip, swallowed up by the impenetrable darkness.

Vidar *howled*. He writhed with abrupt strength, hurling Angrisla from his back, but then his body locked into a rictus; frozen, contorted upon the stone, he was a picture of perfect agony. Then he was insubstantial, then faint as a ghost; then he was gone, leaving blank marble and empty chains where his body had been.

A new light shone within the box, blood-red and murderous.

Lune slammed the lid shut. A spider now stared at her from the formerly blank shield. Shuddering at the sight, she gestured the mortal to retreat. He did so, with visible relief.

No one else looked relieved. But they would not have to endure much longer. "Lord Antony, if you would join me? Let us together place Vidar's prison where it will disturb no one's rest."

A deep line cut between his brows as he approached; she thought he understood her meaning, but doubted whether it would work. *I hope it does. I can think of no better way.* He took up the box, and at Lune's nod replaced it within its hawthorn case.

Her subjects breathed easier with the iron thus shielded, but when Lune reached out to the Onyx Hall, she still felt the taint inside the wood, like poison beneath a sugared coating. Or was that her imagination? Her hand tightened on Antony's, and she heard his breath hiss between his teeth, as if he felt it, too. But the Hall answered when they called; the marble split open, as if it were sand falling away from beneath the box. Down it went; down, and down, deeper into the foundations of the Hall than she had ever gone, until at last it reached some indefinable boundary. The palace lay *beneath* London, but only in a mystical sense; one could not reach it with a shovel. Yet there was a point at which the Hall gave way to ordinary earth once more, the bedrock upon which London sat.

They left the iron box there, and sealed the stone above it.

Every single pair of eyes in the chamber was fixed on the floor, which had swallowed Vidar's prison without a trace. Lune pried her hand free of Antony's, and cast a sideways glance at him. He met it with a faint smile, knowing her concern. But his eyes were clear, and he showed no sign of weakness.

"It is finished," Lune said. "Let Ifarren Vidar be forgotten."

GUILDHALL, LONDON
12 August 1665

The hoof beats of Antony's horse echoed off the walls and overhanging jetties of Ketton Street. He might have been alone in the world, the street devoid of its usual hawkers and housewives. London might as well have been snatched away to a different realm, leaving its people behind; even the Onyx Hall seemed more populous these days than the city above it.

Antony sweated behind the kerchief wrapped over his nose and mouth, and wondered how much it protected him against the infected air. But leaving it off would certainly *not* help, and so he kept it on—just as he rode, instead of hiring a hackney coach, whose previous occupant might have borne the plague. His own coach gathered dust for lack of anyone to drive it. Antony's household was reduced to Burnett and himself, and Burnett had enough to do, keeping his master fed and clothed. He was lucky to still have a horse, so many had been stolen.

A pile of rubbish half blocked the turn onto the narrow lane between the church of St Laurence Jewry and Blackwell Hall—the remnant of some shopkeeper's effort to sweep the street before his house, in accordance with the plague orders. But no one had taken the refuse away, and the shopkeeper had clearly abandoned his effort weeks ago. Antony guided his horse past and emerged a moment later into the tiny courtyard of the Guildhall. On an ordinary day it would have been thronged with men engaged in government and trade; now it stood all but empty under the gaze of the statues adorning the Guildhall porch. Christ and the Virtues, their faces blank and stern. The only living figure in sight was a lone watchman, standing by the Triple Tun, whose door was marked with the familiar red cross and the legend *Lord Have Mercy Upon Us*.

Antony had long since given up shuddering at the sight.

One could hardly find a street in London that did not hold at least one infected house.

The Guildhall itself stood forlorn, nearly as empty as the courtyard outside. Lord Mayor Lawrence had not called a meeting of the aldermen in weeks; half the council was fled. But Antony hoped that very desolation would aid him today. Men feared gathering in public places, where plague might spread. Here, though, their only company would be the spiders spinning their webs undisturbed.

He lit tallow dips in the Court of Aldermen, and brushed dust from his own seat. How many would come today? Sir William Turner for certain; *he* understood that his City needed him. Others had stayed as well. With the help of parish officials, they carried out the plague orders issued by Charles before he withdrew with his court, in the withering hope that it would somehow check the plague's ever-rising tide. Nearly three thousand dead in the last week alone, and no sign of ebb.

Lune's thoughts were elsewhere, waiting to see if Vidar's cruel punishment would satisfy Nicneven and prevent war. But Antony had given up on blaming the fae for their inaction. In the dark of the night, when he lay in his bed alone, he did not believe any effort, faerie or otherwise, could make a difference.

And then the morning came, and he rose, and carried on nonetheless.

Footsteps outside the door. Antony straightened, but could not prevent a slump of disappointment when he saw

Jack Ellin. "I hoped you were an alderman."

"Then I am even sorrier to bring you this news."

The bleak tone pierced Antony's weariness, and he saw in the candlelight that Jack's ironical face was pale and strained. "You—are not *ill?*"

His mind leapt to that conclusion without prodding; it was the obvious one, nowadays. With Jack, more than obvious: the man, in his lunacy, was offering his services as a physician in the parish of St Giles Cripplegate, now among the worst afflicted. Over three hundred and fifty dead there last week, and those were only the ones reported as plague; they were scarcely half the full total. Antony's mind tallied the numbers reflexively.

The doctor shook his head. "Not I. But Burnett, yes."

It should have upset Antony. Perhaps somewhere, far beneath his exhaustion, it did. At the moment, it was a blow to insensate flesh. Impact, without meaning. "How—"

"I called at your house this morning. He answered the door in a fever." Jack's jaw tensed, heralding his next words. "I examined him, and found the tokens."

Hard red spots on the body, like fleabites. Coupled with fever, an infallible sign of the plague.

"Antony." The name broke through his dazed blankness. Jack crossed the room with swift strides, but halted himself before he could take Antony's arm. No doubt the doctor had worn gloves and all the rest of his usual costume when examining Burnett, but even standing this close could be dangerous, if Jack had breathed in the distempered vapours.

How much longer could the man survive, going so often among the diseased?

"Antony," Jack said, softly. "You must send him to a pest-house."

He shook, roused himself. "Incarcerate him among the dying? I might as well shoot him myself."

"He'll likely die anyway," Jack said. The topic was too familiar for tact. "The pest-house will not help his chances—but it will help *yours*. Antony, if you don't send him away, they'll shut up your house. *With you in it.*"

The backbone of all their attempts to stem the plague. A man could carry the distemper without knowing it; anyone who lived under the same roof as a victim must be locked in, until enough time had passed to prove they were not sick.

Or until everyone inside was dead.

Antony swallowed and turned away. "You have said yourself—the pest-houses are overwhelmed." They had managed to build three, supplementing the two left over from the last great visitation, but they were scarce able to hold a few hundred, let alone the stricken thousands.

Jack would not let him dodge the question. "If you will not send him away, then you must leave. Remove yourself from the house, *today*, and go into the countryside. Join Kate. Shutting yourself in with him... you might as well put that pistol to your *own* head."

They had fought this point before. Jack hated that order, and championed the pest-houses. What he advised now was nothing less than the knowing subversion of law.

If Antony already bore the plague, he would carry it with him into the countryside, as others had done before him: the exact situation the plague order was designed to prevent.

That argument would make not a dent in Jack's skull. Instead Antony said, "I cannot leave. We are meeting today to arrange relief; we've found ways to shift collections of coin from the parishes that can spare it to those that cannot, and to delay the payment of certain debts. Half London can scarcely feed itself, Jack, and trade is at a standstill. Would you have me abandon my city to famine and collapse?"

"No." A trace of the old, wry smile crossed Jack's face. "I know you better than that. But you cannot do that work shut up in your house with a red cross on the door, either. You *must* send Burnett away."

The very thought of it ached. Burnett was loyal, and deserved loyalty in return. Antony would gladly have kept him at home, and hired some woman to nurse him—one who had survived the infection already. Far better than sending him into that festering realm of hell in St Giles Cripplegate, where they could almost throw a corpse out a window and have it land in a plague pit.

Where Burnett would die, alone.

But keeping him would mean the end of Antony's own ability to help.

More footsteps outside. Sir William Turner appeared in the doorway, and someone else hovered behind him. Two aldermen, at least; with Antony, three. Perhaps they would get more. And together, they might keep London on her feet.

They would. They had to.

Antony lowered his voice, and hoped that hid the shame in it. "Very well. Do everything you can for him, Jack."

The doctor gripped his arm, heedless of risk. "My oath to God. I will save him if I can."

CHEAP WARD, LONDON
13 September 1665

Despite the oppressive heat, Antony shivered as he made his way on foot down Cheapside. Charred logs still crouched at the corner with Old Change, though the sudden downpour that extinguished the bonfire last week had vanished without a trace, returning the summer's terrible dryness in its wake.

Three days of bonfires, burning throughout the City, ordered by the King from his court at Salisbury. Three days of flame, to purify the air.

Seven thousand dead, that very same week.

He swerved left to give a wide margin to a body slumped against the wall of the Mermaid Tavern. Dead, or dying; it hardly mattered which. The reek of death was in the air, the churchyards filled to overflowing and beyond, despite the orders that insisted all corpses be buried at least six feet deep.

His change of course brought him too close to another man, who shot out bony hands and seized Antony by the front of his waistcoat, crumpling the sweaty cloth in his fingers. "They insist we purge our bodies with potions," the man gasped, foul breath gusting into Antony's face. "They insist we purge the air with fire. But do we purge our *souls*? Do we repent our sins, which have brought this visitation upon us?"

A moment of frozen paralysis; then Antony shoved at the man, struggling to force him away. The buttons of his waistcoat gave way before the stranger did. "Get back! Do not come near me."

The man laughed at him, exposing broken teeth, as if he had been struck in the face. "You have nothing to fear—if you are a righteous man. This is the Lord's will, His divine punishment for a nation that has strayed from the path of holiness."

A filthy, damnable Puritan. Rage flushed Antony to the roots of his thinning hair. "God," he snarled in the man's face, "has nothing to do with it. This? Is random bloody *chance*. It is our physical squalor, the garbage in our streets, the foul air we breathe. The pestilential suburbs we permit to crowd around our walls. *God is not here*. He watches from above as we scream in our agonies and die, begging His mercy or cursing His name, and He has *nothing* to do with any of it!"

The last shouted words echoed in his ears, reflecting off the smoke-stained walls of the shops that lined this once great street. The Puritan was running by then, staggering down Bow Lane, desperate to get away. Antony gasped for breath, his head pounding. When had he last eaten? He could not recall. With Burnett gone, vanished into the maw of the pest-house, no doubt dead by now, he made shift for himself as best he could.

There should still be a cold meat pie for him at home—if he had not eaten it already. Antony could not remember. They could feed him below, but he would not go; he could not bear the sight of the fae anymore, clean and whole and safe from the cataclysm above. If this heat did not break, if the plague did not subside, then even the living few would soon be gone, and London left to the ghosts and the faeries in the shadows.

He set off again, moving more by force of habit than anything else, down Lombard Street to the familiar door. He fumbled a cluster of rue out of his pocket and breathed deeply of its pungent scent, hoping to clear any contagion picked up from that man. Was there anything yet in his house that could take this headache from him? He could scarcely think through its clamour.

The door opened. The interior of the house was blessedly cool, no fire having been lit in the hearth for days, and Antony wrenched off his doublet and waistcoat, baring his sweat-soaked undershirt. The thought of food turned his stomach. He would eat later, after he had rested. Dropping the garments to the floor, Antony sought his bed, where he lay shivering and restless, waiting for his tremors to cease.

THE ONYX HALL, LONDON
14 September 1665

"The problem," Valentin Aspell said patiently, "is that it *fades*, your Majesty."

MARIE BRENNAN

Lune resisted the urge to snarl at him. Instead she forged her irritation into a sharper, cooler edge of condescension. "I am aware of the nature of faerie gold, Lord Valentin. But with judicious timing, we might yet be able to assist Lord Antony in a manner that does not expose us to the threats above. If we can do nothing for the sick, we may at least help those who are still well, by giving them the coin with which to buy food and other necessities."

As her Lord Keeper reminded her, faerie gold would eventually turn back to leaves, and that could draw unwanted attention. But from what Antony said, the chaos above had reached such a pitch that their interference might pass unremarked. He had even named a few fellows that might be suitable targets. One boasted of increasing his personal wealth as he rushed all over London and Westminster to obtain supplies for the Navy in their wars against the Dutch, yet gave only a few pounds for the relief of the afflicted.

"Samuel Pepys," she suggested to Valentin. "In Seething Lane. Substitute faerie gold for some of his own, and I shall give the true coin to Antony, for distribution elsewhere."

The Lord Keeper bowed. He did not see the point of this, Lune knew. To his way of thinking, the plague was a necessary cleansing of the filthy, overcrowded streets of London and its suburbs. Humans were not meant to live like maggots, crawling over the rotting corpse of their home, polluting their houses with their own smoke and waste. He had little understanding of them as people, and no sympathy for their plight.

But Lune did. The carnage above sickened her, evoking the terrifying spectre of mortality; she shuddered at the thought of going above, among the boarded-up windows and the painted crosses and the desperate prayers of the dying. Yet this little thing, she could do. She knew Antony thought her wholly occupied with faerie affairs, the breathless wait for Nicneven's next move, but the waiting threatened to drive her mad. And it would ease his heart to know she had done something, small though it was. When he returned, she would have a surprise for him: a windfall from the men who gilded their own coffers while others starved for want of charity.

"Why are you still here?" she asked Valentin, who flinched. "Find someone to carry this out—or I will send *you*."

"Yes, madam," he murmured, and fled.

LOMBARD STREET, LONDON
15 September 1665

Antony needed water. A raging thirst had scoured him for hours, parching his throat and mouth and gut, while sweat poured off his skin to soak the clinging bedclothes. He had fetched watered wine from the cellar... he could not remember how long ago. The jug sat empty now, knocked onto its side, though he could not recall drinking from it. Perhaps he had spilled it all.

He called weakly for Burnett, in a voice that went no

farther than his bed, before remembering the servant was gone. In the pest-house. Dead, by now.

Pain stabbed upward from his groin, curling his body in protest. Medicine. Was there nothing in the house for pain? For the headache that threatened to split his skull in half? Antony knew dimly that he had a fever, and must bring it down—cool cloths, soaked in water, to lay across his forehead. Kate would do that. She had gentle hands.

No. Kate was not here either. Dead? God forbid... no, she was in Norfolk still. They exchanged letters, but only rarely, since few men were brave enough to carry the post. He prayed the plague had not come to her there. She was safe, as Jack wanted Antony to be.

The stairs creaked. Burnett at last; the servant must have heard him call. No, his voice was gone; but Burnett was a good man, and came to check on him regardless.

"God have mercy..."

Not Burnett. Antony forced his eyes open, and Jack Ellin's face swam into focus. He croaked the name, unsure whether this was another figment of his fever.

Jack had nothing over his mouth; he should be wearing a kerchief, or one of those ridiculous beaked masks some doctors affected, stuffing the front with strong herbs to cleanse the air they breathed. The man's hands felt like ice through Antony's sodden linen shirt. He shivered uncontrollably and tried to push them away, but Jack evaded him with ease and yanked the laces open. Antony gasped in pain as the physician rolled his head to one side and then the other, checking his neck and under his arms; then agony lanced through him again as Jack pulled aside his drawers to examine his thighs.

The doctor growled an oath, and that forced home the truth Antony had been denying all this time. Telling himself it was just a fever. A headache. It would pass.

"I am dying," he whispered.

The pain was unmistakable. Bad now, it would only grow worse, until he ran mad, and thought of ending his own life to end his suffering. Antony could feel the swellings in his groin, not just tokens but the very stamp of the plague.

"You will *not* die," Jack said violently, and shifted his weight back, preparatory to a burst of activity that would bring all his medicinal art to bear on the task of saving Antony's life.

Antony caught his arm before he could stand, digging his fingers in hard. "Listen. You must do something for me. You *must.*"

Jack covered the hand with his own. "Tell me."

"You must do it. Your oath on it. Swear to me, before God, that you will do *exactly* as I bid you. No matter—no matter how strange it seems. No matter what you see."

The physician's face grew hesitant. "Antony—I must fetch my medicines, lance the swellings—"

"*Later,*" Antony rasped. He did not know whether it was sweat or tears that ran down his cheeks. "Swear it!"

Jack swallowed, then nodded once. "As God is

my witness, I will do as you bid me. If it will get you to cooperate, I'll do anything."

Antony sagged back against the pillow, made weak by relief. His hand trembled against Jack's arm, its grip now slackened. "Thank you. God bless you, John Ellin. You may save my life indeed."

THE ANGEL INN, ISLINGTON
15 September 1665

What in the name of the Devil's unholy arsehole am I doing here?

Fulfilling his oath to Antony. Every stride Jack's horse took northward felt like another strip carved out of his heart; he should be back in Lombard Street, burning quicklime and spices to cleanse the room, getting opium and hopefully some food into his afflicted friend.

But Antony would not rest; he kept repeating his feverish words. And so Jack rode north into Islington, on the word of a dying—

Do not say " dying."

On the word of a very sick man.

The faster Jack carried out his duty, the sooner he could get on with his treatment. It had saved some patients, he believed. None of them so old as Antony, true—

He snarled the thought away, and dismounted behind the Angel Inn.

Go to the rosebush, Antony had said, *and tell it your name.*

Jack felt like an ass, but he suspected a secret meaning in the instruction. Antony had friends, he knew, from before the King's restoration, and subtle means of passing information; Jack had long thought some of them associated with the Angel Inn. Speaking to the rosebush was no doubt a signal. But he didn't share Antony's apparent conviction that someone would be watching, ready to receive his message.

Nevertheless, he had sworn it. So, taking a deep breath, Jack bent to one withered, rain-starved blossom and said, "My name is Dr John Ellin. Sir Antony Ware has sent me to say that he has fallen ill with the plague. He is in his house in Lombard Street, and begs—"

He got no further, because the rosebush began to move. The tendrils stretched themselves upward, forming a graceful arch. Jack stumbled backward in surprise, then fell without dignity on his rump as a woman appeared in the arch. "Lord Antony? Sick? Oh, *no*—"

Then *she* stopped, because a familiar sound rang out over the grassy field: the church bell of Islington, tolling the death of a parishioner.

The woman's eyes rolled up in her head, and she crumpled to the ground.

Jack sat in the grass, staring. *Did a three-foot-tall woman just come out of a rosebush and faint at my feet?*

He had his answer an instant later, when a second woman of equally small stature popped out of the arch, looking harassed and bearing a tiny cup in one hand. She made an exasperated noise when she saw the figure on the ground. "Honestly, if she had just listened—I warned her not to come out unprepared."

Reflex took over; Jack crawled forward and supported the unconscious woman—girl? No, she was mature, though dwarfish in size—helping the other pour what looked to be a swallow of milk down her throat. "She fainted—"

"Yes, the bell. I heard it." The woman tucked the cup into her rose-embroidered apron. "Come now, Gertrude, wake up—there's a good girl."

Honey-brown eyes fluttered open. She blinked twice, dazed, before seeming to realise she was lying against Jack's knees. Then she sat bolt upright. "Antony!"

He rose, backing up a pace, and brushed the dirt and dried grass from the knees of his breeches. The two women were so much alike, they could only be sisters; were it not for their different aprons, he would have trouble distinguishing them. Antony had told him to bear this message to "the sisters", and one thing more, to a specific name. If the woman with the daisies was called Gertrude, then the other... "Are you Lune?"

The woman with the roses blinked. "What? No, of course not. She isn't here. Why—"

"I have a message for her as well."

Focusing his mind on that errand helped. As long as he concentrated on his promise to Antony, he could keep the rest of that promise: to carry out his task no matter what he saw.

Both of the women were standing now. "Tell us," Gertrude said.

Their faces were pitiful with concern; whoever else— *whatever* else—they were, Jack believed them true friends of Antony's. But his oath was the only thing holding him together right now. "No. The words are for Lune alone; I'll give them only to her."

"Young man," the rose-woman began, but her sister cut her off. "Rosamund, we haven't the time. Lord Antony sent him; we must trust him. And the Queen will want to know, regardless."

Catherine of Braganza? She was in Salisbury with the King. *Let it pass.* Rosamund fixed him with a piercing glare and said, "For Lord Antony's sake, then—follow us, and do as we bid you, without question."

He'd already sworn it, but there was no point in wasting time telling her that. Jack nodded, and they both sighed in relief. "I will make the horses," Gertrude said, "and we shall go."

THE ONYX HALL, LONDON
15 September 1665

He went along with everything. He didn't ask why Rosamund and Gertrude were taller when they mounted up for the ride. He didn't blink when they stopped at an alder tree along St Martin's Lane and the sisters' horses seemed to vanish into thin air, straws falling to the ground where they had been.

He even managed to keep from screaming when the alder tree swallowed him whole.

A distant, perversely calm part of his mind suggested that his brain was too dazed for questions or even fear, but that when he had a moment to think, he would react very strongly indeed. It was probably true. For now, Jack just gaped at everything, like a clod of a farmer come into London for the first time.

Smooth black walls rose around him, lit by cool lights that seemed to float without support. Creatures stared at him as he passed—beings that made Rosamund and Gertrude look entirely normal by comparison. The very *air* felt different, secret and hushed, as if he walked in a shadow made solid.

Any doubt he might have had as to the nature of this place and its inhabitants fell into dust when he walked into a great, vaulted chamber and saw the woman on the throne.

She sat beneath a glittering canopy of estate that would have beggared Charles to buy, framed by the sweeping arch of silver that formed the throne's back. Her own hair gleamed as brightly beneath the fanlike coronet that capped it, while the midnight silk of her gown provided a splash of jewelled colour. The high bones of her face never belonged to anything human.

The elfin woman was speaking to a serpentine man, her tone quite sharp, but she cut off when the sisters hurtled past a startled and sticklike usher, their shoes tapping a rapid beat against the marble floor. "Gertrude? Rosamund?" she said, in clear, resonant tones. "Is something amiss?"

They dropped perfunctory curtsies, as if begrudging even that instant of delay. "Your Majesty," Rosamund said, "this man bears you a message from Lord Antony."

Immediately, every eye in the chamber was on Jack. He had followed at the sisters' heels, but forgotten in his stupor to bow; he did so now, as clumsily as he had ever done, and felt the amusement of some of the watching courtiers. The resulting spark of anger steadied him, and when he straightened, he met the faerie Queen's gaze without flinching. "Are you Lune?"

"I am," she said, ignoring the gasps at his insolent address.

"Then Sir Antony bids me ask you this: if you will not save London, will you at least save him?"

Dead silence. No one so much as breathed, let alone laughed. Seeing Lune's stricken face, Jack wondered for the first time at the content of Antony's message. He'd taken it without thinking, assuming it all to be part of the man's feverish rantings—but no. Clearly it had meaning.

A meaning that hurt this elfin Queen, struck deeply at her heart. He had not realised, coming here, that his first words to her would be so terribly cruel.

"Madam," Gertrude whispered into that terrible hush, "'tis the plague."

The Queen came to her feet in a movement so swift his eye missed it. "Take me to him."

* * *

LOMBARD STREET, LONDON
15 September 1665

The stench of putrefaction and death filled the house, a foul miasma that choked Lune's breath. The doctor hung back, strangely reluctant, and nodded at the staircase. Covering her mouth, she hurried up the stairs, terrified of what she might find.

His skin was corpse-pale and beaded with sweat, and he did not so much as twitch when she threw the door open. Lune hesitated on the threshold, trembling in every limb. Mortality, in its most dreadful form: the slow rotting of the flesh, with agony as its excruciating handmaiden. Gangrenous black spots marked his throat, striped with red where he had torn at them with his nails. Plague had come to London before, many a time; she knew enough to recognise what she saw.

And to hope, for one awful moment, that he was dead already, and free of this suffering.

The physician was behind her. Lune forced herself forward, one unwilling step at a time. "Is he—"

The man knelt at Antony's side. John Ellin; that was his name. Jack. The memory swam up through her horror. Ellin covered his hand with a kerchief and pressed his fingers into Antony's neck. "His pulse is weak, but he lives."

Her breath rushed out in a gasp. Ellin examined Antony with gentle care, then paused. Not looking at her, he said, "He told me you would save him."

The gasp became almost a sob. *It is the war, all over again. Had I acted more decisively, and sooner—*

She could not have stopped the spread of this plague. The mortals believed it was God's punishment, for the licentious behaviour of the City and its King; whether that was true or not, she had no power to halt it. *But I could have kept him below.*

He would never have stayed there, not when London needed him. If he sheltered in the Onyx Hall, though, where the air was unfouled, where there was no filth to breed disease... or if she had done as he asked, aiding in the mortals' plight, so he did not exhaust himself in a battle he could not win.

Ellin pivoted on his knee, his pale face desperate. "If you have some charm that can save him, *use it.* I don't know how long he has."

Lune forced away her anguished thoughts; there would be time enough for those, later. The reply hurt her throat. "I— disease is not something we know. I cannot make him well."

She watched the light in his eyes die. "But he believed—"

"He *hoped.*" Lune came forward, standing over Ellin's shoulder, unable to look away from her dying Prince. "Had we any charm to dismiss the plague from a man's body, I would have used it ere now. But we do not. The best I can give him..."

She trailed off, lost. Ellin shot upright and seized her by the shoulders. *"What?"*

The sheer affront of his conduct tore her attention away

from Antony at last. "We might strengthen him," she said. "A draught—something to aid him in the fight." Whether it would do any good, she did not know.

"Then fetch it," Ellin said. "At this point, nothing can hurt."

LOMBARD STREET, LONDON
16 September 1665

Cramps bent Antony's legs up to his chest, setting off an agonising fire through his hips and thighs. He cried out, driven from hazy, tormented unconsciousness into a waking state he had not thought he would see again.

Delicate hands touched his face, bathing his brow with blessedly cool water. He wept at the pain, and a voice soothed him, whispering reassurance it did not believe. *I am dreaming,* he thought. *The fever has sent me mad.*

If so, his madness was cruel. It should have brought him both Kate and Lune—though it was not safe for Kate to be here. He did not want her shut in with him.

Lune could not be here, not as he saw her, wearing her own face. But then a bell tolled, black herald of yet another death, and she shuddered; and that convinced him. This was no fancy of his fevered brain. She truly was here, without glamour, without protection, comforting him in his extremity.

"You are awake," she said: an inanity to fill a void that could not be filled.

Somehow, a smile found its way to his face, though he suspected it looked more like a rictus. "Jack found you."

She nodded. "And he is here now, brewing some strange concoction for you. I have never seen the like."

Antony began to laugh, as if the notion were surpassingly funny. God above—had he at last driven Jack into the arms of the chymical physicians, with their inexplicable remedies for bolstering the body's vital spirit? Salts and mercury and Heaven knew what else. Lune smiled at first, but it faded to concern as he continued to laugh, long after he should have stopped. Once he subsided to wheezing, she said, "You must be feeling better, to show such humour."

His breath caught in his throat, and he coughed, rackingly, on his own spit. When he could speak at last, he answered her bluntly. "I am dying."

So he had told Jack, and the doctor denied it. Lune was not so practised at a physician's politic lies. Her eyes told the truth.

"Forgive me," she whispered. Her hands sought out his own and clutched them tight. "I *would* save you, if only I could."

Antony hissed, almost crushing her fingers. The swellings were excruciating, enough to drive a man mad; he wanted to run, scream, do anything to distract himself from the pain. Fling himself into a plague pit, perhaps, and wait for the dirt to blot out the sun. "You cannot. I understand that. And I—I forgive you."

The words cost him. So many years he had stood at

her side, always knowing that he would die, and she would go on. But it was bitter indeed when it came. *I will be forgotten, soon enough. A single name, in a litany that will stretch far beyond my time.*

But he did not want his name remembered, if the cause to which he had dedicated his life fell into ruin. "Lune," he whispered, half-strangled, but determined to get it out. "I am lost. Do not let London be lost with me." What remained of it, after death's scythe had swept across it these long months.

"I will not," Lune promised. Anything, no doubt, to give him peace.

His hands were slick with sweat, although thirst parched his body dry. "The people are what matters. Yours and mine both. *They need you.* They need all who love this City, to preserve it against its fall."

Her silver eyes wavered with shame. He did not hate her for her weakness, the terror that paralysed her—but she hated it in herself. And abruptly, in a voice made strong by wild determination, Lune spoke. "In Mab's name, I swear to you that I will do everything I can to preserve London and its people from disaster—and let fear hinder me no more."

He inhaled sharply. Not the empty assurances she gave before: an oath. Still binding to fae, though mortals broke their sworn word with impunity.

This, then, would be his legacy to the Onyx Court: that he had shamed their Queen into making fast her commitment to the mortal world. Not just the one mortal at her side, but all the ones above.

His time among the fae was one of success and failure so closely interwoven that few strands could be picked out, but this, the last thread, shone gold among them all.

It did nothing to abate the agony of his swollen body, the delirious heat of his fever. It did not make Jack's treatments hurt any less, as the physician lanced the pustules and fed him medicines that burned his throat. Nothing, in the end, could make the remaining span of his life any less of a torture—not even God. He almost asked Lune to end it for him; there would be no stain upon her inhuman soul, and one more could not blacken his by much.

But he had always fought before, and so he fought now, until the last of his strength gave out, and blackness took the pain away forever.

LOMBARD STREET, LONDON
18 September 1665

The silence had lasted for over an hour, and it told Jack everything. He waited in the deserted kitchen, mortar and pestle forgotten in his hands, and stared unseeing at the floor, while periodically his vision blurred with tears.

Guilt gnawed at his insides, inescapable and cruel. Not only had he failed here; how many others had he neglected, in trying to save Antony? What would be the death toll this week? Could he have preserved any of them, if he left this place and went to their aid?

A question not worth asking, for no force in the world could have pried him from this house.

But the footsteps on the stair confirmed what he already knew: that his use here had ended. He put down the mortar and pestle, scrubbed his face dry with one sleeve, and stood to face the door.

The faerie woman looked as haggard as he, as if every vital drop had been drained from her. She met his gaze without flinching and nodded once.

He clenched his teeth and looked down. *Not so ready for it, after all.* And how would he tell Kate?

Lune, it seemed, was thinking of matters even more immediate. "His parish was St Nicholas, was it not?"

The reminder stung Jack. Antony had refused a priest at the end, with bitter words that horrified the physician and put Lune whimpering on the floor. But whatever the man's anger at God, he must be buried. "The churchyard at St Nicholas is full. As they are everywhere."

Her eyes might have been steel instead of silver. "I will not see him flung into a plague pit outside the walls. Antony *will* rest in sanctified ground."

Her concern for such matters surprised him. Jack sighed wearily. The wealthy could afford to buy such concessions, and despite his charity these past months, Antony no doubt still had enough. "I'll see to it."

"Thank you, Dr Ellin." Raggedly spoken, but gracious. Lune sounded far too serene. Was she even capable of grief? Something had torn at her during those long hours at the dying man's side, but he did not think she wept.

He began cleaning away the scattered remnants of his ineffective medicines. "I did little enough."

"You stayed with him," Lune said. "Which is all anyone can do."

It made his hands pause in their task. Another bedside, with Antony lying insensate. Another woman who aided him then. Jack had given his name to the sisters, but not to this woman, and yet she spoke as if she knew him—as if they'd met before.

"You were Mistress Montrose," he said.

A slight intake of breath, audible in the perfect silence of the house. "You have a good eye."

A host of other questions followed on the heels of that one, but he had not the heart to ask them. Antony had spoken of secrets; it seemed Jack had found them. He emptied the mortar into a bucket, wondering what he would do now.

Lune shifted her weight. "Dr Ellin. You've seen a great deal that few others have. I know you have little enough reason to hear me—but I would propose an exchange between us."

His fingers tightened on the stone bowl. Facing her was hard; her inhuman presence unsettled him too much, at a time when he had not much stability to spare. But her words put all his nerves on edge, and he could not stand with her at his back. "What could I give you, that you would desire?"

The sculpted lips tightened in a painful, ironic smile.

"Not your soul, Dr Ellin. Tell me: how large is a penny loaf of bread these days?"

"Nine and a half ounces." What did that have to do with anything?

"Could you afford an extra one each day?"

On the money the City was paying him for his services, no. A bloody *apothecary* was paid more, because of the medicines they mixed; he should give up his place in the College of Physicians and hire himself out as a vendor of drugs instead. But Jack was already bankrupting himself fruitlessly in combating the plague; if this could gain him anything in return, he would do it without hesitation. "To what end?"

"Our greatest obstacle," Lune said, "is a l—" A nearby bell rang, and she staggered. Jack was there before he could think the better of it, taking her arm and lowering her onto a stool. For all her height, she weighed less than a bird. She had fainted, he thought, but she recovered an instant later, and let out a breathy laugh. "My point precisely. We lack protection, as you can see. If you are willing to tithe a loaf of bread to the fae each night, then we will help you."

It sounded simple—which made Jack suspicious. "Did Antony do this?"

"He could not. He was... too close to us."

A phrase with disturbing implications. "What help do you offer?"

Lune lifted her chin. "What do you need?"

The silver eyes chilled him, but Jack forced himself to think past their inhuman touch. "Assistants—ones who need not fear catching the plague. Money for medicines. A place to shelter the sick, *away* from the healthy, instead of shutting them up together so that all will die. Clean places to bury the dead. An end to the arguments between the Galenic physicians and the chymical physicians and the surgeons and the apothecaries, and all the quacks who prey upon the desperate driven out of town with a whip. Rain, to cleanse the air and end this heat that breeds distemper." How much lay within her power, he had no idea—but she *had* asked.

The elfin woman nodded slowly, thinking. "I cannot give you all of that. But if you give us the bread we need... I dislike begging the tithe so baldly, but we have reached a pass where it is necessary. With bread, I can order my people into service."

Jack thought of the disdainful looks he had received from her courtiers. His mouth quirked. "So long as you give me the least resentful ones as my nurses, Lady, we have an accord."

THE ONYX HALL, LONDON
9 December 1665

Dame Segraine stepped ahead to open the bronze-bound door, which meant she did not see the involuntary shudder that rippled across Lune's shoulders. Most of her subjects didn't notice the tremors—not unless they came near this place, and few enough did that without explicit orders. She felt them, no matter where she was.

Despite being alone.

The gravedigger had laid Antony to rest in his parish churchyard. Late at night, in accordance with the plague orders, with no one there to mourn; but Lune and John Ellin watched from the shadows, concealed by a charm, and protected by some of the bread he gave to the court. The ground was clogged with bones and fragments of coffins, past burials broken open by the need to make space for more. It was hardly the dignified end Antony Ware deserved. But he had deserved far better than the death he had, too.

His absence left a hole in her life. Strange as it sounded, she missed their arguments; she missed having someone to confront her when she needed it, even in front of her own courtiers. His solidity had been a foundation she depended on.

And without him, there was likewise a hole in her power. Lune hoped no one guessed just how vulnerable she was, ruling on her own. At least she was still able to command obedience—however much her courtiers resented it.

The door creaked open, and moans ghosted through the gap. Lune went through quickly, and Segraine shut the portal behind them, closing them in with the scent of death.

She'd chosen this area carefully. The twists and turns of the Onyx Hall had no logic to them; some parts were open and airy, while others were confined warrens. This part was accessible from only three points, one of those leading above to Billingsgate. The other two could be closed off, creating a space Dr Ellin could use as his pest-house.

The idea had seemed absurd at first. Bring mortals into

the Onyx Hall? Well enough when they were trusted friends, or passing diversions brought in for brief glimpses, and few in number. Over a hundred lay on pallets throughout these chambers, and they stayed until they recovered or died. They were the poor, the forgotten, those whose families could not care for them. Ellin brought them below, sequestering them so they would not spread their infection to the healthy. With the chambers stripped of all furnishings save those needed for their care, and the doors guarded against their wanderings, there was little enough to tell the patients where they were. And if the otherworldly atmosphere of the place struck them as strange... well, high fevers could explain much.

How much of a difference did it make? Lune wondered if she deluded herself into thinking it too much, assuaging her own guilt through a show of action. Antony had bade her protect the people of London, and so she did what she could. Ellin, who was far more knowledgeable in these matters than she, said it did some good.

Fae moved through the space, carrying water, medicines, food brought from above. Hobs made up the greater part of their number, called to this service by their helpful natures, but there were others as well. Some of the goblins came out of a twisted interest in the suffering and putrefaction of flesh. Ellin hated them, but so long as they followed his orders, they were permitted to stay.

A despairing cry broke the quiet atmosphere. "God help me—please, I beg you, end my pain..." Several fae flinched, purely out of reflex. They were all protected. None of them, though, liked it when the mortals called out in their extremity. And the Onyx Hall's stones trembled, but held.

Lune exhaled slowly. Isolated voices, crying out in delirium, could not destroy this place—but she tensed every time it happened.

She saw Ellin up ahead, wiping sweat from his face despite the cool air. Lune touched Segraine's arm and pointed at an ugly little hob struggling along beneath a copper of water. "Aid him. I will not go far."

Alone, she approached the doctor, who gave her a weary smile. "Did the Goodemeades send you?"

"No one 'sends me' anywhere," Lune said with asperity. The shared misery of easing Antony through his final hours had created a peculiar bond between them, one that bypassed the deference of her rank. They had somehow transformed from strangers to close allies without any intervening stages, as if they had known each other for years. "I keep my own eye on you, Dr Ellin."

"They left here not an hour ago," he said, dropping his sodden handkerchief on a tray carried by a passing puck. "To purchase more food, I think."

Lune raised an eyebrow. "They left nearly half a day ago, and the food came not long after. *They* are resting. As you should be."

His surprise looked genuine. Lune smiled wryly. "Time is strange in this place. You are still not accustomed to it."

"Apparently not." Ellin sank down upon a crate, resting his back against the wall. He could do courtesy when he chose to, but here, working in his element, he lapsed into a more casual manner, sparing his energy for those he tried to save. "I'll rest; you have my word. In fact…"

While he trailed off into thought, Lune snapped her fingers and summoned a hob. Exile in Berkshire had taught her the names of all her subjects who followed her there, but those who stayed apart were often unfamiliar to her. She knew her courtiers, but not those who lived below the glittering beauty of her court, shunning the elegant amusements of the privileged. "Mead, for Dr Ellin," she said. The Goodemeades provided barrels full, though when they had the time to make it, she could not guess.

Ellin accepted the cup when it came. Initially he had feared its effect on him, but Gertrude convinced him it was safe for mortals to drink. After a hearty swallow, he said, "I think it may be time to close this place."

"Oh?"

He nodded, gesturing around. "If you look, you'll see that it's emptier than it was. Plague weakens in the winter months. I don't think this visitation has run its course, but I'm mindful of the dangers posed by keeping people here. G—" He almost choked on the name. "Ah, that is—*someone* forbid that next summer should be as bad as the last, but if it is, we might consider this little pest-house again. But for now, we may return these people to the London they left."

I almost want to argue with him. Having come so late to the defence of the city, Lune was loath to end this service. But if she deferred to Ellin in the creation of the pest-house to begin with, she could hardly disagree when he decided to close it. "I have noticed myself that trade is reviving."

"Yes, and the King may return soon. Nor is he the only one." Ellin contemplated his mead cup for a moment, then muttered, almost too quietly to hear, "Lady Ware has returned."

Lune went still. Then she asked, "Is that safe?"

He snorted. "Safety has rarely been her foremost concern."

Antony's children were grown and gone. The blessings they had received in the cradle would shelter them as much as could be; beyond that, Lune had no interest in them. Some fae assumed she would pursue the eldest as the next Prince of the Stone, but Lune had no such design; Henry's disposition would be far too hostile to her, both as a faerie and a Queen. Antony, however, had loved Katherine Ware, and would want her looked after.

"Thank you for telling me," Lune murmured, then strengthened her voice. "Well. If you are certain it is time to move on, then let us arrange the return of your patients to their homes."

LOMBARD STREET, LONDON
13 December 1665

The church service was a long one, praying for the souls lost to the plague, and beseeching the Lord God to preserve those who remained. Many who filed out of St Nicholas's afterward wore deep mourning; it was a wealthy parish, whose members could afford the black cloth that had grown so dear.

Fortified by the tithe, Lune could have gone in. It felt too great a hypocrisy, though, and so she waited outside in the winter air, watching, until she saw the drawn face and white hair of Lady Ware among the mourners. Then she followed at a discreet distance, from the church to the house on Lombard Street. Once enough time had passed to make it seem she had *not* followed, she crossed the street and knocked on the door.

Lady Ware answered it herself. Her weary eyes hardened at the sight of the face Lune wore: Anne Montrose, a familiar guise for her, and the one Antony's widow would recognise. She had altered it for the years that had passed since their last meeting, but that was not so much.

"What do you want?" Lady Ware asked.

Lune offered her a respectful curtsy. "If it please you—I would beg a moment of your time. Nothing more."

Katherine Ware hesitated, then grudgingly stepped back. "Come in."

The parlour upstairs was a bare place; like so many other Royalists, Antony had been but meanly rewarded by the bankrupt King upon his restoration. What recovery he made through trade, he had spent in parish relief during the long, awful summer. His widow's stiff posture suggested her embarrassment at the spartan furnishings—or perhaps that was hostility.

Lune sat upon a hard chair and doubted her own purpose in coming. What could the two of them say to one another, across the chasm that divided them?

She must say *something*. Smoothing the looped-up layers of her skirt, Lune said, "I am very sorry for your husband's death."

The ageing woman across from her closed her eyes briefly against the grief. "Dr Ellin tells me you were here."

"Yes. I—am not vulnerable to plague. I have survived it already." It happened; Antony's old manservant Burnett was one of Ellin's assistants now, having emerged alive from the pest-house. "If I could have done anything to save him, I would have."

Lady Ware's brown gaze was steady now. "I see. You were close to my husband?"

This, at least, Lune was prepared for. She said, "He was a treasured friend. No less, and no more."

"Yes," the widow said. "Antony told me."

An unspoken world whispered in the name. That was their bridge across the chasm: the man who had been such a vital part of both their lives. And if Lune's own life would go on for ages to come, as Katherine Ware's would not, still, she would not forget the forty years they shared.

Nor the principles he championed, nor the promise he wrung from her at the end.

She stared at her gloves, struggling with herself. When Lune looked up, she saw a faint smile grace Kate's lips. "You are wondering whether you should tell me more," the widow said. "I will save you the trouble: do not. I know something of who you are, and what you did with my husband; some of what I know, he told me, and some I pieced together on my own. I suspect, for example, that the printing press we used during the war belonged to your secret fellowship."

Lune's eyes widened. It deepened the smile briefly. Then the merriment faded, and Kate's chin trembled before she regained control. "I had hoped," the woman went on, "that in time he would find the courage to tell me what secret he kept back. The plague has robbed us of that chance. But if I cannot hear the remainder of it from my husband, then I do not wish to hear it from you. Let it be, Mistress Montrose."

The speech surprised Lune, and she wondered if Lady Ware had rehearsed it against the possibility of this day, so that familiarity wore the most painful edges off her declaration, allowing her to speak it without faltering.

But there was no hostility in it; just sorrow and regret. Lune bent and retrieved the box at her feet. "You may refuse this," she said, "and I will not be offended. But I should like you to have it. I have no family to whom I may pass it on, and it seems to me such a thing should be given as a gift."

Curious, Kate accepted the box, gliding her fingers over the polished holly of its lid. Then she opened it, and lifted out a small bowl, blown from delicate glass, glowing emerald in the light.

"It is a luck," Lune said. "The story is that a faerie woman gave it to a great-grandfather of mine, in exchange for some kind deed on his part. So long as it is not lost or broken, it will bring good fortune to the family that owns it." She permitted herself a brief hesitation, then said, "It is, I suppose, not the most godly object I could offer—"

Kate laughed quietly. "I've had enough of godly folk for a lifetime. But will it not be unwise for you to give it away?"

Lune shook her head. The bowl was made for Lady Ware herself, at Lune's request. She had blessed Antony's three children; now she did what she could to look after his wife.

And not just his kin, of course, but all the City he had placed in her charge.

"I would rather see it passed on to a friend," she said. "Or at least the family of a friend."

Kate answered her with a wavering smile, but an honest one. "Say 'friend'," she replied, and held out her hand to Lune. "You may use that word without fear."

THE ONYX HALL, LONDON
19 December 1665

Irrith did not like the snaky Lord Keeper, Valentin Aspell. He was one of those fae who seemed to take a certain delight in cruelty, though he kept it hidden behind well-oiled courtesy. He bowed often as he conveyed his ill news to the Queen, but it never went deeper than the surface. "The Gyre-Carling's demand is unreasonable, of course, madam. Your own justice has already dealt with Ifarren Vidar, and it is not for another Queen to demand possession of him—most especially when his crimes against this court were so great. But her message was most... insistent."

Lune scowled and spun away from Aspell, skirts whirling in a sapphire blur. She had been pacing the length of the privy chamber through his entire recitation, and showed no sign of stopping. "She can be insistent all she pleases; we will not give her Ifarren Vidar."

Irrith wished she *would*. At least that damn box would be out of the Onyx Hall.

The sprite concealed a shudder. Living in the Vale, she had heard of the Onyx courtiers and their well-crafted intrigues, the poisonous traps they wove for one another. That was under the old Queen, of course, and in Lune's time the stories were not so foul, but everyone agreed the fae of London had learned all the backstabbing, manipulative lessons of their mortal counterparts. In the Vale, if two fae hated one another, they had a duel and ended it. Here, they devised far more intricate ways of making their enemies suffer. *Nothing* she had seen, though, measured up to the terrible fate Lune meted out to Ifarren Vidar.

She had called it mercy, but it was nothing of the sort.

Aspell coughed delicately. "Madam—though the Gyre-Carling cannot mount a second attack, with her Irish allies lost, she will yet find other ways to trouble us. And in this court's, ah, parlous state—"

That stopped Lune's pacing. She glared at the Lord Keeper. "Speak plainly, Valentin; I have no patience for your hesitations."

"Your Majesty has previously forbidden us to speak of such matters."

"I have forbidden you to contrive about them. Speak, before I have that forked tongue of yours torn out."

Irrith sidled backward, wishing she had some excuse to leave the room. The Queen's temper had been uncertain ever since the death of her mortal favourite—and she had not even loved that one.

The Lord Keeper bowed deeply. "Without a Prince, madam, this court is vulnerable. I know Lord Antony was more than a symbol of your Grace's principles; he was essential to the stability of your crown. With the Gyre-Carling threatening us once more, I must beg your Highness to consider the possibilities for his successor."

Lune scowled and gestured sharply for wine. Irrith, unfortunately, was the nearest to it; she had to hurry forward with the cup. But Lune merely took it and drank, without so much as subjecting Irrith to a glare. "We shall take that under advisement, Lord Valentin. But our previous command still holds: this is a matter for us to decide. Anyone who attempts to interfere shall find our displeasure great indeed."

MONKWELL STREET, LONDON
3 January 1666

She showed up on the tenth day of Christmas, wearing the Montrose face, and startled Jack nearly out of his wits.

Christmas it might be, but disease waited neither for man nor for the Son of God; it still brazenly afflicted people, in total disrespect of the holy season. Jack worked every morning in his shop near Cripplegate, and went every afternoon to the houses of those who could not come to him. Though the plague was mostly held in abeyance by the winter cold, there were other complaints, in numbers more than sufficient to keep him busy.

He hadn't been below for weeks, and perhaps some part of his mind had given up on curiosity, and dismissed the whole thing as a delusion.

Mistress Montrose looked so resolutely ordinary, just another gentlewoman come in to consult with a physician, that he would never have connected her with the faerie Queen of London had she not admitted it that day in Antony's house. He even wondered briefly if it might be another; he knew well enough by now that the fae could adopt any face they chose. But she offered him a grave nod when she entered, and he knew it was her.

Jack got rid of his patient as quickly as he could; the man had a cold, nothing more, which his fears had magnified into plague and spotted fever and the old sweating sickness, all at once. Then he offered the disguised Queen a bow. "I… didn't expect to see you here."

She smiled faintly at his restraint. "My apologies; I do not mean to discomfit you. We have not seen you in our halls, though, and I have a question I would put to you—before you grow too far from us, and convince yourself it was all a dream."

Close to the mark; she was sharp, this elfin woman. He supposed she had unknown ages in which to practise. "Then please, come into the back. A poor enough place, compared with your home—"

Lune dismissed that with a wave of her gloved hand. "Hard as it may be to believe, Dr Ellin, a hovel is as interesting to me, in its own way, as a palace. Both are reflections of humanity."

And that, in turn, interested *him*. Jack showed her through into the back room, where a fire warmed the air, and offered her wine, which she accepted.

While he busied himself with such small tasks, Lune waited with the patient air of one who recognised nervous delay when she saw it. What question was pressing enough to send her into his home? Not until he was seated did she speak. "Tell me, Dr Ellin—were you born in London?"

He blinked. "On Gracechurch Street. Is that what you came here to ask?"

She laughed quietly. He heard the faintest undercurrent of tension in it; was she nervous, too? *Something* had ruffled the faerie woman's composure, beneath the mask of her mortal face. "No. But it's a necessary prelude. As is this: how much do you know of Antony's relation to my court?"

"Fragments," Jack said honestly, and took a gulp of his wine while he considered. "I heard a few call him 'the Prince'." Though a man less like a faerie prince, he was hard-pressed to imagine. *I suppose a Puritan would be less like.*

"Prince of the Stone," Lune said. "You will hear some

call that the title of my mortal consort, but the… intimate relationship the word *consort* implies was no part of my dealings with Antony. I swore years ago to always rule the Onyx Court with a mortal at my side, and the Prince is the man who fills that role."

Jack listened with a distracted ear; half his attention was taken up by the light this shed on Antony's behaviour, particularly with regards to Kate. Consort and yet not to a faerie Queen—no wonder he feared to confess it to his wife.

"If you wish it," that self-same faerie Queen said, "the title shall be yours."

He blinked. Then blinked again. Then fought the urge to clean out his ear, as if its physical state could be blamed for what he'd just heard. "I beg your pardon?"

Lune met his gaze without flinching, though her hands were wrapped tight around the wine. "There has been no Prince since Antony's death. Already some of my courtiers whisper that my vow was but a passing fancy, and that henceforth I will rule as our kind usually does— alone, or with a consort more fitting to my nature. Some would like it to be true. But I promised Antony before he died that I would do everything in my power to help London, and I cannot do that without someone to speak for them."

Words fled like startled cats when he reached for them; Jack became aware that he was gaping, and tried to stop. "So—" He trailed off, unsure where to begin. "You need a consort, and so you come to me."

"I need a *Prince*," she said. "I do not offer it to you out of desperation; were you not suitable, I would search until I found another."

"*Suitable?*" The word came out on an undignified laugh. "I'm no Prince. My unsavoury habit of dabbling in surgery and other such matters even tarnishes my name as a gentleman. And I know nothing of your world."

She smiled, with more than a touch of sadness. "Your predecessors learned. I have no doubt that you shall, too."

Did she calculate that response for its effect on him, or speak it without thinking? Either way, its effect was undeniable. The strangeness of that world seemed so distant as he sat here, advising patients on their ills, but it haunted him again and again in dreams, and every morning he woke up with a head full of unanswered questions. Now Lune sat before him, offering the answers to them all—or at least the unfettered opportunity to ask them.

The sudden light in his eyes must have given him away; either that, or he'd begun to visibly salivate at the thought. Lune raised a querying eyebrow, and he responded with a lopsided grin. "Are you familiar with the Royal Society?"

"I have heard the name," she said cautiously. "Some group of learned men."

"Some group of men who *wish* to learn. To increase their store of knowledge, to test it against the world around them, and to share that knowledge with others. I could tell you such stories—"

But his eager chatter cut short at the look on her face.

Lune said, only slightly unsteady, "Have you told them of us?"

"What? Certainly not. When have I had the chance?"

She breathed more easily, but not all the tension left her. "Then I must beg you not to. We live here in *secret*, Dr Ellin. I wish it were not so; it would be a great victory indeed if we could walk the streets in safety. But yours is a world of iron and faith, and these weapons may easily be turned against us. People, some of them, are content to know that the fae live in hollow hills and shaded glens, old peel towers and other remote places. Those same people would not likely rest well if they knew we went about beneath their very feet."

He had never stopped to give it particular consideration. Now that he did...

She spoke of a threat to her kind, but that was not the only danger in play. Though Lune might look like an ordinary gentlewoman, she was not. She was a queen, and if he threatened her realm, he had no doubt this quailing fear would all too quickly turn to action. He did not think the fae would let him speak before the Royal Society.

Even if I did so, I would be laughed out of the room.

Faeries in London—the very thought was preposterous. And yet there they were; and knowing that, Jack could hardly walk away from them. Not with Lune offering this chance to know more. "I hope you would not forbid me to indulge a personal curiosity, at least."

Her eyes weighed him to the last ounce, but she shook her head.

Curiosity had come first, hard on the heels of her offer; now the more sensible part of his mind caught up, and brought with it a question insufficiently answered. "But why me? I'm no great citizen of London, as Antony was. Until I came into your realm, I had never set foot in a royal court. I know little of such grand ways—or such intrigues." He assumed they had intrigues. Every court did.

Lune accepted the protest without concern. "I could answer you at greater length, and I will, if you choose to join me. But for now, I shall put it in plain terms, for they are the most powerful I have: *You love London*. You have stood fast by her side, even in the face of a disaster that surpasses any in living memory. If I am to fulfil my promise to do the same, I will need assistance." A quiet shadow darkened her eyes, and for a brief moment, she looked away. "Each Prince teaches me something new. I should like to learn this dedication from you."

What had she learned from Antony? Jack was not about to ask. For his own part, he felt supremely unqualified to teach anything to a faerie queen, but he believed her words sincere.

She wanted to learn; so did he. Her curiosity was a simple one, his rather more voracious—but they both betokened open minds, and that was not a bad foundation upon which to build.

And a whole world lay beneath his feet, waiting for him to explore it.

An unrestrainable smile spread over his face, as much rueful as amused. *No sense fighting myself, when I've clearly already decided the point.*

Jack drained his wine and said, "Tell me, then—what would this require?"

THE ONYX HALL, LONDON
1 May 1666

Why he expected the creation of a faerie prince to be much less complicated than the coronation of a king, Jack didn't know. Simple-minded hope, perhaps. Lune's visit to him in Monkwell Street, without so much as a single attendant shadowing her heels, had made it seem like all that was needed was the offer and acceptance.

Of course not.

The antechamber he stood in now was too small for satisfying pacing; he could go barely three strides before reaching a wall. At least his boots didn't squeak, for all they were new. Whatever cobbler elf had made them, he knew his craft. The supple leather encased his legs like a glove, and was far from the richest part of his garb.

Fortunately, Jack had won the fight over the style of his clothing. The beauteous lordling in charge of dressing him had fallen victim to the excesses of Charles's court, and would have put Jack in a frothy confection of multi-coloured ribbons, petticoat breeches, shoe roses, scented curls, and worse. Jack could not imagine anyone had ever forced Antony into such nonsense, and stood his ground.

Three shouting matches later, Lune ordered Lewan Erle to dress Jack as the physician pleased, so long as the material was rich.

And so it was. Jack ran one nervous hand down the emerald-green moire of his doublet, fingertips catching on the silver lace that edged it. The buttons on his waistcoat were diamonds—*diamonds,* which the fae accounted not the most precious of their jewels. The brooch on his hat glittered with starlight itself, somehow caught in crystalline form. And the silk of his shirt was so fine, it might have been woven of wind.

He hoped the finery would stand him in good stead today. Jack knew full well that many of Lune's subjects were less than happy at the thought of his elevation.

Somehow, I managed to convince myself there would be no politics. Wilful blindness on his part. How could a Prince *not* get tangled in politics? Aside from the simple fact of his mortality, he was not high-born enough for the courtiers, who considered Antony's baronetcy scarcely acceptable. They would prefer a peer. Jack tried to imagine Lune making her offer to the Duke of Albemarle, and snorted with suppressed laughter.

Lewan Erle gave him a reproving look. The elf's curls hung in golden perfection, and his clothing was even in good taste; it would not be seemly for him to outdo the future Prince in extravagance. He took such matters very seriously, even if Jack did not.

A twinkling light slipped beneath the door and flitted

into the centre of the room, where it dimmed and brightened three times. *Our cue.* The ceremony had begun some time before, Lune speaking in memory of her late Princes—Antony, and the one before—but the time had come for its final scene.

Erle bowed and opened the door. Jack took a deep breath, steeling himself, then went through.

The antechamber stood just off the entrance to the great presence chamber, where a pair of burly creatures like very small giants stood at the bronze doors. At his nod, they grasped the handles and hauled the tremendous weight toward them, creating an impressive frame in which Jack stood for a moment, letting everyone see him.

I am, without doubt, quite mad.

Everyone was gathered inside. Not just Lune's courtiers, but all her lesser subjects as well, and ambassadors from every realm that bothered to maintain relations with the Onyx Court. Half the creatures there, Jack had no name for. They came from all over England, from Wales and Ireland and Scotland, even from the continent. The room was packed to the walls, and rippled with a respectful nod as he passed down the narrow aisle left for him in the centre. Nods, no more; he was not Prince yet.

To remedy that, Lune waited on the dais at the far end. She was a splendid sight, attired in a midnight-blue gown that harmonised beautifully with his own green, with her formal crown upon her head. Silver, surprisingly—he expected a richer metal—but it might have been poured from the moon itself. Perhaps it had. In this world, Jack could take nothing for granted.

Feeling like an explorer greeting some foreign potentate, Jack ascended the dais to a spot one step below the Queen, where he knelt. Her voice rang clear in the silence of the hall. "John Ellin. Do you give your sworn word that you are a mortal man born of London, within hearing of the Bow Bells?"

"I do so swear, by Oak and Ash and Thorn." No invoking God, here; they would not thank him for that. And the "ancient Mab" the fae swore by was apparently not for him.

"John Ellin, do you give your sworn word that you intend no harm to the faerie folk of this court?"

"I do so swear, by Oak and Ash and Thorn."

"John Ellin, do you give your sworn word that you will serve faithfully the interests of the Onyx Court, seeking harmony between the races of London, mortal and immortal alike, speaking on behalf of the humans of this City, and ruling at my side?"

There came a time in every man's life when he had to wonder what he was doing, kneeling in a faerie court, swearing to carry out a strange double existence on behalf of creatures for whom the entirety of his lifespan would be no more than an eye-blink.

Satisfying my curiosity, Jack thought wryly. *And serving, not them, but the ordinary souls who have no idea they're here.*

"I do so swear, by Oak and Ash and Thorn."

Did he imagine the tiny sigh of relief from above? "Then be welcome in our halls, John Ellin, as a knight of our court," Lune said, and a heavy weight struck each of his shoulders, stinging him even through the layers of fabric. He'd seen the sword, waiting in the hands of the captain of her guard, but he hadn't expected Lune to wield it quite so firmly. It seemed she wanted those oaths to leave a mark.

So now he was a faerie knight. Jack felt no different as he rose to his feet. But they were not done; Lune's Lord Keeper, a snakelike fellow, brought forward his burden without Lune having to gesture. The cup he held must have some significance, or someone, Jack imagined, would have repaired its dented rim—or chosen a richer piece to begin with.

Lune took the cup from the Lord Keeper, so smoothly that the wine inside barely trembled. "No man can serve Faerie without knowing its nature," she said. "If you would stand at my side, then drink of this, and bind yourself to us of your own free will."

Until this point, all their ceremony had vaguely amused Jack, unaccustomed as he was to such ritual. Now, looking into the dark wine, he shivered. The months spent wrangling over his elevation had given him time to read, and all the stories told him what an appallingly bad idea this was. Men who tasted of this other world could never leave it again. Lune swore to him he could still go above, that he would not crumble into dust—but the binding was real. It had almost killed Antony during the Protectorate, and the exile of this court.

He could walk away from those oaths just sworn, if he had to. But once he drank, he was trapped forever.

The many eyes on him exerted palpable pressure, weighing every instant of his hesitation. Jack forced himself to reach out and accept the cup, rippling the dark surface.

What price knowledge?

Ah, Hell. Here's to my health...

Jack set the dented rim to his lips and drank.

It tasted of shadows and secrets, hidden knowledge to tantalise the mind. He shivered and sweated at once, feeling the wine as if it went, not into his stomach, but the marrow of his bones. Beautiful, and terrible; somehow both bitter and sweet at once. Too much for a mortal palate, but from the first drop he craved it, tilting the cup back, gulping greedily, like a drowning man gulping for air, filling his mouth until he almost choked.

And then the cup was empty, and he gasped, his heart pounding in his ears.

I would sell my soul for another taste of that wine.

Perhaps I just did.

Lune reclaimed the cup, handing it back to the Lord Keeper, who bowed and retreated. She'd warned him of this, when she admitted he must bind himself to them to become Prince of the Stone. One cup only; henceforth, all his food and drink would be gathered from above, or made in a fashion that rendered it safe. Too much destroyed a man, she said. Jack could believe it.

"You carry now a touch of Faerie," Lune said. He became

aware again of the watching eyes, the audience that had vanished when the wine reached his lips. They smiled now, in a way he did not entirely like. "We create you Prince of the Stone, and co-ruler of our realm. Hail, Lord John Ellin."

As a body, the watching fae knelt, repeating her final words. Lune stepped close and kissed him once, chastely, her lips cool against his. She tasted of Faerie, too, and Jack restrained himself from opening his mouth hungrily to hers. This would take more strength of will than he had realised.

Then she took his hand and turned him so they faced the chamber together. "Our realm is whole once more," Lune said, and the fae dutifully cheered.

The Prince is dead, Jack realised, grieving for his fallen friend. *Long live the Prince.*

THE ONYX HALL, LONDON
1 May 1666

The dazed look in Ellin's eyes, the hectic flush of his cheeks... oh yes, he was bound to them now. It called forth a sharp pang in Lune's heart, of mixed fondness and grief, remembering the men who came before him. Michael Deven stumbled into this life through love, but Antony Ware had chosen it knowingly— or at least as knowingly as any man could. And John Ellin had done the same. It gave reality to her own choices, the presence of a mortal at her side: one could be accident, or even two, but tonight a third Prince walked the realm, and what might seem a whim had become tradition.

Not all of her subjects were pleased, of course, but they swallowed their objections for now. The celebration was in raucous progress, both here and in the Moor Fields north of London's wall, where the fae had taken over the grassy meadows and sheltering trees for their May Day festivities. Dawn was yet some hours away, Ellin's coronation having been carried out just after midnight. Soon enough, they would go above together, and join the courtiers who pretended to like her choice.

First, however, there was one more task to carry out.

They stood alone in the great presence chamber, the bronze doors closed and barred. Around them, the stone reflected back every minute noise, ghostly and faint. "Now," Lune said, "we shall make you Prince of the Stone in truth."

Ellin's eyebrows rose. "How foolish of me—I assumed all that ritual had meaning."

"It did," she agreed. His sharp-edged tongue would make their years together interesting, however many those turned out to be. "All of it was necessary, I assure you. But we are not yet done. What I held back, I did for good reason—for this is the most closely kept secret of our realm." And therefore not something to share with him until she was sure he would not flee.

She beckoned him to follow her down the echoing expanse of marble. Once on the dais, Lune gestured for Ellin to position himself to one side of her throne, while she took the other. He gave the massive silver an extremely dubious glance, and she smiled. "It is not as heavy as it looks."

Which was not to say it was light; he grunted as they slid it forward. But the grunt turned into a speculative breath, as he saw the opening behind the throne's back. "I wondered why it stood against the wall."

"Come and see," Lune said, and went through.

The alcove behind was scarcely large enough for the two of them, and the wooden platform that occupied most of the floor. Above it, from the unadorned ceiling, hung a scarred and pitted block of limestone, with grooves incised deeply into its surface.

Ellin let out a half-laugh. "Is that—"

"The London Stone. Or rather, a reflection of it. I would explain to you its presence here, but showing is easier. Come." Lune mounted the steps. The platform put her high enough that the Stone hung just above her head, within easy reach.

Her companion was taller; he could knock his head against the Stone if he was not careful. "Please don't tell me I have to kiss it. I fear too much that it might also carry a reflection of the filth above."

She smiled again. A sharp tongue, but an amusing one. "Not at all. Simply give me your left hand, and place your right upon the Stone."

He bent to give her a wary look. "That's all?"

"That is all."

After a moment's consideration, Ellin shrugged. "I

should hardly baulk at a simple thing like that, given what else I've done this night." Their left hands crossed beneath the Stone. His palm was dry and bore few calluses, as befit a gentleman, and he held hers with ginger care.

Lune mirrored him as he raised his right hand, and they laid their fingers on the Stone together.

CANNON STREET. LONDON
1 May 1666

"What in the name of—"

The exclamation was enough to draw the disinterested attention of a constable, standing where Walbrook and Dowgate crossed Cannon Street, but after a moment the man continued on his way, swinging his lantern as he went. Other than that, the lane was deserted. And the London Stone, like all entrances to the Onyx Hall, concealed in some measure those who passed through it.

Lune stifled a laugh as Jack Ellin peeled his hand loose from the limestone, as if from a block of ice. "That—"

She let him absorb it for a moment. The London Stone was the linchpin of the Onyx Hall, and touching it communicated a great deal about the palace's structure and nature. They could have stayed below, but she wanted him to see as well as feel that connection, the way the Stone anchored itself into the earth and then reflected below. Here, it did not seem like much—an unremarkable block along the south side of the street, half-buried in the dirt—but it was the key to everything. The Onyx Hall would not recognise him as its master until the Stone knew his touch.

Finally Jack said, breathlessly, "You could warn a man."

"But words would cheapen it," Lune said, letting go of his other hand. "I am sorry for the surprise."

"No, you're not. You enjoyed that."

She could feel the ease between them now, the connection that bound them through their shared realm. It was unlike what she had shared with Antony, as it would be unlike her bond with his successor, whoever that might be. Each mortal felt slightly different, like the same note struck on a variety of instruments.

Jack shook his head as if to clear it, opened his mouth, and choked on a sound. Lune nodded. "It will fade; you have my word. In time you will be able to call on your divine Master again."

He swallowed, like a man swallowing his own tongue. When he could speak, he said, "I suppose I'm grateful it's Tuesday, then. That gives me time."

The reminder of religion put Lune on edge. She was vulnerable, out here; she had not wanted to go through the coronation and this ritual while shielded against mortality. Soon, though, a bell might ring, and there was iron enough to make her shiver regardless. And they were expected in Moor Fields.

Holding out her hand again, she said, "Shall we go back down? Our escort awaits us there."

THE ONYX HALL, LONDON
30 August 1666

"Your Majesty," Valentin Aspell said, "an ambassador has arrived, and begs a grant of safety while he delivers his message to you."

Safety? Lune's curiosity came alight. *I can think of few who would need to* remind *me of the safe conduct owed an embassy. And Valentin looks like he's swallowed a wasp.* "An ambassador from where?"

The Lord Keeper bowed, as if afraid she would strike him for his answer. "From the Gyre-Carling in Fife."

It startled her more than angered. Startled, and somewhat encouraged: since when did Nicneven send ambassadors? Unless this was some diversion, meant to distract from an attack elsewhere—but that was the sort of thing Vidar would have planned, and he was firmly out of the Unseely Queen's reach. "Is the ambassador *here?*"

Valentin shook his head. "He waits beyond the border of your realm, and sent a gruagach in his stead."

Politeness, even—or perhaps just prudence. Either way, the surprises continued. "Grant him passage," she said, "and have him meet me..." Where? The great presence chamber would be the best place to awe him, but that would also make it far more public than she wanted. "In the lesser presence chamber. Have it cleared; we shall speak in private. No sense giving rise to more rumours than we must."

Bowing, Aspell began to retreat. "Also," Lune said,

before he could vanish out the door, "send word to Jack Ellin, requesting his attendance." He needed more seasoning in politics, and she had every intention of forcing the Fife ambassador to acknowledge the Prince's existence. Just because Nicneven had chosen civil conversation was no reason for Lune to back down from those things the Gyre-Carling most hated.

With the Lord Keeper gone, Lune flew to her preparations, summoning her ladies to help her change into a more formal gown and adorn her curls with a crown. *Sun and Moon, I hope Aspell's messenger tells Jack what is afoot, and the man has the sense to dress for it.* Surely he had learned that much already.

She knew to a nicety the time it would take a traveller to reach the wall from any northern approach, and the distance to all the closest entrances. Lune might have insisted on meeting the ambassador above, but beginning with an insult would hardly be auspicious—and besides, there was little to gain in hiding the doors to her realm. Nicneven knew them all by now.

Examining her own thoughts, Lune found in them no small amount of fear. Attacks, she understood and anticipated; the Gyre-Carling was trying something new. She had no idea what to expect from this.

Jack was waiting for her in the chamber, and she breathed a sigh of relief. Perhaps someone had taken clothes to him, for he had changed with tremendous speed. "Do you recall what I told you of Nicneven?" she asked, settling into her chair of estate.

He recited the basic facts back to her in a crisp tone that concealed any nerves he might feel. The man's memory was well trained; he missed nothing. "Do not hesitate to speak if this ambassador says anything touching on the people of London," Lune said when he was done, "but beyond that, I expect to handle this myself. The ambassador *will* acknowledge your presence, even if I must force him, but I doubt he will deign to speak to you."

A hint of relief was in his nod. And that was all they had time for; Aspell entered, received Lune's nod, and threw the door open. "From the Gyre-Carling of Fife, her ambassador, Sir Cerenel."

Only her preformed determination to keep a serene countenance, no matter what happened, kept Lune from staring. It was no trick: her own former knight entered, approached the dais, and made his formal bow. To them both, she saw; whether it was in his instructions or not, Cerenel included Jack in the reverence.

"Be welcome to the Onyx Hall, Sir Cerenel," she managed, and he rose. "We hope you are well?"

"I am, your Majesty." He, too, must have resolved before coming that he would keep the whole encounter polite. Did he feel hostility toward her? Bitterness? Fear? The violet eyes showed no hint.

He had bowed to Jack; Lune decided to press that. "You have not met John Ellin, who is now Prince of the Stone."

A slight tightening of Cerenel's lips, maddeningly

unreadable. "I had heard that Lord Antony died. Please allow me to offer the compliments of my condolence for your loss."

His condolence; not *theirs*. So Nicneven had not been replaced by some soft-hearted human changeling. Oddly, Lune found it reassuring. She made the expected reply to his words, and indicated subtly to Jack that he should do the same; the physician exchanged empty courtesies with the knight, while Lune tried to glean any further clues from Cerenel's manner. He dressed as a Scot again, but that might not mean much.

Or it might mean a great deal. Why was *he*, of all fae, Nicneven's ambassador?

Cerenel at least did not keep her wondering long. "Madam," he said, "my lord—I have been sent hither to bear you a message from my Queen."

The phrase stung, even though she expected it. *Nicneven is his Queen now.* "We are pleased to receive it," Lune said, and waited.

"She bid me say this: that although there has been much strife between your two realms, she will lay that aside and offer you peace, in simple exchange for the person of Ifarren Vidar."

Not a demand. An offer. Trade. Jack was alive with curiosity; he knew Vidar's name, but not all the tortuous details of that war. The man's thirst for knowledge never ended, but now was not the time to sate it. Lune said to Cerenel, "You understand the cynical response this occasions, I trust. Nicneven's hatred preceded Vidar's arrival at her court. Why should she relinquish it now?"

A faint smile ghosted across Cerenel's lips. "If I may speak plainly, madam—this very matter is why I begged her Majesty to send me as her emissary. I understand your suspicion. But the Gyre-Carling is a creature of passions, not politics. Her hatred was born the day the mortal Queen of Scots died, manipulated onto the scaffold in part by the machinations of this court. But Charles Stuart is dead as well, and her revenge complete; what cares she any longer for such matters? Her hatred now is reserved for another."

"Ifarren Vidar."

"He betrayed her, and she does not forgive that lightly. At his urging, she surrendered the Sword of Nuada to the Irish, believing they would help her destroy this place. And in the taking and retaking of the Onyx Hall, she lost warriors—fae she cared for, as any Queen must."

The bitterness Lune might have expected in that last touch was not there. She found, to her surprise, that she sincerely wanted to lay aside this embassy, and speak to Cerenel in his own right. Perhaps they could mend the breach she had created. But Nicneven could not be laid aside, and so Lune answered his point. "I have no doubt of her hatred for Ifarren Vidar. But the substance of the Gyre-Carling's words to me have not changed, have they? She may couch it in terms of offered peace, but that is simply the other face of the original coin. If I do not give her the traitor, then it is war between us once more, and the threatened destruction of the Onyx Hall."

Reluctantly, Cerenel nodded.

"Then my answer is unchanged," Lune said. "I have sentenced Vidar to eternal imprisonment, and there he shall stay."

She could sense Jack's uncertainty; no doubt Cerenel could, as well. Her new Prince did not yet understand these matters, for all he learned as quickly as he could. This was a poor time for him to come among them, as it would have been for any man. Cerenel's reaction was the one that surprised her: disappointment, and worry. Even fear? *He came because he wanted this to succeed, and trusted no other with it. And now he has failed.*

"Madam," Cerenel said, going unexpectedly to one knee, "I do not wish to bear you these words, but my Queen's instructions were clear. I am to tell you that the Gyre-Carling *will* have him, by one means or another."

The threat had never been so deeply concealed, after all. "Has she more soldiers, then?" Lune asked, with contemptuous bravado. "What other treasures has she sold to the Irish, for their aid? It does not matter. The Onyx Hall rose to fight them once before, and it can do so again. Let her waste their lives, if she will."

"Not soldiers, madam." Cerenel's fingers whitened against the carpet, and desperation laced his voice. "She has another ally—one you cannot fight. Even now she comes. Give over Vidar, and your realm will be left unharmed. Remain obstinate, and all will suffer, from you down to your humblest subject."

She could not begin to imagine what he meant, but neither would she ask. Cerenel could not be allowed to know it troubled her. Jack was already showing too much, gaze flicking between the kneeling ambassador and the Queen at his side, hands curling on the arms of his chair. But Lune felt the weight of the Onyx Hall upon her shoulders, the mantle of her sovereignty, and knew herself at the precipice. Whatever ally Nicneven had found, Lune could not acknowledge it as her superior, as a force that held power over her realm.

If only Nicneven had not threatened, she thought with grim resignation. *If I could make this decision on some ground other than coercion.*

But even then, no. She remembered Vidar's words: *It is what Invidiana would have done.* She would not let the Gyre-Carling kill him, just to protect her own power.

Lune rose to her feet, towering over Cerenel; a belated instant later, Jack mirrored her, following the gesture she made behind her back. "We do not fear the Gyre-Carling or her minions," Lune said, pronouncing it with razor clarity. "Return that message to her. Tell her Vidar shall stay imprisoned until it is our pleasure to release him. Tell her that if our presence here, our dealings with mortals, trouble her so greatly, then we invite her to retire from this world into the deep reaches of Faerie, where she need not concern herself with such matters. No threat from her shall shift us from our course."

Bleak with disappointment, but fighting not to show

it, Cerenel bowed his head, rose, and backed from the chamber, leaving Lune and Jack Ellin alone.

"What—" the Prince said, after a moment of staring silence.

"Another time," Lune cut him off, sinking exhausted into her chair and rubbing her brow with one hand. *There must be some way to end this threat, without sacrificing myself and the Onyx Hall to the Gyre-Carling of Fife.* "There is more you should hear, but I have not the will for it now. Please."

He hovered for a moment, obviously frustrated by all he wanted to ask, but finally he nodded. "As you wish." Then he, too, left her, and Lune sagged wearily in her chair, listening to the shadowed silence of her home.

She thought at first she imagined it—the stir of a curl against her cheek. Then it came again, for longer this time, bringing with it a chilling whisper of age and death.

Wind, in the unmoving air of the Onyx Hall.

Wednesday 5 September 1666

THE BATTLE FOR LONDON

"Let water flow from every eye,
Of all good Subjects in the Land,
Mountains of fire were raised high,
Which Londons City did command;
Waste lye those buildings were so good,
And Ashes lye where London stood."

"THE LONDONERS LAMENTATION"

*T*he City still burns.

 The wind has fallen to deathly calm, but in its absence the flames do not simply wink out. Yet at Temple Bar, and Holborn Bridge, and all about the fringes of London, men bend their backs with renewed will, determined to overmaster at last the beast that has driven them so far.

 Gunpowder still shatters the air with its detonations, clearing space the sparks, robbed of their ally the wind, cannot leap. Though at Cripplegate the battle yet rages in strength—led by the Lord Mayor, eager to redeem his earlier ignominy—much of the levelled ground now lies smoking, such that when daybreak comes men will walk across its embers, and see what they have lost.

 An unfortunate few see more than that.

 On the heights around the cathedral, where the ashes of the books still blow, little tongues of flame race along the ground.

 They seek one another, blending together like droplets of water, merging into a greater whole. Salamanders crawl atop each other, the larger consuming the smaller, and growing ever more, until a coiling body takes shape, crusted with black cinders like scales, that crack to reveal the fiery flesh beneath.

It is legion, and too powerful to be slain so simply. Calling all its children from across the City, the Dragon lifts its head from the ashes, and scents its prey once more.

THE ONYX HALL, LONDON
one o'clock in the morning

Armoured in the fine clothes he'd worn for his creation as Prince of the Stone, Jack Ellin went forth to do battle.

Only now, when the breath of the Cailleach Bheur had subsided at last, did he realise how much the Blue Hag's touch had worn on *him,* too. Even if age and the slow decay of flesh were natural to his kind, no one liked to be reminded for days on end of how he would, in time, fall to dust. Free now of that ominous whisper, he felt a tiny surge of life infusing his weary limbs. Enough, he hoped, to see him through this confrontation with the Gyre-Carling.

And before that, a confrontation with Lune.

He found her still dressing in her wardrobe. Her ladies fussed around her, smoothing the fashionably wide neckline of her gown, kneeling to place silver shoes on her feet. Two miniature sprites hovered in the air, tucking the scorched ends of her hair out of sight, until her coiffure gleamed like polished metal under the faerie lights of the chamber. The melting frost on the walls steamed in the warmer air.

"Good, you are prepared," Lune said when she saw him. Nianna dabbed colour on her lips between phrases, trying and failing to conceal her vexation with the Queen's insistence on speaking. "Nicneven should be at Aldgate soon."

"What should I expect of her?"

She gave a tiny shrug, so as not to interfere with Carline sliding an earring into her lobe. "As much as a mouse might. You are beneath her notice. I would say to make her acknowledge you if you can, but tonight of all nights, we might be better served not to annoy her."

If saving what remained of London meant lying down on the presence chamber floor and letting Nicneven walk over his face, he would do it. But Jack had something of far greater use in mind. "Allow me," he said, claiming Lune's rings from Amadea without waiting for the chamberlain to respond. "I would speak with her Majesty alone."

Amadea raised her eyebrows at him again; he wondered if Antony had not claimed private audiences so much. Perhaps the old Prince had not minded public confrontations.

The ladies curtsied and took their leave. When the door closed, Jack came forward and began sliding the rings onto Lune's fingers. She had the bones of a bird, and her skin was cool to the touch. "Do you intend to give her Vidar?" he asked.

"No."

"Why?"

Her fingers curled around his. Jack met the silver gaze squarely, rings clutched in his free hand. Lune stared at him for a moment, then shook her head, curls dancing. "I have not the time to explain."

"You have time for nothing else. This is the thread upon which your kingdom hangs, Lune. Your people cannot endure more of the Cailleach's assault—and why should they? For the sake of a creature I *know* to be your enemy?"

The point edging her sleeve shivered briefly; then she pulled free of his grasp. "Not for his sake," Lune said. "For the sake of the Onyx Hall."

Now it was Jack's turn to raise his eyebrows. "The same Onyx Hall that twice almost became a Dragon's meal? This is how you protect it?"

Lune winced. "I never anticipated that. Had it been just the Cailleach…"

"Then London would not have burnt. But it *has,* and the Onyx Hall very nearly joined it. So tell me, Lune, just how you are protecting *anything* by protecting Ifarren Vidar."

She bowed her head, half-ringed hand closing over the gloved one. "Because that is how faerie sovereignty works," she said, weary and flat. "I cannot bend to Nicneven's will and still be Queen. If she had threatened something other than my realm, perhaps. If she had threatened *me.* But the Onyx Hall is the lever she would use to move me. And if I succumb, then I acknowledge her power over it. I admit that she could destroy it, and give in to prevent that. Which means I surrender it to her."

Lune lifted her gaze at last, and he saw to his great shock that tears rimmed the lids of her eyes. *I did not think she* could *weep.* "She would obliterate this place. But resistance, it seems, will bring about the same end."

Some day, when the two of them sat at peace before a comfortable fire, Jack would question her more; Lune's explanation opened up a wealth of ideas he had never considered before. But he wanted that comfortable fire to be inside the Onyx Hall, and that meant finding a way out of this trap.

"Let me do it," he said, with sudden inspiration. "Let *me* give her Vidar. Then you acknowledge nothing—it is all my doing!" And if it cost him his title, so be it. He didn't mind, so long as he could still come among the fae.

But Lune flinched again, as she had done when he suggested sending knives after Nicneven. "No! She would kill him."

Jack spread his hands in bafflement. "He's a condemned traitor, Lune! From what I gather, you were about to sentence him to death yourself, before you decided it was somehow more *merciful* to stick him in an iron box for all eternity. You would not kill him then; you will not kill him now. *Why?*"

Lune turned her back on him—to conceal, Jack thought, the emotions she was too weary to hide behind her accustomed mask. The long, stiff line of her bodice kept her back straight; above it, her shoulders were rigid with unspoken tension. "You have heard of Invidiana?"

"Some, yes."

"She did not hesitate to kill any she could not use. Any who threatened the security of her power. Killing Vidar..." Lune's breath wavered when she released it. "He said it to me himself, during his trial. It is what she would have done."

Jack's lips parted, but no words came out. He blinked several times, trying to encompass what she said, trying to find some response that would not send her out of the room in a rage. Finally he bowed his head, tucking the forgotten rings into his pocket, lest he drop them. "Let me see if I understand. We have here a fellow who has been traitorous to every sovereign he ever served. He betrayed Invidiana to her enemies and sold Nicneven to the Irish; in fact, he will sell anyone to anybody if it might gain him power. He confessed his guilt during his trial. Your own *people* want him dead. And you can buy peace for your entire realm simply by letting Nicneven carry out the sentence you intended to deliver—had he not said the one thing that would convince you it was wrong. But because he said it, you will not do what you should."

Lune stiffened even further. "Invidiana—"

"Is *gone!* Will you let her shadow dictate your choices?" Jack buried his hands in his hair, and realised too late he had just destroyed Lewan Erle's careful arrangement. *To Hell with elegance.* "Are you Lune, or merely *not* Invidiana?"

She spun to face him, eyes wide. But what answer she would have given, Jack never learned, because at that moment Valentin Aspell bowed himself into the room. He could have strangled the Lord Keeper.

The serpentine fellow's words, though, explained his intrusion all too swiftly. "Your Grace, my lord—the Gyre-Carling has arrived."

Lune had spent hours planning what she would say to Nicneven, and now all the words had fled.

Are you Lune, or merely not Invidiana?

No respite, no time to regain her equilibrium. They could not afford to keep Nicneven waiting. Side by side, Lune and Jack Ellin hurried through the Onyx Hall to the great presence chamber, where they would receive the Gyre-Carling of Fife.

Her subjects were flooding toward the chamber as well, humble and grand alike. Lune even thought she glimpsed the Goodemeades, before taller figures hid them from sight. "We must keep everyone back," she murmured to Aspell, noting more than a few vengeful expressions. *I should order them out, and hold this audience in private.* But that would only raise questions, undermine their trust in her. *If they even trust me at all, after what they have endured.*

I do not even know if they should.

Her breath was coming too fast. "Where is the Onyx Guard?" she demanded, noticing for the first time their absence.

Valentin shook his head. "Madam, they are not returned."

Worry clutched at her gut. She had felt the collapse of St Paul's, but knew nothing more. Prigurd, and her loyal knights—they could all be slain, and she unaware.

More concerns she could not address. For now, the Gyre-Carling was all, and the threat of the Cailleach Bheur. Ahead loomed the bronze doors, and beyond them the great presence chamber, where Ifarren Vidar's spirit lay trapped in iron beneath the stone.

Will you let her shadow dictate your choices?

Quickly as they moved, they were only just in time. One of Aspell's underlings hurried up to his master's side and said, "My lord, the embassy approaches." Running her thumb over the nearly bare fingers of her good hand, Lune hurried onto the dais, Jack at her side. Like actors upon a stage, her courtiers rushed into their places. The last settled just as her herald bellowed out, "The embassy of Fife: her Majesty the Gyre-Carling Nicneven!"

For the first time in decades of conflict, Lune saw the face of her enemy.

Nicneven could never have passed for an Onyx courtier. Her face—neither handsome nor unhandsome—had a wildness to it that made Irrith look tame, from the sweep of her cheekbones to the high wings of her brows. The garb she wore would not have seemed out of place in Scotland these thousand years or more, a kirtle of intense woad blue and leather shoes cross-gartered on her legs. But for all her rustic dress, she carried herself with the presence of a queen.

Lune met the fierce eyes of the Gyre-Carling and understood the truth of Cerenel's words. This was not the cold, passionless evil of Invidiana. Nicneven simply held fast to the old ways of the fae—and hated the lord who had betrayed her.

So fixed was Lune upon her fellow sovereign that she took no notice of anything else, until Jack gasped quietly and nudged her hand.

The attendants behind the Unseely Queen made a surprising crowd, far more numerous than she expected. Lune recognised Sir Cerenel, of course; but it took her a moment longer to realise she recognised others, as well. Not attendants at all. Stumbling forward, prodded by the goblins who followed behind, were the ragged and soot-stained figures of her missing knights.

Her attention leapt back to Nicneven just in time to see the Gyre-Carling smile. "We found them escaping the ashes of your City," she said in her broad Scottish accent, the words carrying to the far corners of the hall. Behind her, Peregrin and all the rest jerked to a halt—but not Prigurd. Lune could not see the giant anywhere among them. "And I thought to myself, this Onyx Queen is reluctant to give up Vidar. Perhaps we shall give her more reason."

The threat struck home. How Nicneven had brought in the prisoners without anyone marking it, Lune could not guess; Aspell looked honestly stunned. Some charm, perhaps. For prisoners they most certainly were: tight twists of grass bound their hands and gagged their leaf-stuffed mouths. All their proud dignity was worn and broken, lost in the exhaustion of their battle above—but if Segraine could have killed with her eyes, the Gyre-Carling would lie cold on the stone.

Instead that Unseely Queen stood in the heart of Lune's own realm and smirked. And this blow, coming without warning, shattered Lune's last attempt at cool serenity. With Jack's words ringing in her ears, she came to one stark realisation, diamond-edged and clear.

Ifarren Vidar was not worth the lives of these loyal subjects.

Indeed, he was worth very little at all. These, who had fought so hard to preserve their home, were worth far more. If by surrendering her throne Lune could preserve the Onyx Hall and its people, she would have done it. Better that than to betray the service these had given, and all the loyalty she had won from her own subjects, both during the exile and after it. They deserved more from her.

Which told her, quite simply, where Ifarren Vidar was wrong.

Not my power. My people. They *are what I wish to protect.*

Lune fought her expression under control. Though her hands shook upon the arms of her throne, she could not simply concede Vidar to Nicneven. Not to save his life, but rather to save the Onyx Hall. It would survive no longer in Scottish hands than it took the Gyre-Carling to break the enchantments. But would it be enough to let Jack capitulate on her behalf?

"My heart," Jack drawled, into the gap left by her faltering. "And here I thought they came under the aegis of a safe conduct."

May all the powers of Faerie bless John Ellin. "Indeed," Lune replied, narrowing her eyes. "I do believe this would violate the terms by which the Gyre-Carling was invited into our court. But I cannot believe she would err so foolishly as to threaten our subjects; why, if she did that, then she in turn could not expect us to keep *our* word as given."

The Onyx Guard might be in Nicneven's grasp, but there were other knights in the chamber, and goblins aplenty. Now all those toothy grins served Lune well. The Scottish folk had been chosen too well to flinch obviously, but she saw them note the odds, and mislike them. Cerenel, to his credit, looked unhappy with the entire affair.

As well he might be. If it *did* come to battle, he would fall with the Scots. And he did not deserve that, either.

But Nicneven simply laughed. "So it would be. Our paths crossed, as I said, and now we return them to you, like lapdogs found wandering. Besides—they have something to tell you." She nodded, and Cerenel leapt to unbind Peregrin, not bothering to hide his relief.

The weary knight spat out the leaves that filled his mouth. Before his hands were even free, he gasped, "Your Grace—the Dragon is not dead!"

Lune's heart might have stopped. All her thoughts were on how to manage Nicneven without surrendering too much; his cry made no sense at first. Then it penetrated, and all her blood went cold. "What?"

"We saw it," Segraine rasped, chafing her freed wrists. "In the ashes of the City. Prigurd cut it to bits before he died, and we thought *it* dead, too. But it has reformed."

Prigurd dead. The tears that threatened took her by surprise; Lune had not thought herself capable of grieving for the giant who had betrayed her. But in the end he was loyal—to the point of reason, and beyond—and the great cruelty was that she could not mourn him as he deserved.

Not with her oath suddenly binding her soul tight.

In Mab's name, I swear to you that I will do everything I can to preserve London and its people from disaster—and let fear hinder me no more.

The Gyre-Carling's smile deepened, as if anticipating blood. "So again you face your choice, as I gave it to you before. Give me Ifarren Vidar—or your realm shall be destroyed."

Not just the Onyx Hall, but the City. The Cailleach alone was no threat to the mortals above, but with the Dragon still alive... Lune had escaped the trap of her oath thus far by seeking parley, by battling it at the Stone, by making plans to slay the beast. Any means of saving London that did not mean giving in to Nicneven. If she had failed, at least she had fought, had done everything she could.

Now only this remained: to surrender her realm and her throne. To sacrifice the Onyx Court for the mortals above.

The oath tightened its grip, forcing the words toward her lips. Lune clenched her teeth until her jaw ached, knuckles rigid and white. Jack Ellin's gaze bored into her, but he could not save her from this; she was caught. It was too late for any more evasions.

She might as well have surrendered days before, when that first street began to burn. Lune wished she *had*. But she had not foreseen the terrible price of resistance—and now she must give her realm into the hands of Nicneven, who was glad to see London burn.

And upon that thought, the pressure vanished.

Breath rushed back into her lungs. Lune released her grip on the arms of her throne, steadied herself, then said, "And when we have given you the traitor—why, then, we still have a Dragon on our doorstep, and the Cailleach under your command. You, madam, have sought the destruction of our realm since first you sent a man to the Aldersgate tree, flint and tinder in hand. What reason have we, in this world or any other, to believe that you will simply take your prize and go home?"

Those who lived in the Onyx Court soon learned to lie very well. Nicneven, Queen of a simpler and more honest land, had no such skill. Anger flared across her wild features, obvious even to the most naïve of hobs.

Lune lifted her chin and turned her attention to those hobs, and the goblins and pucks, the sprites and elves, and those few fae of the natural world who brought themselves within her stone halls. "You see the truth upon her," she said, pitching her voice more loudly. "She would burn us out, with Ifarren Vidar or without him. London lies in ashes because she, seeing the Fire driven on by the wind, refused to spare the City you love. We are twisted, she thinks, every one of us corrupted by the mortal shadow in which we dwell. Nothing less will suffice for her but the utter destruction of our home—below *and* above."

She returned her gaze to Nicneven then, and took strength from the throne on which she sat, the London Stone lying concealed at her back. Lune had travelled the breadth of England as a beggar Queen, a supplicant to the courts in which she dwelt; now, for the first time, she faced a fellow sovereign as an equal, from the seat of her own power.

This is my throne. Not Invidiana's, nor any other.

Her throne, her realm—and her people. Lune let a fierce smile curve her lips, and addressed a question to her subjects, even as she stared unblinking into the Gyre-Carling's wild eyes. "My lord Prince—my lords and ladies of my council and court, my faithful knights, my devoted servants, you who are the humblest of my subjects—I ask you then, what answer shall I make to this threat from the North?"

She meant it to be rhetorical, a mere flourish before she threw her defiance in Nicneven's teeth. But a hoarse voice answered her, from among the battered remains of the Onyx Guard: Segraine, standing proud on the last ragged edge of her will. "Tell her to go home; she'll find no victory here. We'll kill this Dragon for you, madam, and anything else she sends at us."

"Me and my pretty mortal guns will help you," Bonecruncher growled. "They're a corruption I like well."

Nicneven had not expected the responses, either. Until now, she'd spoken only to Lune, not acknowledging with so much as a glance that anyone else stood in the hall; now her hair flew like snakes as she whirled to face the goblin and the knight. "You are mad," the Gyre-Carling said flatly. "Why dwell here, locked in stone, with a hundred churches above your head? This lunatic Queen of yours has robbed you of your common sense."

Angry murmurs greeted her words. Not threats, but arguments: fae speaking in defence of their home, and then a lighter voice rising above them all. "Why?" Irrith asked. "*Because* of the mortals. No one robbed me of anything; I came here by choice, because I was curious." The sprite managed one of her impudent smiles, as if aware of how much it would infuriate Nicneven. "I'm afraid London's not at its best right now—taverns burnt, people camping in fields outside the walls—but if you come back next year, I could guide you around. You might find you like it here."

A handful of pucks took that jibe and embroidered upon it, turning the anger to mocking laughter. Like barbed darts, the laughs pierced the Unseely Queen's skin and lodged there, maddening her like a boar brought to bay. Her attendants drew closer, fearful again of violence—all except Cerenel, who stood apart, unreadable, watching as Nicneven's rage crested and finally broke.

"This *City* of yours," she shouted above the laughs, spitting the word as if it were an obscenity, "is gone! And soon your palace shall be, too."

The laughter stopped. And in that silence, Jack Ellin stepped forward.

For one blind instant, Lune feared he would throw

the courtesies of safe passage into the midden, and incite her subjects into attacking the Scottish party. They would do it, too; Lune had not meant for this to happen, for the confrontation between her and the other Queen to spring so suddenly from her control.

But it was Jack. Not a soldier, but he wielded words like a weapon.

"The houses are burnt," he said, as if it were no great matter. "Some churches are gone, taverns, shops—but not the City. London, madam, is more than its walls and its roofs. So long as there are Londoners, there will be a London."

Then he turned to Lune and made her a courteous bow. "I daresay our subjects are of equally hardy stuff. Perhaps you would care to instruct me in the building of a faerie palace?"

She stared at him, trying not to release the disbelieving laugh that trembled in her throat. *He is mad.* But he was not the only one; from down on the floor, she heard Rosamund Goodemeade say, "We can help you with that, my lord."

"I don't know if we can fit everyone into Rose House," Gertrude said, with artful doubt, "but I'm sure we'll find homes for the rest, while we rebuild."

"Might redesign a few entrances while we're at it," her sister mused.

"And try for something more cheerful than all this black stone."

"Make my bedchamber larger!" one of the pucks called out, and another jested in response, "What for? You're the only one who uses it." As if the floodgates had opened, a hundred other suggestions filled the air, for the improved design of a new Onyx Hall.

They were mad, every last one of them. Lune did not know if it was the strain of living under the Cailleach's assault, or the transmuted fire she and Jack had poured into them, the radiant heart of London. But their madness gave *her* heart, because it meant they stood behind her, even in the face of a Dragon.

Without them, she was Queen of nothing. With them, there was no distance she could fall that she could not climb back up again.

Fierce pride swelled in her heart. Lune waited, letting her subjects have their say, and then when the shouts subsided she spoke once more to the dumbfounded and furious Nicneven.

"You can destroy the Onyx Hall," she admitted, mimicking Jack's casual tone. "But not the Onyx Court. So long as these people call London their home, you cannot destroy us. Not without killing every last fae who chooses to dwell in this city, and every mortal who stands beside us. And that will start a war you *cannot* win.

"So this is *your* choice, Gyre-Carling. You can raise the Cailleach once more and hope the Dragon burns us out. If it does, you lose Ifarren Vidar, for he will be destroyed with the palace. In the aftermath, we will rebuild our home, and you will have nothing but the vindictive satisfaction of putting us to that work.

"Or you can stand aside and let us destroy this beast. When we are done, you shall have Ifarren Vidar—but in exchange, you will return to Fife, and make no further war against us."

Nothing shivered within. Her realm was more than stone; it was her people. And they were outside Nicneven's control; they could not—*would* not—be used to make Lune kneel.

Nicneven did not understand. Lune doubted she was capable of it. That fae should find mortals interesting, *that* was comprehensible. Faerie-kind had always been drawn to their endless passion and capacity for change. But to live so close beside them, and stand so proudly in defence of such a home...

The Gyre-Carling would never understand that choice. But neither could she win against it. No victory was possible, against those who would not admit defeat.

She stood frozen in the centre of the floor, baulked of her prey. She could still drive them out, destroy the Onyx Hall, and retire to Fife with her empty triumph. But it would cost her Ifarren Vidar.

Passions, not politics, Cerenel had said. Vidar's treachery had hurt her far more deeply than the Onyx Hall ever could.

Through teeth clenched hard, the Gyre-Carling said, "How do I know you will give him to me?"

An oath was the easy answer. But Lune was tired of those, tired of cheapening Mab's name by swearing to this and that. She cast about for another solution, and then Rosamund stepped forward. "Madam, if it would be acceptable to you, Gertrude and I will stand surety for your word."

Hostages. Fear stirred in Lune's heart, but Cerenel

bowed to her, and to the Goodemeades. "And I will vouch for their safety, if the Gyre-Carling pleases."

The Gyre-Carling did not please much at all, by the look on her face, but to say so would gain her nothing. "Go kill your Dragon," she spat at last. "If you can."

THE ONYX HALL, LONDON
two o'clock in the morning

"Madam—it cannot be done."

Jack paused, halfway through shrugging out of his stiff doublet, and stared at Sir Peregrin Thorne. The knight was weary, and covered head-to-toe with filth; he hadn't spoken up during the pretty little show out in the presence chamber, when the fae of the Onyx Court defied Nicneven. Standing closer to him now, Jack saw the despair in his eyes. "If anyone could kill the Dragon, Prigurd would have done. I have never seen such strength. But it has devoured so much..." Matted hair swung as he shook his head, except where it had been scorched from one side. "It has grown too great. Not all your knights together could kill it now."

His flat declaration produced an awkward pause. Good humour had been running high among Lune's advisers, gathered for this urgent war council, but it faltered badly under Peregrin's words. Jack finished taking off his doublet and laid it over the back of a chair, less confident than he had been.

"Guns?" Bonecruncher suggested, hopefully. The

barguest liked the weapons rather too well. But Peregrin shook his head.

"If we had iron shot, perhaps," Segraine said, lowering herself into a chair. No one grudged her the comfort—or Peregrin either, though he refused to take it. "It's a mystical being, as we are. But by the time we arm ourselves thus, it will be too late."

Lune laid her hands flat on the surface of the council table, aligning them with exaggerated care along the floral pattern outlined in bright commesso. "Iron," she said.

Everyone except Jack shivered.

She lifted her head, and smiled without mirth. "Not iron shot. It seems Nicneven has done us a favour after all."

By forcing her to give up Vidar. Jack said, "That iron box you locked him in."

The Queen nodded.

"Will it *hold* the thing?" he asked doubtfully. "You've not seen the Dragon, Lune; it's huge."

"The box does not work that way. It is small; what it entraps is the spirit. But yes, it will hold the Dragon."

You think *it will.* Jack would not voice the doubts she kept silent, though. Rolling back the cuffs of his sleeves, he said, "Then once we take Vidar out again, we need two things: a way to force the Dragon inside, and bait to draw it near."

Bonecruncher snorted. "Just offer it what's left of the City."

Jack glared at the goblin. Fortunately, Lune answered before he could speak his mind. "The Dragon does not want the City. Rather, it *does*—but more than that, it craves the power we have here. The Onyx Hall. It has tried for us twice already."

Her mind was on tactics. Jack saw, as she did not, the shudder that rippled through the room. They knew of the battle in the cathedral, and rumours had spread of Lune's defence at the Stone; they saw her crippled hand, and understood what it betokened. Now she wished to bait the Dragon again?

But they had barred the Stone against their enemy, and Prigurd had closed the cathedral door himself. "We need some new lure," the Queen said.

Jack hated to suggest it, but she would think of it regardless. "The Tower?"

He was both relieved and dismayed to see her shake her head. "They've blown up all the houses nearby; the Fire cannot approach. And while a beast of flames might be overlooked in a great inferno, we cannot battle it inside the Tower of London without drawing far too many eyes."

Segraine's head had sagged, until Jack thought her asleep; now she raised it and said, "It is flame no more. Black cinders, like char crusting meat—but beneath is molten flesh."

"We saw it," Peregrin said, though no one had forgotten. "Prowling in the vicinity of Newgate."

Which only lent more weight to Lune's point. Men might convince themselves they saw no shape in the flames, but a giant black beast was rather much to overlook. Jack pressed the heels of his hands against his eyes and thought. *We cannot bring it below. Two of the key points are barred to it, the third unusable—the Thames and the wall will not work—*

But there was one more element of the Onyx Hall the Dragon might hunger after.

"We offer it ourselves," Jack said quietly.

His hands were still blindfolding his eyes; hearing only dead silence, he lowered them and managed an off-balance grin. "I know. In a moment someone will find his tongue and remind me that a Queen is not to be used as bait. But if what the Dragon desires is a conduit to the Onyx Hall... well, at least these conduits can fight back."

The faces surrounding him might have been a painter's study in seventeen kinds of horror. Seventeen of horror, and one of calm understanding. Lune knew as well as he did that they were the tastiest morsels they could dangle before their enemy—and that it had to be both of them, together.

She let her advisers argue it for a moment; then she diverted them down a secondary path, leaving the idea to stew in their minds. By the time she came back to it, they would be more resigned to the notion. Or at least Jack assumed that was her plan. In the meantime—"We must get it outside London, I think," she said. "Outside the wall. Who knows what will happen when we trap it, both above and below. But nowhere that has not burnt already."

"The liberties to the west, then," Jack said. "We find the Dragon, draw its attention, then run for Ludgate or Newgate as if the Devil himself were on our tails." *On the whole, I might prefer the Devil.*

But that left unanswered the question of how to force

it into the trap they hoped would hold it. Lune put it very plainly. "We need some piece of the one to be trapped. With Vidar, it was blood, but the Dragon has none. I think it must be flesh—such as it has. And for a being as powerful as this, I would not trust anything less than its heart to suffice."

"Does it *have* a heart?" Irrith asked.

For some reason everyone looked to Jack, as if a mortal physician knew anything about the organs of elemental beasts. "It has *something* at its core," he said, "that we may as well call the heart." It sounded good, and he prayed it was true.

As for how to get at it... "How did George slay *his* dragon?" Amadea asked.

Jack's breath huffed out in a voiceless laugh. "The princess he was rescuing threw him her girdle, which, placed around the neck of the beast, made it docile as a lamb. Then he led it about for a time before slaying it."

"I do not think we will try that," Lune said dryly. "We need some means to split its breast."

Jack tapped his lip in thought. "It's molten within, you say. Hot glass shatters if swiftly cooled. Might that not work here?"

"Do you have a boulder of ice to throw at it?" Bonecruncher growled.

"I can offer you something better."

That voice came from near the door. When had that ambassador of Nicneven's joined them? Cerenel made the briefest of bows, shoulders stiff under the disapproving stares around him. *Yes—he used to be a knight of this court. Is that why he comes among us now?*

"Your Grace, my lord," the violet-eyed knight said, turning from Lune to Jack, "what you need is the staff of the Cailleach Bheur."

After suffering under her touch for days, no one looked happy at the suggestion. The Cailleach *was* winter, though, and for once that might work to their purpose. "Her staff hardens the ground with frost," Lune murmured, considering. "It would do very well indeed. But we do not have it."

"I shall get it for you."

He spoke with perfect confidence, enough to make Bonecruncher snort again. "Nicneven will just hand it over, will she?"

Jack would not have thought a slender elf-knight could glare down a barguest, but Cerenel managed. "I shall get it," he repeated. "Her Majesty knows my word is good."

For some reason that made Lune flinch. But the tight line of her jaw softened when Cerenel turned back to her; she even offered him a painful, grateful smile. "So it is. If you can bring us the staff of the Cailleach Bheur, then we shall face our enemy at last."

NEWGATE, LONDON
six o'clock in the morning

Swirling ashes choked the dawn air, giving all the light a sullen red glow, as if cast by the fire. The rising sun was a flat disc through the haze, comfortable to the naked eye, though Lune had precious little attention to spare for it. She had to pick her way carefully across the smoking debris, the embers roasting the soles of her boots until she wondered how Jack could stand it. He kept close by her side, one hand always prepared to steady her elbow, though she had dressed herself once more in the clothes she'd worn in retaking the Onyx Hall.

Not the armour, though. It would do her no good against the Dragon, and make running much, much harder.

Running, they would likely have to do. She had never felt so physically vulnerable in her life. Not even when making her stand at the Stone—perhaps because she had thrown herself into that confrontation before she had time to think. Now, wandering the ruin of her City, she felt the Hall's power breathing in her flesh. Hers, and Jack's, and the two of them out here, offering themselves to the Dragon.

Not alone, at least. All around them, slipping like ghosts through the grey air, their companions spread out in search of their enemy. Prey sighted, they would give the cry, and then all would try to harry the beast toward the nearest gate. Fire still raged in the liberties and elsewhere, but on this side of the Fleet it was mostly burnt out. They hoped to make their stand on the near side of the river.

"What sort of sound does one make to call a Dragon?" Jack muttered at her side. "I hear tell there are different calls for cattle, and pigs, and sheep…"

Lune's hands tightened around the staff. She often

enjoyed his levity, but not now. Not with winter itself sending lances of cold through her bones.

The Cailleach's staff was knotted black wood, cold and hard enough to be mistaken for iron. Nor was it much less unpleasant to Lune: all the effects of the wind were nothing compared to this. Jack could not carry it for her; one touch, and he had dropped it screaming. "I saw my death," he whispered, eyes raw, and would not tell her what it was.

So Lune had to bear the staff, and with it, a thousand dreams of what her own death might be. One might expect nineteen of twenty to give the Dragon a prominent role, but in truth they were of all kinds, which was almost a comfort. Every time she imagined drowning or being stabbed through the heart, it distracted her from the very real death that might be just moments away.

For as right as Jack was to suggest the two of them as bait, Lune knew very well the risk they embraced. One or both of them might not survive this encounter.

Her own death was not the only one dancing before her eyes.

"Do you suppose that might kill it?"

Wrapped up in her dismal thoughts, Lune did not understand him at first. *Concentrate. You cannot afford to be distracted.* Following Jack's nod, she glanced down at the staff. The Cailleach was powerful—perhaps even more so than the Dragon—but only the weapon was here, not the Hag herself. "I do not know."

He shrugged, as if it did not especially matter. "If it

does, splendid—we shall go and get drunk. If not, we still have this." Jack patted the empty box cradled in his arms. He carried it as if the iron sides were as fragile as the shell of a blown egg, as if too much pressure from his hands might shatter their one real hope. Lune had spent bread with a prodigal hand, armouring herself and everyone else coming above until their coffers were all but bankrupt, but she remembered what happened the last time she touched iron.

So instead I have the weapon, which I scarcely know how to use.

The gloves on her hands did no good at all. The burned flesh on the left ached from the cold, and the unhealed wound in her shoulder throbbed in response. But the staff was hope, and so she clung to it.

Through the drifting ashes, she heard the whispers. "Do you see it?" "No." "Perhaps it's moved on…"

It could be anywhere. The Onyx Guard had glimpsed it near Newgate, but the Dragon might have gone across the City since then. It could be at the Stone. Or in the liberties, where the fire still raged. Or planning some assault against the Tower.

In this, the City she knew so well, Lune was lost. The streets had vanished beneath fallen timbers and tile; only occasionally did one stumble across a clear patch of cobbles, even that dusted with a layer of cinders and ash. But up ahead she saw the remnants of an arch across the street, and beyond it the corner where the wall turned north from its eastward path. They must be on Foster Lane—

such as it was—and the blackened, smouldering wreck on the right was the Goldsmiths' Hall, where generations of the Ware family had learned their craft, and generations more, members by patrimony, had exercised their influence on London life. Lune's throat closed at the sight. *I have tried to fulfil my promise—but without much success.*

The charred timbers shifted, sending sparks into the air.

Jack halted her with one hand on her arm. The tottering chimneys might yet crumble into their path. But by the tightening of his fingers, he realised at the same instant she did that the debris was not collapsing.

It was rising.

The black, searing bulk of the Dragon rose from its lair.

Liquid gold and silver, the lost treasures of the company hall, dripped from its sides like blood. The jagged head swung around, skin cracking where it bent, exposing the fiery substance beneath. Hellish wind blasted them both as the beast exhaled, and then it opened its eyes.

Pinned beneath that gaze like mice beneath a hawk, neither of them found the voice to speak. They needed no words: the instant their muscles could respond, they fled.

But the flight Lune had imagined was nothing like what they faced. There were no streets to run down; instead they staggered across a treacherous plain, twisting their ankles with every third stride. Lune planted the staff for footing, and the ground cracked beneath the sudden frost. Jack clutched her shoulder to save his own balance. They swerved around a chimney, then heard the bricks crash down behind them a moment later. Bereft of all their landmarks and paths, Jack and Lune sought the gate by instinct, and behind them the Dragon gained.

Shouts in the choking air. The others had noticed their flight, and harried the beast's flanks, as if it needed encouragement to follow. A scream: someone perhaps had come too close. Lune dared not turn to look. They'd passed Aldersgate in their terror, but the unburned houses lay too near outside that wall; Newgate would be safer.

If they could reach it in time.

The shattered bulk stood up ahead, all the prisoners of its jail fled. Gasping for want of clean air, Lune flung herself at it; Jack coughed out something that might have been an oath. They passed through the shadow of its arch, and she thought, *We made it.*

A snarl came from above.

The Dragon coiled atop the scorched and crumbling structure of the gate. Its long neck thrust downward, maw wide to reveal the inferno within. Lune screamed, and then Jack had her sleeve and jerked her to the side. The serrate teeth snapped shut where they had been.

They had meant to go down Snow Hill, and make their stand at Holborn Bridge over the Fleet, where Blacktooth Meg might still lurk. But in their panic, they were running north, along the line of the wall, while the Dragon's bulk thundered down from the gate, shaking the earth with its landing. Up ahead—far too close—sat an unbroken line of houses, preserved with terrible effort from the calamity that even now pursued Lune and Jack.

She dragged him to a halt in the embers. "We cannot go farther! It must be here!"

Jack spun to face the oncoming worm. Lune wrapped her aching hands around the staff and did the same. But not quickly enough, for the Dragon was upon them, and a claw of black heat snapped tight around her body.

PIE CORNER, LONDON
seven o'clock in the morning

Jack leapt without thinking, grabbing hold of Lune's leg. The iron box clanked into the ashes, and for a moment Queen and Prince alike swung in the air, dangling from the Dragon's claw. Then something ripped and they fell. Jack slammed his hip badly against the box, but worse, he heard the staff clatter away.

He inhaled, caught a lungful of dust, and spasmed in a cough. Only instinct made him roll, and an instant later something crushed the ground where he had been. Blind and choking, he scrabbled away, repeating to himself, *This is not the death I saw. This is not the death I saw.* But was the vision he'd seen when he touched the Cailleach's staff prophecy, or merely one possibility out of many?

Through his own coughing he heard other voices. They were not alone. As his streaming eyes cleared, though, he saw that no one could get past the Dragon's lashing tail; he and

Lune were the sole prey for its claws and teeth. *Lucky us.*

His back hit some fragment of wall, and Jack reached for a hold that could help him to his feet. But before he found anything, his body locked in new paralysis.

Above him, the seething face of the Dragon rose.

It was a horror beyond fire, beyond plague, beyond war. *Those* did not have eyes that transfixed a man, that blazed down upon him and hungered for the power his flesh bore. Jack could not breathe; his lungs convulsed, unable to draw air past the constriction in his throat.

Then came a scream unlike any he had heard. Lune—the elegant faerie Queen of the Onyx Court, the silver statue who played politics like chess but knew nothing of battle—had the staff in her hands once more, and she swung it full-armed at the Dragon, fury taking the place of skill. "I shall *not* lose two!"

The Dragon hissed when the staff struck its leg, not from its throat, but from the steaming flesh itself. The Cailleach's winter chill blackened the surface and stiffened the joint. But it didn't slow the beast's other limbs; the undamaged claw slapped Lune down, sending her sprawling across the ground, before seizing her once more in an unbreakable grip.

The staff, knocked from her hands, skidded within Jack's reach.

For one horrific instant, his arms would not move. They refused, knowing the pain that awaited them. But Lune screamed from above, and it turned out that loyalty trumped self-preservation.

Clenching his jaw so hard a tooth split, he grabbed the staff of the Cailleach Bheur.

I know how I will die.

Roaring, Jack thrust the end of the staff at the underbelly of the Dragon, at the place where the heart might be if this were an ordinary creature. The impact made no mark on his numb, insensate hands, but the force travelled through his arms and into his spine, staggering him back a step.

And this time the Dragon screamed.

A crack opened through the chest and belly of the Dragon, like stone contracting beneath a harder frost than the world had ever known. At the very root of that fissure burned a tiny sun, light and heat beyond the ability of the human eye to bear. The Dragon's heart was there for the taking—but it would annihilate mortal flesh at a touch.

He had seen his death twice, and this was not it.

A shadow eclipsed that terrible light. Lune plunged her left hand into the fissure, sinking her arm in up to the shoulder, and when she pulled out again, the sun was in her hand.

The box!

Jack dove into the ashes. He felt but didn't hear his body strike the ground; he couldn't tell whether all the world had gone to clamour or silence, in the dreadful inaudible sound of the Dragon's agonised bellow. *The box, where is the box—Lune will have no hand left at all—*

His fingers stubbed themselves against the iron, then found a corner and pulled.

More ashes flew to choke him as he lurched to his feet, snatching the lid open as he went. Above them, the black mass of the Dragon writhed. Wounded, but not dead. It could live without its heart. He ducked as a claw snatched blindly above his head, and ran for the Queen.

Lune blazed as if the sun had lent the moon all its glory. No time for transmutation now. Jack shoved the iron prison at her. *Christ Almighty, I can see the bones of her hand.* They spasmed just above the black opening, as if Lune could not make her fingers release. Her face was a rictus of agony.

Forgive me—

Jack drove the iron edge against her wrist.

Blackness swallowed the sun. So great was the light of the heart, Jack thought for a moment the light in the sky had gone out. But he didn't need his eyes to feel the metal in his hands, and he slammed the lid shut.

Silence.

His ears popped with it. Squinting in the now dim light, Jack realised that nothing stirred up the dust about them. He could see the wall, and the unburnt houses nearby, and the fae regaining their feet some distance away, but where the black bulk of the Dragon had been, there was nothing. Just a swirl of ash, now settling once more to the ground.

The iron was warm in his hands. The shield on top, he saw, bore a tongue of flame.

Lune swayed. He almost dropped the box again, but caught himself in time to set it down with hasty care. Her hand still hovered in the air; where blistered flesh had been, now there was nothing more than a blackened claw, and a charred ring of leather that was all that remained of the cuff of her glove. Her eyes were wide and staring, as if she could not believe he stood before her.

Jack managed a smile, though when he spoke he discovered he must have been screaming a good deal, for his voice almost did not answer. "You needn't have feared," he said. "This is not how I die."

Then they both sagged down into the ashes, and waited for the others to come help them home.

LONDON AND ISLINGTON
ten o'clock in the evening

She woke so soon only because she must, because she had yet to face the Gyre-Carling.

Lune, who scarcely needed sleep at all, could have remained in her bed for a month. She was still half-blind from the light of the Dragon's heart, her eyes adjusting only slowly to the dimness of her home, and as for her hand...

I thought it ruined before. Perhaps I shall ask Nuada of Temair who made his silver hand.

But had Jack touched the heart, he would be dead. She had feared it too much to say; the thought of losing another Prince so soon after the last was more than she could bear. Jack would not tell her what death he saw in the black wooden staff. She had been so certain it was in battle with the Dragon.

Michael Deven. Antony Ware. Jack Ellin would follow them someday—but not yet.

Amadea helped her sit upright, supporting her left side where her hand no longer could. Once Lune was well propped with pillows, the Lady Chamberlain handed her a cup filled to the brim with the Goodemeades' best brew. "We have taken a cup to the Prince as well," Amadea told her. "For when he wakes."

"Wake him now." Lune's voice was a rasping ghost of its normal quality. "He must be at my side when we face Nicneven."

With help, she struggled into clothing, and pulled a new glove over her hand. It was difficult, the fingers now incapable of bending. Lune saw the delicate bones had fused together, before she concealed the black skeleton from her sight. The glove sat poorly, without skin and flesh to fill it out. But it would have to do.

Sun and Moon. We must return the Cailleach's staff.

She had not asked how Cerenel got it. She was afraid to know. But for the use they had of it, she would pay almost any price; it had saved them all. Irrith brought a report as Lune dressed, with news of fires everywhere beaten down; some few still burned here and there, but the great danger was past. Tomorrow the King would address the people in Moor Fields, and commence the work of rebuilding his great City.

She scarce believed it could be done, despite all Jack's bold words. To hear of the destruction was one thing, to feel its progress above her another; to walk the blowing ashes in person was yet another entirely. When the breeze cleared gaps in the dust, she had looked from Aldersgate down to the river, past the shattered ruin of St Paul's. And the wasteland to either side stretched farther than she could see.

Enough. Nicneven waits.

As did Jack Ellin. Lune met him outside her bedchamber. The man was haggard, but hale; she wondered how much mead his attendant had poured down his throat. Well, when it wore off, he could sleep for a year, if he wished. "Shall we?" he asked, and offered her his arm. Lune wrapped the paralysed claw of her hand around it, and together they went above, into the ashes of London.

The Goodemeades had offered Rose House for the parley, perhaps in a clever scheme to soften Nicneven with hospitality while they awaited the outcome of the battle. Certainly the sisters did not seem hostages when Lune and Jack joined them—though it seemed, by Gertrude's petulance, that she had not convinced the Gyre-Carling to accept any food. The two Queens sat in comfortable chairs, facing one another, both attended by guards, with Jack at Lune's side, and Cerenel at Nicneven's.

"First," the Gyre-Carling said, bypassing all the ordinary courtesies of such a meeting. "You will return the staff of the Cailleach Bheur."

Without the Dragon to fight, Lune had no need to carry it herself; the Onyx Guard had drawn straws, and Segraine had lost. The lady knight presented it with a bow, and either Nicneven was not bothered by its touch, or she was too proud to admit it, for she took the staff in her ungloved hand before passing it to one of her own attendants.

"We are grateful for the use of it," Lune said, and the Gyre-Carling's mouth twisted poisonously. "Moreover we must thank your knight Sir Cerenel, for without his aid, our battle with the Dragon would have gone much harder."

Nicneven glared at Cerenel. *What is here?* The knight bowed to his Queen, then to Lune, and said, "For a past service I rendered to the Court of Fife, her Highness permitted me to claim a boon of her. I chose the staff of the Cailleach. She was most... gracious in granting my wish, but on the understanding that I would leave her service, and her realm, once it was returned."

Lune heard the unspoken implication. He had been a hostage for its safe return, even as the Goodemeades were hostages for Vidar. For the first time, she wondered if contact with the Dragon could have broken even that ancient wood.

Then she noticed the all-too-innocent expressions on the Goodemeades' faces. They had been scheming, it seemed—with Cerenel. Whose exile the sisters had never approved of, either when Lune forced it on him, or when he returned to it in bitter freedom.

Cerenel, who was no longer Nicneven's knight.

"I believe," Lune said, as if just now recalling it, "that we still owe you a boon, as well."

Cerenel bowed again. "Your Majesty is likewise most

gracious. I would be grateful for the hospitality of your court, as I find myself without a home."

All the lingering ache briefly vanished from her hands and shoulder, and Lune smiled at him. Cerenel had a home, as he had told her years before: London. And now, after too many years away, he would at last return to it.

Nicneven had no such joy in her face. She glared again, not blinking as Cerenel offered his last bow, and waited until he was gone from her side before speaking again. "Now. The traitor. So I may be gone from this place."

Lune was more than ready to see her go. Turning to Sir Peregrin, she said, "Bring us Ifarren Vidar."

He came down the staircase with unsteady steps, bound again by the rowan-wood shackles, and haggard as a skeleton from his iron imprisonment. Vidar had come out of the box unconscious, which Lune was grateful for; it allowed her to face the Dragon without distraction. The Scottish and English fae who kept watch over him in his prison said he recovered his senses soon enough, though, and cursed them all with fine inventiveness. Now he merely waited, black and contemptuous.

"I want him to suffer," Nicneven said without preamble.

Lune tried to remember the Scottish policy on torture— not that Nicneven would care what mortal kings and queens considered legal. "He is yours, as promised. What you do with him beyond that is not our concern, save to say that he is a confessed traitor, and worthy of death."

Vidar let out an ugly laugh. "So your fine principles

have fallen to expediency after all. Or was your heart too soft to keep me in that box?"

They had taken him out the Crutched Friars entrance and around the outside of the City; though he must have smelled the smoke, in the darkness he could not see the pall that still hung over London. Locked in iron, Vidar did not know the great changes that had befallen the world outside.

Lune faced him with tranquillity. She did not have to convince Vidar of her principles; it was enough that she knew them, as did those around her. "The Prince and I merely remand you to the justice of the Gyre-Carling, as a gesture of our goodwill."

That got a curled lip from Nicneven, who showed no particular evidence of goodwill. But she surprised Lune by saying, "You shall have your part. Vidar will die, but not by my hand."

Lune blinked. "You wish us to execute him?"

"Not you." Now the other Queen did smile, and it held all the hatred that had been thwarted in the Onyx Hall. "Let the mortals kill him."

"What?" Vidar snarled.

For once, the Gyre-Carling's wolfish look was not turned against Lune. "I have no love for such dealings—but it is a fitting end for you. Let those you despise be your executioners. The Onyx Court can arrange it, I'm sure. A stoning, perhaps; I imagine you have folk enough afraid of witches and uncanny things."

Fury and fear were mingled in equal parts in Vidar's

expression. The Gyre-Carling could not have devised a crueller sentence for him had she tried. The passion of her hatred was fierce indeed.

It made Lune uneasy. While she could do what Nicneven asked, it smelled too much of revenge, instead of justice. *Antony's fine principles left a mark upon me, after all.*

But it was, as Nicneven said, fitting. Vidar had always used mortals in pursuit of his own power, without regard for their well-being. And he went beyond the ordinary cruelty of Invidiana's days during their own years of war: fostering riots, encouraging the Army's madness, feeding all the worst impulses of England's people. He was not the sole author of their suffering, but he played his part.

Perhaps she could consider it *their* justice, too.

But bringing mortals into the process meant bringing in the Prince of the Stone. Lune turned to Jack, and he shrugged. To him, Ifarren Vidar was a name accompanied by a curse, and now a bound prisoner rousing hatred that began long before his birth. Whatever opinion he had, it would be more impartial than hers.

"Mortal affairs are yours to decide, my lord," Lune said, and enjoyed Nicneven's expression of disgust. "The fae of this court accede to the Gyre-Carling's request. Can a suitable way be found?"

Jack gave it a moment's thought. Then a smile spread over his face—a strange one, equal parts amusement and pain. "Yes. I think it can."

TYBURN, LONDON
27 October 1666

A festival atmosphere prevailed around the gallows at Tyburn. It mattered little if four-fifths of the City lay in ruins not far away, and an area outside the walls as large as that remaining fifth; or if thirteen thousand houses were reduced to charcoal and ash, along with churches, livery company halls, and most of London's centres of commerce. The author of it all was soon to hang.

"They don't believe it," Jack murmured to the woman at his side. "And yet, they do; they *choose* to believe it, because it's what they wanted someone to tell them. Now they have someone to blame."

"And to punish." Mistress Montrose stood straight and solemn, hands clasped over her plain bodice. "Because no such disaster could be pure accident."

And yet, accident it had been. The committee set up by the House of Commons knew it full well, despite the scores of accusations that had poured in. But if it was not the work of papist conspirators, then it must be an act of God: a second judgement for London's sinful ways. They had not learned from plague, so now the Almighty tried fire.

The godly were happy to believe that. Others—the ones who enjoyed their sinful ways too much to give them up— insisted on a papist conspiracy. And Robert Hubert was its convenient author.

The man swore blind to the judges, again and again,

that he had thrown a fire-ball through the window of Farynor's bakery. Farynor supported this wholeheartedly, for certainly such a disaster could not be due to *his* negligence, the slovenly keeping of his kitchen. Never mind that Hubert confused details, sometimes contradicted himself; led among the ashes, he could point to where the bakery had been, and that was damning enough.

The judges believed him simple. They knew Hubert wasn't guilty; they tried to get him to admit it. A strange sort of questioning, when the prisoner's jailers wished him to *retract* his confession—but they didn't want to hang an innocent man. The people of London, though, wanted blood, and Hubert seemed determined to offer it to them. In the end, what could they do but accept his martyrdom?

By this disreputable means did Jack tender London his services.

They were leading Hubert onto the scaffold now. There was no trace of Vidar in his body or manner; the enchantments binding his mind might confuse his behaviour at times, but there was nothing to show him for a faerie lord. And though Lune had promised Nicneven that the traitor would scream inside, fully aware of the fate he suffered, in truth they had done what they could to confuse his thoughts as well. Lune did not have it in her nature to torture him thus, enemy though he undoubtedly was.

For the Onyx Court, justice. For the Gyre-Carling, revenge. And for London, a sense of peace: with the guilty punished, they could turn their thoughts from accusing their neighbours to rebuilding the streets they shared.

Soon enough the clearing would begin. Charles had already laid down rules for the restoration of the City; streets were to be widened, all the houses built of brick, so that this calamity could not happen again. Half a dozen men had submitted plans for a comprehensive change, seeing an opportunity to sweep away the detritus of London's ancient past and make it a city worthy to stand alongside the brightest gems of the Continent. Jack didn't know if any of them would bear fruit; too much of London was bound up in its shape, the parishes and ward boundaries and the encircling wall.

But even if no such changes occurred, the City he had known was gone. The half-timbered houses, the overhanging jetties; the churches hundreds of years old. All would be made anew.

What that meant for the Onyx Hall, they would just have to wait and see.

The rope jerked tight. Hubert swung, kicking. Jack closed his ears to the roar of the crowd, and took hold of Lune's hand. Disguised by her glamour, it felt like healthy flesh.

She still could not tighten her fingers on his, but she covered them with her other hand. "We will recover from this," she said, and he nodded. A year of calamities had given him a difficult start in the Onyx Court, but he had no intention of leaving. They had far too much to do.

EPILOGUE
THE PHOENIX

ST PAUL'S CATHEDRAL, LONDON
21 June 1675

For nearly seven years the ground here lay empty and hollowed, after the last of the rubble was cleared away. The corpses jarred so rudely from their homes were removed to a place of more respect, and the unknown body found in the east end given decent burial. Piece by piece, the shattered remnants were demolished. Yellow flowers now starred the earth, as if a tiny meadow would flourish in the heart of the City.

Other gaps still remained, scattered here and there along the newly marked streets and lanes. But London had risen quickly from the barren ground, and a casual eye could miss the empty lots, the gutted churches still awaiting repair. The Fire Courts did their work well, with a fairness that disgruntled many but betrayed few: those who lied or tried to move the boundary markers of their property were punished, and tenants placed in balance with their landlords, so that none would lose more than they must. For those who worked in brick or stone, the surveyors and carters and above all the architects, this was a golden age indeed, full of opportunity and wealth.

Many of the company halls were replaced, and a number of the churches, though some few were gone, never to be built again. A new Exchange stood along Cornhill, watched over by the statue of its founder Gresham, found miraculously preserved among the ashes. The new Custom House was much finer than the old, a splendid sight along the bank of the Thames.

And now the shouts of workmen filled the air atop Ludgate Hill, as a stone slid ponderously along the ground.

The cavity left behind by the destruction of the old cathedral, once filled with rainwater and debris, had since been dug anew. Not to the same shape: Sir Christopher Wren, who among the King's surveyors had taken command of the rebuilding, yearned desperately to bring a fresh elegance to London. His plan for a new City had been discarded, along with several more unusual proposals for the cathedral, but here he had something like a victory.

The architect watched as the workmen coaxed and swore the first foundation stone into place. One stone set; many thousands to come.

It would be a different cathedral than the one London had known for centuries. But it was still St Paul's, standing proudly atop the City's western hill—just as the streets were still the streets, from broad Cheapside down to many of the small lanes and alleys and courts. They stood now dressed in brick instead of the familiar timber and plaster, but even a disaster so great as the terrible Fire could not divide London from itself.

And as above, so below. So long as a cathedral stood on Ludgate Hill, so long as the Tower of London faced it from the east—so long as the wall held its arc, and the London Stone pierced the ground at the City's heart—thus would London's shadow endure.

And rise a fairer phoenix from its ashes.

AUTHOR'S NOTE

If you go looking for the Vale of the White Horse, you will find it in Oxfordshire, not Berkshire (as described in this book). This is because the county boundaries have changed since the seventeenth century. It's a lovely place, and well worth visiting, especially on a fine English summer day.

Alert readers may also notice that the spelling of the Queen of Scots's surname has changed between books. This, believe it or not, is an attempt to *avoid* confusion. Spelling was a flexible thing back then; I've generally chosen to use the forms favoured by the *Oxford Dictionary of National Biography*. They list the Queen of Scots as Mary Stewart, but her grandson as Charles Stuart. Since that relationship is relevant to this story, I decided to bring Mary in line with Charles, even if it meant contradicting my choice in *Midnight Never Come*. Likewise, what was Candlewick Street in the previous novel is Cannon Street in this one; its name changed over time.

Regarding the calendar: my habit has been to follow the convention of most recent history books, which is to date these events as if the year began in January. In the seventeenth-century England still followed a convention wherein the new year began in March, but I decided to forgo that piece of historical accuracy in favour of clarity.

ACKNOWLEDGEMENTS

I habitually put my research bibliography on my website, both to help any reader who wants to know more, and to acknowledge the scholars without whom I could never write these books. Where the latter is concerned, I must single out the late C.V. Wedgwood, who did more than any other historian I read to bring this period to life. Any historian will mention, for example, the attempted arrest of the Five Members, perhaps quoting one or two of the famous lines from the incident; Wedgwood goes on to say that Charles was accompanied by his nephew, and the Earl of Roxburgh was propping the door open, and some of the courtiers in the lobby mimed firing at the men in the Commons. Such details are more valuable than gold to a writer of historical fiction. All of the "real event" scenes in the first half of this book owe their truthfulness to Wedgwood; for the second half of the book and the Great Fire, I refer you to my website, and all the other scholars listed there.

I also owe an enormous debt of gratitude to those who aided me directly. Aside from all the wonderful LiveJournal folk who recommended references to me, I must thank

Meriel Jeater and John Schofield at the Museum of London; Susanne Groom of Historic Royal Palaces; and Gwen Thomas, Robin Pyke, and Kate Robinson of the National Trust at Ham House. Ellen Rawson and Ian Walden rescued me from being at the mercy of the Sunday bus schedule in rural Oxfordshire; John Pritchard supplied me with valuable information about the history of the Vale; and Lothair Biedermann lent me a spot of help in placing labels on the map at the front of this book.

I don't have names for all the individuals at the Guildhall Library and London Metropolitan Archives who aided me in my documentary research while I was in London, but all hail the honourable order of librarians, without whom I would have been lost.

And particular thanks to Kate Walton and Alyc Helms, for more late-night (and sometimes afternoon) conversations about the book. Their comments kept me on course when I was lost in the wilds of seventeenth-century history—and one well-timed question from Kate regarding the Cailleach Bheur saved my sanity when I needed it most. The Kate in this novel is not named for her, but she feeds my general conviction that anyone with that name must be an excellent person indeed.

ABOUT THE AUTHOR

American fantasy writer Marie Brennan habitually pillages her background in anthropology, archaeology and folklore for fictional purposes. In addition to the *Onyx Court* series, she is author of the *Doppelganger* duology of *Warrior* and *Witch*, the urban fantasy *Lies and Prophecy*, and the highly acclaimed *Natural History of Dragons* fantasy series, as well as more than forty short stories.

For more fantastic fiction, author events, competitions,
limited editions and more

VISIT OUR WEBSITE
titanbooks.com

LIKE US ON FACEBOOK
facebook.com/titanbooks

FOLLOW US ON TWITTER
@TitanBooks

EMAIL US
readerfeedback@titanemail.com

IN ASHES LIE